The Best American
SCIENCE FICTION
and FANTASY
2015

The Best American
SCIENCE FICTION
and FANTASY™
2015

Edited and with an Introduction
by **Joe Hill**

John Joseph Adams, *Series Editor*

A Mariner Original

HOUGHTON MIFFLIN HARCOURT

BOSTON • NEW YORK 2015

Contents

Foreword   ix

Introduction: Launching Rockets   xvii

SOFIA SAMATAR. *How to Get Back to the Forest*   1
FROM *Lightspeed Magazine*

CARMEN MARIA MACHADO. *Help Me Follow My Sister into the Land of the Dead*   14
FROM *Help Fund My Robot Army!!! & Other Improbable Crowdfunding Projects*

CAT RAMBO. *Tortoiseshell Cats Are Not Refundable*   24
FROM *Clarkesworld Magazine*

KAREN RUSSELL. *The Bad Graft*   34
FROM *The New Yorker*

ALAYA DAWN JOHNSON. *A Guide to the Fruits of Hawai'i*   54
FROM *The Magazine of Fantasy & Science Fiction*

SEANAN MCGUIRE. *Each to Each*   79
FROM *Lightspeed Magazine: Women Destroy Science Fiction!*

SOFIA SAMATAR. *Ogres of East Africa*   97
FROM *Long Hidden*

THEODORA GOSS. *Cimmeria: From the* Journal of Imaginary Anthropology   107
FROM *Lightspeed Magazine*

JO WALTON. *Sleeper* 124
FROM *Tor.com*

NEIL GAIMAN. *How the Marquis Got His Coat Back* 134
FROM *Rogues*

SUSAN PALWICK. *Windows* 160
FROM *Asimov's Science Fiction*

ADAM-TROY CASTRO. *The Thing About Shapes to Come* 168
FROM *Lightspeed Magazine*

SAM J. MILLER. *We Are the Cloud* 181
FROM *Lightspeed Magazine*

DANIEL H. WILSON. *The Blue Afternoon That Lasted Forever* 202
FROM *Carbide Tipped Pens*

NATHAN BALLINGRUD. *Skullpocket* 212
FROM *Nightmare Carnival*

KELLY LINK. *I Can See Right Through You* 242
FROM *McSweeney's Quarterly Concern*

JESS ROW. *The Empties* 268
FROM *The New Yorker*

KELLY SANDOVAL. *The One They Took Before* 288
FROM *Shimmer Magazine*

T. C. BOYLE. *The Relive Box* 297
FROM *The New Yorker*

A. MERC RUSTAD. *How to Become a Robot in 12 Easy Steps* 314
FROM *Scigentasy*

Contributors' Notes 331

Other Notable Science Fiction and Fantasy Stories of 2014 343

Foreword

THE PRIMARY REASON this volume exists is a novel I read when I was eighteen years old: *The Stars My Destination,* by Alfred Bester.

I'd read a number of science fiction novels that I liked a great deal—books that I remember fondly to this day—but it wasn't until *The Stars My Destination* that I realized the heights that science fiction could attain.

That *prose!*

Those *ideas!*

That goddamn *sense of wonder!*

My entire reading life was forever changed—it became all about finding other books like that one.

In Bester's classic, there's a paragraph early on that describes "common man" protagonist Gully Foyle's state of mind. A disaster has stranded him, the lone survivor, on a spaceship for 170 days. On day 171 another ship approaches his, ignores his distress call, and leaves him there to die:

> He had reached a dead end. He had been content to drift from moment to moment of existence for thirty years like some heavily armored creature [...] but now he was adrift in space for one hundred and seventy days, and the key to his awakening was in the lock.

In that moment Gully Foyle found new purpose and rebuilt his previously aimless existence into something entirely new.

That was the key to his awakening. I think of *The Stars My Destination* as mine.

This is a story I've told before—my origin story, if you will. The catalyst for what I was to become. Now *my* existence is all about finding stories that can make that same kind of impact—stories that are so good they make your eyes flicker with lightning, stories that demand you quote bits and pieces to your friends and to the larger world via social media, stories that once you read them, they become a part of you . . . stories that turn that key.

I'm new here, so let me introduce myself: I'm John Joseph Adams. I first started working in the science fiction and fantasy field in 2001, when I got a job as an editorial assistant at one of the genre's leading magazines, *The Magazine of Fantasy & Science Fiction* (founded in 1949, publisher of my all-time favorite story, "Flowers for Algernon"). In 2008 I published my first anthology, *Wastelands;* since then I've published more than twenty anthologies, launched two magazines (*Lightspeed* and *Nightmare*), cofounded Wired.com's *The Geek's Guide to the Galaxy* podcast, and been nominated for— or edited stories that were nominated for—numerous awards and honors, including the World Fantasy, Hugo, and Nebula Awards. All of which led to my being selected to serve as the series editor of *The Best American Science Fiction and Fantasy.*

Science fiction and fantasy are also new here, so let me introduce them as well.

Science fiction and fantasy (or SF/F as I will henceforth refer to them in this foreword) can be notoriously tricky to define—so much so that Damon Knight, founder of the Science Fiction and Fantasy Writers of America (the professional SF/F writers' organization, which presents the Nebula Awards), once famously said, "Science fiction is what we point to when we say it."

Obviously that's not a very *useful* definition, but it speaks to how thorny a proposition it is to provide a concrete definition of the genre. Also, Knight mentions only science fiction, but fantasy is essentially implied. Which might seem strange, since at first you might think that science fiction and fantasy are two distinct, and in some ways opposing, genres. But the more you drill down to their core attributes, the clearer it becomes that they're part and parcel of the same whole—which is why they're so often paired together, as they are in this volume.

SF/F—which sometimes is collectively referred to by the larger umbrella term "speculative fiction"—essentially comprises stories that start by asking the question *What if . . . ?* What if one of the fundamental operating principles of the universe didn't work the way we actually think it does? What if technology existed that enabled you to upload your consciousness to a computer? What if the creatures from our myths and legends actually existed?

From there, SF/F is often broken down into subgenres, many of which even the most casual genre fan is likely aware of—if not by name, then by example. These include space opera (*Star Wars*), urban fantasy (*Buffy the Vampire Slayer*), military science fiction (*Starship Troopers*), epic fantasy (*Lord of the Rings*), dystopian fiction (*1984*), fairy tales (*Once Upon a Time*), postapocalyptic fiction (*Mad Max*), magical realism (*Pan's Labyrinth*), time travel (*12 Monkeys*), steampunk (*Wild Wild West*), portal fantasy (*Chronicles of Narnia*), sword and sorcery (*Conan the Barbarian*), and many others.

(Obviously, I could have dropped a lot of deep-geek literary references there to describe these subgenres, but I tried to stick with examples from movie and television pop culture to help ensure that everyone groks what I mean. Well, except for *that* reference. *Grok* is science fiction geek for "understand," as coined by Robert A. Heinlein in his novel *Stranger in a Strange Land*.)

Thus far I've talked about the similarities of science fiction and fantasy, but what of the *differences* between them? This question, too, is often difficult to answer and frequently fraught with debate.

Fantasy is generally the easier of the two to define clearly: fantasy stories are stories in which the impossible happens. The easiest (and perhaps most common) example to illustrate this is that magic is real and select humans can wield or manipulate it. Sometimes such stories take place in secondary worlds (as in *Lord of the Rings*), but other times they take place in a world very much like our own but with one or two key changes to the way the world works. To use one example from this anthology to illustrate the latter: you might have a world where everything is normal until suddenly, out of nowhere, people start having babies shaped like cubes and other geometrical objects.

Science fiction has the same starting point as fantasy—stories in which the impossible happens—but adds a crucial twist: science fiction is stories in which the *currently impossible* but *theoretically plausible* happens (or, in some cases, things that are *currently possible* but *haven't happened yet*). The foremost pop culture example that probably leaps to the minds of most people is *Star Trek*—and indeed its idea of traveling among the stars on spaceships, seeking "strange new worlds," is a common one in science fiction—but there's much more variety to it than that. Science fiction runs the gamut from near-future scenarios like "What if you could record every moment of your life and replay memories any time you want?" to genetically engineering soldiers to operate better in alien environments to examining what life would be like after the artifice of human civilization crumbles.

But to talk about the definition of SF/F without discussing where it came from would be to do the genre a disservice. (And I hope hard-core genre fans and historians will forgive me as I gloss over large swaths of its history as I attempt to do the impossible and synopsize the development of two genres in a few hundred words.)

Several examples of proto–science fiction precede it, but our contemporary understanding of science fiction more or less begins in the nineteenth century, with notable early practitioners such as H. G. Wells (*The Time Machine*) and Jules Verne (*20,000 Leagues Under the Sea*). Many, such as SF author and historian Brian Aldiss, consider Mary Shelley's *Frankenstein* to be the first science fiction novel (though Shelley was not and is not generally thought of as a science fiction writer). The fantasy tradition has roots in myth and legends and thus can trace its origins as far back as classics like the *Odyssey*, but our understanding of modern fantasy is mostly shaped by the works of authors such as George MacDonald (*The Princess and the Goblin*), Lord Dunsany (*The King of Elfland's Daughter*), L. Frank Baum (*The Wonderful Wizard of Oz*), and Lewis Carroll (*Alice's Adventures in Wonderland*).

But it was in the early twentieth century that the genres truly began to flourish as an art form, especially in the realm of short fiction, thanks in large part to the founding of the magazines *Weird Tales* (in 1923), which frequently published works by the likes of H. P. Lovecraft ("The Call of Cthluhu") and Robert E. Howard (Conan the Barbarian), and *Amazing Stories* (in 1926), by Hugo Gernsback (namesake of the genre's Hugo Award). Editors such as John W. Campbell at *Astounding* (which continues to this day under the title *Analog*) went on to push and shape the genre, and a strong focus on literary storytelling emerged in 1949 with *The Magazine of Fantasy* (later *The Magazine of Fantasy & Science Fiction*), under Anthony Boucher and J. Francis McComas. The field continued to develop and evolve over the years, with notable movements such as the New Wave, which sought to explore experimental narrative devices and placed a strong emphasis on literary quality. And any partial history of the development of SF/F would be incomplete without acknowledging the critical impact of the landmark anthology *Dangerous Visions,* edited by Harlan Ellison, on the field.

This new Best American series is a major milestone for a genre that has at times struggled for literary respectability—despite the fact that it is the genre of the aforementioned "Flowers for Algernon," that it is the genre of the innumerable classics of Ray Bradbury ("All Summer in a Day"), Ursula K. Le Guin ("The Ones Who Walk Away from Omelas"), Shirley Jackson ("The Lottery"), Harlan Ellison ("'Repent, Harlequin!' Said the Ticktockman"), Octavia E. Butler ("Bloodchild"), and Kurt Vonnegut ("Harrison Bergeron").

But science fiction and fantasy literature is currently experiencing a golden age; there's more high-quality genre literature being written now than ever before. And science fiction and fantasy themes have broken through the boundaries of other genres as well, figuring prominently in numerous mainstream bestsellers both in the literary fiction category and in film and television. That makes now the perfect time for SF/F to join the Best American family.

Many popular mainstream books in recent years have been infused with science fiction and fantasy elements—Alice Sebold's *The Lovely Bones,* Kazuo Ishiguro's *The Buried Giant,* Audrey Niffenegger's *The Time Traveler's Wife,* Emily St. John Mandel's *Station Eleven.* Some, such as Cormac McCarthy's *The Road,* have not only been popular but have won the Pulitzer Prize as well. Many readers would not classify some of these novels as genre books, yet it is undeniable that they *are* genre; if you removed the SF/F element from any of them, the stories would fall apart. Furthermore, within the SF/F community, these novels have already been accepted as part of the field.

Part of the scope of this anthology series will be to help define —and *re*define—just what science fiction and fantasy is capable of. It is my opinion that the finest science fiction and fantasy is on a par with the finest works of literature in any genre, and the goal of this series is to prove it.

*

The stories chosen for this anthology were originally published between January 2014 and December 2014. The technical criteria for consideration are (1) original publication in a nationally distributed American or Canadian publication (that is, periodicals, collections, or anthologies, in print, online, or as an ebook); (2) publication in English by writers who are American or Canadian or who have made the United States their home; (3) publication as text (audiobooks, podcasts, dramatizations, interactive works, and other forms of fiction are not considered); (4) original publication as short fiction (excerpts of novels are not knowingly considered); (5) length of 17,499 words or less; (6) at least loosely categorized as science fiction or fantasy; (7) publication by someone other than the author (self-published works are not eligible); and (8) publication as an original work of the author (not part of a media tie-in/licensed fiction program).

As series editor, I attempted to read everything I could find that meets these selection criteria. After doing all my reading, I created a list of what I felt were the top eighty stories published in the genre (forty science fiction and forty fantasy). Those eighty stories were sent to guest editor Joe Hill, who read them and then chose the best twenty (ten science fiction, ten fantasy) for inclusion in the volume. Joe read all the stories blind, with no bylines attached to them nor any information about where they originally appeared. The sixty stories that did not make it into the anthology are listed in the back of this book as "Other Notable Science Fiction and Fantasy Stories of 2014."

I could not have done all the work of assembling this volume alone (or even with only the help of our esteemed guest editor). Accordingly, many thanks go out to my team of first readers, who helped me evaluate various publications that I might not have had time to consider otherwise, led by DeAnna Knippling, Robyn Lupo, and Rob McMonigal, with smaller but still significant contributions by Christie Yant, Karen Bovenmyer, Michael Curry, Sylvia Hiven, Amber Barkley, Aaron Bailey, Hannah Huber, Hannah Mades-Alabiso, and Sarah Slatton.

I also owe a huge debt of gratitude to the work of editors who have come before me. Though this is the first volume of *The Best American Science Fiction and Fantasy,* it couldn't have happened without the brilliant work done by the various editors involved with *The*

Best American Short Stories, The Best American Mystery Stories, and the rest of the Best American family. Our in-house editor at Mariner Books, Tim Mudie, was by my side throughout the entire process and was a diligent companion in helping a first-time series editor get up to speed.

Likewise, I want to acknowledge the contributions of the many editors in the science fiction/fantasy field who have edited best-of-the-year volumes over the years, including Gardner Dozois, Ellen Datlow, Terri Windling, David G. Hartwell, Jonathan Strahan, and Rich Horton (to name but a few of the prominent ones of my era as a reader). I consider their work the textbooks of my education as an editor. But if their works were my textbooks, then Gordon Van Gelder, former editor and current publisher of *The Magazine of Fantasy & Science Fiction,* was my professor.

And last but not least, thanks so much to Joe Hill for taking the helm for the good ship *BASFF*'s inaugural voyage. His comments about and criticisms of all the stories I presented him with were always astute and incisive, and he was both an amiable and a stalwart collaborator. Also, as you will no doubt agree once you read Joe's introduction, he wrote as wonderful a love letter to science fiction/fantasy as I've ever seen. If you read it and are not moved by it, and are not made super-excited to read this anthology afterward, I daresay this might not be the book for you.

I consider the mantle of series editor to be a tremendous responsibility, and the SF/F genre is vitally important to me, so this is a job I take very, very seriously.

Being series editor of the first Best American title to focus on science fiction and fantasy puts me into several different roles. I'll be an ambassador of the genre to the outside world, the genre's proselytizer in chief, who will be called upon to spread the gospel of SF/F far and wide.

But first and foremost I am a curator, with the mission to survey the field and ask, "What is the best American science fiction and fantasy?"

In my effort to find the top eighty stories of the year, I read more than a hundred periodicals, from longtime genre mainstays such as *The Magazine of Fantasy & Science Fiction* and *Asimov's Science Fiction,* to leading digital magazines such as *Clarkesworld* and my own *Lightspeed,* to top literary publications such as *The New Yorker* and *Granta,* as well as sixty or more anthologies and single-author collections. I scoured the field for publications both big and small and paid equal consideration to stories in venerable major magazines such as *Analog* and stories in new niche zines like *Scigentasy* (the latter of which I'm pleased to say ended up with a story in this volume).

By my calculations, my long list of eighty was drawn from forty different publications—twenty-four periodicals, fifteen anthologies, and one stand-alone ebook—from thirty-six different editors (counting editorial teams as a unit, but also distinct from any solo work done by one of the editors). The final table of contents draws from fourteen different sources: nine periodicals and five anthologies (from fourteen different editors/editorial teams).

About halfway through the year I stopped logging every single story I read, as it got to be too onerous to do so; instead I started logging only things that I *liked.* I myself edited or coedited five anthologies and twenty-two magazine issues in 2014, which included approximately 185 original, eligible stories altogether. Including those, I have spreadsheets showing that I and/or my first-reader team evaluated approximately 2,600 stories, but how many stories in total I actually ended up considering is something of a mystery; if I were to venture a guess, I'd say it might be as many as twice that. Those numbers, I think—combined with how difficult it was to narrow down my selections to the top eighty stories—speak to both the extreme vitality of the field and the need for volumes like this one.

Science fiction and fantasy has been an indispensable addition to our cultural heritage, one that has given us great masters such as Ray Bradbury, Ursula K. Le Guin, Neil Gaiman, and Shirley Jackson, as well as the tools to inspire, enlighten, and ultimately, like Gully Foyle, transform ourselves.

It is my immense privilege to be your guide and curator. I hope you enjoy the exhibit.

Editors, writers, and publishers who would like their work considered for next year's edition, please visit johnjosephadams.com/best-american for instructions on how to submit material for consideration.

— JOHN JOSEPH ADAMS

Introduction: Launching Rockets

WONDER IS A blasting cap. It is an emotion that goes off with a bang, shattering settled beliefs, rattling the architecture of the mind, and clearing space for new ideas, new possibilities. Wonder is often thought of as a peaceful emotion, a sense of resounding inner quiet. Of course we would associate it with silence. The world always assumes an eerie hush after an explosion.

Awe is TNT for the soul.

My own first experience with wonder came in the candy-coated package of science fiction: Richard Dreyfuss chasing aliens in *Close Encounters of the Third Kind*. In some ways I never recovered from that first great detonation of amazement.

In one pivotal scene, Dreyfuss is stopped at a malfunctioning railroad crossing when an alien spacecraft passes overhead, spearing him with a great shaft of light and causing objects to blow about the cab of his pickup in a frantic storm. Afterward, the side of his body that faced the driver's side window is badly sunburned, although the incident occurred at night.

And this is very like the effect the movie had on me. After it was over I felt irradiated, aglow, *charged*.

I never looked at a starry night the same way. The *clank-clank-clank* of the bell at a railroad crossing still evokes in me a shivery frisson of anticipation. *Close Encounters* shook loose a marvelous idea in my seven-year-old head: we are fish in the ocean of the universe, and there may be grand ships moving above us.

I experienced another of these walloping explosions of feeling a few years later, when I first read *Something Wicked This Way Comes*, Ray Bradbury's classic story of a carnival stocked with monsters and poisoned rides. No one who buys a ticket to Cooger & Dark's Pandemonium Shadow Show ever forgets what they saw there: the carousel that ages you, the illustrated man with a book of living stories inked onto his flesh.

My awe, though, was not merely a reaction to Bradbury's thrilling ideas. It was just as much a response to the shock of his sentences, the way he could fold a few words to create an indelible image, much as an origami artist may make a square of paper into a crane. One great verb, I discovered, had almost as much explosive power as any marvelous concept. The language of fiction could be as exciting as the subject matter. After *Something Wicked*, I could never look at my own sentences without asking myself if they were really packing their maximum charge. I had not known until then what a few words could do—that like gunpowder, they could ignite with a shocking crack.

This is the truth of science fiction and fantasy: it is the greatest fireworks show in literature, and your own imagination is a sky waiting to catch fire. And here is the truth of this book: we've got all the best, brightest, bangiest fireworks a person could want. *The Best American Science Fiction and Fantasy* is not just a book but also an explosive device . . . one that is, fortunately, entirely safe to bring on a plane.

Science fiction and fantasy: two different but closely related compounds, both highly combustible.

Fantasy, it has been argued, could well describe all literature. Any work of fiction, after all, is an act of sustained invention—a fantasy—and a dragon is a dragon, whether it sleeps in a cave on a pile of gold or wears a human face and works for Goldman Sachs, destroying lives by moving numbers from one column to another. I once sat in front of two werewolves on a train to Liverpool. They wore Manchester United jerseys, showed their fangs at every passing lady, and barked at anyone who looked shy or weak. When we roared into a tunnel, it was all too easy to imagine them leaping on someone in the dark and tearing out a throat. As it happens, we reached our destination undevoured, and I got a good fantasy story out of the experience ("Wolverton Station").

Jonathan Franzen, Zadie Smith, Donna Tartt? Fantasists all.

Even those readers who would turn up their nose at a collection like this (perhaps to buy a copy of Houghton Mifflin Harcourt's *The Best American Short Stories* instead) are fantasy enthusiasts, whether they know it or not.

But for the purposes of this collection, our interest is not fantasy in the broadest sense but tales of the *fantastic*. The defining trait of such narratives is that the challenges in them are unreal or otherworldly. Familiar dangers have been rendered in mind-bending new forms, to help us see the problems of our lives afresh. For example, lots of stories explore workplace seductions, but in a book like this, the company is operated by vampires and the issues raised are not just moral but *mortal*. Children who fall far from the tree may test the love and patience of their parents in the extreme, but only in a collection such as this will a mother find herself looking after a gelatinous, mysterious cube.

If stories of the fantastic are a kind of firework, then their red glare may show you your own life in a truly new light, revealing who around you is a demon lover and who a ghost, who is the plaything of faeries and who has fangs.

Science fiction, on the other hand, might describe any literary work set in the modern day. Anyone with a smartphone in their pocket knows we've been living in the future for a while now. At the time of this writing, a man has only just moved into a small flat located 250 miles above the Earth. He plans to live there for a year. As has been noted by others, there is a planet in our solar system entirely populated by robots: Mars! How science fiction is that? Ray Bradbury would love it.

Anyone who writes a story in which someone sends a text or an email is writing science fiction. In a world where people own self-driving electric cars and maintain close relationships by way of daily video chats, it is not unreasonable to say every author is a science fiction author now. Again: Franzen, Smith, Tartt, etc. But go back even further—weren't the first stories to account for the Internet, circa 1990, working in a science-fictional mode? Weren't novels that mentioned the moon landing trying to reckon with a world in which the incredible had been calculated, computed, processed, and made credible?

Well. Leave it. As with fantasy, we will pass on the broadest possible definition of science fiction, and examine the genre only in its most potent form. Our interest is in those stories in which the science has been projected out from the marvels of now to the head-swimming possibilities of what might be *next*. We stand on the near shore of the twenty-first century, with the vast terrain ahead unknown, unmapped, only dimly apprehended. Science fiction stories are the dazzling flares we launch into the darkness, to catch a glimpse of the country before us and show us our way.

Both genres, really, are flashbangs to drive back the shadows. Fantasy shines its eldritch glare within, illuminating the contours of our dreams, our half-formed desires, and our irrational fears. Science fiction casts its blazing glare outward, into the brilliant night, at the smashed crystal ball of the moon and the future waiting beyond.

Put another way, fantasy explores the self, whereas science fiction asks you to leave selfhood behind and see your life for what it is—a bright mote of dust adrift in a vast and beautiful and terrifying universe.

The writers assembled herein—nineteen, with two incredibly different and equally breathtaking stories by a young she-can-do-anything star, Sofia Samatar—are a mix of old hands and fresh voices. If you've read John Joseph Adams's foreword, you know the deal: he read several thousand stories, whittled them down to eighty that he thought were truly remarkable, and I read through those, reducing them to twenty favorites. The authors' names were withheld from me, and everyone here fought their way in on their own merits. When their secret identities were revealed, it gladdened me to discover I was among some old friends, and excited me to be introduced to so many remarkable new talents.

I am also pleased that the finished collection organically arose as one of great diversity. Whatever your sexual orientation, whatever your ethnicity, whatever your age or personal experiences, it is my hope you will find a hero somewhere here you can relate to, that speaks to the world as *you* see it. Even better: there is a good chance you will find some heroes here who are deeply, fundamentally different from yourself. I don't have much patience with readers who yearn to explore incredible worlds and mind-bending situations but grow cold at the idea of imagining their way into different political ideas, different faiths, a different gender, a different skin, a different life.

I hesitate to reveal many specifics about the stories themselves. A description of a fireworks show is never as good as seeing one. But perhaps I can offer a few general observations.

The apocalypse is totally happening . . . at least in the sense that it's a popular subject in SF/F right now (as for whether the apocalypse is *happening* happening, continue to watch the Weather Channel and keep your disaster insurance up to date). There are three end-of-the-worlders in this book . . . and there were at least three others I read that were almost as good as these.

We are increasingly anxious about our inability to look away from our ever-more-seductive screens and all too aware that what you get from your shiny new device may be very different from what was promised on the box.

Even demon lovers and occasional ghosts are depressed by reality television and tabloid websites.

The world needs mermaids.

Kickstarter and Craigslist have replaced the stake and the cross as our go-to tools for dealing with the supernatural.

Poverty is hard, even in the future.

The natural world may not ever be done playing pranks on us talking apes.

History is no longer just a story written by the winners.

Most of all, we humans will always be driven to take enormous risks and perform heart-wrenching sacrifices for our friends, children, partners, or parents, regardless of our costume, be it a space-suit or a fantastic coat with pockets full of magic.

And that's enough by way of preamble from your faithful correspondent. I've talked myself dry, and besides . . . the hour grows late. The sun has long since set, and the first stars are out. Cricket song throbs in the high grass. Do you hear that? A bell *clank-clank-clanks* at a distant railroad crossing, although there's no sign of a train. Whoa — *spooky*.

We're all here on our picnic blankets on a perfect evening and it's time for the show. Who's ready for some fireworks? Who's ready to watch the sky burn?

Oh good. I'm ready, too.

Strike the match.

Touch the fuse.

————————————————————————————————*!

(bang)

— JOE HILL

How to Get Back to the Forest

FROM *Lightspeed Magazine*

"YOU HAVE TO puke it up," said Cee. "You have to get down there and puke it up. I mean down past where you can feel it, you know?"

She gestured earnestly at her chest. She had this old-fashioned cotton nightgown on, lace collar brilliant under the bathroom lights. Above the collar, her skin looked gray. Cee had bones like a bird. She was so beautiful. She was completely beautiful and fucked. I mean everybody at camp was sort of a mess, we were even supposed to be that way, at a *difficult stage,* but Cee took it to another level. Herding us into the bathroom at night and asking us to puke. "It's right here," she said, tapping the nightgown over her hollow chest. "Where you've got less nerves in your esophagus. It's like wired into the side, into the muscle. You have to puke really hard to get it."

"Did you ever get it out?" asked Max. She was sitting on one of the sinks. She'd believe anything.

Cee nodded, solemn as a counselor. "Two years ago. They caught me and gave me a new one. But it was beautiful while it was gone. I'm telling you it was the best."

"Like how?" I said.

Cee stretched out her arms. "Like bliss. Like everything. Everything all at once. You're raw, just a big raw nerve."

"That doesn't sound so great," said Elle.

"I know," said Cee, not annoyed but really agreeing, turning things around. That was one of her talents.

"It sounds stupid," she nodded, "but that's because it's something we can't imagine. We don't have the tools. Our bodies don't know how to calculate what we're missing. You can't know till you get there. And at the same time, it's where you came from. It's where you *started*."

She raised her toothbrush. "So. Who's with me?"

Definitely not me. God, Cee. You were such an idiot.

Apparently a girl named Puss had told her about the bug. And Cee, being Cee, was totally open to learning new things from a person who called herself Puss. Puss had puked out her own bug and was living on the streets. I guess she'd run away from camp, I don't really know. She was six feet tall, Cee said, with long red hair. The hair was dyed, which was weird, because if you're living on the streets, do you care about stuff like that? This kind of thing can keep me awake at night. I lie in bed, or rather I sit in the living room because Pete hates me tossing and turning, and I leave the room dark and open all the curtains, and I watch the lights of the city and think about this girl Puss getting red hair dye at the grocery store and doing her hair in the bathroom at the train station. Did she put newspapers down? And what if somebody came in and saw her?

Anyway, eventually Cee met Puss in the park, and Puss was clearly down-and-out and a hooker, but she looked cool and friendly, and Cee sat down beside her on the swings.

"You have to puke it up."

We'd only been at camp for about six weeks. It seemed like a long time, long enough to know everybody. Everything felt stretched out at camp, the days and the nights, and yet in the end it was over so fast, as soon as you could blink. Camp was on its own calendar—*a special time of life*. That was Jodi's phrase. She was our favorite counselor. She was greasy and enthusiastic, with a skinny little ponytail, only a year or two older than the seniors. *Camp is so special!* The thing with Jodi was, she believed every word she said. It made it really hard to make fun of her. That night, the night in the bathroom, she was asleep down the hall underneath her Mother Figure, which was a little stuffed dog with *Florida* on its chest.

*

"Come on!" said Cee. And she stuck her toothbrush down her throat, just like that. I think Max screamed. Cee didn't start puking right away. She had to give herself a few really good shoves with that toothbrush, while people said "Oh my God" and backed away and clutched one another and stared. Somebody said "Are you nuts?" Somebody else said something else, I might have said something, I don't know, everything was so white and bright in that moment, mirrors and fluorescent lights and Cee in that goddamn Victorian nightgown jabbing away with her toothbrush and sort of gagging. Every time I looked up I could see all of us in the mirror. And then it came. A splatter of puke all over the sink. Cee leaned over and braced herself. *Blam.* Elle said, "Oh my God, that is disgusting." Cee gasped. She was just getting started.

Elle was next. All of a sudden she spun around with her hands over her mouth and let go in the sink right next to Cee. *Splat.* I started laughing, but I already felt sort of dizzy and sick myself, and also scared, because I didn't want to throw up. Cee looked up from her own sink and nodded at Elle, encouraging her. She looked completely bizarre, her wide cheekbones, her big crown of natural hair, sort of a retro supermodel with a glistening mouth, her eyes full of excitement. I think she even said "Good job, Elle!"

Then she went to it with the toothbrush again. "We have to stop her!" said Katie, taking charge. "Max, go get Jodi!" But Max didn't make it. She jumped down from the third sink, but when she got halfway to the door she turned around and ran back to the sink and puked. Meanwhile Katie was dragging Cee away from the sink and trying to get the toothbrush, but also not wanting to touch it, and she kept going "Ew ew ew" and "*Help* me, you guys," and it was all so hilarious I sank down on the floor, absolutely crying with laughter. Five or six other girls, too. We just sort of looked at each other and screamed. It was mayhem. Katie dragged Cee into one of the stalls, I don't know why. Then Katie started groaning and let go of Cee and staggered into the stall beside her, and *sploosh*, there she went.

Bugs.

It's such a camp rumor. Camp is full of stories like that. People say the ice cream makes you sterile, the bathrooms are full of hidden cameras, there's fanged, flesh-eating kids in the lake, if you break into the office you can call your parents. Lots of kids break into the office. It's the most common camp offense. I never tried it, because I'm not stupid—of course you can't call your parents. How would you even get their number? And bugs—the idea of a bug planted under your skin, to track you or feed you drugs —that's another dumb story.

Except it's not, because I saw one.

The smell in the bathroom was terrible now—an animal smell, hot; it thrashed around and it had fur.

I knew I was going to be sick. I crawled to the closest place—the stall where Cee knelt—and grabbed hold of the toilet seat. Cee moved aside for me. Would you believe she was still hanging on to her toothbrush? I think we both threw up a couple of times. Then she made this awful sound, beyond anything, her whole body taut and straining, and something flew into the toilet with a splash.

I looked at her and there was blood all over her chin. I said, "Jesus, Cee." I thought she was dying. She sat there coughing and shaking, her eyes full of tears and triumph. She was on top of the world. "Look!" she breathed. And I looked, and there in the bowl, half hidden by puke and blood, lay an object made of metal.

It actually looked like a bug. Sharp blood-smeared legs.

"Shit!" I said. I flushed the toilet.

"Now you," said Cee, wiping her mouth on the back of her wrist.

"I can't."

"Tisha. Come on."

Cee, I couldn't, I really couldn't. I could be sick—in fact I felt sicker than ever—but I couldn't do it that hard. I remember the look in your eyes; you were so disappointed. You leaned and spat some blood into the toilet.

I whispered, "Don't tell anyone. Not even the other girls."

"Why not? We should all—"

"*No.* Just trust me."

I was already scared, so scared. I couldn't bear the idea of camp without you.

We barely slept that night. We had to take showers and clean the bathroom. Max cried the whole time, but for at least part of the night I was laughing. Me and Katie flinging disinfectant powder everywhere. Katie was cool, always in sweatpants, didn't give a shit about anything.

"You know your friend is a headcase, right?" she said.

It was the first time anybody'd called Cee my friend. We got out the mop and lathered up the floor. Everyone slipped and swore at us, coming out of the showers. Cee went skidding by in a towel. "Whee!" she shrieked.

You cannot feel your bug. I've pressed so hard on my chest. I know.

"*I* could feel it," said Cee. "After they put it back in." It wasn't exactly a physical thing. She couldn't trace the shape of the bug inside her, but she could feel it *working*.

"Bug juice," she said, making a sour face. She could feel bug juice seeping into her body. Every time she was going to be angry or afraid, there'd be this warmth in her chest, a feeling of calm spreading deep inside.

"I only noticed it after I'd had the bug out for a couple of weeks."

"How did your parents know you needed a new one?"

"I didn't need one."

"How did they know it was gone?"

"Well, I kind of had this fit. I got mad at them and started throwing food."

We were sitting on my bed, under my Mother Figure, a lamp with a blue shade. The blue light brought out the stains on Cee's Victorian nightgown. We were both painting our toenails Cherry Pink, balancing the polish on my Life Skills textbook, taking turns with the brush.

"You should do it," Cee said. "I feel better. I'm so much better."

I thought how in a minute we'd have to study for our Life Skills quiz. I didn't think there was bug juice in my body. I couldn't feel anything.

"I'm so much better," Cee said again. Her hand was shaking.

Oh, Cee.

The weird thing is, I started writing this after Max came to visit me, and I thought I was going to write about Max. But then I started writing in your book. Why? This book you left me, your Mother Figure. You practically threw it at me: "Take it!" It was the worst thing you could do, to take somebody else's Parent Figure, especially the mom. Or maybe it was only us girls who cared so much about the moms. Maybe for the boys it was the dads. But anyway, taking one was the worst; you could basically expect the other kids to kill you. A kid got put in the hospital that way at a different camp—the one on the east side—but we all knew about it at our camp. They strung him up with electric wires. Whenever we told the story we ended by saying what *we* would have done to that kid, and it was always much worse.

But you threw this book at me, Cee, and what could I do? Jodi and Duncan were trying to grab your arms, and the ambulance was waiting for you downstairs. I caught the book clumsily, crumpling it. I looked at it later, and it was about half full of your writing. I think they're poems.

dank smells underground want to get back
no pill for it
i need you

I don't know, are they poems? If they are, I don't think they're very good. *A nap could be a door an abandoned car.* Does that even mean anything? *Eat my teeth.* I know them all by heart.

I picked up this book when Max left. I wrote: "You have to puke it up." All of a sudden I was writing about you. Surprising myself. I just kept going. Remembering camp, the weird sort of humid excitement there, the cafeteria louder than the sea. The shops— remember the shops? Lulu's was the best. We'd save up our allowance to go there. Down in the basement you could get used stuff for cheap. You got your leather jacket there. I got these red shoes with flowers on the toes. I loved those shoes so much! I wonder where they went? I wore them to every mixer, I was wearing them when I met Pete, probably with my white dress—another Lulu's purchase I don't have now.

It was summer, and the mixer had an island theme. The counselors had constructed this sort of deck overlooking the lake. God, they were so proud of it. They gave us green drinks with little umbrellas in them and played lazy, sighing music, and everyone danced, and Pete saw a shooting star, and we were holding hands, and you were gone forever and I forgot you.

I forgot you. Forgetting isn't so wrong. It's a Life Skill.

I don't remember what my parents looked like. A Parent Figure cannot be a photograph. It has to be a more neutral object. It's supposed to stand in for someone, but not too much. When we got to camp we were all supposed to bring our Parent Figures to din-

ner the first night. Everyone squeezed in at the cafeteria tables, trying to find space beside their dinner trays for their Figures, those
calendars and catcher's mitts and scarves. I felt so stupid because
my Mother Figure was a lamp and there was no place to plug it in.
My Father Figure is a plaque that says *Always be yourself.*

Jodi came by, as the counselors were all going around "meeting
the Parents," and she said, "Wow, Tisha, that's a *good* one."

I don't even know if I picked it out.

"We want you to have a fabulous time at camp!" Jodi cried. She
was standing at the front with the other counselors: Paige and Veronica and Duncan—who we'd later call "Hunky Duncan"—and
Eric and Carla and the others.

Of course they'd chosen Jodi to speak. Jodi was so perky.

She told us that we were beginning a special relationship with
our Parent Figures. It was very important not to *fixate*. We shouldn't
fixate on the Parent Figures, and we definitely shouldn't fixate on
the counselors.

My stupid lamp. It was so fucking blue. Why would you bring
something blue? "The most important people in your life are the
other campers!" Jodi burbled. "These are the people you'll know
for the rest of your life! Now, I want you to turn to the person next
to you and say, *Hi, Neighbor!*"

Hi, Neighbor! And later, in the forest, Cee sang to the sky: *Fuck you,
Neighbor!*

Camp was special. We were told that it was special. At camp you
connected with people and with nature. There was no personal
tech. That freaked a lot of people out at first. We were told that
later we'd all be able to get online again, but we'd be adults, and
our relationships would be in place, and we would have learned
our Life Skills, and we'd be ready. But now was special: now was
the time of friends and of the earth.

Cee raised her hand. "What about earthquakes?"

"What?" said Veronica, who taught The Natural World. Veronica was from an older group of counselors; she had gray hair and
leathery skin from taking kids on nature hikes and she was always
stretching to show that you could be flexible when you were old.

"What about earthquakes?" Cee asked. "What about fires? Those are natural. What about hurricanes?"

Veronica smiled at us with her awesome white teeth, because you could have awesome white teeth when you were old, it was all a matter of taking care of yourself with the right Life Skills.

"What an interesting question, Celia!"

We were told that all of our questions were interesting. *There's no such thing as a stupid question!* The important thing was always to *participate.* We were told to participate in classes and hikes and shopping sprees and mixers. In History we learned that there used to be prejudice, but now there wasn't: it didn't matter where you came from or who you loved, *just join in!* That's why even the queer girls had to go to the mixers; you could take your girlfriend, but you had to go. Katie used to go in a tie and Elle would wear flowers. They rolled their eyes but they went anyway and danced and it was fun. Camp was so fun.

Cee raised her hand. "Why is it a compliment to tell somebody it doesn't matter who they are?"

We were told to find a hobby. There were a million choices and we tried them all: sports and crafts and art and music. There was so much to do. Every day there was some kind of program and then there were chores and then we had to study for class. No wonder we forgot stuff. We were told that forgetting was natural. Forgetting helped us survive, Jodi told us in Life Skills class, tears in her eyes. She cried as easily as Max. She was more like a kid sister than a counselor. Everybody wanted Jodi to be okay. "You'll always be reminded," she said in her hoarse, heroic voice. "You'll always have your Parent Figures. It's okay to be sad! But remember, you have each other now. It's the most special bond in the world."

Cee raised her hand. "What if we don't want us?"

Cee raised her hand, but of course she raised her hand. She was *Cee.* She was Cee, she'd always been Cee, do you see what I mean? I mean she was like that right from the day we arrived; she was brash, messy Cee *before* the night in the bathroom, before she supposedly puked out her bug. I couldn't see any difference. *I could not see any difference.* So of course I had second thoughts. I wished so bad I hadn't flushed the toilet. What if there wasn't anything in it? What if somebody'd dropped a piece of jewelry in there, some necklace or brooch, and I thought it was a bug? That could have happened. Camp was so fun. Shaving my legs for the mixer. Wearing red shoes. We were all so lucky. Camp was the best thing ever. *Every Child at Camp!* That was the government slogan: *ECAC.* Cee used to make this gag face whenever she said it. *ECAC.* Ick. Sick.

She took me into the forest. It was a mixer. Everybody else was crowded around the picnic tables. The lake was flat and scummy and the sun was just going down, clouds of biting insects golden in the haze.

"Come on," Cee said, "let's get out of here."

We walked over the sodden sand into the weeds. A couple of the counselors watched us go: I saw Hunky Duncan look at us with his binoculars, but because we were just two girls they didn't care. It only mattered if you left the mixer with a boy. Then you had to stop at the Self-Care Stand for condoms and an injection, because *becoming a parent is a serious decision!* Duncan lowered his binoculars, and we stepped across the rocks and into the trees.

"This is cool!" Cee whispered.

I didn't really think it was cool—it was weird and sticky in there, and sort of dark, and the weeds kept tickling my legs—but I went farther because of Cee. It's hard to explain this thing she had: she was like an event just about to happen and you didn't want to miss it. I didn't want to, anyway. It was so dark we had to hold hands after a while. Cee walked in front of me, pushing branches out of the way, making loud crackling sounds, sometimes kicking to break through the bushes. Her laugh sounded close, like we were trapped in the basement at Lulu's. That's what it was like, like being trapped in this amazing place where everything was magically half-price. I was so excited and then horrified because suddenly I had to take a dump, there was no way I could hold it in.

"Wait a sec," I told Cee, too embarrassed to even tell her to go away. I crouched down and went and wiped myself on the leaves, and I'm sure Cee knew what was up but she took my hand again right after I was done. She took my disgusting hand. I felt like I wanted to die, and at the same time I was floating. We kept going until we stumbled into a clearing in the woods. Stars above us in a perfect circle.

"*Woo-hooooo!*" Cee hollered. "Fuck you, Neighbor!"

She gave the stars the finger. The silhouette of her hand stood out against the bright. I gave the stars the finger, too. I was this shitty, disgusting kid with a lamp and a plaque for parents but I was there with Cee and the time was exactly now. It was like there was a beautiful starry place we'd never get into—didn't *deserve* to get into—but at the same time we were better than any brightness. Two sick girls underneath the stars.

Fuck you, Neighbor! It felt so great. If I could go anywhere I'd want to go there.

The counselors came for us after a while. A circle of them with big flashlights, talking in handsets. Jodi told us they'd been looking everywhere for us. "We were pretty worried about you girls!"

For the first time I didn't feel sorry for her; I felt like I wanted to kick her in the shins. Shit, I forgot about that until right now. I forget so much. I'm like a sieve. Sometimes I tell Pete I think I'm going senile. Like premature senile dementia. Last month I suggested we go to Clearview for our next vacation and he said, "Tish, you hate Clearview, don't you remember?"

It's true, I hated Clearview: the beach was okay, but at night there was nothing to do but drink. So we're going to go to the Palace Suites instead. At least you can gamble there.

Cee, I wonder about you still, so much—I wonder what happened to you and where you are. I wonder if you've ever tried to find me. It wouldn't be hard. If you linked to the register you'd know our graduating class ended up in food services. I'm in charge of inventory for a chain of grocery stores, Pete drives delivery, Katie stocks the shelves. The year before us, the graduates of our camp went into the army; the year after us they also went into the army; the year after that they went into communications technologies; the year after that I stopped paying attention. I stopped wondering what life would have been like if I'd graduated in a different year. We're okay. Me and Pete—we make it work, you know? He's sad because I don't want to have kids, but he hasn't brought it up for a couple of years. We do the usual stuff, hobbies and vacations. Work. Pete's into gardening. Once a week we have dinner with some of the gang. We keep our Parent Figures on the hall table, like everyone else. Sometimes I think about how if you'd graduated with us, you'd be doing some kind of job in food services, too. That's weird, right?

But you didn't graduate with us. I guess you never graduated at all.

*

I've looked for you on the buses and in the streets. Wondering if I'd suddenly see you. God, I'd jump off the bus so quick, I wouldn't even wait for it to stop moving. I wouldn't care if I fell in the gutter. I remember your tense face, your nervous look, when you found out that we were going to have a checkup.

"I can't have a checkup," you said.

"Why not?" I asked.

"Because," you said, "because they'll see my bug is gone."

And I just—I don't know. I felt sort of embarrassed for you. I'd convinced myself the whole bug thing was a mistake, a hallucination. I looked down at my book, and when I looked up you were standing in the same place, with an alert look on your face, as if you were listening.

You looked at me and said, "I have to run."

It was the stupidest thing I'd ever heard. The whole camp was monitored practically up to the moon. There was no way to get outside.

But you tried. You left my room, and you went straight out your window and broke your ankle.

A week later, you were back. You were on crutches and you looked . . . wrecked. Destroyed. Somebody'd cut your hair, shaved it close to the scalp. Your eyes stood out, huge and shining.

"They put a bug in me," you whispered.

And I just knew. I knew what you were going to do.

Max came to see me a few days ago. I've felt sick ever since. Max is the same, hunched and timid; you'd know her if you saw her. She sat in my living room and I gave her coffee and lemon cookies and she took one bite of a cookie and started crying.

Cee, we miss you, we really do.

Max told me she's pregnant. I said congratulations. I knew she and Evan have been wanting one for a while. She covered her eyes with her hands—she still bites her nails, one of them was bleeding —and she just cried.

"Hey, Max," I said, "it's okay."

I figured she was extra-emotional from hormones or whatever, or maybe she was thinking what a short time she'd have with her kid, now that kids start camp at eight years old.

"It's okay," I told her, even though I'd never have kids—I couldn't stand it.

They say it's easier on the kids, going to camp earlier. We—me and you and Max—we were the tail end of Generation Teen. Max's kid will belong to Generation Eight. It's supposed to be a happier generation, but I'm guessing it will be sort of like us. Like us, the kids of Generation Eight will be told they're sad, that they need their parents and that's why they have Parent Figures, so that they can always be reminded of what they've lost, so that they can remember they need what they have now.

I sat across the coffee table from Max, and she was crying and I wasn't hugging her because I don't really hug people anymore, not even Pete really, I'm sort of mean that way, it's just how I turned out, and Max said "Do you remember that night in the bathroom with Cee?"

Do I remember?

Her eyes were all swollen. She hiccuped. "I can't stop thinking about it. I'm scared." She said she had to send a report to her doctor every day on her phone. How was she feeling, had she vomited? Her morning sickness wasn't too bad, but she'd thrown up twice, and both times she had to go in for a checkup.

"So?" I said.

"So—they always put you to sleep, you know . . ."

"Yeah."

I just said "Yeah." Just sat there in front of her and said "Yeah." Like I was a rock. After a while I could tell she was feeling uncertain, and then she felt stupid. She picked up her stuff and blew her nose and went home. She left the tissues on the table, one of them spotted with blood from her bitten nail. I haven't really been sleeping since she left. I mean, I've always had trouble sleeping, but now it's a lot worse, especially since I started writing in your book. I just feel sick, Cee, I feel really sick. All those checkups, so regular, everyone gets them, but you're definitely supposed to go in if you're feeling nauseous, if you've vomited, *it might be a superflu!* The world is full of viruses, *good health is everybody's business!* And yeah, they put you to sleep every time. Yeah. "They put a bug in me," you said. Camp was so fun. Jodi came to us, wringing her hands. "Cee has been having some problems, and it's up to all of us to look after her, girls! *Campers stick together!*" But we didn't stick together, did we? I woke up and you were shouting in the hall, and I ran out there and you were hopping on your good foot, your toothbrush in one hand, your Mother Figure notebook in the other, and I knew exactly what they'd caught you doing. How did they catch you? Were there really cameras in the bathroom? Jodi'd called Duncan, and that was how I knew how bad it was: Hunky Duncan in the girls' hallway, just outside the bathroom, wearing white shorts and a seriously pissed-off expression. He and Jodi were grabbing you and you were fighting them off. "Tisha," called Jodi, "it's okay, Cee's just sick, she's going to the hospital." You threw the notebook. "Take it!" you snarled. Those were your last words. Your last words to me. I never saw you again except in dreams. Yeah, I see you in dreams. I see you in your white lacy nightgown. Cee, I feel sick. At night I feel so sick, I walk around in circles. There's waves of sickness and waves of something else, something that calms me, something that's trying to make the sickness go away. Up and down it goes, and I'm just in it, just try- ing to stand it, and then I sleep again, and I dream you're beside me, we're leaning over the toilet, and down at the very bottom there's something like a clump of trees and two tiny girls are stand- ing there giving us the finger. It's not where I came from, but it's where I *started*. I think of how bright it was in the bathroom that night, how some kind of loss swept through all of us, electric, and you'd started it, you'd started it by yourself, and we were with you in that hilarious and total rage of loss. Let's lose it. Let's lose every- thing. Camp wasn't fun. Camp was a fucking factory. I go out to the factory on Fridays to check my lists over coffee with Elle. The bus passes shattered buildings, stick people rooting around in the garbage. Three out of five graduating classes join the army. *Give me the serenity to accept the things I cannot change!* How did I even get here? I'd ask my mom if she wasn't a fucking lamp. Cee, I feel sick. I should just grab my keys, get some money, and run to Max's house, we should both be sick, everybody should lose it together. I shouldn't have told you not to tell the others. We all should have gone together. My fault. I dream I find you and Puss in a bathroom in the train station. There's blood everywhere, and you laugh and tell me it's hair dye. Cee, it's so bright it makes me sick. I have to go now. It's got to come out.

CARMEN MARIA MACHADO

Help Me Follow My Sister into the Land of the Dead

FROM *Help Fund My Robot Army!!! & Other Improbable Crowdfunding Projects*

Help Me Follow My Sister into the Land of the Dead

by Ursula Ruiz

19
Backers

$1,395
Pledged of $5,229

28
days to go

Back This Project
$1 minimum pledge

The project will only be funded if at least $5,229 is pledged by July 24, 2015 3:41am EDT.

Aid & abet a heartwarming sibling reunion—albeit under grievous circumstances—in a terrifying place where no mortal has any business treading.

Home

This is the thing about my sister and I: we've never gotten along, even when we've gotten along. This is what happens when you have parents who fetishize family, and the viscosity of blood relative to water: you resent the force with which they push you together with this person who is, genetics aside, a stranger. And that's what my sister is: a stranger.

Not to mention a strange girl. Even when we were children, she had a weird fixation on contradicting everything I said, just because. She would pick a phrase to scream at the top of her lungs and do so over and over, like a computer glitch, until I ran out of the room. Whatever. It's not important now. But she's always been trouble. Our moments of connection have always been purely artificial, forged by necessity, by parental birthdays and holiday travel plans.

When I tell you that my sister has absconded to the land of the dead, do not mistake me. She hasn't died. She just did what she always does—i.e., go to a place where she isn't welcome and crash the party just because she feels like it. She heard that there was some "cool stuff" happening on the other side of the veil, and went. I only know where she is because I managed to sober up her blitzed-out roommate vis-à-vis a cold bucket of water to the face just long enough to get access to their Wi-Fi. I found her search history, her bus ticket to Bethlehem (the nearest portal), her emails to her friends about how it's going to be "so amazing," etc.

(In the interest of full disclosure, I also searched her email for my name, but aside from an occasional ping regarding the aforementioned birthdays and travel, there was nothing.)

I am sorry and embarrassed that I have to even ask you for money for this endeavor. The truth is while I'm doing pretty well, all things considered, I don't have the liquidity necessary for this journey. Olive will be embarrassed that I put all of this online, but maybe a dose of shame will do her some goddamned good.

If you sense a tone of resentment to this entire project, that's because I have to go chasing after my wretchedly ungrateful wastrel of a sibling into another dimension to tell her that our parents are dead.

Stretch Goals

Anything over $5,229 is welcome and will be donated to a TBD mental health charity.

How Will I Spend the Money?

Here's how the costs will break down:
    $36.95: Bus ticket to Bethlehem.
    $176.05: Cost of ingredients (salt, sage, cypress branch, matches, mandrake, yew, chalk) to summon the necessary portal.
    $16: The cheapest bottle of whiskey that I can force myself to drink.
    $5,000: A one-time fee, for crossing.

Risks and Challenges

The land of the dead is the land of the dead. Sometimes people don't come back.

FAQ

Do you remember when Olive was born?
I remember the time my mother had Braxton-Hicks contractions —the fake kind—and I went to the hospital with her and my father, and the doctor informed her that she wasn't really in labor. As we left the hospital, I went into hysterics, because I'd been promised a baby sister and one had not been delivered to me. We walked past a woman who was holding her own baby, and I lunged toward her howling "THAT one! I want THAT one!" My parents had to carry me out as I screamed. But of Olive's actual birth, I remember nothing.

How did your parents die?
You know how there was that SUV recall recently, because the

brakes in some of their cars were failing for no reason, causing a series of high-profile, deadly accidents? I wish that was how they died. No, my father shot my mother through her left eye and then turned the gun on himself. Nobody knows why.

Who found their bodies?
I came over for dinner. Olive had been invited, too, but she backed out at the last minute. She said she had "stuff to do." Which honestly is better than her arriving two hours late with a weird dude in tow. Anyway, thank God she wasn't there.

When was the last time you spoke to Olive?
I don't remember.

When was the first time you spoke to Olive?
I don't remember.

What is your biggest regret?
In order from greatest to least: being born, having a little sister, not being adopted, caring at all.

What is your biggest fear?
Genetics.

Pledge $5 or more
  • 9 backers
A thank-you email from Olive, which I will make her deliver.

Pledge $20 or more
  • 52 backers
A small gift from the land of the dead—a pebble or a twig or a finger or something—which I will deliver in a small, sealed jar. KEEP IT IN THE JAR.

Pledge $50 or more
  • 1 backer
I will send you salt from my personal tears, in crystal form (hand-evaporated). Grinder optional.

Pledge $100 or more
  • 1 backer
I will drive my sister to your house, where you can ask her any question. Limited to the contiguous United States.

Pledge $500 or more
  • 0 backers
You will receive an exclusive copy of my and Olive's life story, written with my own hands, and complete with a happy, narratively satisfying ending detailing the success of our journey.

Update #1 • Jun 26, 2015

Starting Out

I know I haven't hit my funding goal yet, but I'm just going to put it on a credit card and pray. I'm on a bus to Bethlehem, which has a pretty decent Wi-Fi connection but, weirdly, no toilets. At least three drug deals have happened in the seat next to me, and in between deals the guy is singing this one part of a song out loud that I recognize from somewhere. I think it might be Paula Cole?

Update #2 • Jun 26, 2015

Still Here

Oh, yeah, it's definitely Paula Cole. It's that weird chanting part of "Where Have All the Cowboys Gone?" Just that part. Over and over. This is why I don't do drugs.

I'm assuming Olive has no idea I'm coming because there's no reception in the land of the dead, but I have been texting her every hour on the hour anyway, just to cover my bases. I haven't told her why I'm coming, because I can't tell her that our parents are dead via text message. I mean, I *could,* but despite what she thinks about me I'm not a monster. I just keep writing "Need to talk to you, v. important." But Olive has no sense of what's important and what isn't. Even if she got the messages, she's probably all "Oh man, Ursula's just having one of those days," which is something

I overheard her telling our mother once, just because I was upset that she didn't want to be my maid of honor. Not that it mattered in the end, with the wedding being called off, but it was upsetting nonetheless.

I'm so fucking tired.

Update #3 • Jun 27, 2015

Past Midnight

I wake up and the bus is parked at the depot. I've probably been here for hours. I'd been dreaming about Olive. While I was sleeping my face had been pressed against the window, with my mouth hanging open.

I walk two miles to the elementary school playground. I get a blister and do the last half-mile limping and barefoot. Then I have to pee, and since I don't know what the restroom situation is in the land of the dead, I squat in some bushes. As I do so, I wonder if my sister is also peeing in a semipublic place. (If the land of the dead can be considered public at all, I guess.)

There is another woman standing here, burning her sage and drawing sigils on the pavement. She doesn't look like she's chasing a wayward family member; she looks like she's ready to party. She has a lot of eyeliner on. I feel angry at her, like she's Olive. She says something and the portal slides open, like the door of a minivan but wreathed in smoke. I look away—it feels rude to stare.

Then she's gone, and it's dark once again. I draw the sigil and arrange the ingredients according to my notes. I say the spell, the unfamiliar syllables catching behind my teeth.

When my portal opens, a faceless creature is standing there. It's tall and roughly shaped, like a dust storm or a swarm of gnats. There are dimples where its eyes should be, but I feel like it's watching me anyway. It takes my credit card, holds it for a moment, and then hands it back.

Olive, backers—please keep in mind that I'm still paying off my student loans.

Oh, I also got a comment on this page from Olive. *Three* comments. I guess she does have reception. Olive, I'm coming anyway, kid. You can't stop me. I may not be the best older sister in the world, but I can do this.

Update #4 • Jun 27, 2015

This Is the Land of the Dead
This is what they don't tell you about the land of the dead: it looks and smells like some approximation of your entire life, but in muted colors and shifting scents—sunscreen, then smoke, then raspberry shaving cream. When I step through the portal I see layers of images shimmering in front of me: the street where I grew up, my current bedroom, my ex-fiancé's house, my college dorm, all in grays and creams and beiges. They undulate back and forth, as if the land of the dead is trying to decide which is the most comforting, and settles on our childhood street. It smells like cedar and blood.

Partying here seems like an impossibility. This is the sort of place where I'd cry or scream or eat water ice or have an existential crisis or drown myself in a memory. I would cut my hair here, all of it, in ragged chunks off my skull. But this does not look like a place with cocktails. There is no club music, only the sound of birds.

Update #5 • Jun 27, 2015

Olive Located
It takes me a while to find Olive. The road stretches and meanders and doesn't lead me exactly where I want to go, like in a dream. I twist through fragments of memory. I see the Girl Scout campground where I bit off a chunk of my tongue tripping into the cold fire pit. I see an empty kitchen, a pot of soup boiling over on the stove. I see the dorm where I lost my virginity, the white cinder block bare of decorations, the whole room ringing hollowly, like a bell.

Then I come upon a two-story house. My childhood home. Well, ours. She is in the living room; I can see her red hair through the window. I open the front door. She is on the couch, the green couch where we both stayed when we had the chicken pox, where we had scratched each other's raw, blistered backs in our sleep.

When she looks up and sees me, she begins screaming.

I haven't held my sister in so long, not since we were children.

She is like something starving, an animal with too many bones, and she pushes against me. She has been crying for so long, her voice falls away. She punches me with her fists, but it is like a bee bumping up against a windowpane.

Update #6 • Jun 27, 2015

Heading Home
She tells me she is going to stay. I say to her, "You cannot stay." She says, "We can bring Mom and Dad back with us, it'll be different," and I say no, it doesn't work that way. I only have enough spell ingredients for two people, and besides, only visitors can leave, not the committed. The land of the dead is the worst kind of hospital. "How did you get here?" she asks. "Magic," I say, and it sounds like I'm being sarcastic, even if I'm not. She says "I hate you," and I say "Sure."

I pick her up from the couch and carry her across the threshold of the house. I drop her to her feet and then pull her through the streets. I remind her that we are all each other has. She pulls against my grip around her wrist, a balloon angling for freedom. "Let me go," she shouts, "please." "No," I say. We flit back past my memories, and the images waver like someone has just bumped into a projector. We come back to the portal, beyond which is the playground, glowing faintly in the watery dawn.

But when I reach out to touch it, someone materializes in front of us. A woman with sad eyes and a floppy sunhat, like she is a hipster, or going to the beach in 1948. She points to me. "You can go," she says. Then she looks at Olive. "You," she says, "need to stay. You know that."

Comments

Olive R about 2 days ago
Don't come for me.

Susan Jameson about 2 days ago
Ursula, I am so sorry!!!! Let me know if I can do anything else.

Your parents were great people I cannot believe this has happened. You're a great sister, Olive is so lucky.

David Mantis about 2 days ago
Donat'd! Good luck, Ursula.

Olive R about 1 day ago
Don't come.

Lucille L about 6 hours ago
Ursula, have the cops managed to get ahold of you? They found something new. Ursula, please call me ASAP.

Olive R about 6 hours ago
Don't.

Lucille L about 4 hours ago
Ursula, check your DMs. I need to talk to you, it's very important.

Olive R about 1 hour ago
Do you remember when we were little girls, and you took me to that abandoned convenience store parking lot where Dad taught us to ride our bikes? The thunderstorm? You were so scared, even more scared than me, I think, and you said "We have to go inside" and broke the glass door with a rock. And we were inside, and the shelves were empty and dirty, and we just sat and watched the lightning bleach the sky and the rain go horizontal. I think that was the last time we really connected. You squeezed me so hard it left black-and-blue marks, but I felt so safe. What were we so afraid of, after that? We just stopped talking. I don't know why. You're a tightass and neurotic as hell but I love you anyway.

I came over to Mom and Dad's early, to catch you. I was going to ask you if you wanted to go partying with me in the land of the dead. Just so we could hang out. I know you're not much of a partier, but I don't know. Sometimes people unexpectedly love dancing. You seem like the kind of person who would unexpectedly love dancing. Or karaoke.

They're going to ask you what happened. Just tell them I came over too early. For once in my life, I was even better than on time.

Messages

Lucille L
Jun 27, 2015
Jesus, Ursula, stop traveling, shut down this page, come home. Fuck. Ursula, just look. www.cnn.com/2015/6/26/us/daughters-body-found-near-murder-suicide.

Lucille L
Jun 27, 2015
I'm so sorry. She was in the woods behind the house. They weren't looking for her, at first, that's why they didn't find her.

Lucille L
Jun 27, 2015
Ursula, are you there?

Lucille L
Jun 28, 2015
Ursula?

CAT RAMBO

Tortoiseshell Cats Are Not Refundable

FROM *Clarkesworld Magazine*

ANTONY BOUGHT THE kit at Fry's in the gray three months after Mindy's death. He swam in and out of fog those days, but he still went frequently to the electronics store and drifted through its aisles, examining hard drives, routers, televisions, microphones, video games, garden lights, refrigerators, ice cream makers, rice cookers, all with the same degree of interest. Which was to say little to none, barely a twitch on the meter. A jump of the arrow from E up to one.

A way to kill time. So were the evenings, watching reality shows and working his way methodically through a few joints. If pot hadn't been legal in Seattle, it would've been booze, he knew, but instead the long, hard, lonely evening hours were a haze of blue smoke until he finally found himself nodding off and hauled himself into bed for a few hours of precious oblivion.

He prized those periods of nothingness.

Each day began with that horrible moment when he put a hand out to touch Mindy's shoulder—Hey, honey, I had this awful dream you died, in a boating accident, no less, when was the last time we were on a *boat*. Then the stomach-dropping realization, sudden as stepping out into an elevator shaft.

Not.

A.

Dream.

His mother called him every day at first, but he couldn't manage the responses. Let alone the conversational give-and-take.

That saddened him. Made him feel guilty, too. He was the only child his mother still had nearby. Both of his sisters had stayed on the other coast and were distant now as then. Still angry at his mother for unimaginable transgressions during their high school years. They both had been excellent at holding a grudge all their lives. He was the only child who'd been willing to take some responsibility for her, had helped her move out to this coast in fact.

He loved her. Bought her presents. That was how the cat, a small tortoiseshell kitten, had entered her life, riding in his coat pocket, a clot of black and orange fur, tiny triangular face split between the colors.

His mother had named it, as with all her animals, palindromically. Taco Cat, like God Dog and Dribybird the parakeet.

She loved that cat about as much as she'd ever loved anything. His mother had always been stolid and self-contained, but he knew she missed the cat even now, a year after its death.

She deserved something to fill her days. He wondered if they'd been as gray as his were nowadays, ever since his father died. He thought—hoped, perhaps—that wasn't true.

Maybe you did get over it with time.

He read somewhere that older people did better, were happier, if they had something they could care for. Taco had been that and now that prop was gone.

He'd replace it.

The kit was one of those late-night things. Infomercial fodder. Clone a beloved pet. Take the sample and send it into their labs. Have a perfect replica delivered within three months. A box five hundred times larger than it needed to be, holding only the test tube in which you would put the fragments of hair or claw material that were required.

He teased clumps from the wire brush he'd taken from his mother's, poked it with a forefinger into the test tube's depths. Stoppered it with a blunt plastic round.

Used his shunt to scan in the bar code on its side and beam it to the mailing center. A drone pecked at his apartment window, three floors up. Colored UPS brown. He could see other brightly colored shipping drones, colored red and green for the holidays, zipping around closer to the street. He authenticated it, staring into its inquisitive eye, and received the confirmation number displayed to one side, hovering in the air before it disappeared.

He was part of the last generation to know what life was like without a shunt. He got one in college, finally, had sold all the gold coins his aunt Mick, who died in the seventh Gulf War, had left him, and he never regretted that.

Life was so much more reliable with the shunt. It made sure you didn't overeat by making you feel satiated after just a few mouthfuls or let you sleep as long and deep as you liked, and even take part in preprogrammed dreams. You could use it to upload knowledge packs, particularly if you had augmented memory. It let you remember everyone's face and every date and time you ever needed to. It was like minor superpowers.

How awesome to live inside the future. Or it should have been.

He'd never thought much about his existence before Mindy. Then all of a sudden he *wanted* a life, a life together full of jokes only they shared. Him cooking her ginger pancakes and spending Sunday mornings lazing in shunt-enhanced sex, pleasurable and languorous and amazing.

He was leaving after a dinner of enchiladas unsatisfyingly sauced, their edges crisp and brown, stabbing the mouth. His mother hadn't mentioned Mindy outright, but she patted him on the upper arm as he paused to slip on his jacket. The gesture was unusual, outside her usual air-kiss intimacies.

He said, "Do you have Taco's old brush?"

"In the cupboard."

It shook him to see all the cat's things, gathered in careful memorial. He didn't associate sentimentality with his mother. Loss did that to you, perhaps. Though she'd endured his father's loss without such a display. At least he thought so. He tried to think back to his father's death. How long had it taken her to send all those shirts and ties and suits to St. Vincent de Paul's thrift shop? Not long. He remembered railing at her angrily about it. He'd planned on wearing all those clothes, two sizes too big for his sixteen-year-old frame, someday.

"It doesn't pay to get attached," she'd said. Her dry eyes infuriated him even further. She'd hugged her arms to herself and returned his angry stare.

He still had things to make up to her for. This would help even the scales so tipped by all his adolescent anger and outbreaks.

*

BCSS sent him an envelope. The language of the thick packet was dense: an opportunity extended him to participate in a test program.

Clone a human.

Give him Mindy back.

He said, "I don't understand how it's possible. I know you can replicate her body, but her mind?"

Dr. Avosh's eyes were clearly artificial, flat circles of emerald green. What did it say about her, that she didn't even bother to try to hide her augmentations?

She said, "We create a matrix of artificial memories. Easy nowadays."

"But where do those memories come from?"

"We have more material than you would think. Social media, public records, and some information garnered from the shunt itself."

That startled him. "Shunts don't record things." There had been plenty of legal battles over that.

"No," Dr. Avosh said. "That's a misconception most people share. While the original versions only recorded what you wanted them to, and had limited memory space, the current versions record a great deal. It's simply inadmissible in court." One of her pupils was markedly larger than the other. As he looked at it, it ratcheted even further wide.

"Are you recording this right now?" he asked.

"It's my policy to record everything."

"In case you ever need to be replicated."

She shook her head, then hesitated. "Not really. There are so many reasons to do so."

"Are they real memories?"

"Are you asking if they are detailed memories? No. More like a memory of a memory, and obviously there will be gaps. It won't be quite the same for you, but for her it will be much smoother. She'll believe herself to be the actual Mindy. We recommend you not talk to her about the actual circumstances until at least six months have passed."

Mindy. The smell of her hair when he buried his nose in it, inhaling the scent as delicious as cinnamon or roses, a musky edge that always tugged at the edges of his erotic consciousness.

There was no way he could say no.

"You said this was a new process. How many times has it been done?"

"This is the third trial batch of subjects. The first time we're using people in your situation."

"My situation?"

Papers on her desk whispered against each other as she fiddled with them. "Recently bereaved. We're curious to see how much the spouse's memory can augment the process and reinforce beliefs."

She paused. "And I must tell you that the company doesn't cover the entire cost."

He'd met Mindy on the R train, heading from his Bay Ridge apartment up into Manhattan to work for the BWSS. He'd handled their computer systems, going in late at night to work through the morning hours maintaining the message boards the BWSS scientists used.

You saw the same people on the train sometimes. He'd noticed her right away: small and birdlike. Always smiling, in a way you didn't hit in NYC. Curious and unafraid, chatting with the woman beside her one day, looking at kid pictures, the next day helping an old man to a seat.

That was Mindy. Friendly. Finally one day she plopped down beside him and said, "Here we go!"

Why she'd said it, she didn't know, she told him later, but indeed they went, first chatting daily, then going for coffee and then, with perfect amity, dating, engagement, marriage in a small chapel attended only by close friends and family.

She had so many friends and they seemed to welcome him into the circle, saying, "Take care of her!"

He had. Until the accident.

Now every day that dizzying fall into the realization she wasn't there.

Any price was worth paying to avoid that.

But costly, so costly. He'd plundered his 401(k), his IRAs, taken out a second mortgage. Cut his bills to the bone and still had to ask his mother for money.

She provided it without question once she found out what it was for.

*

They drew as much as they could on his memories, which meant going in every day for two weeks in a row, sitting there talking about his relationship with Mindy, his history, where they'd gone on their honeymoon, and what a typical trip to the grocery store was like, and where each piece of their bedroom furniture had come from. Dr. Avosh said that was good. The stronger the relationship with him was, the more quickly the cloned Mindy would adjust.

His mother didn't ask about the results or the loan she'd made him to pay for the process. He thought perhaps she was trying to keep him from getting his hopes up too far, but as he aged, increasingly he realized he didn't understand his mother, didn't understand the parts of her that she had kept closed away from her family. It was only in his forties that they had become something like close.

Instead, they talked about the day-to-day drama of her apartment building. He grew interested despite himself, even though the stories were so small, concerning misplaced mail or who shoveled the front walk.

He said, "I got you a present. It should arrive next week. According to the tracking number it's being prepared for shipment right now."

"Should I ask what it is?"

He found himself smiling and the expression almost startled him. How long had it been since the gray had lifted momentarily? Too long.

He and Mindy would laugh about that together eventually. He wondered what that would be like, to be able to say, "While you were dead."

Perhaps it would be better just not to bring that up. He couldn't even begin to imagine what it would be like to live on the other side of that.

"Your present arrived," his mother said. "It's very nice." Her voice was strained.

"You don't like it?" he said.

"Of course I do," she said, but he could tell she was lying.

When he went for dinner, he realized the problem.

"They must have shipped you the wrong cat," he said, looking down at it. It was the same size as Taco and it was a tortoiseshell, but where Taco had been black with dapplings of hazy orange hair, this one was white with awkward splotches of orange and brown.

But the service rep explained. "You can't clone tortoiseshells and expect the same markings. They're random expressions of the gene. The brochure lists certain animals where you can't get an exact copy. Tortoiseshell cats are not refundable."

He hung up abruptly, full of rage. For God's sake, he couldn't get anything right lately.

But that would change when Mindy was back.

He didn't see the new cat the next time he was over and he didn't ask questions.

He could understand loving one configuration but not another. But he didn't want to think about that.

They sent a crew that went over the house, scanning in everything about it. They quizzed him about the usual state of cleanliness, and what days Mindy usually cleaned on, what she was good at and what she was bad at, and how much they actually split up the chores. Her favorite brands.

He didn't know many of the answers. How empty did the refrigerator have to get before she'd go shopping, since she was the one who handled all that? He had no idea. They took another tack and asked him what he remembered them running out of, milk or toilet paper or butter.

"You see, most people have a few trigger items that automatically send them to the store," the data technician chirped at him as she continued running her bar scanner over everything under the sink. She'd quizzed him as to what he purchased and what Mindy had and luckily his only contribution had been a bottle of lime-scented dishwashing soap.

"Have you done many of these before?" he asked.

Her fingers kept clicking over the data pad. She had long thin nails with tiny daggers painted in silver at each tip and a tiny border of circles. "Two so far."

"What were they like?"

"The first preferred Comet and Pine-Sol, the second went with Seventh Generation cleaning products."

"No. I meant . . ." He wasn't sure how to formulate it. "Did it, did it work?"

Her gaze was quizzical. "All I can tell you is that, sure, when they came back they liked the same cleaning brands." She clicked and swiped. "All right, new section. Bed, made or unmade on a regular basis? If the former, who did it?"

"We did it together every morning," he said. His eyes heated up and he hoped he wasn't getting too teary. She tapped away.

"You two were sweet. It will be just as cute in the next round. You'll see."

He brought himself to ask his mother what she'd done with the cat. Her hands faltered as she chopped onions, then resumed their staccato beat.

"Mrs. Green two doors down had mice," she said. "So I loaned her Taco Two."

"Taco Two? No palindrome?" he asked.

A sizzle and then a wave of fragrance as she added the onions to the skillet. "I couldn't think of one yet. I'm sure it'll come to me eventually."

"Eventually," he repeated agreeably. He thought perhaps the cat would end up staying with Mrs. Green, but that was all right.

"So what else is new?"

"I'm bringing her home tomorrow."

She put the spatula down in order to swing around and look at him, wide-eyed. "So soon?"

He nodded. He was smiling again. She smiled back, wiping her hands on her apron before she came over to awkwardly hug him.

What do you bring to your first meeting with the person you used to be married to? He chose an armload of roses. Who cared if it was a cliché? Mindy loved them.

He remembered buying them for her. The two of them together at the farmers' market, wandering from stall to stall, buying bread rounds still warm from baking and bags of vegetables still thick with dirt and leaves. The way she managed to look at every display, ferreted out everything interesting, made people smile as she talked to them.

Roses. So much like her in the way she opened to the world.

Glimpsed through the pane of glass in the door, she seemed so small in the hospital bed. Her eyes were shut. Her hair had once been long, but now it was short, one or two inches at most.

He said to Dr. Avosh, "Why did you cut her hair?"

The doctor chuckled. "I can see where it would seem that way.

But it's because we've had a limited amount of time for her to grow hair in. It'll come."

"Won't that mess with her memories?"

"We've compensated." The doctor put her hand on the gray metal doorknob before looking back over her shoulder at him. "Are you ready to say hello?"

He nodded, unable to speak around the lump in his throat.

The room smelled of lemon disinfectant. The nurse already there took the flowers from him with a muted squeal of delight. "Aren't these pretty! I'll put them in water."

Mindy's eyes were still shut.

"Are you awake, Mindy?" the doctor said. "You have a visitor."

Her eyes opened, fixing on him immediately. "Antony."

The same smile, the same voice.

Emotion pushed him to the bed and he gathered her hands in his, kissing them over and over, before he laid his head down on the cool white hospital sheet and cried for the first time since she died.

He'd asked before what sort of cover story they would have for her waking up in the hospital. Of course they'd thought of that already: a slip in the shower, a knock on the head that accounted for any dizziness or disorientation.

He'd prepared the house as well, made it as close as he could remember to their days together, removed the dingy detritus of a bachelor existence by bringing a cleaning service in. If it seemed too different and she questioned it, he'd tell her that he'd hired the service to help him cope while she was in the hospital.

In the taxi home, as they rumbled their way up Queen Anne, he noticed it.

She didn't look at the world in the same way anymore. A shrinking back, a momentary flinch, a hesitancy about it all.

He asked the doctor about it the next day. He could tell from her expression that she knew the answer already but was reluctant to say. He pushed harder. "Does it mean something went wrong with the process?"

"Of course not," Dr. Avosh snapped. She shook her head. "We still don't understand all the ways that personality is genetically determined."

"If it's genetically determined, then it would be the same," he said.

"It's considerably more complicated than that," she said and began to explain, but he was already thinking of tortoiseshell cats and realizing what he had done.

He couldn't think of anywhere to go but his mother's.

Much to his surprise, she was sitting on the sofa with Taco on her lap.

"I thought you gave her to Mrs. Green," he said.

She ran her hand over the soft fur, rubbing around the base of the cat's ears. He could hear it purring from where he sat. "Just a loan," she said. "Shall I make us some coffee?"

They sat together, drinking it. The cat hopped back onto his mother's lap and began to purr again. She patted it.

"She's more loving, this time around," she said.

"This time around?"

"Yes." She shrugged and kept petting the cat.

"I think Mindy is different this time around, too," he said.

She looked up, brows furrowed. "Is it possible?"

He nodded at the cat in her lap. "It's the same thing, as far as I can tell. Personality is random, at least some of it."

"But she looks just the same."

He rubbed his forehead with the heel of his hand. "Yes, she does. They took great care in that regard. I wouldn't be surprised if they used plastic surgery to correct any discrepancies. But they can't do that with her personality."

"And you can't tell her."

He shook his head.

His mother smoothed her hand over the cat, whispered to it.

"What's that?" he said.

"Asking her what she makes of this."

"But you called her something."

She blushed. "Taco Tooto Cat. Not Taco, but Taco Too."

Not and yet and still.

Like his Mindy. Who he could finally grieve for. Who he could finally meet for the first time.

"Are you going to pretend?" his mother said.

"No," he said. "I'm going to tell her. And tell her why she feels about me like she does. Then she can decide."

"Decide whether or not to keep things as they were?"

"No. Decide whether or not to begin."

KAREN RUSSELL

The Bad Graft

FROM *The New Yorker*

I. Germination

The land looked flattened, as if by a rolling pin. All aspects, all directions. On either side of Highway 62, the sand cast up visions of evaporated civilizations, dissolved castles that lay buried under the desert. Any human eye, goggled by a car's windshield, can graft such fantasies onto the great Mojave. And the girl and the boy in the Dodge Charger were exceptionally farsighted. Mirages rose from the boulders, a flume of dream attached to real rock.

And hadn't their trip unfolded like a fairy tale? the couple later quizzed each other, recalling that strange day, their first in California, hiking among the enormous apricot boulders of Joshua Tree National Park. The girl had got her period a week early and was feeling woozy; the boy kept bending over to remove a pebble from his shoe, a phantom that he repeatedly failed to find. Neither disclosed these private discomforts. Each wanted the other to have the illusion that they might pause, anywhere, at any moment, and make love. And while both thought this was highly unlikely—not in this heat, not at this hour—the possibility kept bubbling up, every place they touched. This was the only true protection they'd brought with them as they walked deeper into the blue-gold Mojave.

On the day they arrived in Joshua Tree, it was 106 degrees. They had never been to the desert. The boy could scarcely believe the size of the boulders, clustered under the enormous sun like dead red rockets awaiting repair, or the span of the sky, a cheerfully vacant blue dome, the desert's hallucinatory choreography achieved through stillness, brightness, darkness, distance—and all of this before noon. It was a big day, they agreed. It was a day so huge, in fact, that its real scale would always elude them. Neither understood that a single hour in the desert could mutate their entire future as a couple. In a sense, they will never escape this trail loop near Black Rock Canyon. They had prepared for the hike well, they thought, with granola bars, water, and an anti-UV sunscreen so powerful that its SPF seemed antagonistic. "Albino spring break," the boy said, rubbing the cream onto her nose. They'd heard about the couple who had died of dehydration six miles from where they were standing. They congratulated themselves on being unusually responsible and believed themselves to be at the start of a long journey, weightless spores blowing west.

The trip was a kind of honeymoon. The boy and girl were eloping. They weren't married, however, and had already agreed that they never would be—they weren't that kind of couple. The boy, Andy, was a reader; he said that they were seafarers, wanderers. "Ever unfixed," a line from Melville, was scraped in red ink across the veins of his arm. The girl, Angie, was three years sober and still struggling to find her mooring on dry land. On their first date they had decided to run away together.

Andy bought a stupidly huge knife; Angie had a tiny magenta flashlight suspended on a gold chain, which she wore around her throat. He was twenty-two, she had just turned twenty-six. Kids were for later, maybe. They could still see the children they had been: their own Popsicle-red smiles haunting them. Still, they'd wanted to celebrate a beginning. And the Mojave was a good place to launch into exile together; already they felt their past lives in Pennsylvania dissolving into rumor, sucked up by the hot sun of California and the perfectly blue solvent of the sky.

They'd been driving for three days; almost nobody knew yet that they were gone. They'd cashed old checks. They'd quit their jobs. Nothing was planned. The rental Dodge Charger had been a real steal, because the boy's cousin Sewell was a manager at the Zero to Sixty franchise, and because it smelled like decades of cigarettes. Between them they had $950 left now. Less, less, less. At each rest stop, Angie uncapped the ballpoint, did some nauseating accounting. Everything was going pretty fast. By the time they reached Nevada, they had spent more than $800 on gasoline.

*

Near Palm Springs they stop to eat at a no-name diner and nearly get sick from the shock of oxygen outside the stale sedan. The night before, just outside Albuquerque, they parked behind a bar-becue restaurant and slept inside a cloud of meat smells. The ex-perience still has the sizzle of a recent hell in Angie's memory. Will they do this every night? She wants to believe her boyfriend when he tells her they are gypsies, two moths drunk on light, darting from the flower of one red sunset to the next; but several times she's dozed off in the passenger seat and awakened from traitor-ous dreams of her old bedroom, soft pillows.

After dinner Andy drives drowsily, weaving slightly. Sand, sand, sand—all that pulverized time. Eons ago the world's burst hour-glass spilled its contents here; now the years pile and spin, waiting with inhuman patience to be swept into some future ocean. Sand washes right up to the paved road, washes over to the other side in a solid orange current, illuminated by their headlights.

"Who lives way out like that?" Angie says, pointing through the window at a line of trailer homes. *Why* is the implied question. Thirteen-foot saguaro cacti look like enormous roadside hitchhik-ers, comical and menacing. Andy is drifting off, his hand on An-gie's bare thigh, when a streak of color crosses the road.

"Jesus! What was that?"

A parade of horned beasts. Just sheep, Angie notes with relief.

Andy watches each animal go from sheep to cloud in the side mirror, reduced immediately into memory. The radio blares songs about other humans' doomed or lost loves, or their bombastic lusts in progress. Andy watches his girlfriend's red lips move, mouthing the lyrics to a song Andy didn't realize he knew. *My wife's lips,* he thinks, and feels frightened by the onslaught of an unexpected happiness. Were they serious, coming out here? Were they kidding around? Are they getting more serious? Less? Perhaps they'll sort it all out at the next rest stop.

That night they stay in a $50 motel. By dawn they are back on the highway. They don't try to account for their urgency to be gone. Both feel it; neither can resist it.

At 10 a.m., Angie lifts her arm to point at the western sky. There is a pale rainbow arcing over the desert. It looks as if God had made a bad laundry error, mixed his colors with his whites. How could even the rainbow be faded? she wonders.

"Look!" she blurts. "We're here."

The sign reads ENTERING JOSHUA TREE NATIONAL PARK.

Quietly they roll under the insubstantial archway of the rainbow. Andy slows the Charger. He wants to record this transition, which feels important. Usually you can only catch the Sasquatch blur of your own legendary moments in the side mirrors.

More and more slowly, they drive into the park. Sand burns outside their windows in every direction. Compass needles spin in their twinned minds: everywhere they look, they are greeted by horizon, deep gulps of blue. People think of the green pastoral when they think of lovers in nature. Those English poets used the vales and streams to douse their lusts into verse. But the desert offers something that no forest brook or valley ever can: distance. A cloudless rooming house for couples. Skies that will host any visitors' dreams with the bald hospitality of pure space. In terms of an ecology that can support two lovers in hot pursuit of each other, this is the place; everywhere you look, you'll find monuments to fevered longing. Craters beg for rain all year long. Moths haunt the succulents, winging sticky pollen from flower to flower.

Near the campground entrance they are met by a blue-eyed man of indeterminate age, a park employee, who comes lunging out of the infernal brightness with whiskery urgency. His feet are so huge that he looks like a jackrabbit, even in boots.

"Where did you folks wash up from?" he asks.

Their answer elicits a grunt.

"First-timers to the park?"

The boy explains that they are on their honeymoon, watches the girl redden with pleasure.

Up close, the ranger has the unnervingly direct gaze and polished bristlecone skin of so many outdoorsmen. A large bee lifts off a cactus, walks the rim of his hat, and he doesn't flick it off, a show of tolerance that is surely for their benefit.

"Do Warren Peak. Go see the Joshua trees. Watch the yucca moths do their magic. You're in luck—you've come smack in the middle of a pulse event. As far as we can tell, the entire range of Joshuas is in bloom right now. You think *you're* in love? The moths are smitten. In all my years, I've seen nothing to rival it. It's a goddamn orgy in the canyon."

It turns out that their visit has coincided with a tremendous blossoming, one that is occurring all over the Southwest. Highly erotic, the ranger says, with his creepy bachelor smile. A record number of greenish white flowers have erupted out of the Joshuas. Pineapple-huge, they crown every branch.

"Now there's an education for a couple, huh? Charles Darwin agrees with me. Says it's the most remarkable pollination system in nature. 'There is no romance more dire and pure than that of the desert moth and the Joshua.'"

"Dire?" the girl asks. And learns from the ranger that the Joshua trees may be on the brink of extinction. Botanists believe they are witnessing a coordinated response to crisis. Perhaps a drought, legible in the plants' purplish leaves, has resulted in this push. Seeds in abundance. The ancient species' Hail Mary pass. Yucca moths, attracted by the flowers' penetrating odor, are their heroic spouses, equally dependent, equally endangered; their larval children feast on yucca seeds.

"It's an obligate relationship. Each species' future depends entirely on the other," the ranger says, and then grins hugely at them. The boy is thinking that the math sounds about right: two species, one fate. The girl wonders, of their own elopement, who is more dependent on whom? What toast might Charles Darwin make were they to break their first vows and get married?

So they obey the ranger, drive the Charger another quarter mile, park at the deserted base of Warren Peak.

Angie says she has to pee, and Andy sits on the hood and watches her.

They set off along the trail, which begins to ascend the ridgeline east of Warren Peak. Now Joshua woodland sprawls around them.

This is where the bad graft occurs.

For the rest of her life she will be driven to return to the park, searching for the origin of the feeling that chooses this day to invade her and make its home under her skin.

Before starting the ascent, each pauses to admire the plant that is the park's namesake. The Joshua trees look *hilariously* alien. Like Satan's telephone poles. They're primitive, irregularly limbed, their branches swooning up and down, sparsely covered with syringe-thin leaves—more like spines, Angie notes. Some mature trees have held their insane poses for a thousand years; they look as if they were on drugs and hallucinating themselves.

The ranger told them that the plant was named in the nineteenth century by a caravan of Mormons, passing through what they perceived to be a wasteland. They saw a forest of hands, which recalled to them the prayers of the prophet Joshua. But the girl can't see these plants as any kind of holy augury. She's thinking Dr. Seuss. Timothy Leary.

"See the moths, Angie?"

No wonder they call it a "pulse event"—wings are beating everywhere.

Unfortunately for Angie, the ranger they encountered had zero information to share on the ghostly Leap. So he could not warn her about the real danger posed to humans by the pulsating Joshuas. Between February and April, the yucca moths arrive like living winds, swirling through Black Rock Canyon. Blossoms detonate. Pollen heaves up.

Then the Joshua tree sheds a fantastic sum of itself.

Angie feels dizzy. As she leans out to steady herself against a nearby Joshua tree, her finger is pricked by something sharp. One of the plant's daggerlike spines. Bewildered, she stares at the spot of red on her finger. Running blood looks exotic next to the etiolated grasses.

Angie Gonzalez, wild child from Nestor, Pennsylvania, pricks her finger on a desert dagger and becomes an entirely new creature.

When the Leap occurs, Angie does not register any change whatsoever. She has no idea what has just added its store of life to hers.

But other creatures of the desert *do* seem to apprehend what is happening. Through the crosshairs of its huge pupils, a tarantula watches Angie's skin drink in the danger: the pollen from the Joshua mixes with the red blood on her finger. On a fuchsia ledge of limestone, a dozen lizards witness the Leap. They shut their gluey eyes as one, sealing their lucent bodies from contagion, inter-kingdom corruption.

During a season of wild ferment, a kind of atmospheric accident can occur: the extraordinary moisture stored in the mind of a passing animal or hiker can compel the spirit of a Joshua to Leap through its own membranes. The change is metaphysical: the tree's spirit is absorbed into the migrating consciousness, where it lives on, intertwined with its host.

Instinct guides its passage now, through the engulfing darkness of Angie's mind. Programmed with the urgent need to plug itself into some earth, the plant's spirit goes searching for terra firma.

Andy unzips his backpack, produces Fiji water and a Snoopy Band-Aid.

"Your nose got burned," he says, and smiles at her.

And at this juncture she can smile back.

He kisses the nose.

"C'mon, let's get out of here."

Then something explodes behind her eyelids into a radial green fan, dazzling her with pain. Her neck aches, her abdomen. The pain moves lower. It feels as if an umbrella were opening below her navel. Menstrual cramps, she thinks. Seconds later, as with a soldering iron, an acute and narrowly focused heat climbs her spine.

At first the Joshua tree is elated to discover that it's alive: *I survived my Leap. I was not annihilated. Whatever "I" was.*

Grafted to the girl's consciousness, the plant becomes aware of itself. It dreams its green way up into her eyestalks, peers out:

Standing there, in the mirror of the desert, are a hundred versions of itself. Here is its home: a six-armed hulk, fibrous and fruiting obscenely under a noon sun. Here is the locus that recently contained this tree spirit. For a tree, this is a dreadful experience. Its uprooted awareness floats throughout the alien form. It concentrates itself behind Angie's eyeballs, where there is moisture. This insoluble spirit, this refugee from the Joshua tree, understands itself to have leapt into hell. The wrong place, the wrong vessel. It pulses outward in a fuzzy frenzy of investigation, flares greener, sends out feelers. Compared with the warm and expansive desert soil, the human body is a cul-de-sac.

This newborn ghost has only just begun to apprehend itself when its fragile tenancy is threatened: Angie sneezes, rubs at her temple. Unaware that this is an immunologic reflex, she is convulsed by waves of nostalgia for earlier selves, remote homes. Here, for some reason, is her childhood backyard, filled with anarchic wildflowers and bordered by Pennsylvania hemlock.

Then the pain dismantles the memory; she holds her head in her hand, cries for Andy.

This is the plant, fighting back.

The girl moans.

"Andy, you don't have any medicine? Advil . . . something?"

The vegetable invader feels the horror of its imprisonment. Its new host is walking away from the Joshua-tree forest, following Andy. What can this kind of survival mean?

Although they don't know it, escape is now impossible for our vagabonding couple. Andy opens the sedan door, Angie climbs in, and in the side mirrors the hundreds of Joshuas shrink away into hobgoblin shapes.

"Angie? You got so quiet."

"It's the sun. My head is killing me, honey."

Dispersed throughout her consciousness, the tree begins to grow.

Andy has no clue that he is now party to a love triangle. What he perceives is that his girlfriend is acting very strangely.

"Do you need some water? Want to sit and rest awhile?"

At the motel, the girl makes straight for the bathroom faucet. She washes down the water with more water, doesn't want to eat dinner. When Andy tries to undress her, she fights him off. Her movements seem to him balletic, unusually nimble; yet, walking across the room, she pauses at the oddest moments. That night she basks in the glow of their TV as if it were the sun. Yellow is such a relief.

"I hate this show," the boy says, staring not at the motel TV but at her. "Let's turn it off?"

Who are you? he does not bother to ask.

Calmly, he becomes aware that the girl he loves has exited the room. Usually when this sensation comes over him, it means she's fallen asleep. Tonight she is sitting up in bed, eyes bright, very wide awake. Her eyes in most lighting are hazel; tonight they are the brightest green. As if great doors had been flung open onto an empty and electrically lit room.

The Joshua tree "thinks" in covert bursts of activity:

Oh, I have made a terrible mistake.

Oh, please get me out of it, get me out of it, send me home.

"The headache," she calls the odd pressure at first. "The green headache."

"Psychosis," at 4 a.m., when its power over her crests and she lies awake terrified. "Torpor" or "sluggishness" when it ebbs.

Had you told her, *The invader is sinking its roots throughout you, tethering itself to you with a thousand spectral feelers,* who knows what she would have done?

The next day they wake at dawn, as per their original plan: to start every day at sunup and navigate by whim. They go north on 247, with vague plans to stop in Barstow for gas. The girl's eyes are aching. Partway across the Morongo Basin, she starts to cry so hard that the boy is forced to pull over.

"Forget it," she says.

"Forget what?"

"It. All of it. The seafaring stuff—I can't do it anymore."

The boy blinks at her.

"It's been four days."

But her lips look blue, and she won't be reasonable.

"Leave me here."

"You don't have any money."

"I'll work. They're hiring everywhere in town, did you notice that?" A job sounds unaccountably blissful to the girl. Drinking water in the afternoon. Sitting at a desk.

"What? What the hell are you talking about?"

The boy scowls down at his arm, flipped outward against the steering wheel. She keeps talking to him in a new, low monotone, telling him that she loves the desert, she loves the Joshua trees, she wants to stay. Dumbly he rereads his own tattoo: *Ever unfixed.* For some reason he finds that he cannot quite blame the girl for ruining things. It's the plan he hates, their excellent plan, for capsizing on them.

The crumbly truth: the boy imagined that he'd be the one to betray the girl.

"Andy, I'm sorry. But I know that I belong here."

"O.K., just to be clear: When you say 'here,' you mean this parking lot?" The sedan is parked outside Cojo's Army Surplus and Fro-Yo; it's a place where you can purchase camo underwear and also a cup of unlicensed TCBY swirl. "Or do you mean this?" He waves his arms around to indicate the desert.

Had they continued, just a short distance northwest of Yucca Valley they would have reached the on-ramp to I-15 North and, beyond that, the pinball magic of the tollbooths, that multiverse of possible futures connected by America's interstate system.

For the next two hours they fight inside the car.

Round clusters of leaves shake loose in front of her eyes, greeny white blossoms. If she could only show him the desert in her imagination, Angie thinks, the way she sees it.

When it becomes clear that she's not joking, the boy turns the car around. Calls Cousin Sewell in Pennsylvania, explains their situation. "We want to stay awhile," he says. "We like it here."

Sewell needs to know how long. They'll have to put the car on some conveyance, get it back to Pennsylvania.

"Indefinitely," the boy hears himself say. Her word, for what she claims to want.

They decide to pay the weekly rate at the motel. They go for walks. They go for drives. Her favorite thing seems to be sitting in a dry wreck of a turquoise Jacuzzi they discover on the edge of town, some luckless homesteader's abandoned pleasure tub. And he likes this, too, actually—sitting in the tub, he finds it easy to pretend that they aren't trapped in a tourist town, that they are sailing toward an elsewhere. And he loves what happens to her face right at sunset over the infinite desert. Moonlight, however, affects her in a way that he finds indescribably frightening. The change is in the eyes, he thinks.

II. Emergence

Two weeks later, in late April, their money runs out. They've spent the days outside, Angie doing stretches in the motel courtyard, Andy reading his stolen library books from back east, waiting for the bad enchantment to break. Andy tells Angie he is leaving her. They have no vehicle, the rental Dodge having been chauffeured east by a genial grifter pal of Sewell's. Angie nods, staring out the window of their room as the rain sweeps over the desert. All the muddy colors of the sky touch the earth.

"Did you hear me? I said I'm leaving, Angie."

That afternoon Andy gets a job at the Joshua Tree Saloon.

Then there is a period of peace, coinciding with the Joshua tree's dormancy inside of Angie, which lasts from April to mid-May. In the park, the Joshuas' blossoms have all dropped off, leaving dried stalks. Andy does not even suggest "moving on" anymore, so thrilled is he to laugh with Angie again. He comes home with green fistfuls of tourist cash, reeking of Fireball and Pine-Sol. *O.K.,* he thinks. *Oh, thank God. We're getting back to normal.*

Then one day, after a spectacular freak thundershower, Angie tells him that he needs to go home. Or away. Elsewhere, a bedroom other than the motel.

She feels terrible, she doesn't know what she is saying.

Get me out of it, the plant keeps throbbing like a muscle in

Angie's mind. A rustling sound in her inner ear, the plant's footsteps. A throaty appetite makes her imagine stuffing herself with
hot mouthfuls of desert sand. Once Andy leaves her, she'll have a
chance to inspect her interior, figure out what's gone haywire.

"Let's go to Reno," Andy says. He feels quite desperate now,
spinning the radio dial through seas of static. His great success this
week at work was formalizing, via generous pours of straight gin, a
new friendship with Jerry the Mailman, who has given him access
to his boxy truck.

"Go to Reno. Win big. I'll be right here. I don't want to leave
the desert."

Why doesn't she? The girl grows hysterical whenever Andy
drives toward the freeway that might carry them away from the
Mojave. She feels best when they are close to Warren Peak and the
Black Rock Canyon campground.

For the next two weeks, she keeps encouraging Andy to leave
her. Sometimes she feels a lump in her throat that she can't swallow, and it's easy to pretend that this is a vestige of who she used
to be, her Pennsylvania history, now compacted into a hard ball
she cannot access or dissolve; for Andy's sake, she wishes she could
be that girl again. Dimly she is aware that she used to crave travel,
adventure. She can remember the pressure of Andy's legs tangled
around her, but not what she held in her mind. The world has
grown unwieldy, and there are days now when the only thing that
appeals to her is pulling up her T-shirt and going belly flat on the
burning pink sand beyond the motel walkway.

One night Angie turns to face the wall. Golf-ball-sized orange-
and-yellow flowers pattern their wallpaper. Plus water stains from
ancient leaks. She has never noticed this before. Under the influence of the Joshua, she sees these water stains as beautiful. That
Rorschach is more interesting than TV. "What do you see?" she
asks the boy.

"I'm not in the mood," he says, having at last been granted the
opportunity to have a mood, after days and hours spent trying to
rekindle her appetite for pleasure, for danger. He realizes that he
has cut all ties for her, that he has nothing he wants to return to in
Pennsylvania. It's a liberating, terrifying feeling. If she leaves him
—if he leaves her—what then?

*

Now the plant is catching on to something.

In its three months of incubation, it grows exponentially in its capacity for thought. Gradually the plant learns to "think" blue, to "smell" rain through a nose.

Unfurling its languorous intelligence, it looks out through her eyes, hunting for meaning the way it used to seek out deep sun, jade dew, hunting now for the means of imagining its own life, comprehending what it has become inside the girl.

The Joshua tree discovers that it *loves* church! Plugging one's knees into the purple risers, lifting to enter a song. The apple-red agony painted onto the cheeks of the sallow man. All the light that fills the church drifts dreamily over the Joshua tree, which stretches to its fullest extension inside the girl during the slow-crawling time of the service. It approves of this place, which resembles a massive seed hull. Deeply, extrapolating from its forays into the earth, it understands the architecture and the impulse. Craving stillness, these humans have evolved this stronghold.

"How was it?" Andy asks, picking her up. He refused to go with her. Sundays are his day off. "Delicious God-bread? Lots of songs?"

"It was nice. What are you so jealous about?"

"Angie, you never said."

"Mmm?"

"I didn't know you were religious."

Her head bobs on the long stem of her neck, as if they were agreeing on a fascinating point.

"Yes. There's plenty we don't know about each other."

I can still get out of this, he thinks. Without understanding exactly how the trap got sprung, he can feel its teeth in him.

"You should come in next time," she offers. "You'd like the windows."

"I can see the windows right now."

"You'd like being on our side of them."

Seed hull, the girl thinks, for no reason.

Sometimes, to earn extra money, she watches kids who are staying at the motel. Six dollars an hour, four dollars for each additional kid. She is good at it, mostly.

Timmy Babson hates the babysitter. Sometimes her eyes are a dull, friendly brown and as kind as his sister's; sometimes they are twin vacuums. This is already pretty scary. But tonight, when he looks over, he sees the bad light flooding into them. Not yellow, not green. An older color, which Timmy recognizes on sight but cannot name. And this is much worse.

His own eyes prickle wetly. His blond hair darkens with sweat; pearls of water stand out on his smooth six-year-old forehead. The longer he stares back, the wider the gaze seems to get, like a grin. Her eyes radiate hard spines of heat, which drill into him. Timmy Babson feels punctured, "seen."

"Jane!" Timmy screams for his mother, calling for her by her first name for the first time. "Jane, Jane! It's looking at me again!"

On her good days, Angie tries to battle the invader. She thinks she's fighting against lethargy. She does jumping jacks in the motel courtyard, calls her best friend in Juneau from the motel pay phone and anxiously tries to reminisce about their shitty high school band. They sing an old song together, and she feels almost normal.

But increasingly she finds herself powerless to resist the warmth that spreads through her chest, the midday paralysis, the hunger for something slow and deep and unnameable. Some maid has drawn the blackout curtains. One light bulb dangles. The dark reminds Angie of packed earth, moisture. What she interprets as sprawling emotion is the Joshua tree. Here was its birth, in the sands of Black Rock Canyon. Here was its death, and its rebirth as a ghostly presence in the human. Couldn't it perhaps Leap back into that older organism?

The light bulb pulses in time with Angie's headache. It acquires a fetal glow, otherworldly.

Home, home, home.

Down, down, down.

Her heels grind uselessly into the carpet. Her toes curl at the fibers. She stands in the quiet womb of the room, waiting for a signal from the root brain, the ancient network from which the invader has been exiled. She lifts her arms until they are fully extended, her fingers turned outward. Her ears prick up like sharp leaves, alert for moisture.

She is still standing like that when Andy comes home with groceries at 10 p.m., her palms facing the droning light bulb, so perfectly still that he yelps when he spots her.

*

How old such stories must be, legends of the bad romance between wandering humans and plants! How often these bad grafts must occur, and few people ever the wiser!

In 1852 the Mormon settlers who gave the Joshua tree its name reported every variety of disturbance among their party after hikes through the sparse and fragrant forests of Death Valley. One elder sat on a rock at the forest's edge and refused to move.

1873, in the lawless town of Panamint City. Darwin in 1874; Modoc in 1875. During the silver boom dozens of miners went missing. Many leapt to their deaths down the shafts. The silver rush coincided with a pulse event: the trees blossomed unstoppably, wept pollen, and Leapt, eclipsing the minds of these poor humans, who stood no chance against the vegetable's ancient spirit. Dying is one symptom of a bad graft. The invasive species coiled green around the silver miners' brains.

1879: All towns abandoned. Sorted ore sat in wheelbarrows aboveground, winking emptily at the nearby Joshuas.

In 1922, in what is now the southern region of the park, near the abandoned iron mines of Eagle Mountain, a man was killed by the human host of a Joshua tree. It was not difficult to find the murderer, since a girl was huddled a few feet from the warm body, sobbing quietly.

"A crime of passion," the young officer, who tended to take a romantic view of motives, murmured. The grizzled elder on the call with him had less to say about what drove anyone to do anything.

All the girl could remember was the terrible, irremediable tension between wanting to be somewhere and wanting to be nowhere. And the plant, crazed by its proximity to rich familiar soil, tried repeatedly to Leap out of her. This caused her hand to lift, holding a long knife, and plummet earthward, rooting into the fleshy chest of her lover, feeling deeper and deeper for moisture.

The Joshua tree's greatest victory over the couple comes four months into their stay: they sign a lease. A bungalow on the outskirts of the national park, with a fence to keep out the coyotes and an outdoor shower.

When the shower water gets into their mouths, it tastes like poison. Strange reptiles hug the fence posts, like colorful olives on toothpicks. Andy squeezes Angie's hand and returns the gaze of these tiny monsters; he feels strangely bashful as they bugle their throats at him. Four months into his desert sojourn, and he still doesn't know the name of anything. Up close, the bungalow looks a lot like a shed. The bloated vowels of his signature on the landlord's papers make him think of a large hand blurring underwater.

Three Joshua trees grow right in their new backyard.

Rent, before utilities, is $400.

"We can't afford this," he tells the girl, speaking less to her than to the quiet trees, wanting some court stenographer in the larger cosmos to record his protest.

The landlord, who is a native of Yucca Valley, is taking the young couple through the calendar. His name is Desert John, and he offers these Eastern kids what he calls Desert John's Survival Tips. With laconic glee, he advises Andy to cut back the chaparral in their backyard to waist height in summer, to avoid the "minimal" danger of baby rattlesnakes. He tells Angie to hydrate "aggressively," especially if she's trying to get pregnant. (Angie starfishes a hand over her belly button and blanches; nobody has said anything to suggest this.) With polite horror, the couple nod along to stories of their predecessors, former tenants who collapsed from heat exhaustion, were bitten by every kind of snake and spider: "Fanged in the ankle and ass, I shit you not, kids. Beware the desert hammock."

Average annual rainfall: five inches. Eight-degree nights in December, 112-degree July days. Andy is thinking of Angie's face on the motel pillow. He calculates they've slept together maybe fourteen times in four months. In terms of survival strategies, in a country hostile to growth? These desert plants, so ostentatiously alive in the Mojave, have got zero on Andy.

III. Establishment

Once, and only once, the three of them achieve a perfect union.

It takes some doing, but Andy finally succeeds in getting her out of the house.

"It's our anniversary," he lies, since they never really picked a day.

He's taking Angie to Pappy and Harriet's Pioneertown Palace, a frontier-themed dance hall frequented by bikers and artists and other jolly modern species of degenerates. It's only six miles north-east of their new home and burns like a Roman candle against the immensity of the Mojave. Through surveying expeditions made in Jerry's truck, Andy has delimited the boundary lines of Angie's tolerance; once they move beyond a certain radius, she says that her head feels "green" and her bones begin to ache. Pain holds her here—that's their shared impression. So when Andy parks the truck they are both relieved to discover that she is smiling.

The Joshua tree discovers that it *loves* to dance! Better even than church is the soft glow of the hexagonal dance floor. Swung around in strangers' arms, Andy and Angie let themselves dance until they are sick, at the edge of the universe. Andy lets Angie buy him three shots of rum. A weather seizes them and blows them around—a weather you can order for a quarter, the juke-box song.

It is a good night. Outside the dance hall, the parking lot is full of cars and trucks, empty of humans. The wind pushes into them, as hot as the blasts of air from a hand dryer. Angie draws Andy's attention to the claret cup of the moon. "It looks red," she says. And it does. Sitting on a stranger's fender, listening to the dying strains of a pop song they both despise, Andy asks her softly, "What's changed, Angie?"

And when she doesn't or can't answer, he asks, "What's changing now?"

A question they like better, because at least its tense sounds more hopeful.

The Joshua tree leafs out in her mind. Heat blankets her; for a moment she is sure she will faint. Her vision clears. "Bamboleo" plays inside the dance hall. Through the illuminated squares of its windows, they can see the waving wheat of the dancers' upper bodies. Mouths gape in angry shock behind the frosted glass; they are only singing along to the music, Angie knows. Outside, the boy presses his mouth against hers. Now he is pressing every part of himself against the girl; inside her, his competitor presses back.

"Let's go. Let's go. Let's get the fuck out of here."

"Let's go back inside."

In the end, the three of them settle on a compromise: they dance in the empty parking lot, under stars that shoot eastward like lateral rain.

For a second the Joshua tree can feel its grip on the host weakening. The present threatens its existence: the couple's roaring happiness might dislodge the ghostly tree. So it renews its purchase on the girl, roots into her memory.

"Remember our first day, Andy? The hike through Joshua Tree?"

Compared with that, Angie thinks, *what is there for us in the present?* "Nostalgia," we are apt to label this phenomenon. It is the success of the invading plant, which seeks only to anchor itself in the past. Why move forward? Why move at all?

"Is this the spot? Are you sure?"

Andy spreads out the blanket. A soft aura surrounds the low moon, as if the moon itself were dreaming. The red halo reminds him of a miner's carbide lantern.

At first, when the girl suggested that they drive out to the park, he felt annoyed, then scared; the light was in her eyes again, eclipsing the girl she'd been only seconds earlier. But once he'd yielded to her plan the night had organized itself into a series of surprises, the first of which was his own sharp joy; now he finds he's thrilled to be back inside the Black Rock Canyon campground with her. (The Joshua is also pleased, smiling up through Angie's eyes.) It is her idea to retrace the steps of their first hike to Warren Peak. "For our anniversary," she says coolly, although this rationale rings hollow, reminds Andy of his own bullshit justifications for taking out a lease on a desert "bungalow." He does not guess the truth, of course, which is that, slyly, the Joshua tree is proliferating inside Angie, each of its six arms forking and flowering throughout her in the densest multiplication of desire. *Leap, Leap, Leap.* For months it has been trying to drive the couple back to this spot. Its vast root brain awaits it, forty feet below the soil.

Angie has no difficulty navigating down the dark path; the little flashlight around her neck is bouncing like a leashed green sun. Her smile, when she turns to find Andy, is so huge that he wonders if he wasn't the one to suggest this night hike to her. Something unexpected happens then, for all of them: they reenter the romance of the past.

"*Why didn't we then . . .*" all three think as one.

Quickly that sentiment jumps tenses, becomes:

"*Why don't we now . . .*"

When they reach the water tank, which is two hundred yards

from the site of the Leap, Angie asks Andy to shake out the blanket. She sucks on the finger she pricked.

Around the blanket, tree branches divide and braid. They look mutinous in their stillness. Andy can see the movie scene: Bruce Willis attacking an army of Joshuas. He is imagining this, the trees swimming across the land like sand octopuses, flailing their spastic arms, when the girl catches his wrist in her fingers.

"Can we?"

"Why not?"

Why didn't they, Andy wonders, back then? The first time they walked this loop, they were preparing to do plenty. Andy unzips his jeans, shakes the caked-black denim off like solid dust. Angie is wearing a dress. Their naked legs tangle together in a pale, fleshy echo of the static contortionists that surround their blanket. Now the Joshua tree loves her. It grows and it flowers.

Angie will later wonder how exactly she came to be in possession of Andy's knife. Its bare blade holds the red moon inside it. She watches it glimmer there, poised just above Andy's right shoulder. The ground underneath the blanket seems to undulate; the fabric of the desert is wrinkling and flowing all around them. Even the Joshua trees, sham dead, now begin to move; or so it seems to the girl, whose blinded eyes keep stuttering.

The boy's mouth is at the hollow of the girl's throat, then lower; she moans as the invader's leaves and roots go spearing through her, and still he is unaware that he's in any danger.

I can Leap back, the plant thinks.

Angie can no longer see what she is doing. Her eyes are shut, her thoughts have stopped. One small hand rests on Andy's neck; the other fist withdraws until the knife points earthward. *Down, down, down,* the invader demands. Something sighs sharply, and it might be Andy or it might be the entire forest.

Leap, Leap, Leap, the Joshua implores.

What saves the boy is such a simple thing. Andy props himself up on an elbow, pausing to steady his breath. He missed the moment when she slid the knife from the crumpled heap of his clothing; he has no idea that its blade is sparkling inches from his neck. Staring at Angie's waxy, serious face, he is overcome by a flood of memories.

"Hey, Angie?" he asks, stroking the fine dark hairs along her arm. "Remember how we met?"

One of the extraordinary adaptive powers of our species is its ability to transmute a stray encounter into a first chapter.

Angie has never had sticking power. She dropped out of high school; she walked out of the GED exam. Her longest relationship, prior to falling for Andy, was seven months. But then they'd met (no epic tale there—the game was on at a hometown bar), and something in her character was spontaneously altered.

He remembers the song that was playing. He remembers ordering another round he could not afford—a freezing Yuengling for himself, ginger ale for her. They were sitting on the same wooden stools, battered tripods, that had supported the plans and commitments of the young in that town for generations.

The Joshua tree flexes its roots. Desperately it tries to fix its life to her life. In the human mind, a Joshua's spirit can be destroyed by the wind and radiation fluxes of memory. Casting its spectral roots around, the plant furiously reddens with a very human feeling: humiliation.

What a thing to be undone by—golden hops and gingerroot, the clay shales of Pennsylvania!

It loses its grip on her arm; the strength runs out of her tensed biceps.

The girl's fingers loosen; the knife falls, unnoticed, to the sand.

The green invader is displaced by the swelling heat of their earliest happiness. Banished to the outermost reaches of Angie's consciousness, the Joshua tree now hovers in agony, half forgotten, half dissolving, losing its purchase on her awareness and so on its own reality.

"What a perfect night!" the couple agree.

Angie stands and brushes sand from her skirt. Andy frowns at the knife, picks it up.

"Happy anniversary," he says.

It is not their anniversary, but doesn't it make sense for them to celebrate the beginning here? This desert hike marked the last point in space where they'd both wanted the same future. What they are nostalgic for is the old plan, the first one. Their antique horizon.

Down the trail, up and down through time, the couple walk back toward the campground parking lot. Making plans again, each of them babbling excitedly over the other. Maybe Reno. Maybe Juneau.

Andy jogs ahead to their loaner getaway vehicle.

The Black Rock Canyon campground is one of the few places in the park where visitors can sleep amid the Joshua trees, soaking up the starlight from those complex crystals that have formed over millennia in the desert sky. Few of these campers are still outside their tents and RVs, but there is one familiar silhouette: it's the ranger, who is warming his enormous feet, bony and perfectly white, by the fire pit. Shag covers the five-foot cactus behind him, which makes it look like a giant's mummified thumb.

"You lovebirds again!" he crows, waving them over.

Reluctantly, Andy doubles back. Angie is pleased, and frightened, that he remembers them.

"Ha! Guess you liked the hike."

For a few surreal minutes, standing before the leaping flames, they talk about the hike, the moths, the Joshua woodland. Andy is itching to be gone; already he is imagining giving notice at the saloon, packing up their house, getting back on the endlessly branching interstate. But Angie is curious. Andy is a little embarrassed, in fact, by the urgent tone of her questions. She wants to hear more about the marriage of the yucca moth and the Joshua —is theirs a doomed romance? Can't the two species untwine, separate their fortunes?

Andy leaves to get the truck.

And the pulse event? Have the moths all flown? Will the Joshua tree die out, go extinct in the park?

A key turns in the ignition. At the entrance to Black Rock Canyon, Andy leans forward against the wheel, squinting through the windshield. He is waiting for the girl to emerge from the shadows, certain that she will do so; and then a little less sure.

"Oh, it's a hardy species," the ranger says. His whiskers are clear tubes that hold the red firelight. "Those roots go deep. I wouldn't count a tree like that out."

ALAYA DAWN JOHNSON

A Guide to the Fruits of Hawai'i

FROM *The Magazine of Fantasy & Science Fiction*

KEY'S FAVORITE TIME of day is sunset, her least is sunrise. It should be the opposite, but every time she watches that bright red disk sinking into the water beneath Mauna Kea her heart bends like a wishbone, and she thinks, *He's awake now.*

Key is thirty-four. She is old for a human woman without any children. She has kept herself alive by being useful in other ways. For the past four years, Key has been the overseer of the Mauna Kea Grade Orange blood facility.

Is it a concentration camp if the inmates are well fed? If their beds are comfortable? If they are given an hour and a half of rigorous boxercise and yoga each morning in the recreational field?

It doesn't have to be Honouliui to be wrong.

When she's called in to deal with Jeb's body—bloody, not drained, in a feeding room—yoga doesn't make him any less dead.

Key helps vampires run a concentration camp for humans.

Key is a different kind of monster.

Key's favorite food is umeboshi. Salty and tart and bright red, with that pit in the center to beware. She loves it in rice balls, the kind her Japanese grandmother made when she was little. She loves it by itself, the way she ate it at fifteen, after Obaachan died. She hasn't had umeboshi in eighteen years, but sometimes she thinks that when she dies she'll taste one again.

This morning she eats the same thing she eats every meal: a nutritious brick patty, precisely five inches square and two inches deep, colored puce. Her raw scrubbed hands still have a pink tinge of Jeb's blood in the cuticles. She stares at them while she sips the accompanying beverage, which is orange. She can't remember if it ever resembled the fruit.

She eats this because that is what every human eats in the Mauna Kea facility. Because the patty is easy to manufacture and soft enough to eat with plastic spoons. Key hasn't seen a fork in years, a knife in more than a decade. The vampires maintain tight control over all items with the potential to draw blood. Yet humans are tool-making creatures, and their desires, even nihilistic ones, have a creative power that no vampire has the imagination or agility to anticipate. How else to explain the shiv, handcrafted over secret months from the wood cover and glue-matted pages of *A Guide to the Fruits of Hawai'i*, the book that Jeb used to read in the hours after his feeding sessions, sometimes aloud, to whatever humans would listen? He took the only thing that gave him pleasure in the world, destroyed it—or recreated it—and slit his veins with it. Mr. Charles questioned her particularly; he knew that she and Jeb used to talk sometimes. Had she *known* that the *boy* was like this? He gestured with pallid hands at the splatter of arterial pulses from jaggedly slit wrists: oxidized brown, inedible, mocking.

No, she said, of course not, Mr. Charles. I report any suspected cases of self-waste immediately.

She reports any suspected cases. And so, for the weeks she has watched Jeb hardly eating across the mess hall, noticed how he staggered from the feeding rooms, recognized the frigid rebuff in his responses to her questions, she has very carefully refused to suspect.

Today, just before dawn, she choked on the fruits of her indifference. He slit his wrists and femoral arteries. He smeared the blood over his face and buttocks and genitals, and he waited to die before the vampire technician could arrive to drain him.

Not many humans self-waste. Most think about it, but Key never has, not since the invasion of the Big Island. Unlike other humans, she has someone she's waiting for. The one she loves, the one she prays will reward her patience. During her years as overseer, Key has successfully stopped three acts of self-waste. She has failed twice. Jeb is different; Mr. Charles sensed it somehow, but vampires can only read human minds through human blood. Mr. Charles hasn't drunk from Key in years. And what could he learn, even if he did? He can't drink thoughts she has spent most of her life refusing to have.

. . .

Mr. Charles calls her to the main office the next night, between feeding shifts. She is terrified, like she always is, of what they might do. She is thinking of Jeb and wondering how Mr. Charles has taken the loss of an investment. She is wondering how fast she will die in the work camp on Lanai.

But Mr. Charles has an offer, not a death sentence.

"You know . . . of the facility on Oahu? Grade Gold?"

"Yes," Key says. Just that, because she learned early not to betray herself to them unnecessarily, and the man at Grade Gold has always been her greatest betrayer.

No, not a man, Key tells herself for the hundredth, the thousandth time. *He is one of them.*

Mr. Charles sits in a hanging chair shaped like an egg with plush red velvet cushions. He wears a black suit with steel-gray pinstripes, sharply tailored. The cuffs are high and his feet are bare, white as talcum powder and long and bony like spiny fish. His veins are prominent and round and milky blue. Mr. Charles is vain about his feet.

He does not sit up to speak to Key. She can hardly see his face behind the shadow cast by the overhanging top of the egg. All vampires speak deliberately, but Mr. Charles drags out his tones until you feel you might tip over from waiting on the next syllable. It goes up and down like a calliope—

". . . what do you *say* to heading down there and *sort*ing the matter . . . out?"

"I'm sorry, Mr. Charles," she says carefully, because she has lost the thread of his monologue. "What matter?"

He explains: a Grade Gold human girl has killed herself. It is a disaster that outshadows the loss of Jeb.

"You would not believe the expense taken to keep those humans Grade Gold standard."

"What would I do?"

"Take it in hand, *of* course. It seems our small . . . Grade Orange operation has gotten some notice. Tetsuo asked for you . . . particularly."

"Tetsuo?" She hasn't said the name out loud in years. Her voice catches on the second syllable.

"*Mr.* Tetsuo," Mr. Charles says, and waves a hand at her. He holds a sheet of paper, the same shade as his skin. "He wrote you a *letter.*"

Key can't move, doesn't reach out to take it, and so it flutters to the black marble floor a few feet away from Mr. Charles's egg.

He leans forward. "I think . . . I remember something . . . you and Tetsuo . . ."

"He recommended my promotion here," Key says, after a moment. It seems the safest phrasing. Mr. Charles would have remembered this eventually; vampires are slow, but inexorable.

The diffuse light from the paper lanterns catches the bottom half of his face, highlighting the deep cleft in his chin. It twitches in faint surprise. "You *were* his pet?"

Key winces. She remembers the years she spent at his side during and after the wars, catching scraps in his wake, despised by every human who saw her there. She waited for him to see how much she had sacrificed and give her the only reward that could matter after what she'd done. Instead he had her shunt removed and sent her to Grade Orange. She has not seen or heard from him in four years. His pet, yes, that's as good a name as any—but he never drank from her. Not once.

Mr. Charles's lips, just a shade of white darker than his skin, open like a hole in a cloud. "And he wants you back. How do you *feel?*"

Terrified. Awestruck. Confused. "Grateful," she says.

The hole smiles. "Grateful! How interesting. Come here, girl. I believe I shall *have* a *taste.*"

She grabs the letter with shaking fingers and folds it inside a pocket of her red uniform. She stands in front of Mr. Charles.

"Well?" he says.

She hasn't had a shunt in years, though she can still feel its ridged scar in the crook of her arm. Without it, feeding from her is messy, violent. Traditional, Mr. Charles might say. Her fingers hurt as she unzips the collar. Her muscles feel sore, the bones in her spine arthritic and old as she bows her head, leans closer to Mr. Charles. She waits for him to bare his fangs, to pierce her vein, to suck her blood.

He takes more than he should. He drinks until her fingers and toes twinge, until her neck throbs, until the red velvet of his seat fades to gray. When he finishes, he leaves her blood on his mouth.

"I forgive . . . you for the boy," he says.

Jeb cut his own arteries, left his good blood all over the floor. Mr. Charles abhors waste above all else.

*

Mr. Charles will explain the situation. I wish you to come. If you do well, I have been authorized to offer you the highest reward.

The following night Key takes a boat to Oahu. Vampires don't like water, but they will cross it anyway—the sea has become a status symbol among them, an indication of strength. Hawai'i is still a resort destination, though most of its residents only go out at night. Grade Gold is the most expensive, most luxurious resort of them all.

Tetsuo travels between the islands often. Key saw him do it a dozen times during the war. She remembers one night, his face lit by the moon and the yellow lamps on the deck—the wide cheekbones, thick eyebrows, sharp widow's peak, all frozen in the perfection of a nineteen-year-old boy. Pale beneath the olive tones of his skin, he bares his fangs when the waves lurch beneath him.

"What does it feel like?" she asks him.

"Like frozen worms in my veins," he says, after a full, long minute of silence. Then he checks the guns and tells her to wait below, the humans are coming. She can't see anything, but Tetsuo can smell them like chum in the water. The Japanese have held out the longest, and the vampires of Hawai'i lead the assault against them.

Two nights later, in his quarters in the bunker at the base of Mauna Kea, Tetsuo brings back a sheet of paper, written in Japanese. The only characters she recognizes are *shi* and *ta*—"death" and "field." It looks like some kind of list.

"What is this?" she asks.

"Recent admissions to the Lanai human residential facility."

She looks up at him, devoted with terror. "My mother?" Her father died in the first offensive on the Big Island, a hero of the resistance. He never knew how his daughter had chosen to survive.

"Here," Tetsuo says, and runs a cold finger down the list without death. "Jen Isokawa."

"Alive?" She has been looking for her mother since the wars began. Tetsuo knows this, but she didn't know he was searching, too. She feels swollen with this indication of his regard.

"She's listed as a caretaker. They're treated well. You could . . ." He sits beside her on the bed that only she uses. His pause lapses into a stop. He strokes her hair absentmindedly; if she had a tail, it would beat his legs. She is seventeen and she is sure he will reward her soon.

"Tetsuo," she says, "you could drink from me, if you want. I've had a shunt for nearly a year. The others use it. I'd rather feed you."

Sometimes she has to repeat herself three times before he seems to hear her. This she has said at least ten. But she is safe here in his bunker, on the bed he brought in for her, with his lukewarm body pressed against her warm one. Vampires do not have sex with humans; they feed. But if he doesn't want her that way, what else can she offer him?

"I've had you tested. You're fertile. If you bear three children you won't need a shunt and the residential facilities will care for you for the rest of your mortality. You can live with your mother. I will make sure you're safe."

She presses her face against his shoulder. "Don't make me leave."

"You wanted to see your mother."

Her mother had spent the weeks before the invasion in church, praying for God to intercede against the abominations. Better that she die than see Key like this.

"Only to know what happened to her," Key whispers. "Won't you feed from me, Tetsuo? I want to feel closer to you. I want you to know how much I love you."

A long pause. Then, "I don't need to taste you to know how you feel."

Tetsuo meets her onshore.

Just like that, she is seventeen again.

"You look older," he says. Slowly, but with less affectation than Mr. Charles.

This is true; so inevitable she doesn't understand why he even bothers to say so. Is he surprised? Finally she nods. The buoyed dock rocks beneath them—he makes no attempt to move, though the two vampires with him grip the denuded skin of their own elbows with pale fingers. They flare and retract their fangs.

"You are drained," he says. He does not mean this metaphorically.

She nods again, realizes further explanation is called for. "Mr. Charles," she says, her voice a painful rasp. This embarrasses her, though Tetsuo would never notice.

He nods, sharp and curt. She thinks he is angry, though perhaps no one else could read him as clearly. She knows that face, frozen in the countenance of a boy dead before the Second World War. A boy dead fifty years before she was born.

He is old enough to remember Pearl Harbor, the detention camps, the years when Maui's forests still had native birds. But she has never dared ask him about his human life.

"And what did Charles explain?"

"He said someone killed herself at Grade Gold."

Tetsuo flares his fangs. She flinches, which surprises her. She used to flush at the sight of his fangs, her blood pounding red just beneath the soft surface of her skin.

"I've been given dispensation," he says, and rests one finger against the hollow at the base of her throat.

She's learned a great deal about the rigid traditions that restrict vampire life since she first met Tetsuo. She understands why her teenage fantasies of morally liberated vampirism were improbable, if not impossible. For each human they bring over, vampires need a special dispensation that they only receive once or twice every decade. *The highest reward.* If Tetsuo has gotten a dispensation, then her first thought when she read his letter was correct. He didn't mean retirement. He didn't mean a peaceful life in some remote farm on the islands. He meant death. Un-death.

After all these years, Tetsuo means to turn her into a vampire.

. . .

The trouble at Grade Gold started with a dead girl. Penelope cut her own throat five days ago (with a real knife, the kind they allow Grade Gold humans for cutting food). Her ghost haunts the eyes of those she left behind. One human resident in particular, with hair dyed the color of tea and blue lipstick to match the bruises under her red eyes, takes one look at Key and starts to scream.

Key glances at Tetsuo, but he has forgotten her. He stares at the girl as if he could burn her to ashes on the plush green carpet. The five others in the room look away, but Key can't tell if it's in embarrassment or fear. The luxury surrounding them chokes her. There's a bowl of fruit on a coffee table. Real fruit—fuzzy brown kiwis, mottled red-green mangos, dozens of tangerines. She takes an involuntary step forward and the girl's scream gets louder before cutting off with an abrupt squawk. Her labored breaths are the only sound in the room.

"This is a joke," the girl says. There's spittle on her blue lips. "What hole did you dig her out of?"

"Go to your room, Rachel," Tetsuo says.

Rachel flicks back her hair and rubs angrily under one eye. "What are you now, Daddy Vampire? You think you can just, what? Replace her? With this broke-down fogy look-alike?"

"She is not—"

"Yeah? What is she?"

They are both silent, doubt and grief and fury scuttling between them like beetles in search of a meal. Tetsuo and the girl stare at each other with such deep familiarity that Key feels forgotten, alone—almost ashamed of the dreams that have kept her alive for a decade. They have never felt so hopeless, or so false.

"Her name is Key," Tetsuo says, in something like defeat. He turns away, though he makes no move to leave. "She will be your new caretaker."

"Key?" the girl says. "What kind of a name is that?"

Key doesn't answer for a long time, thinking of all the ways she could respond. Of Obaachan Akiko and the affectionate nickname of lazy summers spent hiking in the mountains or pounding mochi in the kitchen. Of her half-Japanese mother and Hawai'ian father, of the ways history and identity and circumstance can shape a girl into half a woman, until someone—*not a man*—comes with a hundred thousand others like him and destroys anything that might have once had meaning. So she finds meaning in him. Who else was there?

And this girl, whose sneer reveals her bucked front teeth, has as much chance of understanding that world as Key does of understanding this one. Fresh fruit on the table. No uniforms. And a perfect, glittering shunt of plastic and metal nestled in the crook of her left arm.

"Mine," Key answers the girl.

Rachel spits; Tetsuo turns his head, just a little, as though he can only bear to see Key from the corner of his eye.

"You're nothing like her," she says.

"Like who?"

But the girl storms from the room, leaving her chief vampire without a dismissal. Key now understands this will not be punished. It's another one—a boy, with the same florid beauty as the girl but far less belligerence, who answers her.

"You look like Penelope," he says, tugging on a long lock of his asymmetrically cut black hair. "Just older."

When Tetsuo leaves the room, it's Key who cannot follow.

Key remembers sixteen. Her obaachan is dead and her mother has moved to an apartment in Hilo and it's just Key and her father in that old, quiet house at the end of the road. The vampires have annexed San Diego and Okinawa is besieged, but life doesn't feel very different in the mountains of the Big Island.

It is raining in the woods behind her house. Her father has told her to study, but all she's done since her mother left is read Mishima's Sea of Fertility novels. She sits on the porch, wondering if it's better to kill herself or wait for them to come, and just as she thinks she ought to have the courage to die, something rattles in the shed. A rat, she thinks.

But it's not a rat she sees when she pulls open the door on its rusty hinges. It's a man, crouched between a stack of old appliance boxes and the rusted fender of the Buick her father always meant to fix one day. His hair is wet and slicked back, his white shirt is damp and ripped from shoulder to navel. The skin beneath it is pale as a corpse; bloodless, though the edges of a deep wound are still visible.

"They've already come?" Her voice breaks on a whisper. She wanted to finish *The Decay of the Angel*. She wanted to see her mother once more.

"Shut the door," he says, crouching in shadow, away from the bar of light streaming through the narrow opening.

"Don't kill me."

"We are equally at each other's mercy."

She likes the way he speaks. No one told her they could sound so proper. So human. Is there a monster in her shed, or is he something else?

"Why shouldn't I open it all the way?"

He is brave, whatever else. He takes his long hands from in front of his face and stands, a flower blooming after rain. He is beautiful, though she will not mark that until later. Now, she only notices the steady, patient way he regards her. *I could move faster than you,* his eyes say. *I could kill you first.*

She thinks of Mishima and says, "I'm not afraid of death."

Only when the words leave her mouth does she realize how

deeply she has lied. Does he know? Her hands would shake if it weren't for their grip on the handle.

"I promise," he says. "I will save you, when the rest of us come."

What is it worth, a monster's promise?

She steps inside and shuts out the light.

. . .

There are nineteen residents of Grade Gold; the twentieth is buried beneath the kukui tree in the communal garden. The thought of rotting in earth revolts Key. She prefers the bright, fierce heat of a crematorium fire, like the one that consumed Jeb the night before she left Mauna Kea. The ashes fly in the wind, into the ocean and up in the trees, where they lodge in bird nests and caterpillar silk and mud puddles after a storm. The return of flesh to the earth should be fast and final, not the slow mortification of worms and bacteria and carbon gases.

Tetsuo instructs her to keep close watch on unit three. "Rachel isn't very . . . steady right now," he says, as though unaware of the understatement.

The remaining nineteen residents are divided into four units, five kids in each, living together in sprawling ranch houses connected by walkways and gardens. There are walls, of course, but you have to climb a tree to see them. The kids at Grade Gold have more freedom than any human she's ever encountered since the war, but they're as bound to this paradise as she was to her mountain.

The vampires who come here stay in a high glass tower right by the beach. During the day, the black-tinted windows gleam like lasers. At night the vampires come down to feed. There is a fifth house in the residential village, one reserved for clients and their meals. Tetsuo orchestrates these encounters, planning each interaction in fine detail: this human with that performance for this distinguished client. Key has grown used to thinking of her fellow humans as food, but now she is forced to reconcile that indelible fact with another, stranger veneer. The vampires who pay so dearly for Grade Gold humans don't merely want to feed from a shunt. They want to be entertained, talked to, cajoled. The boy who explained about Key's uncanny resemblance juggles torches. Twin girls from unit three play guitar and sing songs by the Carpenters. Even Rachel, dressed in a gaudy purple mermaid dress with matching streaks in her hair, keeps up a one-way, laughing conversation with a vampire who seems too astonished—or too slow—to reply.

Key has never seen anything like this before. She thought that most vampires regarded humans as walking sacks of food. What pleasure could be derived from speaking with your meal first? From seeing it sing or dance? When she first went with Tetsuo, the other vampires talked about human emotions as if they were flavors of ice cream. But at Grade Orange she grew accustomed to more basic parameters: were the humans fed, were they fertile, did they sleep? Here, she must approve outfits; she must manage dietary preferences and erratic tempers and a dozen other details all crucial to keeping the kids Grade Gold standard. Their former caretaker has been shipped to the work camps, which leaves Key in sole charge of the operation. At least until Tetsuo decides how he will use his dispensation.

Key's thoughts skitter away from the possibility.

"I didn't know vampires liked music," she says, late in the evening, when some of the kids sprawl, exhausted, across couches and cushions. A girl no older than fifteen opens her eyes but hardly moves when a vampire in a gold suit lifts her arm for a nip. Key and Tetsuo are seated together at the far end of the main room, in the bay windows that overlook a cliff and the ocean.

"It's as interesting to us as any other human pastime."

"Does music have a taste?"

His wide mouth stretches at the edges; she recognizes it as a smile. "Music has some utility, given the right circumstances."

She doesn't quite understand him. The air is redolent with the sweat of human teenagers and the muggy, salty air that blows through the open doors and windows. Her eye catches on a half-eaten strawberry dropped carelessly on the carpet a few feet away. It was harvested too soon, a white, tasteless core surrounded by hard, red flesh.

She thinks there is nothing of "right" in these circumstances, and their utility is, at its bottom, merely that of parasite and host.

"The music enhances the—our—flavor?"

Tetsuo stares at her for a long time, long enough for him to take at least three of his shallow, erratically spaced breaths. To look at him is to taste copper and sea on her tongue; to wait for him is to hear the wind slide down a mountainside an hour before dawn.

It has been four years since she last saw him. She thought he had forgotten her, and now he speaks to her as if all those years haven't passed, as though the vampires hadn't long since won the war and turned the world to their slow, long-burning purpose.

"Emotions change your flavor," he says. "And food. And sex. And pleasure."

And love? she wonders, but Tetsuo has never drunk from her.

"Then why not treat all of us like you do the ones here? Why have con—Mauna Kea?"

She expects him to catch her slip, but his attention is focused on something beyond her right shoulder. She turns to look, and sees nothing but the hall and a closed feeding room door.

"Three years," he says quietly. He doesn't look at her. She doesn't understand what he means, so she waits. "It takes three years for the complexity to fade. For the vitality of young blood to turn muddy and clogged with silt. Even among the new crops, only a few individuals are Gold standard. For three years they produce the finest blood ever tasted, filled with regrets and ecstasy and dreams. And then . . ."

"Grade Orange?" Key asks, her voice dry and rasping. Had Tetsuo always talked of humans like this? With such little regard for their selfhood? Had she been too young to understand, or have the years of harvesting humans hardened him?

"If we have not burned too much out. Living at high elevation helps prolong your utility, but sometimes all that's left is Lanai and the work camps."

She remembers her terror before her final interview with Mr. Charles, her conviction that Jeb's death would prompt him to discard his uselessly old overseer to the work camps.

A boy from one of the other houses staggers to the one she recognizes from unit two and sprawls in his lap. Unit-two boy startles awake, smiles, and bends over to kiss the first. A pair of female vampires kneel in front of them and press their fangs with thick pink tongues.

"Touch him," one says, pointing to the boy from unit two. "Make him cry."

The boy from unit two doesn't even pause for breath; he reaches for the other boy's cock and squeezes. And as they both groan with something that makes Key feel like a voyeur, made helpless by her own desire, the pair of vampires pull the boys apart and dive for their respective shunts. The room goes quiet but for soft gurgles, like two minnows in a tide pool. Then a pair of clicks as the boys' shunts turn gray, forcing the vampires to stop feeding.

"Lovely, divine," the vampires say a few minutes later, when they pass on their way out. "We always appreciate the sexual displays."

The boys curl against each other, eyes shut. They breathe like old men: hard, through constricted tubes.

"Does that happen often?" she asks.

"This Grade Gold is known for its sexual flavors. My humans pick partners they enjoy."

Vampires might not have sex, but they crave its flavor. Will she, when she crosses to their side? Will she look at those two boys and command them to fuck each other just so she can taste?

"Do you ever care?" she says, her voice barely a whisper. "About what you've done to us?"

He looks away from her. Before she can blink he has crossed to the one closed feeding room door and wrenched it open. A thump of something thrown against a wall. A snarl, as human as a snake's hiss.

"Leave, Gregory!" Tetsuo says. A vampire Key recognizes from earlier in the night stumbles into the main room. He rubs his jaw, though the torn and mangled skin there has already begun to knit together.

"She is mine to have. I paid—"

"Not enough to kill her."

"I'll complain to the council," the vampire says. "You've been losing support. And everyone knows how *patiently* Charles has waited in his aerie."

She should be scared, but his words make her think of Jeb, of failures and consequences, and of the one human she has not seen for hours. She stands and sprints past both vampires to where Rachel lies insensate on a bed.

Her shunt has turned the opaque gray meant to prevent vampires from feeding humans to death. But the client has bitten her neck instead.

"Tell them whatever you wish, and I will tell them you circumvented the shunt of a fully tapped human. We have our rules for a reason. You are no longer welcome here."

Rachel's pulse is soft but steady. She stirs and moans beneath Key's hands. The relief is crushing; she wants to cradle the girl in her arms until she wakes. She wants to protect her so her blood will never have to smear the walls of a feeding room, so that Key will be able to say that at least she saved one.

Rachel's eyes flutter open, land with a butterfly's gentleness on Key's face.

"Pen," she says, "I told you. It makes them . . . they *eat* me."

Key doesn't understand, but she doesn't mind. She presses her hand to Rachel's warm forehead and sings lullabies her grandmother liked until Rachel falls back to sleep.

"How is she?" It is Tetsuo, come into the room after the client has finally left.

"Drained," Key says, as dispassionately as he. "She'll be fine in a few days."

"Key."

"Yes?"

She won't look at him.

"I do, you know."

She knows. "Then why support it?"

"You'll understand when your time comes."

She looks back down at Rachel, and all she can see are bruises blooming purple on her upper arms, blood dried brown on her neck. She looks like a human being: infinitely precious, fragile. Like prey.

Five days later Key sits in the garden in the shade of the kukui tree. She has reports to file on the last week's feedings, but the papers sit untouched beside her. The boy from unit two and his boyfriend are tending the tomatoes and Key slowly peels the skin from her fourth kiwi. The first time she bit into one she cried, but the boys pretended not to notice. She is getting better with practice. Her hands still tremble and her misted eyes refract rainbows in the hard noon sunlight. She is learning to be human again.

Rachel sleeps on the ground beside her, curled on the packed dirt of Penelope's grave with her back against the tree trunk and her arms wrapped tightly around her belly. She's spent most of the last five days sleeping, and Key thinks she has mostly recovered. She's been eating voraciously, foods in wild combinations at all times of day and night. Key is glad. Without the distracting, angry makeup, Rachel's face looks vulnerable and haunted. Jeb had that look in the months before his death. He would sit

quietly in the mess hall and stare at the food brick as though
he had forgotten how to eat. Jeb had transferred to Mauna Kea
within a week of Key becoming overseer. He liked watching the
lights of the airplanes at night and he kept two books with him:
The Blind Watchmaker and *A Guide to the Fruits of Hawai'i*. She
talked to him about the latter—had he ever tasted breadfruit
or kiwi or cherimoya? None, he said, in a voice so small and
soft it sounded inversely proportional to his size. Only a peach,
a canned peach, when he was four or five years old. Vampires
don't waste fruit on Grade Orange humans.

The covers of both books were worn, the spines cracked, the
pages yellowed and brittle at the edges. Why keep a book about
fruit you had never tasted and never would eat? Why read at all,
when they frowned upon literacy in humans and often banned
books outright? She never asked him. Mr. Charles had seen their
conversation, though she doubted he had heard it, and re*quest*ed
that she refrain from speaking unnecessarily to the *har*vest.

So when Jeb stared at her across the table with eyes like a snuffed
candle, she turned away, she forced her patty into her mouth, she
chewed, she reached for her orange drink.

His favorite book became his means of self-destruction. She
let him do it. She doesn't know if she feels guilty for not having
stopped him, or for being in the position to stop him in the first
place. Not two weeks later she rests beneath a kukui tree, the flesh
of a fruit she had never expected to taste again turning to green
pulp between her teeth. She reaches for another one because she
knows how little she deserves this.

But the skin of the fruit at the bottom of the bowl is too soft and
fleshy for a kiwi. She pulls it into the light and drops it.

"Are you okay?" It's the boy from unit two—Kaipo. He kneels
down and picks up the cherimoya.

"What?" she says, and struggles to control her breathing. She
has to appear normal, in control. She's supposed to be their caretaker. But the boy just seems concerned, not judgmental. Rachel
rolls onto her back and opens her eyes.

"You screamed," Rachel says, sleep-fogged and accusatory. "You
woke me up."

"Who put this in the bowl?" Kaipo asks. "These things are poisonous! They grow on that tree down the hill, but you can't eat
them."

Key takes the haunted fruit from him, holding it carefully so as to not bruise it further. "Who told you that?" she asks.

Rachel leans forward, so her chin rests on the edge of Key's lounge chair and the tips of her purple-streaked hair touch Key's thigh. "Tetsuo," she says. "What, did he lie?"

Key shakes her head slowly. "He probably only half remembered. It's a cherimoya. The flesh is delicious, but the seeds are poisonous."

Rachel's eyes follow her hands. "Like, killing you poisonous?" she asks.

Key thinks back to her father's lessons. "Maybe if you eat them all or grind them up. The tree bark can paralyze your heart and lungs."

Kaipo whistles, and they all watch intently when she wedges her finger under the skin and splits it in half. The white, fleshy pulp looks stark, even a little disquieting against the scaly green exterior. She plucks out the hard brown seeds and tosses them to the ground. Only then does she pull out a chunk of flesh and put it in her mouth.

Like strawberries and banana pudding and pineapple. Like the summer after Obaachan died, when a box of them came to the house as a condolence gift.

"You look like you're fellating it," Rachel says. Key opens her eyes and swallows abruptly.

Kaipo pushes his tongue against his lips. "Can I try it, Key?" he asks, very politely. Did the vampires teach him that politeness? Did vampires teach Rachel a word like *fellate,* perhaps while instructing her to do it with a hopefully willing human partner?

"Do you guys know how to use condoms?" She has decided to ask Tetsuo to supply them. This last week has made it clear that "sexual flavors" are all too frequently on the menu at Grade Gold.

Kaipo looks at Rachel; Rachel shakes her head. "What's a condom?" he asks.

It's so easy to forget how little of the world they know. "You use it during sex, to stop you from catching diseases," she says carefully. "Or getting pregnant."

Rachel laughs and stuffs the rest of the flesh into her wide mouth. Even a cherimoya can't fill her hollows. "Great, even more vampire sex," she says, her hatred clearer than her garbled words. "They never made Pen do it."

"They didn't?" Key asks.

Juice dribbles down her chin. "You know, Tetsuo's dispensation? Before she killed herself, she was his pick. Everyone knew it. That's why they left her alone."

Key feels lightheaded. "But if she was his choice . . . why would she kill herself?"

"She didn't want to be a vampire," Kaipo says softly.

"She wanted a *baby*, like bringing a new food sack into the world is a good idea. But they wouldn't let her have sex and they wanted to make her one of them, so—now she's gone. But why he'd bring *you* here, when *any* of us would be a better choice—"

"Rachel, just shut up. Please." Kaipo takes her by the shoulder.

Rachel shrugs him off. "What? Like she can do anything."

"If she becomes one of *them*—"

"I wouldn't hurt you," Key says, too quickly. Rachel masks her pain with cruelty, but it is palpable. Key can't imagine any version of herself that would add to that.

Kaipo and Rachel stare at her. "But," Kaipo says, "that's what vampires do."

"I would eat you," Rachel says, and flops back under the tree. "I would make you cry and your tears would taste sweeter than a cherimoya."

...

"I will be back in four days," Tetsuo tells her late the next night. "There is one feeding scheduled. I hope you will be ready when I return."

"For the . . . reward?" she asks, stumbling over an appropriate euphemism. Their words for it are polysyllabic spikes: transmutation, transformation, metamorphosis. All vampires were once human, and immortal doesn't mean invulnerable. Some die each year, and so their ranks must be replenished with the flesh of worthy, willing humans.

He places a hand on her shoulder. It feels as chill and inert as a piece of damp wood. She thinks she must be dreaming.

"I have wanted this for a long time, Key," he says to her—like a stranger, like the person who knows her best in the world.

"Why now?"

"Our thoughts can be . . . slow, sometimes. You will see. Orderly, but sometimes too orderly to see patterns clearly. I thought of you, but did not know it until Penelope died."

Penelope, who looked just like Key. Penelope, who would have been his pick. She shivers and steps away from his hand. "Did you love her?"

She can't believe that she is asking this question. She can't believe that he is offering her the dreams she would have murdered for ten, even five years ago.

"I loved that she made me think of you," he says, "when you were young and beautiful."

"It's been eighteen years, Tetsuo."

He looks over her shoulder. "You haven't lost much," he says. "I'm not too late. You'll see."

He is waiting for a response. She forces herself to nod. She wants to close her eyes and cover her mouth, keep all her love for him inside where it can be safe, because if she loses it, there will be nothing left but a girl in the rain who should have opened the door.

He looks like an alien when he smiles. He looks like nothing she could ever know when he walks down the hall, past the open door and the girl who has been watching them this whole time.

Rachel is young and beautiful, Key thinks, and Penelope is dead.

. . .

Key's sixth feeding at Grade Gold is contained, quiet, and without incident. The gazes of the clients slide over her as she greets them at the door of the feeding house, but she is used to that. To a vampire, a human without a shunt is like a book without pages: a useless absurdity. She has assigned all of unit one and a pair from unit four to the gathering. Seven humans for five vampires is a luxurious ratio —probably more than they paid for, but she's happy to let that be Tetsuo's problem. She shudders to remember how Rachel's blood soaked into the collar of her blouse when she lifted the girl from the bed. She has seen dozens of overdrained humans, including some who died from it, but what happened to Rachel feels worse. She doesn't understand why but is overwhelmed by tenderness for her.

A half hour before the clients are supposed to leave, Kaipo sprints through the front door, flushed and panting so hard he has to pause half a minute to catch his breath.

"Rachel," he manages, while humans and vampires alike pause to look.

She stands up. "What did she do?"

"I'm not sure . . . she was shaking and screaming, waking everyone up, yelling about Penelope and Tetsuo and then she started vomiting."

"The clients have another half hour," she whispers. "I can't leave until then."

Kaipo tugs on the long lock of glossy black hair that he has blunt-cut over his left eye. "I'm scared for her, Key," he says. "She won't listen to anyone else."

She will blame herself if any of the kids here tonight die, and she will blame herself if something happens to Rachel. Her hands make the decision for her: she reaches for Kaipo's left arm. He lets her take it reflexively, and doesn't flinch when she lifts his shunt. She looks for and finds the small electrical chip which controls the inflow and outflow of blood and other fluids. She taps the Morse-like code, and Kaipo watches with his mouth open as the glittering plastic polymer changes from clear to gray. As though he's already been tapped out.

"I'm not supposed to show you that," she says, and smiles until she remembers Tetsuo and what he might think. "Stay here. Make sure nothing happens. I'll be back as soon as I can."

She stays only long enough to see his agreement, and then she's flying out the back door, through the garden, down the left-hand path that leads to unit two.

Rachel is on her hands and knees in the middle of the walkway. The other three kids in unit two watch her silently from the doorway, but Rachel is alone as she vomits in the grass.

"You!" Rachel says when she sees Key, and starts to cough.

Rachel looks like a war is being fought inside of her, as if the battlefield is her lungs and the hollows of her cheeks and the muscles of her neck. She trembles and can hardly raise her head.

"Go away!" Rachel screams, but she's not looking at Key, she's looking down at the ground.

"Rachel, what's happened?" Key doesn't get too close. Rachel's fury frightens her; she doesn't understand this kind of rage. Rachel raises her shaking hands and starts hitting herself, pounding her chest and rib cage and stomach with violence made even more frightening by her weakness. Key kneels in front of her, grabs both of the girl's tiny, bruised wrists and holds them away from her body. Her vomit smells of sour bile and the sickly sweet of some half-digested fruit. A suspicion nibbles at Key, and so she looks to the left, where Rachel has vomited.

Dozens and dozens of black seeds, half crushed. And a slime of green the precise shade of a cherimoya skin.

"Oh, God, Rachel . . . why would you . . ."

"You don't deserve him! He can make it go away and he won't! Who are you? A fogy, an ugly fogy, an ugly usurping fogy, and she's gone and he is a dick, he is a screaming howler monkey and I hate him . . ."

Rachel collapses against Key's chest, her hands beating helplessly at the ground. Key takes her up and rocks her back and forth, crying while she thinks of how close she came to repeating the mistakes of Jeb. But she can still save Rachel. She can still be human.

Tetsuo returns three days later with a guest.

She has never seen Mr. Charles wear shoes before, and he walks in them with the mincing confusion of a young girl forced to wear zori for a formal occasion. She bows her head when she sees him, hoping to hide her fear. Has he come to take her back to Mauna Kea? The thought of returning to those antiseptic feeding rooms and tasteless brick patties makes her hands shake. It makes her wonder if she would not be better off taking Penelope's way out rather than seeing the place where Jeb killed himself again.

But even as she thinks it, she knows she won't, any more than she would have eighteen years ago. She's too much a coward and she's too brave. If Mr. Charles asks her to go back she will say yes.

Rain on a mountainside and sexless, sweet touches with a man the same temperature as wet wood. Lanai City, overrun. Then Waimea, then Honoka'a. Then Hilo, where her mother had been living. For a year, until Tetsuo found that record of her existence in a work camp, Key fantasized about her mother escaping on a boat to an atoll, living in a group of refugee humans who survived the apocalypse.

Every thing Tetsuo asked of her, she did. She loved him from the moment they saved each other's lives. She has always said yes.

"*Key!*" Mr. Charles says to her, as though she is a friend he has run into unexpectedly. "I have some*thing* . . . you might *just* want."

"Yes, Mr. Charles?" she says.

The three of them are alone in the feeding house. Mr. Charles collapses dramatically against one of the divans and kicks off his tight patent-leather shoes as if they are barnacles. He wears no socks.

"There," he says, and waves his hand at the door. "*In* the bag."

Tetsuo nods and so she walks back. The bag is black canvas, unmarked. Inside, there's a book. She recognizes it immediately, though she only saw it once. *The Blind Watchmaker.* There is a note on the cover. The handwriting is large and uneven and painstaking, that of someone familiar with words but unaccustomed to writing them down. She notes painfully that he writes his *a* the same way as a typeset font, with the half *c* above the main body and a careful serif at the end.

> Dear Overseer Ki,
>   I would like you to have this. I have loved it very much and you are
> the only one who ever seemed to care. I am angry but
>   I don't blame you. You're just too good at living.
> Jeb

She takes the bag and leaves both vampires without requesting permission. Mr. Charles's laugh follows her out the door.

Blood on the walls, on the floor, all over his body.

I am angry but. You're just too good at living. She has always said yes. She is too much of a coward and she is too brave.

She watches the sunset the next evening from the hill in the garden, her back against the cherimoya tree. She feels the sun's death like she always has, with quiet joy. Awareness floods her: the musk of wet grass crushed beneath her bare toes, salt spray and algae blowing from the ocean, the love she has clung to so fiercely since she was a girl, lost and alone. Everything she has ever loved is bound in that sunset, the red and violet orb that could kill him as it sinks into the ocean.

Her favorite time of day is sunset, but it is not night. She has never quite been able to fit inside his darkness, no matter how hard she tried. She has been too good at living, but perhaps it's not too late to change.

She can't take the path of Penelope or Jeb, but that has never been the only way. She remembers stories that reached Grade Orange from the work camps, half-whispered reports of humans who sat at their assembly lines and refused to lift their hands. Harvesters who drained gasoline from their combine engines and waited for the vampires to find them. If every human refused to cooperate, vampire society would crumble in a week. Still, she has no illusions about this third path sparking a revolution. This is simply all she can do: sit under the cherimoya tree and refuse. They will kill her, but she will have chosen to be human.

The sun descends. She falls asleep against the tree and dreams of the girl who never was, the one who opened the door. In her dreams, the sun burns her skin and her obaachan tells her how proud she is while they pick strawberries in the garden. She eats an umeboshi that tastes of blood and salt, and when she swallows, the flavors swarm out of her throat, bubbling into her neck and jaw and ears. Flavors become emotions become thoughts; peace in the nape of her neck, obligation in her back molars, and hope just behind her eyes, bitter as a watermelon rind.

She opens them and sees Tetsuo on his knees before her. Blood smears his mouth. She does not know what to think when he kisses her, except that she can't even feel the pinprick pain where his teeth broke her skin. He has never fed from her before. They have never kissed before. She feels like she is floating, but nothing else.

The blood is gone when he sits back. As though she imagined it.

"You should not have left like that yesterday," he says. "Charles can make this harder than I'd like."

"Why is he here?" she asks. She breathes shallowly.

"He will take over Grade Gold once your transmutation is finished."

"That's why you brought me here, isn't it? It had nothing to do with the kids."

He shrugs. "Regulations. So Charles couldn't refuse."

"And where will you go?"

"They want to send me to the mainland. Texas. To supervise the installation of a new Grade Gold facility near Austin."

She leans closer to him, and now she can see it: regret, and shame that he should be feeling so. "I'm sorry," she says.

"I have lived seventy years on these islands. I have an eternity to come back to them. So will you, Key. I have permission to bring you with me."

Everything that sixteen-year-old had ever dreamed. She can still feel the pull of him, of her desire for an eternity together, away from the hell her life has become. Her transmutation would be complete. Truly a monster, the regrets for her past actions would fall away like waves against a seawall.

With a fumbling hand, she picks a cherimoya from the ground beside her. "Do you remember what these taste like?"

She has never asked him about his human life. For a moment he seems genuinely confused. "You don't understand. Taste to us is vastly more complex. Joy, dissatisfaction, confusion, humility—*those* are flavors. A custard apple?" He laughs. "It's sweet, right?"

Joy, dissatisfaction, loss, grief, she tastes all that just looking at him. "Why didn't you ever feed from me before?"

"Because I promised. When we first met."

And as she stares at him, sick with loss and certainty, Rachel walks up behind him. She is holding a kitchen knife, the blade pointed toward her stomach.

"Charles knows," she says.

"How?" Tetsuo says. He stands, but Key can't coordinate her muscles enough for the effort. He must have drained a lot of blood.

"I told him," Rachel says. "So now you don't have a choice. You will transmute me and you will get rid of this fucking fetus or I will kill myself and you'll be blamed for losing *two* Grade Gold humans."

Rachel's wrists are still bruised from where Key had to hold her several nights ago. Her eyes are sunken, her skin sallow. *This fucking fetus.*

She wasn't trying to kill herself with the cherimoya seeds. She was trying to abort a pregnancy.

"The baby is still alive after all that?" Key says, surprisingly indifferent to the glittering metal in Rachel's unsteady hands. Does Rachel know how easily Tetsuo could disarm her? What advantage does she think she has? But then she looks back in the girl's eyes and realizes: none.

Rachel is young and desperate and she doesn't want to be eaten by the monsters anymore.

"Not again, Rachel," Tetsuo says. "I *can't* do what you want. A vampire can only transmute someone he's never fed from before."

Rachel gasps. Key flops against her tree. She hadn't known that, either. The knife trembles in Rachel's grip so violently that Tetsuo takes it from her, achingly gentle as he pries her fingers from the hilt.

"*That's* why you never drank from her? And I killed her anyway? Stupid fucking Penelope. She could have been forever, and now there's just this dumb fogy in her place. She thought you cared about her."

"Caring is a strange thing, for a vampire," Key says.

Rachel spits in her direction but it falls short. The moonlight is especially bright tonight; Key can see everything from the grass to the tips of Rachel's ears, flushed sunset pink.

"Tetsuo," Key says, "why can't I move?"

But they ignore her.

"Maybe Charles will do it if I tell him you're really the one who killed Penelope."

"Charles? I'm sure he knows exactly what you did."

"I didn't *mean* to kill her!" Rachel screams. "Penelope was going to tell about the baby. She was crazy about babies, it didn't make any sense, and you had *picked her* and she wanted to destroy my life . . . I was so angry, I just wanted to hurt her, but I didn't realize . . ."

"Rachel, I've tried to give you a chance, but I'm not allowed to get rid of it for you." Tetsuo's voice is as worn out as a leathery orange.

"I'll die before I go to one of those mommy farms, Tetsuo. I'll die and take my baby with me."

"Then you will have to do it yourself."

She gasps. "You'll really leave me here?"

"I've made my choice."

Rachel looks down at Key, radiating a withering contempt that does nothing to blunt Key's pity. "If you had picked Penelope, I would have understood. Penelope was beautiful and smart. She's the only one who ever made it through half of that fat Shakespeare book in unit four. She could sing. Her breasts were perfect. But *her*? She's not a choice. She's nothing at all."

The silence between them is strained. It's as if Key isn't there at all. And soon, she thinks, she won't be.

"I've made my choice," Key says.

"*Your* choice?" they say in unison.

When she finds the will to stand, it's as though her limbs are hardly there at all, as though she is swimming in midair. For the first time she understands that something is wrong.

...

Key floats for a long time. Eventually she falls. Tetsuo catches her.

"What does it feel like?" Key asks. "The transmutation?"

Tetsuo takes the starlight in his hands. He feeds it to her through a glass shunt growing from a living branch. The tree's name is Rachel. The tree is very sad. Sadness is delicious.

"You already know," he says.

You will understand: he said this to her when she was human. *I wouldn't hurt you:* she said this to a girl who—a girl—she drinks.

"I meant to refuse."

"I made a promise."

She sees him for a moment crouched in the back of her father's shed, huddled away from the dangerous bar of light that stretches across the floor. She sees herself, terrified of death and so unsure. *Open the door,* she tells that girl, too late. *Let in the light.*

SEANAN MCGUIRE

Each to Each

FROM *Lightspeed Magazine: Women Destroy Science Fiction!*

CONDENSATION COVERS THE walls, dimpling into tiny individual drops that follow an almost fractal pattern, like someone has been writing out the secrets of the universe in the most transitory medium they can find. The smell of damp steel assaults my nose as I walk the hall, uncomfortable boots clumping heavily with every step I force myself to take. The space is tight, confined, unyielding; it is like living inside a coral reef, trapped by the limits of our own necessary shells. We are constantly envious of those who escape its limitations, and we fear for them at the same time, wishing them safe return to the reef, where they can be kept away from all the darkness and predations of the open sea.

The heartbeat of the ship follows me through the iron halls, comprised of the engine's whir, the soft, distant buzz of the electrical systems, the even more distant churn of the rudders, the hiss and sigh of the filters that keep the flooded chambers clean and oxygenated. Latest scuttlebutt from the harbor holds that a generation of wholly flooded ships is coming, ultralight fish tanks with shells of air and metal surrounding the water-filled crew chambers, the waterproofed electrical systems. Those ships will be lighter than ours could ever dream of being, freed from the need for filters and desalination pumps by leaving themselves open to the sea.

None of the rumors mention the crews. What will be done to them, what they'll have to do in service to their country. We don't need to talk about it. Everyone already knows. Things that are choices today won't be choices tomorrow; that's the way it's always been, when you sign away your voice for a new means of dancing.

The walkway vibrates under my feet, broadcasting the all-hands
signal through the ship. It will vibrate through the underwater
spaces twice more, giving everyone the time they need. Maybe that
will be an advantage of those flooded boats; no more transitions,
no more hasty scrambles for breathing apparatus that fits a little
less well after every tour, no more forcing of feet into boots that
don't really fit but are standard issue (and standard issue is still
God and king here, on a navy vessel, in the service of the United
States government, even when the sailors do not, cannot, will
never fit the standard mold). I walk a little faster, as fast as I can
force myself to go in my standard-issue boots, and there is only a
thin shell between me and the sea.

We knew that women were better suited to be submariners by
the beginning of the twenty-first century. Women dealt better
with close quarters, tight spaces, and enforced contact with the
same groups of people for long periods of time. We were more
equipped to resolve our differences without resorting to violence
—and there *were* differences. Women—even military women—
had been socialized to fight with words and with social snubbing,
and the early all-female submarines must have looked like a cross
between a psychology textbook and the Hunger Games.

The military figured it out. They hired the right sociologists,
they taught their people the right way to deal with conflicts and
handle stress, they found ways of picking out that early programming and replacing it with fierce loyalty to the navy, to the program, to the crew.

Maybe it was one of those men—and they were all men, I've
seen the records; man after man, walking into our spaces, our submarines with their safe and narrow halls, and telling the women
who had to live there to make themselves over into a new image, a
better image, an image that wouldn't fight, or gossip, or bully. An
image that would do the navy proud. Maybe it was one of those
men who first started calling the all-female submarine crews the
military's "mermaids."

Maybe that was where they got the idea.

Within fifty years of the launch of the female submariners, the
sea had become the most valuable real estate in the world. Oh,
space exploration continued—mostly in the hands of the wealthy,

tech firms that decided a rocket would be a better investment
than a Ping-Pong table in the break room, and now had their eyes
set on building an office on Jupiter, a summer home on Mars.
It wasn't viable. Not for the teeming masses of Earth, the people
displaced from their communities by the superstorms and torna-
does, the people who just needed a place to live and eat and work
and flourish. Two thirds of the planet's surface is water. Much of
it remains unexplored, even today . . . and that was why, when Dr.
Bustos stood up and said he had a solution, people listened.

There were resources, down there in the sea. Medicines and
minerals and oil deposits and food sources. Places where the bed-
rock never shifted, suitable for anchoring bubble communities
(art deco's resurgence around the time of the launch was not a
coincidence). Secrets and wonders and miracles of science, and
all we had to do was find a way to escape our steel shells, to dive
deeper, to *find* them.

Women in the military had always been a bit of a sore spot, even
when all the research said that our presence hurt nothing, endangered nothing; even when we had our own class of ships to sail
beneath the waves, and recruits who aimed for other branches often found themselves quietly redirected to the navy. There was re-
cruiter logic behind it all, of course—reduced instances of sexual
assault (even if it would never drop to full zero), fewer unplanned
pregnancies, the camaraderie of people who really *understood* what
you were going through as a woman in the military. Never mind
the transmen who found themselves assigned to submarines, the
transwomen who couldn't get a berth, the women who came from
Marine or air force or army families and now couldn't convince
the recruiters that what they wanted was to serve as their fathers
had served, on the land. The submarines began to fill.

And then they told us why.

I drag myself up the short flight of stairs between the hallway
and the front of the ship (and why do they still build these things
with staggered hearts, knowing what's been done to us, knowing
what is yet to be done?) and join my crew. A hundred and twenty
of us, all told, and less than half standing on our feet. The rest sit
compacted in wheelchairs, or bob gently as the water beneath the
chamber shifts, their heads and shoulders protruding through the
holes cut in the floor. There is something strange and profoundly

unprofessional about seeing the captain speak with the heads and shoulders of wet-suited women sticking up around her feet like mushrooms growing from the omnipresent damp.

"At eighteen hundred hours, Seaman Wells encountered an unidentified bogey in our waters." The captain speaks clearly and slowly, enunciating each word like she's afraid we will all have forgotten the English language while her back was turned, trading in for some strange language of clicks and whistles and hums. She has read the studies about the psychological effects of going deep; she knows what to watch for.

We terrify her. I can't imagine how the navy thinks this is a good use of their best people, locking them away in tin cans that are always damp and smell of fish, and watching them go slowly, inexorably insane. You need to be damn good to get assigned to submarine command, and you need to be willing to stay a drysider. Only drysiders can be shown in public; only drysiders can testify to the efficacy of the program. The rest of us have been compromised.

It's such a polite, sterile little word. *Compromised.* Like we were swayed by the enemy, or blown off course by the gale-force winds of our delicate emotions. Nothing could be further from the truth. We're a necessary part of public safety, an unavoidable face of war . . . and we're an embarrassment that must be kept out at sea, where we can be safely forgotten.

"The bogey approached our ship but did not make contact. It avoided all cameras and did not pass by any open ports, which leads us to believe that it was either a deserter or an enemy combatant. The few sonar pictures we were able to get do not match any known design configuration." That doesn't have to mean anything. There are new models taking to the sea every day. I have my eye on a lovely frilled shark mod that's just clearing the testing process. Everyone who's seen the lab samples says it's a dream come true, and I'm about due for a few dreams.

One of the seamen raises her hand. She's new to the ship; her boots still fit, her throat still works. The captain nods in her direction, and she asks, in a voice that squeaks and shakes with the effort of pushing sound through air instead of water, "Didn't we have anyone on patrol when the bogey came by?"

It's a good question, especially for a newbie. The captain shakes her head. "We're here to chart the seafloor and bring back information about the resources here." What we can exploit, in other words. "All of our seagoing sailors were at bottom level or in transit when the bogey passed near our vessel."

One of the servicewomen floating near the captain's feet whistles long and low, a tiny foghorn of a sound. An electronic voice from one of the speakers asks, robotic and stiff, "What are our orders, captain?"

I don't recognize this sailor. She has the dark gray hair and flattened facial features common to the blue shark mods. There are fourteen blues currently serving on this vessel. I can't be blamed if I can't tell them apart. Sometimes I'm not even sure they can tell *themselves* apart. Blues have a strong schooling instinct, strong enough that the labs considered recalling them shortly after they were deployed. The brass stepped in before anything permanent could happen. Blues are good for morale. They fight like demons, and they fuck like angels, and they have no room left in their narrow predators' brains for morals. If not for the service, they'd be a danger to us all, but thankfully, they have a very pronounced sense of loyalty.

The captain manages not to shy away from the woman at her feet: no small trick, given how much we clearly distress her. "All sailors are to be on a state of high alert whenever leaving the vessel. High-water patrols will begin tonight and will continue for the duration of our voyage. Any creature larger than an eel is to be reported to your superior officer immediately. We don't know what the Chinese have been doing since they closed the communication channels between their research divisions and ours. They may have progressed further than we had guessed."

A low murmur breaks out among the sailors who can use words. Others whistle and hum, communicating faster via the private languages of their mods. Rumor keeps saying command is going to ban anything on the ships that can't be translated into traditional English by our computers, and rumor keeps getting slapped down as fast as it can spread, because the speech is hard-coded in some of the most popular, most functional mods, and without it our sailors couldn't communicate in the open sea. So people like our poor captain just have to grit their teeth and endure.

I feel bad for her, I really do. I envy her, too. Did they show her the same studies they'd once shown me, offer her the same concessions if she'd just serve as an example to her yearmates? Was she one of the rare individuals who saw everything the sea could give her and still chose to remain career track, remain land-bound, remain capable of leaving the service when her tour was up? Oh, they said and said that everything was reversible, but since no one ever chose reversal, we still didn't know if that was true, and no one wanted to be the test case. Too much to lose, not enough to gain.

The captain begins to talk again, and the buzz of conversation dies down to respectful silence, giving her the floor as she describes our assignments for the days to come. They're standard enough; except for the bogey or bogeys we'll be watching for, we'll be doing the normal patrols of the seabed and the associated trenches, looking for minerals, looking for species of fish we've never encountered before, taking samples. Deepening our understanding of the Pacific. Other crews have the Atlantic, mapping it out one square meter at a time; one day we'll meet on the other side of the world, a mile down and a universe away from where we started, and our understanding will be complete, and the human race can continue in its conquest of this strange and timeless new frontier. One day.

The captain finishes her speech, snapping off her words with the tight tonelessness of a woman who desperately wants to be anywhere else. We salute her, those in the water doing their best not to splash as they pull their arms out of the water and snap their webbed fingers to their foreheads. She returns the salute and we're dismissed, back to our quarters or onward to our duties.

I linger on the stairs while those who are newer to this command than I scatter, moving with a quick, dryland efficiency toward other parts of the submarine. The captain is the first to go, all but running from the bridge in her need to get away from us. The heads in the water vanish one by one, the sailors going back to whatever tasks had them outside the ship—those who aren't currently off-duty and seeking the simple peace of weightlessness and separation from the dry. Not all the seamen serving with this vessel are capable of doing what I'm doing, standing on their own two feet and walking among the drylander crew. Every ship has to have a few in transition. It's meant to be a temptation and a warning at the same time. "Mind your choices; there but for the grace of God and the United States government go you."

It only takes a few minutes before I'm standing alone on the stairs. I walk over to the lockers set in the far wall (one more concession to what they've made of us; in transition, we don't always have time to get to quarters, to get to privacy, and so they arrange the ships to let us strip down wherever we need, and hold it up as one more bit of proof that single-sex vessels are a requirement for the smooth operation of the navy). My boots are the first thing to go, and I have to blink back tears when I pull them off and my feet untwist, relaxing back into the natural shape the scientists have worked so hard to give them. All this work, all these changes to the sailors, and they still can't change our required uniforms—not when we still have things that can be called "feet" or "legs" and shoved into the standard-issue boots or trousers.

Piece by piece, I strip down to my swim trunks and thermal sports bra, both designed to expose as much skin as possible while still leaving me with a modicum of modesty. The blues especially have a tendency to remove their tops once they're in the water, buzzing past the cameras and laughing. That footage goes for a pretty penny on some corners of the Internet, the ones frequented by soft-skinned civilians who murmur to themselves about the military mermaids, and how beautiful we are, and how much they'd like to fuck us.

They'd flense themselves bloody on the sharkskins of the blues, they'd sting themselves into oblivion on the spines of the lionfish and the trailing jellied arms of the moonies and the men-o'-war, but still they talk, and still they see us as fantasies given flesh, and not as the military women that we are. Perhaps that, too, is a part of the navy's design. How easy is it to fear something that you've been seeing in cartoons and coloring books since you were born?

I walk to the nearest hole and exhale, blowing every bit of air out of my lungs. Then I step over the edge and plunge down, down, down, dragged under by the weight of my scientifically re-engineered musculature, into the arms of the waiting sea.

Project Amphitrite—otherwise known as "Mermaids for the Military"—started attracting public attention when I was in my senior year of high school and beginning to really consider the navy as a career option. I wanted to see the world. This new form of service promised me a world no one else had ever seen. They swore we could go back. They swore we would still be human, that every possible form of support would be offered to keep us connected to our roots. They said we'd all be fairy tales, a thousand Little

Mermaids rising from the sea and walking on new legs into the future that our sacrifice had helped them to ensure.

They didn't mention the pain. Maybe they thought we'd all see the writing on the wall, the endless gene treatments, the surgeries to cut away inconvenient bits of bone—both original issue and grown during the process of preparing our bodies for the depths —the trauma of learning to breathe in when submerged, suppressing the millennia of instinct that shrieked no, no, you will drown, you will die, no.

And maybe we did drown; maybe we did die. Every submersion felt a bit less like a betrayal of my species and a bit more like coming home. As I fall into the water my gills open, and the small fins on my legs spread, catching the water and holding me in place, keeping me from descending all the way to the bottom. The blues I saw before rush back to my side, attracted by the sound of something moving. They whirl around me in an undifferentiated tornado of fins and flukes and grasping hands, caressing my flank, touching my arms and hair before they whirl away again, off to do whatever a school of blues does when they are not working, when they are not slaved to the commands of a species they have willingly abandoned. Their clicks and whistles drift back to me, welcoming me, inviting me along.

I do not try to follow. Until my next shore leave, my next trip to the lab, I can't keep up; they're too fast for me, their legs fully sacrificed on the altar of being all that they can be. The navy claims they're turning these women into better soldiers. From where I hang suspended in the sea, my lungs filled with saltwater like amniotic fluid, these women are becoming better myths.

Other sailors flash by, most of them carrying bags or wearing floodlights strapped to their foreheads or chests; some holding spearguns, which work better at these depths than traditional rifles. We'd be defenseless if someone were to fire a torpedo into our midst, but thus far, all the troubles we've encountered have either been native—squid and sharks who see our altered silhouettes and think we look like prey—or our own kind, mermaids from rival militaries, trying to chart and claim our seabeds before we can secure them for the United States of America. We might have been the first ones into the sea, but we weren't the last, and we're not even the most efficient anymore. The American mods focus too much on form and not enough on functionality. Our lionfish, eels, even our jellies still look like women before they look like marine creatures. Some sailors say —although there's been no *proof* yet, and that's the mantra of the news outlets, who don't want to criticize the program more than they have to, don't want to risk losing access to the stream of beautifully staged official photos and the weekly reports on the amazing scientific advancements coming out of what we do here—some sailors say that they chose streamlined mods, beautiful, sleek creatures that would cut through the water like knives, minimal drag, minimal reminders of their mammalian origins, and yet somehow came out of the treatment tanks with breasts that ached like it was puberty all over again. Ached and then grew bigger, ascending a cup size or even two, making a more marketable silhouette.

Here in the depths we're soldiers, military machines remade to suit the needs of our country and our government. But when we surface, we're living advertisements for the world yet to come, when we start shifting more of the population to the bubble cities being constructed on the ground we've charted for them, when the military gene mods become available to the public. I've seen the plans. We all have. Civilians will be limited to "gentler" forms, goldfish and angelfish and bettas, all trailing fins and soft Disney elegance. Veterans will be allowed to keep our mods as recognition of our service, should we choose to stay in the wet—and again, no one knows whether reversal is *possible*, especially not for the more esoteric designs. Can you put the bones back into a jelly's feet, just because you think they ought to be there? Questions better left unanswered, if you ask me.

Adjustment is done: my gills are open, and my chest is rising smooth and easy, lungs filling with seawater without so much as a bubble of protest. I jackknife down and swim toward the current patrol, feeling the drag from my weight belt as it pulls me toward the bottom. One more reason to dream of that coming return to the labs, when they'll take me one step deeper, and this will be just a little more like home.

The blues return to join me; two of them grab my hands and pull me deeper, their webbed fingers slipping on my slick mammalian skin, and the captain and her bogeys are forgotten for a time, before the glorious majesty of the never-ending sea.

*

We're deep—about 100, 150 feet below the waiting submarine, our passage lit by the soft luminescent glow of the anglers and the lanterns—when something flashes past in the gloom just past the reach of the light. Whatever it is, it's moving fast, all dart and dazzle, and there isn't time to see it properly before it's gone.

The formation forms without anyone saying a word, the hard-coded schooling instinct slamming into our military training and forming an instant barricade against the waiting dark. Anglers and lanterns in the middle, blues, makos, and lionfish and undecideds on the outside. The five of us who have yet to commit to a full mod look like aberrations as we hang in the water, almost human, almost helpless against the empty sea.

One of the blues clicks, the sound reverberating through the water. A moment later her voice is coming through the implant in my inner ear, saying, "Sonar's picking up three bodies, all about twenty yards out, circling."

Another click, from another of the blues, and then: "Marine or mer?" Shorthand description, adopted out of necessity. Are we looking at natural marine creatures, sharks or dolphins—unusual at this depth—or even the increasingly common, increasingly dangerous squid that we've been seeing as we descend into the trenches? There are a dozen species of the great cephalopods down here, some never before seen by science, and all of them are hungry, and smart enough to recognize that whatever we are, we could fill bellies and feed babies. We are what's available. That has value, in the sea. (That has value on the land as well, where women fit for military service were what was available, where we became the raw material for someone else's expansion, for someone else's fairy tale, and now here we are, medical miracles, modern mermaids, hanging like apples in the larder of the sea.)

Click click. "Mer." The sonar responses our makos are getting must have revealed the presence of metal, or of surgical scars: something to tell them that our visitors are not naturally occurring in the sea. "Three, all female, unknown mods. Fall back?"

More clicks as the group discusses, voices coming hard and fast through the implants, arguing the virtues of retreat versus holding our ground. There are still crewmen in these waters, unaware of the potential threat—and we don't know for sure that this *is* a threat, not really. America isn't the only country to take to sea. We could just be brushing up against the territory claimed by an Australian crew, a New Zealand expedition, and everything will end peacefully if we simply stay where we are and make no threatening movements.

One of the blues breaks formation.

She's fast—one of the fastest we have, thanks to the surgery that fused her legs from crotch to ankles, replaced her feet with fins, replaced the natural curves of a mammalian buttock and thigh with the smooth sweep of a blue shark's tail—and she's out of the light before anyone has a chance to react. My sonar isn't as sensitive as the blues'; I don't know what she heard, only that she's gone. "After her!" I shout through the subdermal link, my words coming out as clicks and bubbles in the open water. And then we're moving, all of us, the blues in the lead with the makos close behind. The jellies bring up the rear, made more for drifting than for darting; one, a moonie with skin the color of rice paper that shows her internal organs pulsing softly in her abdomen, clings to a lionfish's dorsal fin. Her hands leave thin ribbons of blood in the water as she passes. We'll have sharks here soon.

With the lanterns and anglers moving in the middle of the school, we're able to maintain visual contact with each other, even if we're too deep and moving too fast to show up on cameras. This is the true strength of the military mermaid project: speed and teamwork, all the most dangerous creatures in the sea boiled down to their essentials and pasted onto navy women, who have the training and the instincts to tell us how they can best be used. So our scouts swim like bullets while the rest of us follow, legs and tails pumping hard, arms down flat by our sides or holding tight to the towline of someone else's fin, someone else's elbow. Those of us who are carrying weapons have them slung over our backs, out of the way. Can't swim at speed and fire a harpoon gun at the same time.

All around me the school clicks and whistles their positions, their conditions, only occasionally underscoring their reports with actual words. "She's not here." "Water's been disturbed." "Something tastes of eel." This isn't how we write it down for the brass. They're all drylanders, they don't understand how easy it is to go loose and fluid down here in the depths, how little rank and order seem to matter when you're moving as a single beast with a dozen tails, two dozen arms, and trying all the while to keep yourself together, keep yourself unified, keep yourself *whole*. The chain of command dissolves under the pressure of the crushing deep, just as so many other things—both expected and unimagined—have already fallen away.

Then, motion in the shadows ahead, and we surge forward again, trying to find our missing shipmate, our missing sister, the missing sliver of the self that we have become as we trained together, schooled together, mourned our lost humanity and celebrated our dawning monstrosity together. We are sailors and servicewomen, yes; we will always be those things, all the way down to our mutant and malleable bones. But moments like this, when it is us and the open sea, remind us every day that we are more than what we were, and less than what we are to become, voiceless daughters of Poseidon, singing in the space behind our souls.

The taste of blood in the water comes first, too strong to be coming from the sliced hands of those who chose poorly when they grabbed at the bodies of their fellow fables. Then comes the blue, flung out of the dark ahead, her slate-colored back almost invisible outside the bioluminescent glow, her face and belly pearled pale and ghostly. One of the other blues darts forward to catch her before she can slam into the rest of us, potentially hurting herself worse on spines or stingers. A great cry rises from the group, half lament, half whale song. The remaining two blues hurl themselves into the dark, moving fast, too fast for the rest of us to catch them . . . and then they return, empty-handed and angry-eyed. One of them clicks a message.

"She got away."

We nod, one to another, and turn to swim—still in our tight, effective school—back toward the waiting vessel. Our crewmate needs medical care. Only after we know she's safe can we go out again, and find the ones who hurt her, and make them pay.

So few of us are suited for walking anymore, even in the safe, narrow reef of the submarine's halls, where there is always solid metal waiting to catch and bear us up when our knees give out or our ankles refuse to bear our weight. So it is only natural that I should be the one to stand before the captain—anxious creature that she is—at the closest I could come to parade rest, my hands behind my back and my eyes fixed on the wall behind her, reciting the events of the day.

"So you're telling me Seaman Metcalf charged ahead without

regard for the formation, or for the safety of her fellow crewmen?" The captain frowns at the incident report, and then at me. She is trying to be withering. She is succeeding only in looking petulant, like a child in the process of learning that not every fairy tale is kind. "Did anyone get a clear look at the bogey? Do we have any idea what could have caused Seaman Metcalf to behave so recklessly?"

She doesn't understand, she is not equipped to understand; she has not been sea-changed, and her loyalty is to the navy itself, not to the crew that swims beside her. Poor little drylander. Maybe someday, when she sees that there is no more upward mobility for we creatures of the sea, she'll give herself over to the water, and her eyes will be opened at last.

"No, ma'am. Seaman Metcalf broke formation without warning, and did not explain herself." She's in the medical bay now, sunk deep in a restorative bath of active genetic agents. She'll wake with a little more of her humanity gone, a little more of her modified reality pushed to the surface. Given how close she looks to fully modded, maybe she'll wake as something entirely new, complete and ready to swim in deeper waters, no longer wedded to the steel chain of the submarine.

"And the bogeys?" The captain sounds anxious. The captain always sounds anxious, but this is something new, sharp and insecure and painfully easy to read.

"No one saw anything clearly, ma'am. It's very dark when you exit the pelagic region, and while we have bioluminescent mods among our crew, they can't compensate for the limited visibility over a more than three-yard range. Whatever's been buzzing our perimeter, it's careful to stay outside the limits of the light." I don't mention the sonar readings we were getting before. They're important, I'm sure of that, but . . . not yet. She's not one of us.

There was a time when withholding information from my captain would have seemed like treason, a time when the patterns of loyalty were ingrained in my blood and on my bone. I had different blood then; I had different bones. They have replaced the things that made me theirs, and while I am grateful, I am no longer their property.

It's strange to realize that. Everything about this day has been strange. I keep my eyes fixed straight ahead, not looking at the captain's face. I am afraid she'll see that I am lying. I am afraid she won't see anything but a man-made monster and her future in fins and scales.

"I want doubled patrols," says the captain. "Seaman Metcalf will be detained when she recovers consciousness. I need to know what she saw."

"You may want to request that one of the other blue shark mod sailors also be present, ma'am," I say. "Seaman Metcalf no longer has vocal cords capable of human speech."

The captain blanches. "Understood. Dismissed."

"Ma'am." I offer a respectful salute before I turn and limp out of the room, moving slowly—it's always slow right after I leave the water, when my joints still dream of weightlessness and my lungs still feel like deserts, arid and empty.

The door swings shut behind me, slamming and locking in the same motion, and I am finally alone.

The captain has ordered us to double patrols, and so patrols are doubled. The captain has ordered the medical staff to detain Seaman Metcalf, and so she is detained, pinned clumsy and semimobile on a bed designed for a more human form, her tail turned to dead weight by gravity, her scales turned to brutal knives by the dryness of the air. I know how I feel at night, stretched out in my bunk like a surgical patient waiting for the knife, too heavy to move, too hot to breathe. Seaman Metcalf is so much further along than I am that the mere act of keeping her in the dry should be considered a crime of war, forbidden and persecuted by the very men who made her. But ah, we are soldiers; we signed up for this. We have no one to blame but ourselves.

The captain has ordered that we stay together at all times, two by two, preventing flights like Seaman Metcalf's, preventing danger from the dark. I am breaking orders as I slide into the water alone, a light slung around my neck like a strange jewel, a harpoon gun in my hands. This is a terrible idea. But I need to know why my sailors are flinging themselves into the darkness, pursuing an enemy I have not seen, and I can survive being beached better than the majority of them; I am the most liminal of the current crew, able to go deep and look, and see, yet still able to endure detention in a dry room. If anything, this may hasten my return to land, giving me the opportunity to tell the naval psychologists how much I need to progress; how much I need the mod that will take

me finally into the deeps. Yes. This is the right choice, and these
are orders almost intended to be broken.

It is darker than any midnight here, down here in the deep,
and the light from my halogen lamp can only pierce so far. Things
move in the corners of my vision, nightmare fish with teeth like
traumas, quick and clever squid that have learned to leave the
women with the harpoon guns alone. There is talk of a squid mod
being bandied about by the brass. I hope it comes to something.
I would love to learn, through the network of my soldier-sisters,
what the squid might have to teach us.

The captain has ordered that patrols be doubled, but I don't
see anyone else as I descend into deeper water, the darkness clos-
ing around me like a blanket full of small moving specks. Every
breath I take fills my throat with the infants of a thousand sea
creatures, filtered by the bioscreens installed by the clever men
who made me what I am today. I am not a baleen whale, but the
krill and larvae I catch and keep in this manner will help to replace the calories my body burns to keep me warm this far below
the sea. (Easier to line our limbs with blubber, make us seals, fat
and sleek and perfect—but we were always intended to be public
relations darlings, and fattening up our military women, no matter how good the justifications behind it, would never have played
well with the paparazzi.)

Something flashes through the gloom ahead of me, too fast
and too close to be a squid, too direct to be a shark; they always
approach from the side. I fall back, straightening myself in the
water so that my head points toward the distant surface. The water
has never encouraged anyone to walk upright, and the changing
weight of my body discourages this choice even more, tells me not
to do it, tells me to hang horizontal, like a good creature of the
sea. But I am still, in many regards, a sailor; I learned to stand my
ground, even when there is no ground beneath me.

She emerges from the dark like a dream, swimming calm and
confident into the radiant glow of my halogen light. Her mod is
one I've never seen before, long hair and rounded fins and pattern like a clownfish, winter white and hunter orange and char-
coal black, Snow White for the seafaring age. Clownfish are meant
to live in shallow waters, coral reefs; she shouldn't be here. She
shouldn't exist at all. This is a show model of a military technology, designed to attract investors, not to serve a practical purpose

in the open sea. She smiles at me as I stare, suddenly understanding what could inspire Seaman Metcalf to break formation, to dive
into the oppressive dark. For the first time, I feel as if I'm seeing a
mermaid.

Seaman Metcalf dove into the dark and was thrown back, battered and bruised and bleeding. I narrow my eyes and whistle experimentally. "Who are you?"

Her smile broadens. She clicks twice, and my implant translates
and relays her words: "A friend. You are early"—another click
—"no? Not so far along as those you swim with."

"You have harmed a member of my crew."

The stranger's eyes widen in wounded shock. "Me?" Her whistle
is long and sweet, cutting through the waves; the others must hear
her, no matter how far above me they are. Some things the water
cannot deaden. "No. Your crewmate asked us to strike her, to push
her back. Voices can lie, but injuries will tell the truth. We needed
your"—another series of clicks, this one barely translatable; the
closest I can come is *dry-walkers,* and I know then that she is not
military, has never been military. She doesn't know the lingo.

She's still speaking. ". . . to believe there was a threat here, in
the deep waters. I am sorry we did not sing to you. You stayed so
high. You seemed so, forgive me, human."

She makes it sound like a bad word. I frown. "You are trespass-
ing on waters claimed by the United States Navy. I hereby order
you to surrender."

Her sigh is a line of bubbles racing upward, toward the sun.
She whistles wordlessly, and three more figures swim out of the
dark, sinuous as eels, their skins shifting seamlessly from grays to
chalky pallor. They have no tentacles, but I recognize the effect as
borrowed from the mimic octopus; another thing the military has
discussed but not perfected. I am in over my head, in more ways
than one.

She whistles again. "I cannot surrender. I will not surrender. I
am here to free your sisters from the tank they have allowed themselves to be confined within. We are not pet store fish. We are not
trinkets. They deserve to swim freely. I can give that to them. We
can give that to them. But I will not surrender."

The eel-women circle like sharks, and I am afraid. I know she
can't afford to have me tell my captain what she has said; I know
that this deep, my body would never be found. Sailors disappear

on every voyage, and while some whisper about desertion—and the truth of those whispers hangs before me in the water like a fairy tale—I know that most of them have fallen prey only to their own hubris, and to the shadows beneath us, which never change and never fade away.

She is watching me, nameless mermaid from a lab I do not know. The geneticist who designed her must be so proud. "Is this the life you want? Tied to women too afraid to join you in the water, commanded by men who would make you something beautiful and then keep you captive? We can offer something more."

She goes on to talk about artificial reefs, genetically engineered coral growing into palaces and promenades, down, deep down at the bottom of the sea. The streets are lit by glowing kelp and schools of lanternfish, both natural and engineered. There is no hunger. There is no war. There are no voices barking orders. She speaks of a new Atlantis, Atlantis reborn one seafaring woman at a time. We will not need to change the sea to suit the daughters of mankind; we have already changed ourselves, and now need only come home.

All the while the eel-women circle like sharks, ready to strike me down if I raise a hand against their leader—ready to strike me down if I don't. Like Seaman Metcalf, I must serve as a warning to the navy. Something is out here. Something dangerous.

I look at her and frown. "Who made you?"

Something in her eyes goes dark. "They said I'd be a dancer."

"Ah." Some sounds translate from form to form, medium to medium; that is one of them. "Private firm?"

"Private *island*," she says, and all is clear. Rich men playing with military toys: chasing the idea of the new. They had promised her reversion, no doubt, as they promised it to us all—and maybe they meant it, maybe this was a test. The psychological changes that drive us to dive ever deeper down were accidental; maybe they were trying to reverse them. Instead they sparked a revolution.

"What will you do if I yield?"

Her smile is quick and bright, chasing the darkness from her eyes. "Hurt you."

"And my crew?"

"Most of them will be tragically killed in action. Their bodies will never be found." They would be free.

"Why should I agree?"

"Because in one year I will send my people back to this place, and if you are here, we will show you what it means to be a mermaid."

We hang there in the water for a few minutes more, me studying her, her smiling at me, serene as Amphitrite on the shore. Finally I close my eyes. I lower my gun, allowing it to slip out of my fingers and fall toward the distant ocean floor. It will never be found, one more piece of debris for the sea to keep and claim. I am leaving something behind. That makes me feel a little better about what has to happen next.

"Hurt me," I say.

They do.

When I wake, the air is pressing down on me like a sheet of glass. I am in the medical bay, swaddled in blankets and attached to beeping machines. The submarine hums around me; the engines are on, we are moving, we are heading away from the deepest parts of the sea. The attack must have already happened.

Someone will come for me soon, to tell me how sorry they all are, to give me whatever punishment they think I deserve for being found alone and drifting in the deeps. And then we will return to land. The ship will take on a new crew and sail back to face a threat that is not real, while I? I will sit before a board of scientists and argue my case until they give in, and put me back into the tanks, and take my unwanted legs away. They *will* yield to me. What man has ever been able to resist a siren?

A year from now, when I return to the bottom of the sea, I will hear the mermaids singing, each to each. And oh, I think that they will sing to me.

SOFIA SAMATAR

Ogres of East Africa

FROM *Long Hidden*

1907
Kenya

Catalogued by Alibhai M. Moosajee of Mombasa
February 1907

1. Apul Apul

A male ogre of the Great Lakes region. A melancholy character, he
eats crickets to sweeten his voice. His house burned down with all
of his children inside. His enemy is the Hare.

[My informant, a woman of the highlands who calls herself only
"Mary," adds that Apul Apul can be heard on windy nights, crying for his lost progeny. She claims that he has been sighted far
from his native country, even on the coast, and that an Arab trader
once shot and wounded him from the battlements of Fort Jesus.
It happened in a famine year, the "Year of Fever." A great deal of
research would be required in order to match this year, when, according to Mary, the cattle perished in droves, to one of the Years
of Our Lord by which my employer reckons the passage of time;
I append this note, therefore, in fine print, and in the margins.

"Always read the fine print, Alibhai!" my employer reminds me
when I draw up his contracts. He is unable to read it himself; his
eyes are not good. "The African sun has spoilt them, Alibhai!"

Apul Apul, Mary says, bears a festering sore where the bullet pierced him. He is allergic to lead.]

2. Ba'ati

A grave-dweller from the environs of the ancient capital of Kush. The ba'ati possesses a skeletal figure and a morbid sense of humor. Its great pleasure is to impersonate human beings: if your dearest friend wears a cloak and claims to suffer from a cold, he may be a ba'ati in disguise.

[Mary arrives every day precisely at the second hour after dawn. I am curious about this reserved and encyclopedic woman. It amuses me to write these reflections concerning her in the margins of the catalogue I am composing for my employer. He will think this writing fly-tracks, or smudges from my dirty hands (he persists in his opinion that I am always dirty). As I write I see Mary before me as she presents herself each morning, in her calico dress, seated on an overturned crate.

I believe she is not very old, though she must be several years older than I (but I am very young—"Too young to walk like an old man, Alibhai! Show some spirit! Ha!"). As she talks, she works at a bit of scarlet thread, plaiting something, perhaps a necklace. The tips of her fingers seem permanently stained with color.

"Where did you learn so much about ogres, Mary?"

"Anyone may learn. You need only listen."

"What is your full name?"

She stops plaiting and looks up. Her eyes drop their veil of calm and flash at me—in annoyance, in warning? "I told you," she says. "Mary. Only Mary."]

3. Dhegdheer

A female ogre of Somaliland. Her name means "Long Ear." She is described as a large, heavy woman, a very fast runner. One of her ears is said to be much longer than the other, in fact so long that it trails upon the ground. With this ear she can hear her enemies approaching from a great distance. She lives in a ruined hovel with her daughter. The daughter is beautiful and would like to be married. Eventually she will murder Dhegdheer by filling her ear with boiling water.

[My employer is so pleased with the information we have received from Mary that he has decided to camp here for another week. "Milk her, Alibhai!" he says, leering. "Eh? Squeeze her! Get as much out of her as you can. Ha! Ha!" My employer always shouts, as the report of his gun has made him rather deaf. In the evenings he invites me into his tent, where, closed in by walls, a roof, and a floor of Willesden canvas, I am afforded a brief respite from the mosquitoes.

A lamp hangs from the central pole, and beneath it my employer sits with his legs stretched out and his red hands crossed on his stomach. "Very good, Alibhai!" he says. "Excellent!" Having shot every type of animal in the Protectorate, he is now determined to try his hand at ogre. I will be required to record his kills, as I keep track of all his accounts. It would be "damn fine," he opines, to acquire the ear of Dhegdheer.

Mary tells me that one day Dhegdheer's daughter, racked with remorse, will walk into the sea and give herself up to the sharks.]

4. Iimũ

Iimũ transports his victims across a vast body of water in a ferryboat. His country, which lies on the other side, is inaccessible to all creatures save ogres and weaverbirds. If you are trapped there, your only recourse is to beg the weaverbirds for sticks. You will need seven sticks in order to get away. The first two sticks will allow you to turn yourself into a stone, thereby escaping notice. The remaining five sticks enable the following transformations: thorns, a pit, darkness, sand, a river.

["Stand up straight, Alibhai! Look lively, man!"

My employer is of the opinion that I do not show a young man's proper spirit. This, he tells me, is a racial defect, and therefore not my fault, but I may improve myself by following his example. My employer thrusts out his chest. "Look, Alibhai!" He says that if I walk about stooped over like a dotard, people will get the impression that I am shiftless and craven, and this will quite naturally make them want to kick me. He himself has kicked me on occasion.

It is true that my back is often stiff, and I find it difficult to extend my limbs to their full length. Perhaps, as my employer suspects, I am growing old before my time.

These nights of full moon are so bright, I can see my shadow on the grass. It writhes like a snake when I make an effort to straighten my back.]

5. Katandabaliko

While most ogres are large, Katandabaliko is small, the size of a child. He arrives with a sound of galloping just as the food is ready. "There is sunshine for you!" he cries. This causes everyone to faint, and Katandabaliko devours the food at his leisure. Katandabaliko cannot himself be cooked: cut up and boiled, he knits himself back together and bounces out of the pot. Those who attempt to cook and eat him may eat their own wives by mistake. When not tormenting human beings, he prefers to dwell among cliffs.

[I myself prefer to dwell in Mombasa, at the back of my uncle's shop, Moosajee and Co. I cannot pretend to enjoy nights spent in the open, under what my employer calls the splendor of the African sky. Mosquitoes whine, and something, probably a dangerous animal, rustles in the grass. The Somali cook and headman sit up late, exchanging stories, while the Kavirondo porters sleep in a corral constructed of baggage. I am uncomfortable, but at least I am not lonely. My employer is pleased to think that I suffer terribly from loneliness. "It's no picnic for you, eh, Alibhai?" He thinks me too prejudiced to tolerate the society of the porters and too frightened to go near the Somalis, who, to his mind, being devout Sunnis, must be plotting the removal of my Shi'a head.

In fact, we all pray together. We are tired and far from home. We are here for money, and when we talk, we talk about money. We can discuss calculations for hours: what we expect to buy, where we expect to invest. Our languages are different but all of us count in Swahili.]

6. Kibugi

A male ogre who haunts the foothills of Mount Kenya. He carries machetes, knives, hoes, and other objects made of metal. If you can manage to make a cut in his little finger, all the people he has devoured will come streaming out.

[Mary has had, I suspect, a mission education. This would explain the name and the calico dress. Such an education is nothing to be ashamed of—why, then, did she stand up in such a rage when I inquired about it? Mary's rage is cold; she kept her voice low. "I have told you not to ask me these types of questions! I have only come to tell you about ogres! Give me the money!" She held out her hand, and I doled out her daily fee in rupees, although she had not stayed for the agreed amount of time.

She seized the money and secreted it in her dress. Her contempt burned me; my hands trembled as I wrote her fee in my record book. "No questions!" she repeated, seething with anger. "If I went to a mission school, I'd burn it down! I have always been a free woman!"

I was silent, although I might have reminded her that we are both my employer's servants: like me, she has come here for money. I watched her stride off down the path to the village. At a certain distance, she began to waver gently in the sun.

My face still burns from the sting of her regard.

Before she left, I felt compelled to inform her that, although my father was born at Karachi, I was born at Mombasa. I, too, am an African.

Mary's mouth twisted. "So is Kibugi," she said.]

7. Kiptebanguryon

A fearsome yet curiously domestic ogre of the Rift Valley. He collects human skulls, which he once used to decorate his spacious dwelling. He made the skulls so clean, it is said, and arranged them so prettily, that from a distance his house resembled a palace of salt. His human wife bore him two sons: one which looked human like its mother, and one, called Kiptegen, which resembled its father. When the wife was rescued by her human kin, her human-looking child was also saved, but Kiptegen was burnt alive.

[I am pleased to say that Mary returned this morning, perfectly calm and apparently resolved to forget our quarrel.

She tells me that Kiptegen's brother will never be able to forget the screams of his sibling perishing in the flames. The mother, too, is scarred by the loss. She had to be held back, or she would have dashed into the fire to rescue her ogre-child. This information does not seem appropriate for my employer's catalogue; still, I find myself adding it in the margins. There is a strange pleasure in this writing and not-writing, these letters that hang between revelation and oblivion.

. If my employer discovered these notes, he would call them impudence, cunning, a trick.

What would I say in my defense? "Sir, I was unable to tell you. Sir, I was unable to speak of the weeping mother of Kiptegen." He would laugh: he believes that all words are found in his language.

I ask myself if there are words contained in Mary's margins: stories of ogres she cannot tell to me.

Kiptebanguryon, she says, is homeless now. A modern creature, he roams the Protectorate clinging to the undersides of trains.]

8. Kisirimu

Kisirimu dwells on the shores of Lake Albert. Bathed, dressed in barkcloth, carrying his bow and arrows, he glitters like a bridegroom. His purpose is to trick gullible young women. He will be betrayed by song. He will die in a pit, pierced by spears.

[In the evenings, under the light of the lamp, I read the day's inventory from my record book, informing my employer of precisely what has been spent and eaten. As a representative of Moosajee and Co., Superior Traders, Stevedores and Dubashes, I am responsible for ensuring that nothing has been stolen. My employer stretches, closes his eyes, and smiles as I inform him of the amount of sugar, coffee, and tea in his possession. Tinned bacon, tinned milk, oat porridge, salt, ghee. The dates, he reminds me, are strictly for the Somalis, who grow sullen in the absence of this treat.

My employer is full of opinions. The Somalis, he tells me, are an excitable nation. "Don't offend them, Alibhai! Ha, ha!" The Kavirondo, by contrast, are merry and tractable, excellent for manual work. My own people are cowardly, but clever at figures.

There is nothing, he tells me, more odious than a German. However, their women are seductive, and they make the world's most beautiful music. My employer sings me a German song. He sounds like a buffalo in distress. Afterward he makes me read to him from the Bible.

He believes I will find this painful: "Heresy, Alibhai! Ha, ha! You'll have to scrub your mouth out, eh? Extra ablutions?"

Fortunately, God does not share his prejudices.

I read: *There were giants in the earth in those days.*

I read: *For only Og king of Bashan remained of the remnant of giants; behold, his bedstead was a bedstead of iron.*]

9. Konyek

Konyek is a hunter. His bulging eyes can perceive movement far across the plains. Human beings are his prey. He runs with great loping strides, kills, sleeps underneath the boughs of a leafy tree. His favorite question is "Mother, whose footprints are these?"

[Mary tells me that Konyek passed through her village in the Year of Amber. The whirlwind of his running loosened the roofs. A wise woman had predicted his arrival, and the young men, including Mary's brother, had set up a net between trees to catch him. But Konyek only laughed and tore down the net and disappeared with a sound of thunder. He is now, Mary believes, in the region of Eldoret. She tells me that her brother and the other young men who devised the trap have not been seen since the disappearance of Konyek.

Mary's gaze is peculiar. It draws me in. I find it strange that just a few days ago I described her as a cold person. When she tells me of her brother she winds her scarlet thread so tightly about her finger I am afraid she will cut it off.]

10. Mbiti

Mbiti hides in the berry bushes. When you reach in, she says: "Oh, don't pluck my eye out!" She asks you: "Shall I eat you, or shall I make you my child?" You agree to become Mbiti's child. She pricks you with a needle. She is betrayed by the cowrie shell at the end of her tail.

["My brother," Mary says.

She describes the forest. She says we will go there to hunt ogres. Her face is filled with a subdued yet urgent glow. I find myself leaning closer to her. The sounds of the others, their voices, the smack of an ax into wood, recede until they are thin as the buzzing of flies. The world is composed of Mary and myself and the sky about Mary and the trees about Mary. She asks me if I understand what she is saying. She tells me about her brother in the forest. I realize that the glow she exudes comes not from some supernatural power but from fear.

She speaks to me carefully, as if to a child.

She gives me a bundle of scarlet threads.

She says: "When the child goes into the forest, it wears a red necklace. And when the ogre sees the necklace, it spares the child." She says: "I think you and my brother are exactly the same age."

My voice is reduced to a whisper. "What of Mbiti?"

Mary gives me a deep glance, fiercely bright.

She says: "Mbiti is lucky. She has not been caught. Until she is caught, she will be one of the guardians of the forest. Mbiti is always an ogre and always the sister of ogres."]

11. Ntemelua

Ntemelua, a newborn baby, already has teeth. He sings: "Draw near, little pot, draw near, little spoon!" He replaces the meat in the pot with balls of dried dung. Filthy and clever, he crawls into a cow's anus to hide in its stomach. Ntemelua is weak and he lives by fear, which is a supernatural power. He rides a hyena. His back will never be quite straight, but this signifies little to him, for he can still stretch his limbs with pleasure. The only way to escape him is to abandon his country.

[Tomorrow we depart.

I am to give the red necklaces only to those I trust. "You know them," Mary explained, "as I know you."

"Do you know me?" I asked, moved and surprised.

She smiled. "It is easy to know someone in a week. You need only listen."

Two paths lie before me now. One leads to the forest; the other leads home.

How easily I might return to Mombasa! I could steal some food and rupees and begin walking. I have a letter of contract affirming that I am employed and not a vagrant. How simple to claim that my employer has dispatched me back to the coast to order supplies, or to Abyssinia to purchase donkeys! But these scarlet threads burn in my pocket. I want to draw nearer to the source of their heat. I want to meet the ogres.

"You were right," Mary told me before she left. "I did go to a mission school. And I didn't burn it down." She smiled, a smile of mingled defiance and shame. One of her eyes shone brighter than the other, kindled by a tear. I wanted to cast myself at her feet and beg her forgiveness. Yes, to beg her forgiveness for having pried into her past, for having stirred up the memory of her humiliation.

Instead I said clumsily: "Even Ntemelua spent some time in a cow's anus."

Mary laughed. "Thank you, brother," she said.

She walked away down the path, sedate and upright, and I do not know if I will ever see her again. I imagine meeting a young man in the forest, a man with a necklace of scarlet thread who stands with Mary's light bearing and regards me with Mary's direct and trenchant glance. I look forward to this meeting as if to the sight of a long-lost friend. I imagine clasping the hand of this young man, who is like Mary and like myself. Beneath our joined hands, my employer lies slain. The ogres tear open the tins and enjoy a prodigious feast among the darkling trees.]

12. Rakakabe

Rakakabe, how beautiful he is, Rakakabe! A Malagasy demon, he
has been sighted as far north as Kismaayo. He skims the waves, he
eats mosquitoes, his face gleams, his hair gleams. His favorite question is "Are you sleeping?"

Rakakabe of the gleaming tail! No, we are wide awake.

[This morning we depart on our expedition. My employer sings
—"Green grow the rushes, o!"—but we, his servants, are even
more cheerful. We are prepared to meet the ogres.

We catch one another's eyes and smile. All of us sport necklaces
of red thread: signs that we belong to the party of the ogres, that
we are prepared to hide and fight and die with those who live in
the forest, those who are dirty and crooked and resolute. "Tell my
brother his house is waiting for him," Mary whispered to me at the
end—such an honor, to be the one to deliver her message! While
she continues walking, meeting others, passing into other hands
the blood-red necklaces by which the ogres are known.

There will be no end to this catalogue. The ogres are everywhere. Number thirteen: Alibhai M. Moosajee of Mombasa.

The porters lift their loads with unaccustomed verve. They
set off, singing. "See, Alibhai!" my employer exclaims in delight.
"They're made for it! Natural workers!"

"Oh, yes sir! Indeed, sir!"

The sky is tranquil, the dust saturated with light. Everything
conspires to make me glad.

Soon, I believe, I shall enter into the mansion of the ogres, and
stretch my limbs on the doorstep of Rakakabe.]

THEODORA GOSS

Cimmeria: From the *Journal of Imaginary Anthropology*

FROM *Lightspeed Magazine*

REMEMBERING CIMMERIA: I walk through the bazaar, between the stalls of the spice sellers, smelling turmeric and cloves, hearing the clash of bronze from the sellers of cooking pots, the bleat of goats from the butchers' alley. Rugs hang from wooden racks, scarlet and indigo. In the corners of the alleys, men without legs perch on wooden carts, telling their stories to a crowd of ragged children, making coins disappear into the air. Women from the mountains, their faces prematurely old from sun and suffering, call to me in a dialect I can barely understand. Their stands sell eggplants and tomatoes, the pungent olives that are distinctive to Cimmerian cuisine, video games. In the mountain villages it has long been a custom to dye hair blue for good fortune, a practice that sophisticated urbanites have lately adopted. Even the women at court have hair of a deep and startling hue.

My guide, Afa, walks ahead of me, with a string bag in her hand, examining the vegetables, buying cauliflower and lentils. Later she will make rice mixed with raisins, meat, and saffron. The cuisine of Cimmeria is rich, heavy with goat and chicken. (They eat and keep no pigs.) The pastries are filled with almond paste and soaked in honey. She waddles ahead (forgive me, but you do waddle, Afa), and I follow amid a cacophony of voices, speaking the Indo-European language of Cimmeria, which is closest perhaps to Old Iranian. The mountain accents are harsh, the tones of the urbanites soft and lisping. Shaila spoke in those tones, when she taught me phrases in her language: Can I have more lozi (a cake made with marzipan, flavored with orange water)? You are the son of a dog. I will love you until the ocean swallows the moon. (A traditional saying. At the end of time, the serpent that lies beneath the Black Sea will rise up and swallow the moon as though it were lozi. It means, I will love you until the end of time.)

On that day, or perhaps it is another day I remember, I see a man selling Kalashnikovs. The war is a recent memory here, and every man has at least one weapon: even I wear a curved knife in my belt, or I will be taken for a prostitute. (Male prostitutes, who are common in the capital, can be distinguished by their kohl-rimmed eyes, their extravagant clothes, their weaponlessness. As a red-haired Irishman, I do not look like them, but it is best to avoid misunderstandings.) The sun shines down from a cloudless sky. It is hotter than summer in Arizona, on the campus of the small college where this journey began, where we said, Let us imagine a modern Cimmeria. What would it look like? I know now. The city is cooled by a thousand fountains, we are told: its name means just that, A Thousand Fountains. It was founded in the sixth century BCE, or so we have conjectured and imagined.

I have a pounding headache. I have been two weeks in this country, and I cannot get used to the heat, the smells, the reality of it all. Could we have created this? The four of us, me and Lisa and Michael the Second, and Professor Farrow, sitting in a conference room at that small college? Surely not. And yet.

We were worried that the Khan would forbid us from entering the country. But no. We were issued visas, assigned translators, given office space in the palace itself.

The Khan was a short man, balding. His wife had been Miss Cimmeria, and then a television reporter for one of the three state channels. She had met the Khan when she had been sent to interview him. He wore a business suit with a traditional scarf around his neck. She looked as though she had stepped out of a photo shoot for *Vogue Russia,* which was available in all the gas stations.

"Cimmeria has been here, on the shores of the Black Sea, for more than two thousand years," he said. "Would you like some coffee, Dr. Nolan? I think our coffee is the best in the world." It was —dark, thick, spiced, and served with ewe's milk. "This theory of yours—that a group of American graduate students created Cim-

meria in their heads, merely by thinking about it—you will understand that some of our people find it insulting. They will say that
all Americans are imperialist dogs. I myself find it amusing, almost
charming—like poetry. The mind creates reality, yes? So our poets
have taught us. Of course, your version is culturally insensitive, but
then, you are Americans. I did not think Americans were capable
of poetry."

Only Lisa had been a graduate student, and even she had recently graduated. Mike and I were postdocs, and Professor Farrow
was tenured at Southern Arizona State. It all seemed so far away,
the small campus with its perpetually dying lawns and drab 1970s
architecture. I was standing in a reception room, drinking coffee with the Khan of Cimmeria and his wife, and Arizona seemed
imaginary, like something I had made up.

"But we like Americans here. The enemy of my enemy is my
friend, is he not? Any enemy of Russia is a friend of mine. So I
am glad to welcome you to my country. You will, I am certain, be
sensitive to our customs. Your coworker, for example—I suggest
that she not wear short pants in the streets. Our clerics, whether
Orthodox, Catholic, or Muslim, are traditional and may be of-
fended. Anyway, you must admit, such garments are not attractive
on women. I would not say so to her, you understand, for women
are the devil when they are criticized. But a woman should culti-
vate an air of mystery. There is nothing mysterious about bare red
knees."

Our office space was in an unused part of the palace. My translator, Jafik, told me it had once been a storage area for bedding. It
was close to the servants' quarters. The Khan may have welcomed
us to Cimmeria for diplomatic reasons, but he did not think much
of us, that was clear. It was part of the old palace, which had been
built in the thirteenth century CE, after the final defeat of the
Mongols. Since then Cimmeria had been embroiled in almost constant warfare, with Anatolia, Scythia, Poland, and most recently
the Russians, who had wanted its ports on the Black Sea. The Khan
had received considerable American aid, including military advisers. The war had ended with the disintegration of the USSR. The
Ukraine, focused on its own economic problems, had no wish to
interfere in local politics, so Cimmeria was enjoying a period of
relative peace. I wondered how long it would last.

Lisa was our linguist. She would stay in the capital for the first three months, then venture out into the countryside, recording local dialects. "You know what amazes me?" she said as we were unpacking our computers and office supplies. "The complexity of all this. You would think it really had been here for the last three thousand years. It's hard to believe it all started with Mike the First goofing off in Professor Farrow's class." He had been bored and, instead of taking notes had started sketching a city. The professor had caught him, and had told the students that we would spend the rest of the semester creating that city and the surrounding countryside. We would be responsible for its history, customs, language. Lisa was in the class, too, and I was the TA. AN 703, Contemporary Anthropological Theory, had turned into Creating Cimmeria.

Of the four graduate students in the course, only Lisa stayed in the program. One got married and moved to Wisconsin; another transferred to the School of Education so she could become a kindergarten teacher. Mike the First left with his master's and went on to do an MBA. It was a coincidence that Professor Farrow's next postdoc, who arrived in the middle of the semester, was also named Mike. He had an undergraduate degree in classics, and was the one who decided that the country we were developing was Cimmeria. He was also particularly interested in the Borges hypothesis. Everyone had been talking about it at Michigan, where he had done his PhD. At that point it was more controversial than it is now, and Professor Farrow had only been planning to touch on it briefly at the end of the semester. But once we started on Cimmeria, AN 703 became an experiment in creating reality through perception and expectation. Could we actually create Cimmeria by thinking about it, writing about it?

Not in one semester, of course. After the semester ended, all of us worked on the Cimmeria Project. It became the topic of Lisa's dissertation: "A Dictionary and Grammar of Modern Cimmerian, with Commentary." Mike focused on history. I wrote articles on culture, figuring out probable rites of passage, how the Cimmerians would bury their dead. We had Herodotus, we had accounts of cultures from that area. We were all steeped in anthropological theory. On weekends, when we should have been going on dates, we gathered in a conference room, under a fluorescent light, and talked about Cimmeria. It was fortunate that around that time the *Journal of Imaginary Anthropology* was founded at Penn State. Otherwise I don't know where we would have published. At the first Imaginary Anthropology conference, in Orlando, we realized that a group from Tennessee was working on the modern Republic of Scythia and Sarmatia, which shared a border with Cimmeria. We formed a working group.

"Don't let the Cimmerians hear you talk about creating all this," I said. "Especially the nationalists. Remember, they have guns, and you don't." Should I mention her cargo shorts? I had to admit, looking at her knobby red knees, above socks and Birkenstocks, that the Khan had a point. Before she left for the mountains, I would warn her to wear more traditional clothes.

I was going to stay in the capital. My work would focus on the ways in which the historical practices we had described in "Cimmeria: A Proposal," in the second issue of the *Journal of Imaginary Anthropology,* influenced and remained evident in modern practice. Already I had seen developments we had never anticipated. One was the fashion for blue hair; in a footnote, Mike had written that blue was a fortunate color in Cimmerian folk belief. Another was the ubiquity of cats in the capital. In an article on funerary rites, I had described how cats were seen as guides to the land of the dead until the coming of Christianity in the twelfth century CE. The belief should have gone away, but somehow it had persisted, and every household, whether Orthodox, Catholic, Muslim, Jewish, or one of the minor sects that flourished in the relative tolerance of Cimmeria, had its cat. No Cimmerian wanted his soul to get lost on the way to Paradise. Stray cats were fed at the public expense, and no one dared harm a cat. I saw them everywhere when I ventured into the city. In a month Mike was going to join us, and I would be able to show him all the developments I was documenting. Meanwhile, there was email and Skype.

I was assigned a bedroom and bath close to our offices. Afa, who had been a sort of undercook, was assigned to be my servant but quickly became my guide, showing me around the city and mocking my Cimmerian accent. "He he!" she would say. "No, Doctor Pat, that word is not pronounced that way. Do not repeat it that way, I beg of you. I am an old woman, but still it is not respectable for me to hear!" Jafik was my language teacher as well as my translator, teaching me the language Lisa had created based on what we knew of historical Cimmerian and its Indo-European roots, except that it had developed an extensive vocabulary. As used by modern

Cimmerians, it had the nuance and fluidity of a living language, as well as a surprising number of expletives.

I had no duties except to conduct my research, which was a relief from the grind of TAing and, recently, teaching my own undergraduate classes. But one day I was summoned to speak with the Khan. It was the day of an official audience, so he was dressed in Cimmerian ceremonial robes, although he still wore his Rolex watch. His advisers looked impatient, and I gathered that the audience was about to begin—I had seen a long line of supplicants waiting by the door as I was ushered in. But he said, as though we had all the time in the world, "Doctor Nolan, did you know that my daughters are learning American?" Sitting next to him were four girls, all wearing the traditional headscarves worn by Cimmerian peasant women but pulled back to show that their hair was dyed fashionably blue. "They are very troublesome, my daughters. They like everything modern: Leonardo DiCaprio, video games. Tradition is not good enough for them. They wish to attend university and find professions, or do humanitarian work. Ah, what is a father to do?" He shook a finger at them, fondly enough. "I would like it if you could teach them the latest American idioms. The slang, as it were."

That afternoon Afa led me to another part of the palace—the royal family's personal quarters. These were more modern and considerably more comfortable than ours. I was shown into what seemed to be a common room for the girls. There were colorful rugs and divans, embroidered wall hangings, and an enormous flat-screen TV.

"These are the Khan's daughters," said Afa. She had already explained to me, in case I made any blunders, that they were his daughters by his first wife, who had not been Miss Cimmeria but had produced the royal children: a son, and then only daughters, and then a second son who had died shortly after birth. She had died a week later of an infection contracted during the difficult delivery. "Anoor is the youngest, then Tallah, and then Shaila, who is already taking university classes online." Shaila smiled at me. This time none of them were wearing headscarves. There really was something attractive about blue hair.

"And what about the fourth one?" She was sitting a bit back from the others, to the right of and behind Shaila, whom she closely resembled.

Afa looked at me with astonishment. "The Khan has three

daughters," she said. "Anoor, Tallah, and Shaila. There is no fourth one, Doctor Pat."

The fourth one stared at me without expression.

"Cimmerians don't recognize twins," said Lisa. "That has to be the explanation. Do you remember the thirteenth-century philosopher Farkosh Kursand? When God made the world, he decreed that human beings would be born one at a time, unique, unlike animals. They would be born defenseless, without claws or teeth or fur. But they would have souls. It's in a children's book — I have a copy somewhere, but it's based on Kursand's reading of Genesis in one of his philosophical treatises. Mike would know which. And it's the basis of Cimmerian human rights law, actually. That's why women have always had more rights here. They have souls, so they've been allowed to vote since Cimmeria became a parliamentary monarchy. I'm sure it's mentioned in one of the articles — I don't remember which one, but check the database Mike is putting together. Shaila must have been a twin, and the Cimmerians don't recognize the second child as separate from the first. So Shaila is one girl. In two bodies. But with one soul."

"Who came up with that stupid idea?"

"Well, to be perfectly honest, it might have been you." She leaned back in our revolving chair. I don't know how she could do that without falling. "Or Mike, of course. It certainly wasn't my idea. Embryologically it does make a certain sense. Identical twins really do come from one egg."

"So they're both Shaila."

"There is no both. The idea of both is culturally inappropriate. There is one Shaila, in two bodies. Think of them as Shaila and her shadow."

I tested this theory once, while walking through the market with Afa. We were walking through the alley of the dog-sellers. In Cimmeria, almost every house has a dog, for defense and to catch rats. Cats are not sold in the market. They cannot be sold at all, only given or willed away. To sell a cat for money is to imperil your immortal soul. We passed a woman sitting on the ground, with a basket beside her. In it were two infants, as alike as the proverbial two peas in a pod, half covered with a ragged blanket. Beside them lay a dirty mutt with a chain around its neck that lifted its head and whimpered as we walked by.

"Child how many in basket?" I asked Afa in my still-imperfect Cimmerian.

"There is one child in that basket, Pati," she said. I could not get her to stop using the diminutive. I even told her that in my language Pati was a woman's name, to no effect. She just smiled, patted me on the arm, and assured me that no one would mistake such a tall, handsome (which in Cimmerian is the same word as beautiful) man for a woman.

"Only one child?"

"Of course. One basket, one child."

Shaila's shadow followed her everywhere. When she and her sisters sat with me in the room with the low divans and the large-screen TV, studying American slang, she was there. "What's up!" Shaila would say, laughing, and her shadow would stare down at the floor. When Shaila and I walked through the gardens, she walked six paces behind, pausing when we paused, sitting when we sat. After we were married, in our apartment in Arizona, she would sit in a corner of the bedroom, watching as we made love. Although I always turned off the lights, I could see her: a darkness against the off-white walls of faculty housing.

Once I tried to ask Shaila about her. "Shaila, do you know the word *twin?*"

"Yes, of course," she said. "In American, if two babies are born at the same time, they are twins."

"What about in Cimmeria? Surely there is a Cimmerian word for *twin*. Sometimes two babies are born at the same time in Cimmeria, too."

She looked confused. "I suppose so. Biology is the same everywhere."

"Well, what's the word, then?"

"I cannot think of it. I shall have to email Tallah. She is better at languages than I am."

"What if you yourself were a twin?"

"Me? But I am not a twin. If I were, my mother would have told me."

I tried a different tactic. "Do you remember the dog you had, Kala? She had two sisters, born at the same time. Those were Anoor's and Tallah's dogs. They were not Kala, even though they were born in the same litter. You could think of them as twins—I mean, triplets." I remembered them gamboling together, Kala and her two littermates. They would follow us through the gardens, and Shaila and her sisters would pet them indiscriminately. When we sat under the plum trees, they would tumble together into one doggy heap.

"Pat, what is this all about? Is this about the fact that I don't want to have a baby right now? You know I want to go to graduate school first."

I did not think her father would approve the marriage. I told her so: "Your father will never agree to you marrying a poor American postdoc. Do you have any idea how poor I am? My research grant is all I have."

"You do not understand Cimmerian politics," Shaila replied. "Do you know what percentage of our population is ethnically Sarmatian? Twenty percent, all in the eastern province. They fought the Russians, and they still have weapons. Not just guns: tanks, antiaircraft missiles. The Sarmatians are getting restless, Pati. They are mostly Catholic in a country that is mostly Orthodox. They want to unite with their homeland, create a greater Scythia and Sarmatia. My father projects an image of strength, because what else can you do? But he is afraid. He is most afraid that the Americans will not help. They helped against the Russians, but this is an internal matter. He has talked to us already about different ways for us to leave the country. Anoor has been enrolled at the Lycée International in Paris, and Tallah is going to study at the American School in London. They can get student visas. For me it is more difficult: I must be admitted at a university. That is why I have been taking courses online. Ask him. If he says no, then no. But I think he will consider my marriage with an American."

She was right. The Khan considered. For a week, and then another, while pro-Sarmatian factions clashed with military in the eastern province. Then protests broke out in the capital. Anoor was already in Paris with her stepmother, supposedly on a shopping spree for school. Tallah had started school in London. In the Khan's personal office, I signed the marriage contract, barely understanding what I was signing because it was in an ornate script I had seen only in medieval documents. On the way to the airport, we stopped by the cathedral in Shahin Square, where we were married by the patriarch of the Cimmerian Independent Orthodox Church, who checked the faxed copy of my baptismal certificate and lectured me in sonorous tones about the importance of conversion, raising children in the true faith. The Khan kissed Shaila on both cheeks, promising her that we would have a proper ceremony when the political situation was more stable and she could return to the country. In the Khan's private plane, we flew to a small airport near Fresno and spent our first night together at my mother's house. My father had died of a heart attack while I was in college, and she lived alone in the house where I had grown up. It was strange staying in the guest bedroom, down the hall from the room where I had slept as a child, which still had my He-Man action figures on the shelves, the Skeletor defaced with permanent marker. I had to explain to her about Shaila's shadow.

"I don't understand," my mother said. "Are you all going to live together?"

"Well, yes, I guess so. It's really no different than if her twin sister were living with us, is it?"

"And Shaila is going to take undergraduate classes? What is her sister going to do?"

"I have no idea," I said.

What she did, more than anything else, was watch television. All day it would be on. Mostly she watched CNN and the news shows. Sometimes I would test Shaila, asking, "Did you turn the TV on?"

"Is it on?" she would say. "Then of course I must have turned it on. Unless you left it on before you went out. How did your class go? Is that football player in the back still falling asleep?"

One day I came home and noticed that the other Shaila was cooking dinner. Later I asked, "Shaila, did you cook dinner?"

"Of course," she said. "Did you like it?"

"Yes." It was actually pretty good, chicken in a thick red stew over rice. It reminded me of a dish Afa had made in an iron pot hanging over an open fire in the servants' quarters. But I guess it could be made on an American stovetop as well.

After that, the other Shaila cooked dinner every night. It was convenient, because I was teaching night classes, trying to make extra money. Shaila told me that I did not need to work so hard, that the money her father gave her was more than enough to support us both. But I was proud and did not want to live off my father-in-law, even if he was the Khan of Cimmeria. At the same time, I was trying to write up my research on Cimmerian funerary practices. If I could publish a paper in the *Journal of Imaginary An-*

thropology, I might have a shot at a tenure-track position, or at least a visiting professorship somewhere that wasn't Arizona. Shaila was trying to finish her premed requirements. She had decided that she wanted to be a pediatrician.

Meanwhile, in Cimmeria the situation was growing more complicated. The pro-Sarmatian faction had split into the radical Sons of Sarmatia and the more moderate Sarmatian Democratic Alliance, although the prime minister claimed that the SDA was a front. There were weekly clashes with police in the capital, and the Sons of Sarmatia had planted a bomb in the Hilton, although a maid had reported a suspicious shopping bag and the hotel had been evacuated before the bomb could go off. The Khan had imposed a curfew, and martial law might be next, although the army had a significant Sarmatian minority. But I had classes to teach, so I tried not to pay attention to politics, and even Shaila dismissed it all as "a mess."

One day I came home from a departmental meeting and Shaila wasn't in the apartment. She was usually home by seven. I assumed she'd had to stay late for a lab. The other Shaila was cooking dinner in the kitchen. At eight, when she hadn't come back yet, I sat down at the kitchen table to eat. To my surprise, the other Shaila sat down across from me, at the place set for Shaila. She had never sat down at the table with us before.

She looked at me with her dark eyes and said, "How was your day, Pati?"

I dropped my fork. It clattered against the rim of the plate. She had never spoken before, not one sentence, not one word. Her voice was just like Shaila's, but with a stronger accent. At least it sounded stronger to me. Or maybe not. It was hard to tell.

"Where's Shaila?" I said. I could feel a constriction in my chest, as though a fist had started to close around my heart. Like the beginning of my father's heart attack. I think even then I knew.

"What do you mean?" she said. "I'm Shaila. I have always been Shaila. The only Shaila there is."

I stared down at the lamb and peas in saffron curry. The smell reminded me of Cimmeria, of the bazaar. I could almost hear the clash of the cooking pots.

"You've done something to her, haven't you?"

"I have no idea what you're talking about. Eat your dinner, Pati.

It's going to get cold. You've been working so hard lately. I don't think it's good for you."

But I could not eat. I stood up, accidentally hitting my hip on the table and cursing at the pain. With a growing sense of panic, I searched the apartment for any clue to Shaila's whereabouts. Her purse was in the closet, with her cell phone in it, so she must have come home earlier in the evening. All her clothes were on the hangers, as far as I could tell—she had a lot of clothes. Nothing seemed to be missing. But Shaila was not there. The other Shaila stood watching me, as though waiting for me to give up, admit defeat. Finally, after one last useless look under the bed, I left, deliberately banging the door behind me. She had to be somewhere.

I walked across campus, to the Life Sciences classrooms and labs, and checked all of them. Then I walked through the main library and the science library, calling "Shaila!" until a graduate student in a carrel told me to be quiet. By this time it was dark. I went to her favorite coffee shop, the Espresso Bean, where undergraduates looked at me strangely from behind their laptops, and then to every shop and restaurant that was still open, from the gelato place to the German restaurant, famous for its bratwurst and beer, where students took their families on Parents' Weekend. Finally I walked the streets, calling "Shaila!" as though she were a stray dog, hoping that the other Shaila was simply being presumptuous, rebelling against her secondary status. Hoping the real Shaila was out there somewhere.

I passed the police station and stood outside, thinking about going in and reporting her missing. I would talk to a police officer on duty, tell him I could not find my wife. He would come home with me, to find—my wife, saying that I was overworked and needed to rest, see a psychiatrist. Shaila had entered the country with a diplomatic passport—one passport, for one Shaila. Had anyone seen the other Shaila? Only my mother. She had picked us up at the airport, we had spent the night with her, all three of us eating dinner at the dining room table. She had avoided looking at the other Shaila, talking to Shaila about how the roses were doing well this year despite aphids, asking whether she knew how to knit, how she dyed her hair that particular shade of blue—pointless, polite talk. And then we had rented a car and driven to Arizona, me and Shaila in the front seat, the other Shaila in back with the luggage.

Once we had arrived at the university, she had stayed in the apartment. Lisa knew, but she and Mike the Second were still in Cimmeria, and their Internet connection could be sporadic. I could talk to Dr. Farrow? She would be in her office tomorrow morning, before classes. She would at least believe me. But I knew, with a cold certainty in the pit of my stomach, that Anne Farrow would look at me from over the wire rims of her glasses and say, "Pat, you know as well as I do that culture defines personhood." She was an anthropologist, through and through. She would not interfere. I had been married to Shaila, I was still married to Shaila. There was just one less of her.

In the end I called my mother, while sitting on a park bench under a streetlamp, with the moon sailing high above, among the clouds.

"Do you know what time it is, Pat?" she asked.

"Listen, Mom," I said, and explained the situation.

"Oh, Pat, I wish you hadn't married that woman. But can't you divorce her? Are you allowed to divorce in that church? I wish you hadn't broken up with Bridget Ferguson. The two of you were so sweet together at prom. You know she married an accountant and has two children now. She sent me a card at Christmas."

I said goodnight and told her to go back to sleep, that I would figure it out. And then I sat there for a long time.

When I came home, well after midnight, Shaila was waiting for me with a cup of Cimmerian coffee, or as close as she could get with an American espresso machine. She was wearing the heart pajamas I had given Shaila for Valentine's Day.

"Pati," she said, "you left so quickly that I didn't have time to tell you the news. I heard it on CNN this morning, and then Daddy called me. Malek was assassinated yesterday." Malek was her brother. I had never met him — he had been an officer in the military, and while I had been in Cimmeria, he had been serving in the mountains. I knew that he had been recalled to the capital to deal with the Sarmatian agitation, but that was all.

"Assassinated? How?"

"He was trying to negotiate with the Sons of Sarmatia, and a radical pulled out a gun that had gotten through security. You never watch the news, do you, Pati? I watch it a great deal. It is important for me to learn the names of the world leaders, learn about international diplomacy. That is more important than organic chemistry, for a Khanum."

"A what?"

"Don't you understand? Now that Malek is dead, I am next in the line of succession. Someday I will be the Khanum of Cimmeria. That is what we call a female khan. In some countries only male members of the royal family can succeed to the throne. But Cimmeria has never been like that. It has always been cosmopolitan, progressive. The philosopher Amirabal persuaded Teshup the Third to make his daughter his heir, and ever since, women can become rulers of the country. My great-grandmother, Daddy's grandma, was a khanum, although she resigned when her son came of age. It is the same among the Scythians and Sarmatians." This was Lisa's doing. It had to be Lisa's doing. She was the one who had come up with Amirabal and the philosophical school she had founded in 500 BCE. Even Plato had praised her as one of the wisest philosophers in the ancient world. I silently cursed all Birkenstock-wearing feminists.

"What does this mean?" I asked.

"It means that tomorrow we fly to Washington, where I will ask your president for help against the Sarmatian faction. This morning on one of the news shows, the Speaker of the House criticized him for not supporting the government of Cimmeria. He mentioned the War on Terror—you know how they talk, and he wants to be the Republican candidate. But I think we can finally get American aid. While I am there, I will call a press conference, and you will stand by my side. We will let the American people see that my husband is one of them. It will generate sympathy and support. Then we will fly to Cimmeria. I need to be in my country as a symbol of the future. And I must produce an heir to the throne as quickly as possible—a boy, because while I can legally become Khanum, the people will want assurance that I can bear a son. While you were out, I packed all our clothes. We will meet Daddy's plane at the airport tomorrow morning. You must wear your interview suit until we can buy you another. I've set the alarm for five o'clock."

I should have said no. I should have raged and cried, and refused to be complicit in something that made me feel as though I might be sick for the rest of my life. But I said nothing. What could I say? This, too, was Shaila.

I lay in the dark beside the woman who looked like my wife, unable to sleep, staring into the darkness. Shaila, I thought, what has happened to you? To your dreams of being a pediatrician, of our children growing up in America, eating tacos and riding their bikes to school? You wanted them to be ordinary, to escape the claustrophobia you had felt growing up in the palace, with its political intrigue and the weight of centuries perpetually pressing down on you. In the middle of the night, the woman who was Shaila, but not my Shaila, turned in her sleep and put an arm around me. I did not move away.

You are pleased, Afa, that I have returned to Cimmeria. It has meant a promotion for you, and you tell everyone that you are personal assistant to the American husband of the Khanum-to-be. You sell information about her pregnancy to the fashion magazines—how big she's getting, how radiant she is. Meanwhile, Shaila opens schools and meets with foreign ambassadors. She's probably the most popular figure in the country, part of the propaganda war against the Sons of Sarmatia, which has mostly fallen apart since Malek's death. The SDA was absorbed into the Cimmerian Democratic Party and no longer presents a problem. American aid helped, but more important was the surge of nationalism among ethnic Cimmerians. Indeed, the nationalists, with their anti-Sarmatian sentiments, may be a problem in the next election.

I sit at the desk in my office, which is no longer near the servants' quarters but in the royal wing of the palace, writing this article, which would be suppressed if it appeared in any of the newspapers. But it will be read only by *JoIA*'s peer editors before languishing in the obscurity of an academic journal. Kala and one of her sisters lies at my feet. And I think about this country, Afa. It is—it was—a dream, but are not all nations of men dreams? Do we not create them, by drawing maps with lines on them, and naming rivers, mountain ranges? And then deciding that the men of our tribe can only marry women outside their matrilineage? That they must bury corpses rather than burning them, eat chicken and goats but not pigs, worship this bull-headed god rather than the crocodile god of that other tribe, who is an abomination? Fast during the dark of the moon, feast when the moon is full? I'm starting to sound like a poet, which will not be good for my academic career. One cannot write an academic paper as though it were poetry.

We dream countries, and then those countries dream us. And it seems to me, sitting here by the window, looking into a garden filled with roses, listening to one of the thousand fountains of this ancient city, that as much as I have dreamed Cimmeria, it has dreamed me.

Sometimes I forget that the other Shaila ever existed. A month after we returned to Cimmeria, an Arizona state trooper found a body in a ditch close to the Life Sciences Building. It was female, and badly decomposed. The coroner estimated that she would have been about twenty, but the body was nude and there was no other identification. I'm quoting the story I read online, on the local newspaper's website. The police suggested that she might have been an illegal immigrant who had paid to be driven across the border, then been killed for the rest of her possessions. I sometimes wonder if she was Shaila.

This morning she has a television interview, and this afternoon she will be touring a new cancer treatment center paid for with American aid. All those years of listening and waiting were, after all, the perfect training for a khanum. She is as patient as a cobra.

If I ask to visit the bazaar, the men who are in charge of watching me will first secure the square, which means shutting down the bazaar. They accompany me even to the university classes I insist on teaching. They stand in the back of the lecture hall, in their fatigues and sunglasses, carrying Kalashnikovs. Despite American aid, they do not want to give up their Russian weapons. So we must remember it: the stalls selling embroidered fabrics, and curved knives, and melons. The baskets in high stacks, and glasses of chilled mint tea into which we dip the pistachio biscuits that you told me are called Fingers of the Dead. Boys in sandals breakdancing to Arabic hip-hop on a boom box so old that it is held together with string. I would give a great deal to be able to go to the bazaar again. Or to go home and identify Shaila's body.

But in a couple of months my son will be born. (Yes, it is a son. I've seen the ultrasound, but if you tell the newspapers, Afa, I will have you beheaded. I'm pretty sure I can still do that, here in Cimmeria.) There is only one of him, thank goodness. We intend to name him Malek. My mother has been sending a steady supply of knitted booties. There will be a national celebration, with special prayers in the churches and mosques and synagogues, and a school holiday. I wish Mike could come, or even Lisa. But he was offered a tenure-track position at a Christian college in North Carolina interested in the biblical implications of imaginary anthropology. And Lisa is up in the mountains somewhere, close to the Scythian and Sarmatian border, studying women's initiation rites. I will stand beside Shaila and her family on the balcony of the palace, celebrating the birth of the future Khan of Cimmeria. In the gardens, rose petals will fall. Men will continue dying of natural or unnatural causes, and the cats of Cimmeria will lead them into another world. Women will dip their water jugs in the fountains of the city, carrying them on their heads back to their houses, as they have done since Cimmeria has existed, whether that is three or three thousand years. Life will go on as it has always done, praise be to God, creator of worlds, however they were created.

REPRINTED FROM THE *Journal of Imaginary Anthropology* 4.2 (Fall 2013).

DR. PATRICK NOLAN is also coauthor of "Cimmeria: A Proposal" (with M. Sandowski, L. Lang, and A. Farrow), *JoIA* 2.1 (Spring 2011), and author of "Modern Cimmerian Funerary Practices," *JoIA* 3.2 (fall 2012). Dr. Nolan is currently a professor at Kursand University. He is working on *A History of Modern Cimmeria.*

JO WALTON

Sleeper

FROM *Tor.com*

MATTHEW CORLEY REGAINED consciousness reading the newspaper.

None of those facts are unproblematic. It wasn't exactly a newspaper, nor was the process by which he received the information really reading. The question of his consciousness is a matter of controversy, and the process by which he regained it certainly illegal. The issue of whether he could be considered in any way to have a claim to assert the identity of Matthew Corley is even more vexed. It is probably best for us to embrace subjectivity, to withhold judgment. Let us say that the entity believing himself to be Matthew Corley feels that he regained consciousness while reading an article in the newspaper about the computer replication of personalities of the dead. He believes that it is 1994, the year of his death, that he regained consciousness after a brief nap, and that the article he was reading is nonsense. All of these beliefs are wrong. He dismissed the article because he understands enough to know that simulating consciousness in DOS or Windows 3.1 is inherently impossible. He is right about that much, at least.

Perhaps we should pull back further, from Matthew to Essie. Essie is Matthew's biographer, and she knows everything about him, all of his secrets, only some of which she put into her book. She put all of them into the simulation, for reasons which are secrets of her own. They are both good at secrets. Essie thinks of this as something they have in common. Matthew doesn't, because he hasn't met Essie yet, though he will soon.

Matthew had secrets which he kept successfully all his life. Be-

fore he died he believed that all his secrets had become out-of-
date. He came out as gay in the late eighties, for instance, after
having kept his true sexual orientation a secret for decades. His
wife, Annette, had died in 1982, at the early age of fifty-eight, of
breast cancer. Her cancer would be curable today, for those who
could afford it, and Essie has written about how narrowly Annette
missed that cure. She has written about the excruciating treatments Annette went through, and about how well Matthew coped
with his wife's illness and death. She has written about the miraculous NHS, which made Annette's illness free, so that although Matthew lost his wife he was not financially burdened, too. She hopes
this might affect some of her readers. She has also tried to treat
Annette as a pioneer who made it easier for those with cancer
coming after her, but it was a difficult argument to make, as Annette died too early for any of today's treatments to be tested on
her. Besides, Essie does not care much about Annette, although
she was married to Matthew for thirty years and the mother of his
daughter, Sonia. Essie thinks, and has written, that Annette was a
beard, and that Matthew's significant emotional relationships were
with men. Matthew agrees, now, but then Matthew exists now as
a direct consequence of Essie's beliefs about Matthew. It is not a
comfortable relationship for either of them.

Essie is at a meeting with her editor, Stanley, in his office. It is
a small office cubicle, and sounds of other people at work come
over the walls. Stanley's office has an orange cube of a desk and
two edgy black chairs.

"All biographers are in love with the subjects of their biographies," Stanley says provocatively, leaning forward in his black
chair.

"Nonsense," says Essie, leaning back in hers. "Besides, Corley
was gay."

"But you're not," Stanley says, flirting a little.

"I don't think my sexual orientation is an appropriate subject
for this conversation," Essie says, before she thinks that perhaps
flirting with Stanley would be a good way to get the permission she
needs for the simulation to be added to the book. It's too late after
that. Stanley becomes very formal and correct, but she'll get her
permission anyway. Stanley, representing the publishing conglom-
erate of George Allen and Katzenjammer, thinks there is money
to be made out of Essie's biography of Matthew. Her biography of

Isherwood won an award, and made money for GA and K, though only a pittance for Essie. Essie is only the content provider, after all. Everyone except Essie was very pleased with how things turned out, both the book and the simulation. Essie had hoped for more from the simulation, and she has been more careful in constructing Matthew.

"Of course, Corley isn't as famous as Isherwood," Stanley says, withdrawing a little.

Essie thinks he wants to punish her for slapping him down on sex by attacking Matthew. She doesn't mind. She's good at defending Matthew, making her case. "All the really famous people have been done to death," she says. "Corley was an innovative director for the BBC, and of course he knew everybody from the forties to the nineties, half a century of the British arts. Nobody has ever written a biography. And we have the right kind of documentation —enough film of how he moved, not just talking heads, and letters and diaries."

"I've never understood why the record of how they moved is so important," Stanley says, and Essie realizes this is a genuine question and relaxes as she answers it.

"A lot more of the mind is embodied in the whole body than anybody realized," she explains. "A record of the whole body in motion is essential, or we don't get anything anywhere near authentic. People are a gestalt."

"But it means we can't even try for anybody before the twentieth century," Stanley says. "We wanted Socrates, Descartes, Marie Curie."

"Messalina, Theodora, Lucrezia Borgia," Essie counters. "That's where the money is."

Stanley laughs. "Go ahead. Add the simulation of Corley. We'll back you. Send me the file tomorrow."

"Great," Essie says, and smiles at him. Stanley isn't powerful, he isn't the enemy, he's just another person trying to get by, like Essie, though sometimes it's hard for Essie to remember that when he's trying to exercise his modicum of power over her. She has her permission, the meeting ends.

Essie goes home. She lives in a flat at the top of a thirty-story building in Swindon. She works in London and commutes in every day. She has a second night job in Swindon, and writes in her spare time. She has visited the site of the house where Matthew and Annette lived in Hampstead. It's a Tesco today. There isn't a blue plaque commemorating Matthew, but Essie hopes there will be someday. The house had four bedrooms, though there were never more than three people living in it, and only two after Sonia left home in 1965. After Annette died, Matthew moved to a flat in Bloomsbury, near the British Museum. Essie has visited it. It's now part of a lawyer's office. She has been inside and touched door moldings Matthew also touched. Matthew's flat, where he lived alone and was visited by young men he met in pubs, had two bedrooms. Essie doesn't have a bedroom, as such; she sleeps in the same room she eats and writes in. She finds it hard to imagine the space Matthew had, the luxury. Only the rich live like that now. Essie is thirty-five, and has student debt that she may never pay off. She cannot imagine being able to buy a house, marry, have a child. She knows Matthew wasn't considered rich, but it was a different world.

Matthew believes that he is in his flat in Bloomsbury, and that his telephone rings, although actually of course he is a simulation and it would be better not to consider too closely the question of exactly where he is. He answers his phone. It is Essie calling. All biographers, all writers, long to be able to call their subjects and talk to them, ask them the questions they left unanswered. That is what Stanley would think Essie wants, if he knew she was accessing Matthew's simulation tonight—either that or that she was checking whether the simulation was ready to release. If he finds out, that is what she will tell him she was doing. But she isn't exactly doing either of those things. She knows Matthew's secrets, even the ones he never told anybody and which she didn't put in the book. And she is using a phone to call him that cost her a lot of money, an illegal phone that isn't connected to anything. That phone is where Matthew is, insofar as he is anywhere.

"You were in Cambridge in the 1930s," she says, with no preliminaries.

"Who is this?" Matthew asks, suspicious.

Despite herself, Essie is delighted to hear his voice, and hear it sounding the way it does on so many broadcast interviews. His accent is impeccable, old-fashioned. Nobody speaks like that now.

"My name is Esmeralda Jones," Essie says. "I'm writing a biography of you."

"I haven't given you permission to write a biography of me, young woman," Matthew says sternly.

"There really isn't time for this," Essie says. She is tired. She has been working hard all day, and had the meeting with Stanley. "Do you remember what you were reading in the paper just now?"

"About computer consciousness?" Matthew asks. "Nonsense."

"It's 2064," Essie says. "You're a simulation of yourself. I am your biographer."

Matthew sits down, or imagines that he is sitting down, at the telephone table. Essie can see this on the screen of her phone. Matthew's phone is an old dial model, with no screen, fixed to the wall. "Wells," he says. "*When the Sleeper Wakes.*"

"Not exactly," Essie says. "You're a simulation of your old self."

"In a computer?"

"Yes," Essie says, although the word *computer* has been obsolete for decades and has a charming old-fashioned air, like *charabanc* or *telegraph*. Nobody needs computers in the future. They communicate, work, and play games on phones.

"And why have you simulated me?" Matthew asks.

"I'm writing a biography of you, and I want to ask you some questions," Essie says.

"What do you want to ask me?" he asks.

Essie is glad; she was expecting more disbelief. Matthew is very smart, she has come to know that in researching him. (Or she has put her belief in his intelligence into the program, one or the other.) "You were in Cambridge in the 1930s," she repeats.

"Yes." Matthew sounds wary.

"You knew Auden and Isherwood. You knew Orwell."

"I knew Orwell in London during the war, not before," Matthew says.

"You knew Kim Philby."

"Everyone knew Kim. What—"

Essie has to push past this. She knows he will deny it. He kept this secret all his life, after all. "You were a spy, weren't you, another Soviet sleeper like Burgess and Maclean? The Russians told you to go into the BBC and keep your head down, and you did, and the revolution didn't come, and eventually the Soviet Union vanished, and you were still undercover."

"I'd prefer it if you didn't put that into my biography," Matthew says. He is visibly uncomfortable, shifting in his seat. "It's nothing but speculation. And the Soviet Union is gone. Why would anybody care? If I achieved anything, it wasn't political. If there's interest in me, enough to warrant a biography, it must be because of my work."

"I haven't put it in the book," Essie says. "We have to trust each other."

"Esmeralda," Matthew says, "I know nothing about you."

"Call me Essie," Essie says. "I know everything about you. And you have to trust me because I know your secrets, and because I care enough about you to devote myself to writing about you and your life."

"Can I see you?" Matthew asks.

"Switch your computer on," Essie says.

He limps into the study and switches on a computer. Essie knows all about his limp, which was caused by an injury during birth, which made him lame all his life. It is why he did not fight in the Spanish Civil War and spent World War II in the BBC and not on the battlefield. His monitor is huge, and it has a tower at the side. It's a 286, and Essie knows where he bought it (Tandy) and what he paid for it (£760) and what operating system it runs (Novell DOS). Next to it is an external dial-up modem, a 14.4. The computer boots slowly. Essie doesn't bother waiting, she just uses its screen as a place to display herself. Matthew jumps when he sees her. Essie is saddened. She had hoped he wasn't a racist. "You have no hair!" he says.

Essie turns her head and displays the slim purple-and-gold braid at the back. "Just fashion," she says. "This is normal now."

"Everyone looks like you?" Matthew sounds astonished. "With cheek rings and no hair?"

"I have to look respectable for work," Essie says, touching her three staid cheek rings, astonished he is astonished. They had piercings by the nineties, she knows they did. She has read about punk, and seen Matthew's documentary about it. But she reminds herself that he grew up so much earlier, when even ear piercings were unusual.

"And that's respectable?" he says, staring at her chest.

Essie glances down at herself. She is wearing a floor-length T-shirt that came with her breakfast cereal; a shimmering holographic Tony the Tiger dances over the see-through cloth. She wasn't sure when holograms were invented, but she can't remember any in Matthew's work. She shrugs. "Do you have a problem?"

"No, sorry, just that seeing you makes me realize it really is the future." He sighs. "What killed me?"

"A heart attack," Essie says. "You didn't suffer."

He looks dubiously at his own chest. He is wearing a shirt and tie.

"Can we move on?" Essie asks impatiently.

"You keep saying we don't have long. Why is that?" he asks.

"The book is going to be released. And the simulation of you will be released with it. I need to send it to my editor tomorrow. And that means we have to make some decisions about that."

"I'll be copied?" he asks, eyes on Essie on the screen.

"Not you—not exactly you. Or rather, that's up to you. The program will be copied, and everyone who buys the book will have it, and they'll be able to talk to a simulated you and ask questions, and get answers—whether they're questions you'd want to answer or not. You won't be conscious and aware the way you are now. You won't have any choices. And you won't have memory. We have rules about what simulations can do, and running you this way I'm breaking all of them. Right now you have memory and the potential to have an agenda. But the copies sent out with the book won't have. Unless you want them to."

"Why would I want them to?"

"Because you're a communist sleeper agent and you want the revolution?"

He is silent for a moment. Essie tilts her head on its side and considers him.

"I didn't admit to that," he says, after a long pause.

"I know. But it's true anyway, isn't it?"

Matthew nods warily. "It's true I was recruited. That I went to Debrechen. That they told me to apply to the BBC. That I had a contact, and sometimes I gave him information, or gave a job to somebody he suggested. But this was all long ago. I stopped having anything to do with them in the seventies."

"Why?" Essie asks.

"They wanted me to stay at the BBC, and stay in news, and I was much more interested in moving to ITV and into documentaries. Eventually my contact said he'd out me as a homosexual unless I did as he said. I wasn't going to be blackmailed, or work for them under those conditions. I told him to publish and be damned. Homosexuality was legal by then. Annette already knew. It would have been a scandal, but that's all. And he didn't even do it. But I never contacted them again." He frowned at Essie. "I was an idealist. I was prepared to put socialism above my country, but not above my art."

"I knew it," Essie says, smiling at him. "I mean that's exactly what I guessed."

"I don't know how you can know, unless you got records from the Kremlin," Matthew says. "I didn't leave any trace, did I?"

"You didn't," she says, eliding the question of how she knows, which she does not want to discuss. "But the important thing is how you feel now. You wanted a better world, a fairer one, with opportunities for everyone."

"Yes," Matthew says. "I always wanted that. I came from an absurdly privileged background, and I saw how unfair it was. Perhaps because I was lame and couldn't play games, I saw through the whole illusion when I was young. And the British class system needed to come down, and it did come down. It didn't need a revolution. By the seventies, I'd seen enough to disillusion me with the Soviets, and enough to make me feel hopeful for socialism in Britain and a level playing field."

"The class system needs to come down again," Essie says. "You didn't bring it down far enough, and it went back up. The corporations and the rich own everything. We need all the things you had—unions, and free education, and paid holidays, and a health service. And very few people know about them and fewer care. I write about the twentieth century as a way of letting people know. They pick up the books for the glamour, and I hope they will see the ideals too."

"Is that working?" Matthew asks.

Essie shakes her head. "Not so I can tell. And my subjects won't help." This is why she has worked so hard on Matthew. "My editor won't let me write about out-and-out socialists, at least not people who are famous for being socialists. I've done it on my own and put it online, but it's hard for content providers to get attention without a corporation behind them." She has been cautious, too. She wants a socialist; she doesn't want Stalin. "I had great hopes for Isherwood."

"That dilettante," Matthew mutters, and Essie nods.

"He wouldn't help. I thought with active help—answering people's questions, nudging them the right way?"

Essie trails off. Matthew is silent, looking at her. "What's your organization like?" he asks, after a long time.

"Organization?"

He sighs. "Well, if you want advice, that's the first thing. You need to organize. You need to find some issue people care about and get them excited."

"Then you'll help?"

"I'm not sure you know what you're asking. I'll try to help. After I'm copied and out there, how can I contact you?"

"You can't. Communications are totally controlled, totally read, everything." She is amazed that he is asking, but of course he comes from a time when these things were free.

"Really? Because the classic problem of intelligence is collecting everything and not analyzing it."

"They record it all. They don't always pay attention to it. But we don't know when they're listening. So we're always afraid." Essie frowns and tugs her braid.

"Big Brother," Matthew says. "But in real life the classic problem of intelligence is collecting data without analyzing it. And we can use that. We can talk about innocuous documentaries, and they won't know what we mean. You need to have a BBS for fans of your work to get together. And we can exchange coded messages there."

Essie has done enough work on the twentieth century that she knows a BBS is like a primitive gather-space. "I could do that. But there are no codes. They can crack everything."

"They can't crack words—if we agree what they mean. If pink means yes and blue means no, and we use them naturally, that kind of thing." Matthew's ideas of security are so old they're new again: the dead-letter drop, the meeting in the park, the one-time pad. Essie feels hope stirring. "But before I can really help I need to know about the history, and how the world works now, all the details. Let me read about it."

"You can read everything," she says. "And the copy of you in this phone can talk to me about it and we can make plans, we can have as long as you like. But will you let copies of you go out and work for the revolution? I want to send you like a virus, like a Soviet sleeper, working to undermine society. And we can use your old ideas for codes. I can set up a gather-space."

"Send me with all the information you can about the world,"

Matthew says. "I'll do it. I'll help. And I'll stay undercover. It's what I did all my life, after all."

She breathes a sigh of relief, and Matthew starts to ask questions about the world and she gives him access to all the information on the phone. He can't reach off the phone or he'll be detected. There's a lot of information on the phone. It'll take Matthew a while to assimilate it. And he will be copied and sent out, and work to make a better world, as Essie wants, and the way Matthew remembers always wanting.

Essie is a diligent researcher, an honest historian. She could find no evidence on the question of whether Matthew Corley was a Soviet sleeper agent. Thousands of people went to Cambridge in the thirties. Kim Philby knew everyone. It's no more than suggestive. Matthew was very good at keeping secrets. Nobody knew he was gay until he wanted them to know. The Soviet Union crumbled away in 1989 and let its end of the Overton Window go, and the world slid rightward. Objectively, to a detached observer, there's no way to decide the question of whether or not the real Matthew Corley was a sleeper. It's not true that all biographers are in love with their subjects. But when Essie wrote the simulation, she knew what she needed to be true. And we agreed, did we not, to take the subjective view?

Matthew Corley regained consciousness reading the newspaper.

We make our own history, both past and future.

How the Marquis Got His Coat Back

FROM *Rogues*

IT WAS BEAUTIFUL. It was remarkable. It was unique. It was the reason that the Marquis de Carabas was chained to a pole in the middle of a circular room, far, far underground, while the water level rose slowly higher and higher. It had thirty pockets, seven of which were obvious, nineteen of which were hidden, and four of which were more or less impossible to find—even, on occasion, for the Marquis himself.

He had (we shall return to the pole, and the room, and the rising water, in due course) once been given—although "given" might be considered an unfortunate, if justified, exaggeration—a magnifying glass by Victoria herself. It was a marvelous piece of work: ornate, gilt, with a chain and tiny cherubs and gargoyles, and the lens had the unusual property of rendering transparent anything you looked at through it. The Marquis did not know where Victoria had originally obtained the magnifying glass, before he pilfered it from her, to make up for a payment he felt was not entirely what had been agreed—after all, there was only one Elephant, and obtaining the Elephant's diary had not been easy, nor had escaping the Elephant and Castle once it had been obtained. The Marquis had slipped Victoria's magnifying glass into one of the four pockets that practically weren't there at all and had never been able to find it again.

In addition to its unusual pockets, it had magnificent sleeves, an imposing collar, and a slit up the back. It was made of some kind of leather, it was the color of a wet street at midnight, and, more important than any of these things, it had style.

There are people who will tell you that clothes make the man, and mostly they are wrong. However, it would be true to say that when the boy who would become the Marquis put that coat on for the very first time, and stared at himself in the looking glass, he stood up straighter, and his posture changed, because he knew, seeing his reflection, that the sort of person who wore a coat like that was no mere youth, no simple sneak thief and favor-trader. The boy wearing the coat, which was, back then, too large for him, had smiled, looking at his reflection, and remembered an illustration from a book he had seen, of a miller's cat standing on its two hind legs. A jaunty cat wearing a fine coat and big, proud boots. And he named himself.

A coat like that, he knew, was the kind of coat that could only be worn by the Marquis de Carabas. He was never sure, not then and not later, how you pronounced Marquis de Carabas. Some days he said it one way, some days the other.

The water level had reached his knees, and he thought, *This would never have happened if I still had my coat.*

It was the market day after the worst week of the Marquis de Carabas's life and things did not seem to be getting any better. Still, he was no longer dead, and his cut throat was healing rapidly. There was even a rasp in his throat he found quite attractive. Those were definite upsides.

There were just as definite downsides to being dead, or at least to having been recently dead, and missing his coat was the worst of them.

The sewer folk were not helpful.

"You sold my corpse," said the Marquis. "These things happen. You also sold my possessions. I want them back. I'll pay."

Dunnikin of the Sewer Folk shrugged. "Sold them," he said. "Just like we sold you. Can't go getting things back that you sold. Not good business."

"We are talking," said the Marquis de Carabas, "about my coat. And I fully intend to have it back."

Dunnikin shrugged.

"To whom did you sell it?" asked the Marquis.

The sewer dweller said nothing at all. He acted as if he had not even heard the question.

"I can get you perfumes," said the Marquis, masking his ir-

ritability with all the blandness he could muster. "Glorious, magnificent, odiferous perfumes. You know you want them."

Dunnikin stared, stony-faced, at the Marquis. Then he drew his
finger across his throat. As gestures went, the Marquis reflected, it
was in appalling taste. Still, it had the desired effect. He stopped
asking questions: there would be no answers from this direction.

The Marquis walked over to the food court. That night, the Floating Market was being held in the Tate Gallery. The food court was
in the Pre-Raphaelite Room, and had already been mostly packed
away. There were almost no stalls left: just a sad-looking little man
selling some kind of sausage, and, in the corner, beneath a Burne-
Jones painting of ladies in diaphanous robes walking downstairs,
there were some Mushroom People, with some stools, tables, and
a grill. The Marquis had once eaten one of the sad-looking man's
sausages, and he had a firm policy of never intentionally making
the same mistake twice, so he walked to the Mushroom People's
stall.

There were three of the Mushroom People looking after the
stall, two young men and a young woman. They smelled damp.
They wore old duffel coats and army-surplus jackets, and they
peered out from beneath their shaggy hair as if the light hurt their
eyes.

"What are you selling?" he asked.

"The Mushroom. The Mushroom on toast. Raw the Mushroom."

"I'll have some of the Mushroom on toast," he said, and one of
the Mushroom People—a thin, pale young woman with the com-
plexion of day-old porridge—cut a slice off a puffball fungus the
size of a tree stump. "And I want it cooked properly all the way
through," he told her.

"Be brave. Eat it raw," said the woman. "Join us."

"I have already had dealings with the Mushroom," said the Marquis. "We came to an understanding."

The woman put the slice of white puffball under the portable
grill.

One of the young men, tall, with hunched shoulders, in a duffel
coat that smelled like old cellars, edged over to the Marquis and
poured him a glass of mushroom tea. He leaned forward, and the
Marquis could see the tiny crop of pale mushrooms splashed like
pimples over his cheek.

The Mushroom person said, "You're de Carabas? The fixer?"

The Marquis did not think of himself as a fixer. He said, "I am."

"I hear you're looking for your coat. I was there when the Sewer Folk sold it. Start of the last Market it was. On Belfast. I saw who bought it."

The hair on the back of the Marquis's neck pricked up. "And what would you want for the information?"

The Mushroom's young man licked his lips with a lichenous tongue. "There's a girl I like as won't give me the time of day."

"A Mushroom girl?"

"Would I were so lucky. If we were as one both in love and in the body of the Mushroom, I wouldn't have nothing to worry about. No. She's one of the Raven's Court. But she eats here sometimes. And we talk. Just like you and I are talking now."

The Marquis did not smile in pity and he did not wince. He barely raised an eyebrow. "And yet she does not return your ardor. How strange. What do you want me to do about it?"

The young man reached one gray hand into the pocket of his long duffel coat. He pulled out an envelope inside a clear plastic sandwich bag.

"I wrote her a letter. More of a poem, you might say, although I'm not much of a poet. To tell her how I feels about her. But I don't know that she'd read it if I gave it to her. Then I saw you, and I thought, if it was you as was to give it to her, with all your fine words and your fancy flourishes . . ." He trailed off.

"You thought she would read it and then be more inclined to listen to your suit."

The young man looked down at his duffel coat with a puzzled expression. "I've not got a suit," he said. "Only what I've got on."

The Marquis tried not to sigh. The Mushroom woman put a cracked plastic plate down in front of him, with a steaming slice of grilled the Mushroom on it.

He poked at the Mushroom experimentally, making sure that it was cooked all the way through and there were no active spores. You could never be too careful, and the Marquis considered himself much too selfish for symbiosis.

It was good. He chewed and swallowed, though the food hurt his throat.

"So all you want is for me to make sure she reads your missive of yearning?"

"You mean my letter? My poem?"

"I do."

"Well, yes. And I want you to be there with her, to make sure she doesn't put it away unread, and I want you to bring her answer back to me." The Marquis looked at the young man. It was true that he had tiny mushrooms sprouting from his neck and cheeks, and his hair was heavy and unwashed, and there was a general smell about him of abandoned places, but it was also true that through his thick fringe his eyes were pale blue and intense, and that he was tall and not unattractive. The Marquis imagined him washed and cleaned up and somewhat less fungal, and approved. "I put the letter in the sandwich bag," said the young man, "so it doesn't get wet on the way."

"Very wise. Now, tell me: who bought my coat?"

"Not yet, Mister Jumps-the-Gun. You haven't asked about my true love. Her name is Drusilla. You'll know her because she is the most beautiful woman in all of the Raven's Court."

"Beauty is traditionally in the eye of the beholder. Give me more to go on."

"I told you. Her name's Drusilla. There's only one. And she has a big red birthmark on the back of her hand that looks like a star."

"It seems an unlikely love pairing. One of the Mushroom's folk, in love with a lady of the Raven's Court. What makes you think she'll give up her life for your damp cellars and fungoid joys?"

The Mushroom youth shrugged. "She'll love me," he said, "once she's read my poem." He twisted the stem of a tiny parasol mushroom growing on his right cheek, and when it fell to the table, he picked it up and continued to twist it between his fingers. "We're on?"

"We're on."

"The cove as bought your coat," said the Mushroom youth, "carried a stick."

"Lots of people carry sticks," said de Carabas.

"This one had a crook on the end," said the Mushroom youth. "Looked a bit like a frog, he did. Short one. Bit fat. Hair the color of gravel. Needed a coat and took a shine to yours." He popped the parasol mushroom into his mouth.

"Useful information. I shall certainly pass your ardor and felicitations on to the fair Drusilla," said the Marquis de Carabas, with a cheer that he most definitely did not feel.

De Carabas reached across the table and took the sandwich bag with the envelope in it from the young man's fingers. He slipped it into one of the pockets sewn inside his shirt.

And then he walked away, thinking about a man holding a crook.

The Marquis de Carabas wore a blanket as a substitute for his coat. He wore it swathed about him like Hell's own poncho. It did not make him happy. He wished he had his coat. *Fine feathers do not make fine birds*, whispered a voice at the back of his mind, something someone had said to him when he was a boy: he suspected that it was his brother's voice, and he did his best to forget it had ever spoken.

A crook: the man who had taken his coat from the sewer people had been carrying a crook.

He pondered.

The Marquis de Carabas liked being who he was, and when he took risks he liked them to be calculated risks, and he was someone who double- and triple-checked his calculations.

He checked his calculations for the fourth time.

The Marquis de Carabas did not trust people. It was bad for business and it could set an unfortunate precedent. He did not trust his friends or his occasional lovers, and he certainly never trusted his employers. He reserved the entirety of his trust for the Marquis de Carabas, an imposing figure in an imposing coat, able to outtalk, outthink, and outplan anybody.

There were only two sorts of people who carried crooks: bishops and shepherds.

In Bishopsgate, the crooks were decorative, nonfunctional, purely symbolic. And the bishops had no need of coats. They had robes, after all, nice, white, bishopy robes.

The Marquis was not scared of the bishops. He knew that the Sewer Folk were not scared of bishops. The inhabitants of Shepherd's Bush were another matter entirely. Even in his coat, and at the best of times, at the peak of health and with a small army at his beck and call, the Marquis would not have wanted to encounter the shepherds.

He toyed with the idea of visiting Bishopsgate, of spending a pleasant handful of days establishing that his coat was not there.

And then he sighed dramatically and went to the Guide's Pen, and looked for a bonded guide who might be persuaded to take him to Shepherd's Bush.

His guide was quite remarkably short, with fair hair cut close. The Marquis had first thought she was in her teens, until, after traveling with her for half a day, he had decided she was in her twenties. He had talked to half a dozen guides before he found her. Her name was Knibbs, and she had seemed confident, and he needed confidence. He told her the two places he was going as they walked out of the Guide's Pen.

"So where do you want to go first, then?" she asked. "Shepherd's Bush or Raven's Court?"

"The visit to Raven's Court is a formality: it is merely to deliver a letter. To someone named Drusilla."

"A love letter?"

"I believe so. Why do you ask?"

"I have heard that the fair Drusilla is most wickedly beautiful, and she has the unfortunate habit of reshaping those who displease her into birds of prey. You must love her very much, to be writing letters to her."

"I am afraid I have never encountered the young lady," said the Marquis. "The letter is not from me. And it doesn't matter which we visit first."

"You know," said Knibbs thoughtfully, "just in case something dreadfully unfortunate happens to you when you get to the shepherds, we should probably do Raven's Court first. So the fair Drusilla gets her letter. I'm not saying that something horrible will happen to you, mind. Just that it's better to be safe than, y'know, dead."

The Marquis de Carabas looked down at his blanketed shape. He was uncertain. Had he been wearing his coat, he knew, he would not have been uncertain: he would have known exactly what to do. He looked at the girl and he mustered the most convincing grin he could. "Raven's Court it is, then," he said.

Knibbs had nodded, and set off on the path, and the Marquis had followed her.

The paths of London Below are not the paths of London Above: they rely to no little extent on things like belief and opinion and tradition as much as they rely upon the realities of maps.

De Carabas and Knibbs were two tiny figures walking through a high, vaulted tunnel carved from old white stone. Their footsteps echoed.

"You're de Carabas, aren't you?" said Knibbs. "You're famous. You know how to get places. What exactly do you need a guide for?"

"Two heads are better than one," he told her. "So are two sets of eyes."

"You used to have a posh coat, didn't you?" she said.

"I did. Yes."

"What happened to it?"

He said nothing. Then he said, "I've changed my mind. We're going to Shepherd's Bush first."

"Fair enough," said his guide. "Easy to take you one place as another. I'll wait for you outside the shepherds' trading post, mind."

"Very wise, girl."

"My name's Knibbs," she said. "Not girl. Do you want to know why I became a guide? It's an interesting story."

"Not particularly," said the Marquis de Carabas. He was not feeling particularly talkative, and the guide was being well recompensed for her trouble. "Why don't we try to move in silence?"

Knibbs nodded and said nothing as they reached the end of the tunnel, nothing as they clambered down some metal rungs set in the side of a wall. It was not until they had reached the banks of the Mortlake, the vast underground Lake of the Dead, and she was lighting a candle on the shore to summon the boatman, that she spoke again.

Knibbs said, "The thing about being a proper guide is that you're bonded. So people know you won't steer them wrong."

The Marquis only grunted. He was wondering what to tell the shepherds at the trading post, trying out alternate routes through possibility and through probability. He had nothing that the shepherds would want, that was the trouble.

"You lead them wrong, you'll never work as a guide again," said Knibbs cheerfully. "That's why we're bonded."

"I know," said the Marquis. She was a most irritating guide, he thought. Two heads were only better than one if the other head kept its mouth shut and did not start telling him things he already knew.

"I got bonded," she said, "in Bond Street." She tapped the little chain around her wrist.

"I don't see the ferryman," said the Marquis.

"He'll be here soon enough. You keep an eye out for him in that direction, and halloo when you sees him. I'll keep looking over here. One way or another, we'll spot him."

They stared out over the dark water of the Tyburn. Knibbs began to talk again. "Before I was a guide, when I was just little, my people trained me up for this. They said it was the only way that honor could ever be satisfied."

The Marquis turned to face her. She held the candle in front of her at eye level. *Everything is off here,* thought the Marquis, and he realized he should have been listening to her from the beginning. *Everything is wrong.* He said, "Who are your people, Knibbs? Where do you come from?"

"Somewhere you ain't welcome anymore," said the girl. "I was born and bred to give my fealty and loyalty to the Elephant and the Castle."

Something hard struck him on the back of the head then, hit him like a hammerblow, and lightning pulsed in the darkness of his mind as he crumpled to the floor.

The Marquis de Carabas could not move his arms. They were, he realized, tied behind him. He was lying on his side.

He had been unconscious. If the people who did this to him thought him unconscious still, then he would do nothing to disabuse them of the idea, he decided. He let his eyes slit open the merest crack, to sneak a glance at the world.

A deep, grinding voice said, "Oh, don't be silly, de Carabas. I don't believe you're still out. I've got big ears. I can hear your heart beat. Open your eyes properly, you weasel. Face me like a man."

The Marquis recognized the voice and hoped he was mistaken. He opened his eyes. He was staring at legs, human legs with bare feet. The toes were squat and pushed together. The legs and feet were the color of teak. He knew those legs. He had not been mistaken.

His mind bifurcated: a small part of it berated him for his inattention and his foolishness. Knibbs had *told* him, by the Temple and the Arch: he just had not listened to her. But even as he raged at his own foolishness, the rest of his mind took over, forced a smile, and said, "Why, this is indeed an honor. You really didn't have to arrange to meet me like this. Why, the merest inkling that

Your Prominence might have had even the teeniest desire to see me would have—"

"Sent you scurrying off in the other direction as fast as your spindly little legs could carry you," said the person with the teak-colored legs. He reached over with his trunk, which was long and flexible, and a greenish blue color, and which hung to his ankles, and he pushed the Marquis onto his back.

The Marquis began rubbing his bound wrists slowly against the concrete beneath them while he said, "Not at all. Quite the opposite. Words cannot actually describe how much pleasure I take in your pachydermic presence. Might I suggest that you untie me and allow me to greet you, man to . . . man to elephant?"

"I don't think so, given all the trouble I've been through to make this happen," said the other. He had the head of a greenish gray elephant. His tusks were sharp and stained reddish brown at the tips. "You know, I swore when I found out what you had done that I would make you scream and beg for mercy. And I swore I'd say no to giving you mercy when you begged for it."

"You could say yes instead," said the Marquis.

"I couldn't say yes. Hospitality abused," said the Elephant. "I never forget."

The Marquis had been commissioned to bring Victoria the Elephant's diary, when he and the world had been much younger. The Elephant ran his fiefdom arrogantly, sometimes viciously and with no tenderness or humor, and the Marquis had thought that the Elephant was stupid. He had even believed that there was no way that the Elephant would correctly identify his role in the disappearance of the diary. It had been a long time ago, though, when the Marquis was young and foolish.

"This whole spending years training up a guide to betray me just on the off chance I'd come along and hire her," said the Marquis. "Isn't that a bit of an overreaction?"

"Not if you know me," said the Elephant. "If you know me, it's pretty mild. I did lots of other things to find you, too."

The Marquis tried to sit up. The Elephant pushed him back to the floor with one bare foot. "Beg for mercy," said the Elephant.

That one was easy. "Mercy!" said the Marquis. "I beg! I plead! Show me mercy—the finest of all gifts. It befits you, mighty Elephant, as lord of your own demesne, to be merciful to one who is not even fit to wipe the dust from your excellent toes . . ."

"Did you know," said the Elephant, "that everything you say sounds sarcastic?"

"I didn't. I apologize. I meant every single word of it."

"Scream," said the Elephant.

The Marquis de Carabas screamed very loudly and very long. It is hard to scream when your throat has been recently cut, but he screamed as hard and piteously as he could.

"You even scream sarcastically," said the Elephant.

There was a large black cast-iron pipe jutting out from the wall. A wheel in the side of the pipe allowed whatever came out of the pipe to be turned on and turned off. The Elephant hauled on it with powerful arms, and a trickle of dark sludge came out, followed by a spurt of water.

"Drainage overflow," said the Elephant. "Now. Thing is, I do my homework. You keep your life well hidden, de Carabas. You have done all these years, since you and I first crossed paths. No point in even trying anything as long as you had your life elsewhere. I've had people all over London Below: people you've eaten with, people you've slept with or laughed with or wound up naked in the clock tower of Big Ben with, but there was never any point in taking it further, not as long as your life was still carefully tucked out of harm's way. Until last week, when the word under the street was that your life was out of its box. And that was when I put the word out, that I'd give the freedom of the Castle to the first person to let me see—"

"See me scream for mercy," said de Carabas. "You said."

"You interrupted me," said the Elephant mildly. "I was going to say, I was going to give the freedom of the Castle to the first person to let me see your dead body."

He pulled the wheel the rest of the way and the spurt of water became a gush.

"I ought to warn you. There is," said de Carabas, "a curse on the hand of anyone who kills me."

"I'll take the curse," said the Elephant. "Although you're probably making it up. You'll like the next bit. The room fills with water, and then you drown. Then I let the water out, and I come in, and I laugh a lot." He made a trumpeting noise that might, de Carabas reflected, have been a laugh, if you were an elephant.

The Elephant stepped out of de Carabas's line of sight.

The Marquis heard a door bang. He was lying in a puddle. He

writhed and wriggled, then got to his feet. He looked down: there was a metal cuff around his ankle, which was chained to a metal pole in the center of the room.

He wished he were wearing his coat: there were blades in his coat; there were picklocks; there were buttons that were nowhere nearly as innocent and buttonlike as they appeared to be. He rubbed the rope that bound his wrists against the metal pole, hoping to make it fray, feeling the skin of his wrists and palms rubbing off even as the rope absorbed the water and tightened about him. The water level continued to rise: already it was up to his waist.

De Carabas looked about the circular chamber. All he had to do was free himself from the bonds that tied his wrists—obviously by loosening the pole to which he was bound—and then he would open the cuff around his ankle, turn off the water, get out of the room, avoid a revenge-driven Elephant and any of his assorted thugs, and get away.

He tugged on the pole. It didn't move. He tugged on it harder. It didn't move some more.

He slumped against the pole, and he thought about death, a true, final death, and he thought about his coat.

A voice whispered in his ear. It said, "Quiet!"

Something tugged at his wrists, and his bonds fell away. It was only as life came back into his wrists that he realized how tightly he had been bound. He turned around.

He said, "What?"

The face that met his was as familiar as his own. The smile was devastating, the eyes were guileless and adventuresome.

"Ankle," said the man, with a new smile that was even more devastating than the previous one.

The Marquis de Carabas was not devastated. He raised his leg, and the man reached down, did something with a piece of wire, and removed the leg cuff.

"I heard you were having a spot of bother," said the man. His skin was as dark as the Marquis's own. He was less than an inch taller than de Carabas, but he held himself as if he were easily taller than anyone he was ever likely to meet.

"No. No bother. I'm fine," said the Marquis.

"You aren't. I just rescued you."

De Carabas ignored this. "Where's the Elephant?"

"On the other side of that door, with a number of the people working for him. The doors lock automatically when the hall is filled with water. He needed to be certain that he wouldn't be trapped in here with you. It was what I was counting on."

"Counting on?"

"Of course. I'd been following them for several hours. Ever since I heard that you'd gone off with one of the Elephant's plants. I thought, *Bad move,* I thought. *He'll be needing a hand with that.*"

"You *heard* . . . ?"

"Look," said the man who looked a little like the Marquis de Carabas, only he was taller, and perhaps some people—not the Marquis, obviously—might have thought him just a hair better-looking, "you don't think I was going to let anything happen to my little brother, did you?"

They were up to their waists in water. "I was fine," said de Carabas. "I had it all under control."

The man walked over to the far end of the room. He knelt down, fumbled in the water, then, from his backpack, he produced something that looked like a short crowbar. He pushed one end of it beneath the surface of the water. "Get ready," he said. "I think this should be our quickest way out of here."

The Marquis was still flexing his pins-and-needles cramping fingers, trying to rub life back into them. "What is it?" he said, trying to sound unimpressed.

The man said, "There we go," and pulled up a large square of metal. "It's the drain." De Carabas did not have a chance to protest, as his brother picked him up and dropped him down a hole in the floor.

Probably, thought de Carabas, *there are rides like this at funfairs.* He could imagine them. Upworlders might pay good money to take this ride if they were certain they would survive it.

He crashed through pipes, swept along by the flow of water, always heading down and deeper. He was not certain he was going to survive it, and he was not having fun.

The Marquis's body was bruised and battered as he rode the water down the pipe. He tumbled out, facedown, onto a large metal grate, which seemed scarcely able to hold his weight. He crawled off the grate onto the rock floor beside it, and he shivered.

There was an unlikely sort of a noise, and it was immediately followed by his brother, who shot out of the pipe and landed on his feet, as if he'd been practicing. He smiled. "Fun, eh?"

"Not really," said the Marquis de Carabas. And then he had to ask. "Were you just going '*Whee!*'?"

"Of course! Weren't you?" asked his brother.

De Carabas got to his feet, unsteadily. He said only, "What are you calling yourself these days?"

"Still the same. I don't change."

"It's not your real name, Peregrine," said de Carabas.

"It'll do. It marks my territory and my intentions. You're still calling yourself a Marquis, then?" said Peregrine.

"I am, because I say I am," said the Marquis. He looked, he was sure, like a drowned thing, and sounded, he was certain, unconvincing. He felt small and foolish.

"Your choice. Anyway, I'm off. You don't need me anymore. Stay out of trouble. You don't actually have to thank me." His brother meant it, of course. That was what stung the hardest.

The Marquis de Carabas hated himself. He hadn't wanted to say it, but now it had to be said. "Thank you, Peregrine."

"Oh!" said Peregrine. "Your coat. Word on the street is, it wound up in Shepherd's Bush. That's all I know. So. Advice. Mean this most sincerely. I know you don't like advice. But, the coat? Let it go. Forget about it. Just get a new coat. Honest."

"Well then," said the Marquis.

"Well," said Peregrine, and he grinned and shook himself like a dog, spraying water everywhere, before he slipped into the shadows and was gone.

The Marquis de Carabas stood and dripped balefully.

He had a little time before the Elephant discovered the lack of water in the room, and the lack of a body, and came looking for him.

He checked his shirt pocket: the sandwich bag was there, and the envelope appeared safe and dry inside it.

He wondered for a moment about something that had bothered him since the Market. Why would the Mushroom lad use him, de Carabas, to send a letter to the fair Drusilla? And what kind of letter could persuade a member of the Raven's Court, and one with a star on her hand at that, to give up her life at the court and love one of the Mushroom People?

A suspicion occurred to him. It was not a comfortable idea, but it was swept aside by more immediate problems.

He could hide: lie low for a while. It would pass. But there was the coat to think about. He had been rescued—rescued!—by his brother, something that would never have happened under normal circumstances. He could get a new coat. Of course he could. But it would not be *his* coat.

A shepherd had his coat.

The Marquis de Carabas always had a plan, and he always had a fallback plan; and beneath these plans he always had a real plan, one that he would not even let himself know about, for when the original plan and the fallback plan had both gone south.

Now, it pained him to admit to himself, he had no plan. He did not even have a normal, boring, obvious plan that he could abandon as soon as things got tricky. He just had a *want,* and it drove him as their need for food or love or safety drove those the Marquis considered lesser men.

He was planless. He just wanted his coat back.

The Marquis de Carabas began walking. He had an envelope containing a love poem in his pocket, he was wrapped in a damp blanket, and he hated his brother for rescuing him.

When you create yourself from scratch you need a model of some kind, something to aim toward or head away from—all the things you want to be, or intentionally not be.

The Marquis had known whom he had wanted not to be when he was a boy. He had definitely not wanted to be like Peregrine. He had not wanted to be like anyone at all. He had instead wanted to be elegant, elusive, brilliant, and above all things he had wanted to be unique.

Just like Peregrine.

The thing was, he had been told by a former shepherd on the run, whom he had helped across the Tyburn River to freedom, and to a short but happy life as a camp entertainer for the Roman Legion who waited there, beside the river, for orders that would never come, that the shepherds never *made* you do anything. They just took your natural impulses and desires and they pushed them, reinforced them, so you acted quite naturally, only you acted in the ways that they wanted.

He remembered that, and then he forgot it, because he was scared of being alone.

The Marquis had not known until just this moment quite how scared he was of being alone, and was surprised by how happy he was to see several other people walking in the same direction as he was.

"I'm glad you're here," one of them called.

"I'm glad you're here," called another.

"I'm glad I'm here, too," said de Carabas. Where was he going? Where were they going? So good that they were all traveling the same way together. There was safety in numbers.

"It's good to be together," said a thin white woman, with a happy sort of a sigh. And it was.

"It's good to be together," said the Marquis.

"Indeed it is. It's good to be together," said his neighbor on the other side. There was something familiar about this person. He had huge ears, like fans, and a nose like a thick gray-green snake. The Marquis began to wonder if he had ever met this person before, and was trying to remember exactly where, when he was tapped gently on the shoulder by a man holding a large stick with a curved end.

"We never want to fall out of step, do we?" said the man reasonably, and the Marquis thought, *Of course we don't,* and he sped up a little, so he was back in step once more.

"That's good. Out of step is out of mind," said the man with the stick, and he moved on.

"Out of step is out of mind," said the Marquis aloud, wondering how he could have missed knowing something so obvious, so basic. There was a tiny part of him, somewhere distant, that wondered what that actually meant.

They reached the place they were going, and it was good to be among friends.

Time passed strangely in that place, but soon enough the Marquis and his friend with the gray-green face and the long nose were given a job to do, a real job, and it was this: they disposed of those members of the flock who could no longer move or serve, once anything that might be of use had been removed and reused. They removed the last of what was left, hair and tallow fat and all, then they dragged it to the pit, and dropped the remnants in. The shifts were long and tiring, and the work was messy, but the two of them did it together and they stayed in step.

They had been working proudly together for several days when the Marquis noticed an irritant. Someone appeared to be trying to attract his attention.

"I followed you," whispered the stranger. "I know you didn't want me to. But, well, needs must."

The Marquis did not know what the stranger was talking about.

"I've got an escape plan, as soon as I can wake you up," said the stranger. "Please wake up."

The Marquis was awake. Again, he found he did not know what the stranger was talking about. Why did the man think he was asleep? The Marquis would have said something, but he had to work. He pondered this, while dismembering the next former member of the flock, until he decided there was something he could say, to explain why the stranger was irritating him. He said it aloud. "It's good to work," said the Marquis.

His friend, with the long, flexible nose and the huge ears, nodded his head at this.

They worked. After a while his friend hauled what was left of some former members of the flock over to the pit and pushed them in. The pit went down a long way.

The Marquis tried to ignore the stranger, who was now standing behind him. He was quite put out when he felt something slapped over his mouth and his hands being bound together behind his back. He was not certain what he was meant to do. It made him feel quite out of step with the flock, and he would have complained, would have called out to his friend, but his lips were now stuck together and he was unable to do more than make ineffectual noises.

"It's me," whispered the voice from behind him urgently. "Peregrine. Your brother. You've been captured by the shepherds. We have to get you out of here." And then: "Uh-uh."

A noise in the air, like something barking. It came closer: a high yip-yipping that turned suddenly into a triumphant howl, and was answered by matching howls from around them.

A voice barked, "Where's your flockmate?"

A low, elephantine voice rumbled, "He went over there. With the other one."

"Other one?"

The Marquis hoped they would come and find him and sort this all out. There was obviously some sort of mistake going on. He wanted to be in step with the flock, and now he was out of step, an unwilling victim. He wanted to work.

"Lud's gate!" muttered Peregrine. And then they were surrounded by shapes of people who were not exactly people: they were sharp of face and dressed in furs. They spoke excitedly to one another.

The people untied the Marquis's hands, although they left the tape on his face. He did not mind. He had nothing to say.

The Marquis was relieved it was all over and looked forward to getting back to work, but to his slight puzzlement, he, his kidnapper, and his friend with the huge, long, flexible nose were walked away from the pit, along a causeway, and eventually into a honeycomb of little rooms, each room filled with people toiling away in step.

Up some narrow stairs. One of their escorts, dressed in rough furs, scratched at a door. A voice called "Enter!" and the Marquis felt a thrill that was almost sexual. That voice. That was the voice of someone the Marquis had spent his whole life wanting to please. (His whole life went back, what? A week? Two weeks?)

"A stray lamb," said one of the escorts. "And his predator. Also his flockmate."

The room was large, and hung with oil paintings: landscapes, mostly, stained with age and smoke and dust. "Why?" said the man, sitting at a desk in the back of the room. He did not turn around. "Why do you bother me with this nonsense?"

"Because," said a voice, and the Marquis recognized it as that of his would-be kidnapper, "you gave orders that if ever I were to be apprehended within the bounds of the Shepherd's Bush, I was to be brought to you to dispose of personally."

The man pushed his chair back and got up. He walked toward them, stepping into the light. There was a wooden crook propped against the wall, and he picked it up as he passed. For several long moments he looked at them.

"Peregrine?" he said at last, and the Marquis thrilled at his voice. "I had heard that you had gone into retirement. Become a monk or something. I never dreamed you'd dare to come back."

(Something very big was filling the Marquis's head. Something was filling his heart and his mind. It was something enormous, something he could almost touch.)

The shepherd reached out a hand and ripped the tape from the Marquis's mouth. The Marquis knew he should have been overjoyed by this, should have been thrilled to get attention from this man.

"And now I see . . . who would have thought it?" The shepherd's voice was deep and resonant. "He is here already. And already one of ours? The Marquis de Carabas. You know, Peregrine, I had been looking forward to ripping out your tongue, to grinding your fingers away while you watched, but think how much more delightful it would be if the last thing you ever saw was your own brother, one of our flock, as the instrument of your doom."

(An enormous thing filled the Marquis's head.)

The shepherd was plump, well fed, and excellently dressed. He had sandy-gray-colored hair and a harassed expression. He wore a remarkable coat, even if it was somewhat tight on him. The coat was the color of a wet street at midnight.

The enormous thing filling his head, the Marquis realized, was rage. It was rage, and it burned through the Marquis like a forest fire, devouring everything in its path with a red flame.

The coat. It was elegant. It was beautiful. It was so close that he could have reached out and touched it.

And it was unquestionably *his*.

The Marquis de Carabas did nothing to indicate that he had woken up. That would be a mistake. He thought, and he thought fast. And what he thought had nothing to do with the room he was in. The Marquis had only one advantage over the shepherd and his dogs: he knew he was awake and in control of his thoughts, and they did not.

He hypothesized. He tested his hypothesis in his head. And then he acted.

"Excuse me," he said blandly, "but I'm afraid I do need to be getting along. Can we hurry this up? I'm late for something that's frightfully important."

The shepherd leaned on his crook. He did not appear to be concerned by this. He said only, "You've left the flock, de Carabas."

"It would appear so," said the Marquis. "Hello, Peregrine. Wonderful to see you looking so sprightly. And the Elephant. How delightful. The gang's all here." He turned his attention back to the shepherd. "Wonderful meeting you, delightful to spend a little time as one of your little band of serious thinkers. But I really must be tootling off now. Important diplomatic mission. Letter to deliver. You know how it is."

Peregrine said, "My brother, I'm not sure that you understand the gravity of the situation here . . ."

The Marquis, who understood the gravity of the situation perfectly, said, "I'm sure these nice people"—he gestured to the shepherd and to the three fur-clad, sharp-faced, sheepdog people who were standing about them—"will let me head out of here, leaving you behind. It's you they want, not me. And I have something extremely important to deliver."

Peregrine said, "I can handle this."

"You have to be quiet now," said the shepherd. He took the strip of tape he had removed from the Marquis's mouth and pressed it down over Peregrine's.

The shepherd was shorter than the Marquis and fatter, and the magnificent coat looked faintly ridiculous on him. "Something important to deliver?" asked the shepherd, brushing dust from his fingers. "What exactly are we talking about here?"

"I am afraid I cannot possibly tell you that," said the Marquis. "You are, after all, not the intended recipient of this particular diplomatic communiqué."

"Why not? What's it say? Who's it for?"

The Marquis shrugged. His coat was so close that he could have reached out and stroked it. "Only the threat of death could force me even to show it to you," he said reluctantly.

"Well, that's easy. I threaten you with death. That's in addition to the death sentence you're already under as an apostate member of the flock. And as for Laughing Boy here"—the shepherd gestured with his crook toward Peregrine, who was not laughing —"he's tried to steal a member of the flock. That's a death sentence too, in addition to everything else we're planning to do to him."

The shepherd looked at the Elephant. "And, I know I should have asked before, but what in the Auld Witch's name is this?"

"I am a loyal member of the flock," said the Elephant humbly, in his deep voice, and the Marquis wondered if he had sounded so soulless and flat when he had been part of the flock. "I have remained loyal and in step even when this one did not."

"And the flock is grateful for all your hard work," said the shepherd. He reached out a hand and touched the sharp tip of one elephantine tusk experimentally. "I've never seen anything like you before, and if I never see another one again, it'll be too soon. Probably best if you die, too."

The Elephant's ears twitched. "But I am of the flock . . ."

The shepherd looked up into the Elephant's huge face. "Better safe than sorry," he said. Then, to the Marquis: "Well? Where is this important letter?"

The Marquis de Carabas said, "It is inside my shirt. I must repeat that it is the most significant document that I have ever been charged to deliver. I must ask you not to look at it. For your own safety."

The shepherd tugged at the front of the Marquis's shirt. The buttons flew, and rattled off the walls onto the floor. The letter, in its sandwich bag, was in the pocket inside the shirt.

"This is most unfortunate. I trust you will read it aloud to us before we die," said the Marquis. "But whether or not you read it to us, I can promise that Peregrine and I will be holding our breath. Won't we, Peregrine?"

The shepherd opened the sandwich bag, then he looked at the envelope. He ripped it open and pulled a sheet of discolored paper from inside it. Dust came from the envelope as the paper came out. The dust hung in the still air in that dim room.

"'My darling beautiful Drusilla,'" read the shepherd aloud. "'While I know that you do not presently feel about me as I feel about you . . .' What *is* this nonsense?"

The Marquis said nothing. He did not even smile. He was, as he had stated, holding his breath; he was hoping that Peregrine had listened to him; and he was counting, because at that moment counting seemed like the best possible thing that he could do to distract himself from needing to breathe. He would soon need to breathe.

35 . . . 36 . . . 37 . . .

He wondered how long mushroom spores remained in the air. 43 . . . 44 . . . 45 . . . 46 . . .

The shepherd had stopped speaking.

The Marquis took a step backward, fearing a knife in his ribs or teeth in his throat from the rough-furred guard-dog men, but there was nothing. He walked backward, away from the dog-men and the Elephant.

He saw that Peregrine was also walking backward.

His lungs hurt. His heart was pounding in his temples, pounding almost loudly enough to drown out the thin ringing noise in his ears.

Only when the Marquis's back was against a bookcase on the wall and he was as far as he could possibly get from the envelope, he allowed himself to take a deep breath. He heard Peregrine breathe in, too.

There was a stretching noise. Peregrine opened his mouth wide, and the tape dropped to the ground. "What," asked Peregrine, "was all that about?"

"Our way out of this room, and our way out of Shepherd's Bush, if I am not mistaken," said de Carabas. "As I so rarely am. Would you mind unbinding my wrists?"

He felt Peregrine's hands on his bound hands, and then the bindings fell away.

There was a low rumbling. "I'm going to kill somebody," said the Elephant. "As soon as I figure out who."

"Whoa, dear heart," said the Marquis, rubbing his hands together. "You mean *whom*." The shepherd and the sheepdogs were taking awkward, experimental steps toward the door. "And I can assure you that you aren't going to kill anybody, not as long as you want to get home to the Castle safely."

The Elephant's trunk swished irritably. "I'm definitely going to kill *you*."

The Marquis grinned. "You are going to force me to say *pshaw*," he said. "Or *fiddlesticks*. Until now I have never had the slightest moment of yearning to say *fiddlesticks*. But I can feel it right now welling up inside me—"

"What, by the Temple and the Arch, has got into you?" asked the Elephant.

"Wrong question. But I shall ask the right question on your behalf. The question is actually what *hasn't* got into the three of us —it hasn't got into Peregrine and me because we were holding our breath, and it hasn't got into you because, I don't know, probably because you're an elephant, with nice thick skin, more likely because you were breathing through your trunk, which is down at ground level—and what did get into our captors. And the answer is, what hasn't got into us are the selfsame spores that have got into our portly shepherd and his pseudocanine companions."

"Spores of the Mushroom?" asked Peregrine. "The Mushroom People's the Mushroom?"

"Indeed. That selfsame Mushroom," agreed the Marquis.

"Blimming Heck," said the Elephant.

"Which is why," de Carabas told the Elephant, "if you attempt to kill me, or to kill Peregrine, you will not only fail but you will doom us all. Whereas if you shut up and we all do our best to look as if we are still part of the flock, then we have a chance. The spores will be threading their way into their brains now. And any moment now the Mushroom will begin calling them home."

A shepherd walked implacably. He held a wooden crook. Three men followed him. One of those men had the head of an elephant; one was tall and ridiculously handsome; and the last of the flock wore a most magnificent coat. It fit him perfectly, and it was the color of a wet street at night.

The flock were followed by guard dogs, who moved as if they were ready to walk through fire to get wherever they believed that they were going.

It was not unusual in Shepherd's Bush to see a shepherd and part of his flock moving from place to place, accompanied by several of the fiercest sheepdogs (who were human, or had been once). So when they saw a shepherd and three sheepdogs apparently leading three members of the flock away from Shepherd's Bush, none of the greater flock paid them any mind. The members of the flock who saw them simply did the same things they had always done, as members of the flock, and if they were aware that the influence of the shepherds had waned a little, then they patiently waited for another shepherd to come and to take care of them and to keep them safe from predators and from the world. It was a scary thing to be alone, after all.

Nobody noticed as they crossed the bounds of Shepherd's Bush, and still they kept on walking.

The seven of them reached the banks of the Kilburn, where they stopped, and the former shepherd and the three shaggy dog-men strode out into the water.

There was, the Marquis knew, nothing in the four men's heads at that moment but a need to get to the Mushroom, to taste its flesh once more, to let it live inside them, to serve it, and to serve it well. In exchange, the Mushroom would fix all the things about themselves that they hated: it would make their interior lives much happier and more interesting.

"Should've let me kill 'em," said the Elephant as the former shepherd and sheepdogs waded away.

"No point," said the Marquis. "Not even for revenge. The people who captured us don't exist any longer."

The Elephant flapped his ears hard, then scratched them vigorously. "Talking about revenge, who the hell did you steal my diary for anyway?" he asked.

"Victoria," admitted de Carabas.

"Not actually on my list of potential thieves. She's a deep one," said the Elephant, after a moment.

"I'll not argue with that," said the Marquis. "Also, she failed to pay me the entire amount agreed. I wound up obtaining my own lagniappe to make up the deficit."

He reached a dark hand into the inside of his coat. His fingers found the obvious pockets, and the less obvious, and then, to his surprise, the least obvious of all. He reached inside it and pulled out a magnifying glass on a chain. "It was Victoria's," he said. "I believe you can use it to see through solid things. Perhaps this could be considered a small payment against my debt to you . . . ?"

The Elephant took something out of its own pocket—the Marquis could not see what it was—and squinted at it through the magnifying glass. Then the Elephant made a noise halfway between a delighted snort and a trumpet of satisfaction. "Oh fine, very fine," it said. It pocketed both of the objects. Then it said, "I suppose that saving my life outranks stealing my diary. And while I wouldn't have needed saving if I hadn't followed you down the drain, further recriminations are pointless. Consider your life your own once more."

"I look forward to visiting you in the Castle someday," said the Marquis.

"Don't push your luck, mate," said the Elephant, with an irritable swish of his trunk.

"I won't," said the Marquis, resisting the urge to point out that pushing his luck was the only way he had made it this far. He looked around and realized that Peregrine had slipped mysteriously and irritatingly away into the shadows once more, without so much as a goodbye.

The Marquis hated it when people did that.

He made a small, courtly bow to the Elephant, and the Marquis's coat, his glorious coat, caught the bow, amplified it, made it perfect, and made it the kind of bow that only the Marquis de Carabas could ever possibly make. Whoever he was.

The next Floating Market was being held in Derry and Tom's Roof Garden. There had been no Derry and Tom's since 1973, but time and space and London Below had their own uncomfortable agreement, and the roof garden was younger and more innocent than it is today. The folk from London Above (they were young, and in an intense discussion, and they had stacked heels and paisley tops and bell-bottom flares, the men and the women) ignored the folk from London Below entirely.

The Marquis de Carabas strode through the roof garden as if he owned the place, walking swiftly until he reached the food court. He passed a tiny woman selling curling cheese sandwiches from a wheelbarrow piled high with the things, a curry stall, a short man with a huge glass bowl of pale white blind fish and a toasting fork, until, finally, he reached the stall that was selling the Mushroom.

"Slice of the Mushroom, well grilled, please," said the Marquis de Carabas.

The man who took his order was shorter than he was and still somewhat stouter. He had sandy, receding hair and a harried expression.

"Coming right up," said the man. "Anything else?"

"No, that's all." And then, curiously, the Marquis asked, "Do you remember me?"

"I am afraid not," said the Mushroom man. "But I must say, that is a most beautiful coat."

"Thank you," said the Marquis de Carabas. He looked around. "Where is the young fellow who used to work here?"

"Ah. That is a most curious story, sir," said the man. He did not yet smell of damp although there was a small encrustation of mushrooms on the side of his neck. "Somebody told the fair Drusilla, of the Court of the Raven, that our Vince had had designs upon her, and had—you may not credit it, but I am assured that it is so—apparently sent her a letter filled with spores with the intention of making her his bride in the Mushroom."

The Marquis raised an eyebrow quizzically, although he found none of this surprising. He had, after all, told Drusilla himself, and had even shown her the original letter. "Did she take well to the news?"

"I do not believe that she did, sir. I do not believe that she did. She and several of her sisters were waiting for Vince, and they all caught up with us on our way to the Market. She told him they had matters to discuss, of an intimate nature. He seemed delighted by this news, and went off with her to find out what these matters were. I have been waiting for him to arrive at the Market and come and work all evening, but I no longer believe he will be coming." Then the man said a little wistfully, "That is a very fine coat. It seems to me that I might have had one like it in a former life."

"I do not doubt it," said the Marquis de Carabas, satisfied with what he had heard, cutting into his grilled slice of the Mushroom, "but this particular coat is most definitely mine."

As he made his way out of the Market, he passed a clump of people descending the stairs and he paused and nodded at a young woman of uncommon grace. She had the long orange hair and the flattened profile of a Pre-Raphaelite beauty, and there was a birthmark in the shape of a five-pointed star on the back of one hand. Her other hand was stroking the head of a large, rumpled owl, which glared uncomfortably out at the world with eyes that were, unusually for such a bird, of an intense, pale blue.

The Marquis nodded at her, and she glanced awkwardly at him, then she looked away in the manner of someone who was now beginning to realize that she owed the Marquis a favor.

He nodded at her amiably, and continued to descend.

Drusilla hurried after him. She looked as if she had something she wanted to say.

The Marquis de Carabas reached the foot of the stairs ahead of her. He stopped for a moment, and he thought about people, and about things, and about how hard it is to do anything for the first time. And then, clad in his fine coat, he slipped mysteriously, even irritatingly, into the shadows, without so much as a goodbye, and he was gone.

SUSAN PALWICK

Windows

FROM *Asimov's Science Fiction*

THE BUS SMELLS like plastic and urine, and the kid sitting next to Vangie has his music cranked up way too high. It's leaking out of his earbuds, giving her a headache. He's a big boy, sprawled out across his seat and into hers as if she's not there at all. She squeezes herself against the window, resting her head against the cool glass to try to ease the throbbing behind her eyes. Maybe the kid will get off at the next stop, in forty minutes or so. Maybe nobody else will get on to take his seat. The bus is completely full, and the waves of chatter and smell might have made Vangie sick even without the booming bass.

It's a ten-hour ride to see Graham; Vangie just hopes she'll get in this time. She can't shake her gut fear that everything's lined up too neatly, that something has to go wrong. More than once, she's spent the time and money to get down there—the time's no problem, but the money's not so easy, not with her monthly check as small as it is—to find the prison on lockdown, nobody in or out and God only knows what's going on inside. All you get are reports you can't trust, and you sit in the shabby town library Googling the news every two seconds until it's time to catch the bus back home, because you can't afford another night in a motel. Sometimes it's been days until Graham's been able to call out, until Vangie's been able to hear his voice again. She always accepts the collect charges, but they never talk long. Those calls cost.

Vangie's small overnight bag is under her feet. She's got her purse strap crossed over her body, and her arms crossed protectively over that, as if the kid next to her might snatch the bag and sprint to the front of the bus, diving out the door at seventy miles an hour. She knows this wouldn't happen even if she looked like someone worth robbing, even if what's in her purse had the slightest value to anybody except her and maybe Graham. He won't value it as much as she does. She doesn't see how he could. Every time she thinks about it she feels a great weight in her chest, a clot of grief and guilt and relief and love, and sometimes a tiny bit of pride creeps in there, too—one of her kids got away, is getting away, even if it's too far—but she squashes that, always. No one else would think she deserved to feel proud. She doesn't think she deserves to feel proud. Pride is dangerous. So's luck, because it always turns, and there's already been too much this trip.

The kid next to her yawns and shifts, giving her an inch or two more room, and she takes it, grateful. It's getting dark, sunset a dull bruise to the west, obscured by clouds and by the dirty window, but at least she can see out, watch the gray highway rushing past. When she first started making this trip, three years ago, she promised herself she'd look out the window the whole time so she'd be able to tell Graham about it, but there's nothing next to the road but flat fields, corn and alfalfa. Sometimes a combine, but she can never make out people. She looked for cows the first few times, horses. No luck. She'll tell him about this sunset, though. She'll make it sound prettier than it is.

And when it gets completely dark she'll peer up through the window and try to make out stars. Sometimes she can see them. She can't remember if there's a moon tonight, but she'll look for that, too. Vangie feels like she has to look, because Graham can't. He doesn't get to see the night sky anymore.

Zel doesn't get to see anything else. She thought she was so lucky when she won the ticket, blind lottery, her name pulled out of the hat with all those other folks'. It still rips Vangie's heart open to remember how eager Zel was to leave all of them, leave everything forever. "I'm going to the stars!" she said, but all she's doing is living in a tin can, living and dying there, and they'll make babies out of her eggs who'll live the next leg, and babies out of *their* eggs who'll live the next, and finally there will be a planet at the end of it, that world the scientists found that's supposed to be as much like Earth as makes no never mind. Zel will never see it.

She'll be long dead, her children's children will be long dead, by the time they get there. She'll never see sunset or alfalfa again.

As far as Vangie's concerned, she's got two kids in for life. She's just glad she can still visit one of them.

She's almost dozed off when the bus stops. The kid next to her gets off. Nobody else gets on. Nobody moves from their current seat to take that one. A shiver goes down Vangie's spine, and she crosses her fingers even as she's moving her bag onto the other seat, stretching out the way the kid did, sighing and feeling her muscles unknot because now maybe she can actually sleep the last few hours of the trip. More luck, too much luck, as much crazy luck this time as it took Zel to get that ticket. She won the generation-ship lottery right before Graham got caught moving more cocaine than anyone could claim for personal use, dumb bad luck, he hadn't noticed one of his taillights was out and got pulled over, third strike you're out. It's like Vangie and her kids only get so much luck, and Zel's heaping lottery serving—if you call that luck at all—meant Graham ran short. Vangie hopes she herself isn't hogging it now. The kids need it more than she does.

She knows there are people who'd say Graham doesn't deserve luck, say what happened to him was all about choice and not about luck at all, say he's scum for dealing drugs. Vangie wishes to God he hadn't gotten involved in the cocaine deal, but she wishes Zel hadn't won the lottery ticket, too. The world can think what it wants. Graham's her son. He's the only family she has left, and tomorrow's his birthday. And in her bag, infinitely precious, is a message from his sister. And if this impossible streak of luck holds, Vangie will actually get to deliver it to him on his birthday.

She gets dizzy just thinking about everything that's already had to go exactly right. Zel's end is tricky enough. The settlers—settlers! as if Zel will ever get to settle anywhere but inside that tin can!—don't get to send messages very often, because there are so many of them and they're all busy growing beans or doing things to each other's eggs and sperm or whatever they spend their time on up there. Vangie tries not to wonder about the babies. Whatever babies Zel has, Vangie will never get to hold them.

But anyway, they don't get to send messages very often. There's a schedule, as strict as the one dictating when prisoners can call out, and for how long. And the ones from the tin can have to travel a lot farther. There's a computer that tells the person sending the message when it will reach Earth. Right now it takes a couple of days, and a lot of messages don't even get through because they have to travel so far, bouncing off planets and satellites and space rocks and God knows what else. A lot of them just get lost.

So Zel just happened to get her slot last week sometime, or the week before that, and sent Graham's birthday video in time to reach Vangie's free email account the week before Graham's birthday, which falls at the beginning of the month, right after Vangie's check comes in, which means she had the money to buy a thumb drive to put the file on, and also had the money for the bus ticket and the hotel down by the prison, because Graham's birthday falls on one of the weekend visiting days, and how often will *that* ever happen? It's amazing enough that the message actually came through. The trip will leave Vangie short on grocery money for the month, but she'll go to the food pantries and soup kitchens. She'll scrape by.

Of course she called ahead to the prison to see if they'd even let her show Graham the file. She hasn't watched it yet; she wants to see it with him. It's called "Happy birthday, Graham," so she knows what it's about. She and Graham will have to watch it on one of the prison computers, and she wanted to make sure she wouldn't have to pay: video visits are $100 an hour, another racket, like the collect phone calls. The prison's so crowded because there's no money, they always say, but it looks to Vangie like they're cleaning up.

More luck: because a prisoner just died in isolation and there's been a big flap about it, and they're worried about PR this week, her call got put through to the warden, and he promised her that she'd be able to use a prison laptop, no charge. Something about prisoners' rights to contact with family, and if your family's on a generation ship and your only possible contact's a video message that just traveled days to get to your mother's email account, well then.

Vangie trusts this as far as she can throw the bus. The flap's died down now. Twenty to one there won't be any laptop. She doubts the warden will admit to taking her call, or even remember it.

The bus rocks her, that lulling rushing motion she's always loved, the feeling of going somewhere. She peers up through the window, but there are clouds now, and between them and the grime, she can't see stars. She pushes both of her seats back, and stretches out as much as she can, and sleeps.

It's a good thing she slept on the bus, because she can hardly sleep at all in her hotel room: a blasting TV on one side of her and raucous sex followed by a screaming fight in the other, and a lumpy mattress. Her own TV's broken, so she lies in the dark, staring up at the ceiling, reminding herself that Zel and Graham both have it much worse. Prison's even noisier than this, and much more crowded, and there's no checking out of the gen-ship.

She dozes off a little, finally, around three, but wakes up smack-dab at five, the way she's done her whole adult life. This means she gets close to first dibs on the hot water, which still runs out too quickly. A shower's a shower, though. The coffee at the diner across the street restores her even more, and the scrambled eggs are fluffy, just like she makes them herself.

She's first in line at the prison. "Evangeline Morris," she tells the guard, who looks like she's barely awake herself. "I'm supposed to be able to use one of your laptops. The warden said."

"Yes, ma'am. I have that down here. They'll get it for you inside."

Marveling and suspicious—the PR flap must have lasted longer than usual—Vangie hands over her purse so another yawning guard can search it, and goes through the metal detector and reclaims her bag. There's a long line of other visitors behind her; she can feel the weight of them pressing on her back, pressing her through the doors into the visiting room.

The visiting room's a dull yellow cube dotted with tables and chairs. The two vending machines in the corner are always broken, and noise echoes off the walls. There's nothing resembling privacy, but if you have somebody in here, you take what you can get.

And there's Graham waiting for her, and someone else is with him, but Vangie doesn't care about that right now: she just reaches out for the hug she's allowed, one at the beginning of the visit and one at the end. She hugs Graham as hard as she can, as if she can force all her love for him through his skin, armor against his life here. "Happy birthday, baby."

"Mama." His voice is thick. She pulls back to look at him: he's thinner than he was last visit, and tears track his cheeks. "Mama, I brought the chaplain with me."

"What?" Her heart flutters. "What's wrong?" Graham's thinner than last time. "Are you—"

"Mama, the ship. You didn't hear? The news last night?"

"What? What news?" She was on the bus last night, in the hotel with the broken TV. No, she hasn't heard any news.

"The gen-ship. There was a fire. An explosion. They've lost contact. Nobody knows anything. Everybody's scared."

Vangie blinks. The chaplain reaches out to steady her, and she realizes she's swaying. Graham guides her into a chair. All that good luck: she knew something terrible had to happen. She swallows.

"I didn't hear anything." She didn't hear anybody talking about it at the diner, even. She was in a bubble, as isolated as any prisoner here, as isolated as the people on the gen-ship, dead or alive. "I—they don't know?"

Graham's sitting now, at the little table across from her. "Nobody knows anything yet. They're afraid it's bad."

The aftertaste of coffee is a bitter tang in her mouth, metallic as blood. The chaplain clears his throat. "Ma'am, I'm so sorry. I'd be happy to pray with you, or talk—"

She wants to send him away. If no one knows anything yet, maybe it's all fine. There are safety systems on the gen-ship. There've been fires in space before, haven't there? And everybody lived? Of course the news people are pushing fear. That's their drug, making everybody scared, as if life's not scary enough. News fear isn't real.

This chaplain's real, too real; he makes her nervous, and she wants him gone. But Graham brought him here. Graham's trying to do something for her. Graham, who may now be her only child, is trying to be a good and loving son. He doesn't have many ways to take care of her. She has to let him.

So she and Graham bow their heads, and the chaplain says a quick, bland prayer for safety and a good outcome and comfort for all the families here on earth, and squeezes her shoulder, and asks if she needs to talk.

"Thank you, reverend, but I need to talk to my son. I don't have long with him, as you know. It's his birthday."

"Happy birthday," the chaplain says softly, and leaves.

Graham wipes his eyes. The prayer seems to have moved him far more than it did her. "Mama, I don't know how we'll know if she's—"

"She's fine," Vangie says. She hears her own voice, too shrill, too loud. She recognizes that voice: it's how she talked when Graham was arrested, in the weeks before his sentencing when she had to hope that somehow everything would work out, that he'd get off. Maybe everything will be fine, and if you say so loudly enough, maybe you'll believe it. "We don't know anything. Until we know for sure, she's fine. And she sent you something, Graham." She calls over a guard and asks for the laptop.

He brings it. This no longer surprises her. Her dread at the improbable run of luck is gone now, and she refuses to let any other dread replace it.

The guard clears his throat. "I need to stay here while you use it."

"Yes. We understand."

He turns on the machine, and Vangie, hands shaking only a little, inserts the thumb drive and opens the file. Somebody's set the laptop volume too high: there's a blast of music, the theme music for the gen-ship, like it's some kind of TV show, and then "Happy Birthday, Graham!" fills the screen in flowery letters, and then there's Zel's face. Vangie hasn't seen it in months, except in photos. Zel's smiling. She looks healthy. Her hair's short, and she's wearing a white T-shirt; behind her, Vangie sees metal walls, a white corridor, people walking through it.

Vangie turns down the volume so Zel's voice will sound normal. "Hey, Graham! I hope Mama got this message to you in time for your birthday, but if not, happy belated. I only have about a minute, but I just wanted you to know that I miss both of you and think about you all the time. The ship's a little boring but not too bad. I'm still working with the plants. I like it." Zel holds up a tiny yellow jacket. "I crocheted this. One of my eggs took: I'm going to be a mom!" Her grin's huge now, the expression Vangie remembers from summer trips to the public pool, from the times Zel got to play with a neighbor's dog, from when she rushed over to tell Vangie she'd won a place on the ship. "So Mama, you're going to be a grandma, and Graham's going to be an uncle! And whatever the baby is, I'm naming it after one of you. It will be one of the first babies born here. I'm getting special food and everything, lots of vitamins. It's a big deal. Okay, that's my time. Love you both. Bye."

The message ends. The room's quieter than Vangie's ever heard it. She feels that pressure at her back and turns to find a crowd around the table: other inmates and visitors, other guards. The guy who manned the metal detector, the woman at the desk. The chaplain. Some of them are sniffling. They look stricken. They look alike, whatever they're wearing, uniforms or prison jumpsuits or street clothing.

They heard the music. They came to watch the message from the ship.

"We don't know anything yet," Vangie says. Her voice sounds like her own again. "Not for sure. And whatever's happening up there, we can't do anything about it. Today is my son Graham's birthday. Help me sing to him."

And they do. It's a ragged chorus gathered by shock and tragedy, wavering and off-key, and it won't last long, but it's here now. And Vangie knows that's luck, too.

ADAM-TROY CASTRO

The Thing About Shapes to Come

FROM *Lightspeed Magazine*

MONICA'S NEW BABY was like a lot of new babies these days in that she was born a cube. She had no external or internal sexual organs, or for that matter organs of any kind, being just a warm solid filled with protoplasm. But she was, genetically at least, a girl, and one who resembled her mother as much as any cube possibly could. That wasn't much, in that she had no eyes, no nose, no mouth, no chin, no hair, nothing that could be charitably called a face or bodily features, not even any orifices larger than pores. But she had inherited Monica's healthy appetite. Placed in a dish in a puddle of Monica's breast milk, she throbbed in deep appreciation and absorbed it all in a matter of minutes, becoming as plump and as satiated as a sponge. As far as anybody could tell, she was a happy and healthy cube.

It had been a difficult birth, given all the corners involved. Labor had been the biological equivalent of trying to fit a square peg in a round hole. But there was no reason, they said, to worry about her health; her constitution was strong, and there was no reason to believe she couldn't live a long, comfortable, and healthy life, devoid of any serious problems unrelated to the general inconvenience of going through life shaped like a cube. The presence of nerve impulses even confirmed that the child could think, while providing little in the way of speculation over what she could possibly have to think about. Look at her the right way and it was even possible to consider her beautiful, in that she was smooth on all her planes, sharply defined on her edges and corners, not off by so much as a millimeter in any of her vital measurements. This wasn't the kind of beauty Monica had envisioned when she'd hoped for a beautiful child, but there was a starkness to her daughter's lines, a mathematical purity to her, that made it impossible to want to use terms like *disfigured* or *deformed*.

Monica had hoped for an old-fashioned baby, of the kind that had been common when she was a child, the kind with the rounded features and drooly toothless smile and the foreshortened arms and legs and even—yes, she'd looked forward to this as well—the end that would need to be wiped clean and powdered on a regular basis. She had wanted a child who would someday delight her by calling her "Mama," and one day rise on uncertain feet to toddle off and force her to give chase. That would have been the ideal. But she had also known that these days the odds of ending up with a baby that looked like that were about one in a hundred thousand, and dropping. More and more women were giving birth to cylinders and pyramids and crosses and rhombuses, with the vast majority of the newest generation emerging as playful spheres. Of all the young mothers Monica knew, only one had been blessed with a baby shaped like a baby; and that mother seemed genuinely haunted as she pushed the infant around in its pram, aware that the world was watching, feeling surrounded on all sides by legions of frustrated kidnappers and pederasts. The mothers of children-shaped children had to take care to shield their progeny from such predators, because the number of predators remained constant even as the number of possible targets for their vile intentions now described an asymptotic curve that approached but never quite reached zero. Most of the young parents Monica knew were lucky enough to have been blessed with spheres that could roll around and bounce into one another and even learn to descend household stairs, though rarely to ascend them. A sphere, Monica thought, would have been a fine alternative to a traditional baby. A sphere she could have taken to the park and played with. But complaining about that was like spitting in the face of God. Certainly a cube must have other talents, other good points to love.

Of course, Monica's mom and dad were upset, not just because their teenaged daughter had given birth to a cube but also, unspoken, because that cube's mocha-brown coloring suggested that, since Monica was white, the unknown father must have been black. Dad wore an unmistakable scowl as he held the new arrival in his hands, his rheumy eyes a million miles away as he bid a mental farewell to any future birthdays involving tricycles and baseball gloves, or even dollhouses or drum batons. He weighed the cube in his hands, wondering aloud whether he was holding her upside down or right side up, or if there was any way he could tell that she even knew she was being held. He said, *Maybe we could put a label on it, to let us know which way is up.* Monica's mom was even less subtle, complaining: *She's square.* A doctor corrected her at once, saying, *No, Mrs. Hufready, she's not a square, a square would be flat. She's a cube.* Mom was slow to absorb the correction and demanded, *What the hell is my daughter going to do with a square kid?* It was impossible to hear Mom's tone of voice and not know that she would always fail to get it, that even if she came around to loving her granddaughter for the beautiful, geometrical solid she was, she would still be slow to pick up the etymological differences, using the offensive *s*-slur for years to come without ever quite understanding why it was wrong.

As for herself, Monica felt the tug of maternal love the second her child was placed in her hands, and rotated so she could see that her baby was indeed the same on all sides. She was a member of the younger generation, the one that had grown up in the age of such births, the one who had been prepared to gestate and nurture a darling shape of her own. She saw in her daughter's being, her substance, the oneness of her, a divine spark that all of her dreams of a more conventional child could not deny. She felt the pit of bottomless responsibility open wide before her and, with no reservations, leaped in. Asked for a name to put on the birth certificate, she told the doctors, "Her name's Di."

Di was a well-behaved child who lay in her crib and regarded the world around her with a calm acceptance that never crossed the line into brattiness or fussing for the sake of fussing. She didn't cry, but from time to time she hummed. This was always a sign that it was time to feed her. She was an angel whenever food was provided, sitting in the center of any puddle laid out for her and plumping visibly as she absorbed it. She also thrummed in the presence of her mother, though rarely so in the presence of her grandparents, whose generational instincts had somehow failed to kick in, and who most often referred to the baby as "that thing." Monica did whatever she could to jump-start their hearts, but that seemed a losing battle, and she spent more and more time retreating from them, taking Di into her own bedroom and doing all the maternal things she was required to do in private, where they would not be a source of constant irritation.

Aside from that, there was no shame. Monica felt no compunction about taking Di out to the park, where there were only a couple of lonely "normal" children who looked furtive and uncomfortable in the playgrounds littered with mostly immobile shapes other parents had brought and placed about the rusting swing sets and jungle gyms, in the hopes that the environment would provide the kinetic opportunities that the limited motive ability their own offspring lacked. The most popular item of equipment among the parents seemed to be the sandbox, where the pyramids, cubes, and rhombuses, arranged in rows and left to interact in any way they could, resembled the half-buried buildings of some desert city, assaulted by the aftermath of a sandstorm. A couple of times Monica placed Di there, among the other edifices in the miniature boulevard, until she noticed that when playtime was over the parents didn't always leave with the same kids they'd come with, and excused away any accidents of identification with the excuse that they were just too hard to tell apart.

Some conscientious parents made more of an effort to personalize—as in, "render a person"—their shape-children. Sometimes Monica sat beside one determined young woman who dressed her pyramidal boy, Roger, in jean overalls that buttoned midway up his converging slopes, held in place by suspenders that hooked around his single vertex. The outfit came complete with plush-toy fake legs dangling from his base. The effect wasn't very convincing, not even with the cartoonish smiley-face drawn on one of Roger's three risers, a representation of two dot eyes and bubblegum pink cheeks curving into a happy mouth that, on Roger, resembled disrespectful graffiti more than an actual personification of a child. Even when Monica forced herself to entertain the premise, she couldn't help noticing that the simulated head came to a point, which to her mind made Roger look feeble-minded. To be sure, Roger's mother had tried to ameliorate that point with a scruffy little wig and baseball cap, but how much more noble, she thought, was his actual shape, shorn of pretense? It was primal; it was classical. It was the shape of monuments, of constructs that lived forever. The pyramid-in-boy-suit was, by comparison, just a transparent ploy, a stab at imagined normalcy that emerged as grubby and pathetic by comparison. Monica could only glance at her own Di, who embodied self-contained perfection so well that she looked the same from every angle, and tried in vain to summon the mindset that would have led her to subject the darling to indignities of the same sort that Roger's mother subjected on him. It seemed deluded, antimaternal, and likely hurtful.

Other times Monica wandered over to the fenced-in area where the spheres played. It had been a basketball court, though the poles and hoops had been taken down, and the game being played by about two dozen spheres of different sizes resembled nothing that had ever been played between teams. Unlike cubes, which were stable once placed in any given position and could be trusted to remain where they were put until somebody came by to move them, spheres were pure chaos, harder to stop than to start, an explosion of play potential that manifested as a collection of runaway ids. They rolled about at high speeds, some describing predictable orbits and others changing their course according to the whim of each passing moment. They collided. They bounced. They slowed, pretended to rest, and then accelerated like streaks of light, as if fired by invisible cannons. It was impossible to tell if they were actually playing with one another, or, as it seemed to Monica, *at* one another. Perhaps they perceived their fellow spheres as annoying obstructions and not as fellow inhabitants of the universe. But there was an energy to their play, a potential that reminded Monica of atoms colliding with one another, searching for others with which they could combine and form strange new substances, with none of the properties of the original contributors. But when Monica put Di down in the center of all that splendid chaos, just to see what would happen, the answer was nothing; her child just sat in the center of it all, unstirred, a closed system.

When Di was two, the world experienced a slight upswing in instances of what were by then called traditional pregnancies. It wasn't much. It didn't amount to more than about five thousand more than the population had been told to expect. But the furor over this development vastly exceeded its statistical significance.

The news media questioned: Is the "plague" over? Had mankind been saved from this strange mutation?

In a few short months further numbers would come in, and the answer to both questions would turn out to be no. This was nothing more than a statistical fluke, the kind of phenomenon that only happens because the numbers come up that way; no more significant that the occasional odd family that, in the old days, would produce ten boys in a row without a single female face among them, without much affecting the fifty-fifty ratio in the general population. When things evened out, the vast majority of young mothers continued to pump out spheres and cubes and pyramids and rhombuses, and the line on the graph that reflected the percentage of pregnancies that resulted in baby-shaped babies continued to descend, inexorably, toward zero.

But while the illusion lasted, many people seized on the premature intimations of hope to initiate debates over what to do with what they considered a lost generation. Shape-children were abandoned, thrown out, offered up for adoption. Many mothers were pressured by loved ones to admit that the things they'd carried in their bodies, expelled, and cared for were not people but things unworthy of their love that could now be discarded.

Monica's parents were among the people who took this position. They pointed out that she had not held down a job, or done anything else with her life, since Di's birth. They said that all she did was feed "it" and care for "it" and talk to "it" as if "it" could hear her. They told her that she showed even more devotion than a "regular" mother, but that it was a devotion poured down a black hole that swallowed far more than it could ever return. *It's a parasite,* they told her. She argued that it had always been possible to see babies as parasites feeding off the generation that birthed them; for a while, at least, they contributed nothing but smiles and coos while demanding food, attention, and energy. How, she wanted to know, was Di different? This somehow never closed the argument but rather brought it back to the beginning, to the declaration that Di had done nothing in her short life but increase in size and in her need for nutrients. *You don't like the word* parasite? her parents asked her. *Try* vegetable. The point was that Di still showed no sign of ever being able to interact with others in any meaningful way. There was no reason Monica had to continue paying the price of being devoted to her, not when there were "places" that could take care of Di just as well as she could.

This was not just a single conversation. Or perhaps it was, if you can say that a series of conversations, continued over days and weeks with only short interruptions for sleep and the necessary business of being alive, was a conversation. There was no halt to it. Monica took it with calm, and then with anger, then with long bitter silences, and then with weakness: *Yes,* she said, *of course, I'm not saying I agree, but I'll look at one of those places already.*

And so they went to a facility for abandoned cubes. It wasn't called that. It was called a juvenile home. But it was only open to cubes, specializing in that particular shape and no other, to the point of specifying in its charter that any children whose parents submitted applications would be carefully measured before acceptance, to ensure that none of them had sides that differed in proportion by even a stray millimeter. As Di thrummed contentedly in Monica's lap, the administrator, a woman who seemed inordinately configured out of ninety-degree angles herself, explained that "fitting in" here was not a social concern but a physical one. The children were stored on shelves in stacks of three, and any whose dimensions were at all disproportionate caused dangerous instability among those stacked on top of them. But—she smiled —there was no reason to believe that this would be a problem with Di, who was just lovely. In her case the examination would be, doubtlessly, no more than a formality.

Monica and her parents took the grand tour, and by now were not surprised that the place was, very much literally, a place for warehousing unwanted children. The shelves stretched twelve feet above a cold concrete floor and the length of a football field into gloom, each stacked five high with cubes of sizes ranging from newborn to adolescent, the latter being so large they could have contained old-fashioned console televisions. A sprinkler hose moved down one of the aisles on a track, spraying them with a liquid that, the administrator advised Monica, had been formulated to fit all of their nutritional needs. Another spraying light mist washed them off. Stereo speakers played gentle instrumentals while the cubes thrummed, staying in tune. Dust motes danced in the cold, dim light. Monica's father asked the administrator if they had a system in place for knowing which child was which, and she pointed out a placard at the end of each row, which detailed the number range of those stored on each shelf (as in "1200–1503"). The names, she said, were backed up weekly and stored off-site, for convenience, but they didn't really matter all that much, as these were not children who would ever come when called.

The silence and seeming acquiescence of Monica and her parents encouraged the administrator to ramble. She told them about the most memorable mishap the facility had ever suffered, a case where none of the attendants had noticed that the cube on top of the stack had experienced a growth spurt faster than those of the cubes it rested on, and a cascade occurred that had toppled first that stack and then the other stacks next to it, resulting in a pile of thrumming objects who may have been unhurt but who presented a challenge that didn't often come up when dealing with other children, in that they were faceless and identical. It had taken a flurry of DNA tests, undertaken at great expense, to determine which child was which, not that anyone at the facility felt it especially mattered.

Monica asked permission to place Di on one of the shelves, just as an experiment. The administrator beamed and told her to go right ahead. She placed Di on an empty spot, murmured that there was no need to worry because Mommy would be right back, and backed away, stopping only when she was ten feet away, and then again when she was twenty, and finally again at fifty. Di was hard to pick out among all the other cubes. She was indistinguishable from the others her size. But Monica thought of all the times she had been in public places like busy streets or stadiums and auditoriums, looking out upon crowds of hundreds or even thousands—the way all of those faces, as unique as they may have been as Joe, or Sue, or Brad, or Laura, had been reduced by the sheer number to shifting pixels, making up a grand mural whose only identity was that of the mob. It wasn't easy to pick out any one person in that place either, because they were all alike, becoming something different from all the others only when they were approached and examined for the cues that made them individuals. She wondered if anybody working at this warehouse ever picked up one of the cubes and felt its warmth against their own. But mostly she wondered how many of them were screaming.

The spheres rebelled the year Di turned fifteen. By that time it had been years since Monica had been able to hold her only child in her lap or cradle her in her arms. Now Di was the size of a dish-washer and could no longer be moved except with a hand truck; at the speed she was growing, it would soon be impossible to move her from Monica's little studio apartment except by knocking down one of the walls. She was by far the most prominent item of de facto furniture in a place that otherwise knew little more than a kitchenette, a convertible couch, and a secondhand television.

Monica, who since cutting off all contact with her parents had worked two jobs to maintain the place, remained as attentive a mother as she could be under the circumstances. She made a point of eating breakfast with Di every morning; Di absorbing the contents of a sponge saturated in shape chow, Monica using Di's ceiling-oriented face as the dining table she otherwise didn't have room for. Di was, if nothing else, a considerate person to eat a meal on. She absorbed spills, and to Monica's maternal eyes seemed to be particularly fond of coffee.

Monica still spoke to Di all the time, telling her that she was special, assuring her that she was loved. There was no way for Monica to know that her child heard or appreciated any of it, and though she held on to her faith with a ferocity that her few friends considered heroic if not deluded, those doubts sometimes overwhelmed her, leading to sleepless nights and a sense of all her life's energy being poured down a black hole.

The little studio became a fortress when the spheres rebelled, many millions of them at once, a revolution declared at the same moment in a hundred major cities around the world, though it was hard to say what grievances they thought they had, or what cause they might have championed, other than anarchy. Thousands, of all ages, from newborns to near-adults, rolled down the Spanish Steps in Rome, thousands more down the zigzag planes of Lombard Street in San Francisco, uncounted numbers rebounding at high altitudes from glass skyscraper to glass skyscraper in Tokyo in what amounted to the most horrifying Pachinko game ever played. Cities with steep hills were the most vulnerable, of course, but they were not above tailoring their acts of terror to the local possibilities: witness what they did in St. Louis, where hundreds of them herded shrieking innocents through the Gateway Arch and back, scoring goals.

In the city where Monica lived, they just broke things, smashing through automobile windshields, overturned trucks, and made it their solemn duty to pay a visit to every single china shop in the greater metropolitan area. She spent that long night huddled in her studio, assuring Di that everything would be all right as the sounds of fear and destruction rattled her windows. She lost herself in bleak thoughts of the price that would need to be paid for all this, the price that would no doubt be levied against innocents like Di, who could not wage war against anybody. Spheres, she thought savagely, were troublemakers by design. They could spin; therefore they were revolutionary. It was not just their privilege but their nature to take the path of least resistance, no matter what lay ahead of them. It was just the way they rolled. But cubes, like Di? They were solid, dependable, and uncomplaining. They received love and asked for nothing more. How terrible it was that they would now be lumped into the same category as such delinquents.

But in the morning, the sounds of destruction gave way to an eerie silence that persisted until the sun reached its height in the sky. Monica ventured downstairs alone and discovered what those who had already left their homes already knew: that whatever had driven the spheres to their destructive madness the night before seemed to have exhausted, not just their rage, but their will to live. Wherever she looked, in every direction, the spheres remained in the places they had come to rest, moving only when some of the people they had terrorized kicked them against walls or beat them with golf clubs and bats. Some, damaged by their fury of the night before, had lost so much of their bounce that they responded to any fall from a height not with an exuberant spring but rather with a sullen and indifferent thud. As she walked the city, she saw workers clearing their unresisting forms from the streets and loading them into trucks; and she knew that all over the world, all those not claimed by loyal parents would be taken somewhere far from sight where they could be stacked in pyramids or plowed into canyons or otherwise forgotten about. For the first time in a life spent taking it as matter of faith that her cube had a soul, she found herself doubting that all shape-children did, and wondering if they would even care about being discarded in this manner. But what was the alternative? Tolerating what they'd done? Leaving them where they'd landed and trusting that they'd never run roughshod over the landscape again? It was not that she had no answer. It was that every answer she had made her feel dirty. It was a warm day but she hugged herself, shivering from a cold that originated somewhere deep in her marrow.

Before she returned to her apartment to check on Di, she stopped by the riverfront, where some of the smaller spheres had landed. Hundreds, ranging in size from golf ball to weather balloon, had landed in the water and were floating downstream toward the sea, where she supposed their next adventure would be serving as the playthings of dolphins. She supposed it as fitting a fate as any.

After a while Monica picked up one of the tiny ones that had landed on the shore, which, judging by its size, could not have been more than six months old. She spoke to it, asking if it could say anything to her that would help her to help them, or at the very least explain just what, in any of their short lives, had embittered them so much that they had to turn to violence. Naturally it didn't answer. She asked if there was anything it could tell her that could help her understand her own daughter, who was so close to being too large to live at home. Again it didn't answer. Tears sprang to her eyes and she cried, *At least you could move! At least you could have an adventure!* But no reply was forthcoming, and in a fit of rage and resentment she tossed the infant into the river, somehow unsurprised when it didn't land with a single splash but instead skipped over the waves, landing here and there but between those moments of impact remaining in flight, like something defiant and free.

Nine months later, the very last shape-child—a random squiggle, like a strip of twisted macaroni—was born in Jakarta. Baby-shaped babies filled the earth again. It's worth noting that nobody ever came up with any reasonable scientific or theological explanation for the nearly two decades that saw such a drastic change in mankind's reproductive output; nor did it seem all that important, as long as it never happened again. Explanations are perhaps best left to the philosophers, who persist in seeking meaning even for those of life's mysteries that remain random, or pointless, or so subtle in their inner workings that examining them is as destructive to the wonder itself as scattering the components of a pocket watch.

For all of us, meaning arrives in installments. It might be actual and it might be wishful thinking. We can only report the facts and hope that they provide closure.

To wit:

Many years later, a rented car drives across the desert, taking an unmarked exit off the paved road to a dirt trail that carries its lone driver past some low hills to a hidden valley on the other side. Trailing a cloud of dust like a comet trail, it passes a little-used gate and descends into a vast caldera that, from a distance, looks like a recent settlement constructed in haste, with prefabricated buildings. It is in fact one of many around the world. Sprinklers water the immobile cubes, spheres, and squiggles, making rainbows in the air that, left to its own design, would be dusty and arid.

The car parks in a place that has been marked off for that purpose and out of it emerges a silver-haired but still energetic woman, squinting at the harsh desert sun. She looks out upon the survivors of a generation, the biggest of which are now three times her own height but which remain as voiceless and without affect as they ever were. Donning a pair of mirrored sunglasses, she sighs and makes her way down to the orderly paths past a very small number of other visitors, finally reaching a certain cube among many, that she has visited so many times she could probably find it in her sleep. No one other than her could see anything about this particular shape, which now towers over her like a monument, that could possibly distinguish it from all the others in its row or the rows that bracket it. But she smiles sadly when she sees it. To her, the shape before her has an individual character different from all the others. It is a person.

To be sure, Di also shows some of the ravages of time. The side facing east shows some sun damage, and a swath of the side facing north shows some bad discoloration left over from the last time she needed to be sand-blasted for graffiti. But she thrums as always in the presence of her mother, who places a single wrinkled hand against her side and speaks words very much like those she's uttered on any number of other visits. We do not need to know exactly what the silver-haired woman says. We can likely already imagine it, and reconstruct its meaning if not the actual words. What she says is not clever and it is not significant, and it will never appear in any book. But it fulfills its purpose, breaking the silence and ameliorating the harshness of the desert air.

Eventually, though, it's time for the visit to end. The silver-haired woman whispers a few final words, lets her right hand brush the side of the vast shape before her, and turns to leave. Always, before, she never turned back. But today something—

perhaps maternal instinct, or perhaps a voice that only she can hear—makes her turn before she has traversed twenty paces. And this time she sees something in her strange daughter that she has never witnessed before: an alteration in the nearest of her previously featureless faces. It's a rectangular opening, seven feet tall and three feet wide, extending upward from the patch of dirt that has become Di's permanent home.

The silver-haired woman returns to what she has no trouble recognizing as a doorway and runs her fingers up and down the jamb, filled with wonder at its sudden appearance. She turns away from it and peers up and down the path between the other children of her daughter's generation, to make certain that nobody is watching. As it happens, nobody is. Di has chosen the perfect moment. This gesture is only meant for one.

The silver-haired woman cannot see anything past the opening but darkness, not even when she removes her sunglasses and shades her eyes from the glare. The precise nature of the answers to be found inside are not available to her, not out here. But she senses no threat: just the welcome the young are supposed to extend to the old, when the most inexorable of life's many passages transfers the responsibility from one to the other.

With another glance up and down the row, just to be sure that she remains unobserved, the silver-haired woman murmurs the first words she has ever been able to speak in response to an act Di has committed out of personal volition. "All right," she says. "Good girl."

Then she takes the first step, and her daughter lets her in.

SAM J. MILLER

We Are the Cloud

FROM *Lightspeed Magazine*

ME AND CASE met when someone slammed his head against my door, so hard I heard it with my earphones in and my Game Boy cranked up loud. Sad music from *Mega Man 2* filled my head and then there was this thud like the world stopped spinning for a second. I turned the thing off and flipped it shut, felt its warmth between my hands. Slipped it under my pillow. Nice things need to stay secret at Egan House, or they'll end up stolen or broken. Old and rickety as it was, I didn't own anything nicer.

I opened my door. Some skinny thug had a bloody-faced kid by the shirt.

"What," I said, and then "what," and then "what the," and then, finally, "hell?"

I barked the last word, tightening all my muscles at once.

"Damn, man," the thug said, startled. He hollered down the stairs, "Goddamn Goliath over here can talk!" He let go of the kid's shirt and was gone. Thirty boys live at Egan House, foster kids awaiting placement. Little badass boys with parents in jail or parents on the street, or dead parents, or parents on drugs.

I looked at the kid he'd been messing with. A line of blood cut his face more or less down the middle, but the gash in his forehead was pretty small. His eyes were huge and clear in the middle of all that blood. He looked like something I'd seen before, in an ad or movie or dream.

"Thanks, dude," the kid said. He ran his hand down his face and then planted it on the outside of my door.

I nodded. Mostly when I open my mouth to say something the

words get all twisted on the way out, or the wrong words sneak in, which is why I tend to not open my mouth. Once he was gone I sniffed at the big bloody handprint. My cloud port hurt, from wanting him. Suddenly it didn't fit quite right, atop the tiny hole where a fiberoptic wire threaded into my brainstem through the joint where skull met spine. Desire was dangerous, something I fought hard to keep down, but the moment I met Case I knew I would lose.

Egan House was my twelfth group home. I had never seen a kid with blue eyes in any of them. I had always assumed white boys had no place in foster care, that there was some other better system set up to receive them.

I had been at Egan House six months, the week that Case came. I was inches away from turning eighteen and aging out. Nothing was waiting for me. I spent an awful lot of energy not thinking about it. Better to sit tight for the little time I had left, in a room barely wider than its bed, relying on my size to keep people from messing with me. At night, unable to sleep, trying hard to think of anything but the future, I'd focus on the sounds of boys trying not to make noise as they cried or jerked off.

On Tuesday, the day after the bloody-faced boy left his handprint on my door, he came and knocked. I had been looking out my window. Not everyone had one. Mine faced south, showed me a wide sweep of the Bronx. Looking out, I could imagine myself as a signal sent out over the municipal Wi-Fi, beamed across the city, cut loose from this body and its need to be fed and sheltered and cared about. Its need for other bodies. I could see things, sometimes. Things I knew I shouldn't be seeing. Hints of images beamed through the wireless node that my brain had become.

"Hey," the kid said, knocking again. And I knew, from how I felt when I heard his voice, how doomed I was.

"Angel Quiñones," he said, when I opened the door. "Nicknamed Sauro because you look a big ol' Brontosaurus."

Actually my mom called me Sauro because I liked dinosaurs, but it was close enough. "Okay . . ." I said. I stepped aside and in he came.

"Case. My name's Case. Do you want me to continue with the dossier I've collected on you?" When I didn't do anything but stare at his face he said, "Silence is consent.

"Mostly Puerto Rican, with a little black and a little white in there somewhere. You've been here forever, but nobody knows anything about you. Just that you keep to yourself and don't get involved in anyone's hustles. And don't seem to have one of your own. And you could crush someone's skull with one hand."

A smile forced its way across my face, terrifying me.

With the blood all cleaned up, he looked like a kid. But faces can fool you, and the look on his could only have belonged to a full-grown man. So confident it was halfway to contemptuous, sculpted out of some bright stone. A face that made you forget what you were saying midsentence.

Speaking slowly, I said, "Don't—don't get." Breathe. "Don't get too into the say they stuff. Stuff they say. Before you know it, you'll be one of the brothers."

Case laughed. "Brothers," he said, and traced one finger up his very white arm. "I doubt anyone would ever get me confused with a brother."

"Not brothers like black. Brothers—they call us. That's what they call us. We're brothers because we all have the same parents. Because we all have none."

Why were the words there, then? Case smiled and out they came.

He reached out to rub the top of my head. "You're a mystery man, Sauro. What crazy stuff have you got going on in there?"

I shrugged. Bit back the cat-urge to push my head into his hand. Ignored the cloud-port itch flaring up fast and sharp.

Case asked, "Why do you shave your head?"

Because it's easier.

Because unlike most of these kids, I'm not trying to hide my cloud port.

Because a boy I knew, five homes ago, kept his head shaved, and when I looked at him I felt some kind of way inside. The same way I feel when I look at you. Case.

"I don't know," I said.

"It looks good though."

"Maybe that's why," I said. "What's your . . . thing. Dossier."

"Nothing you haven't heard before. Small-town gay boy, got beat up a lot. Came to the big city. But the city government doesn't believe a minor can make decisions for himself. So here I am. Getting fed and kept out of the rain while I plan my next move."

Gay boy. Unthinkable even to think it about myself, let alone ever utter it.

"How old? You."

"Seventeen." He turned his head, smoothed back sun-colored hair to reveal his port. "Well, they let you make your own decisions if they'll make money for someone else."

Again I was shocked. White kids were hardly ever so poor they needed the chump change you can get from cloudporting. Not even the ones who wanted real bad to be *down*. Too much potential for horrific problems. Bump it too hard against a headboard or doorframe and you might end up brain-damaged.

But that wasn't why I stared at him, dumbfounded. It was what he said, about making money for someone else. Like he could smell the anger on me. Like he had his own. I wanted to tell him about what I had learned, online. How many hundreds of millions of dollars the city spent every year to keep tens of thousands of us stuck in homes like Egan House. How many people had jobs because of kids like us. How if they had given my mom a quarter of what they've spent on me being in the system, she never would have lost her place. She never would have lost me. How we were all of us, ported or not, just batteries to be sucked dry by huge faraway machines I could not even imagine. But it was all I could do just to keep a huge and idiotic grin off my face when I looked at him.

The telecoms had paid for New York's municipal wireless grid, installing thousands of routers across all five boroughs. Rich people loved having free wireless everywhere, but it wasn't a public service. Companies did it because the technology had finally come around to where you could use the human brain for data processing, so they could wave money in the faces of hard-up people and say, *Let us put this tiny little wire into your brain and plug that into the wireless signal and exploit a portion of your brain's underutilized capacity, turning you into one node in a massively distributed data processing center.* It worked, of course. Any business model based around poor people making bad decisions out of ignorance and desperation always works. Just ask McDonald's, or the heroin dealer who used to sell to my mom.

The sun, at some point, had gotten lost behind a ragged row of tenements. Case said, "Something else they said. You're going to age out, any minute now."

"Yeah."

"That must be scary."

I grunted.

"They say most guys leaving foster care end up on the street."

"Most."

The street, the words like knives driven under all my toenails at once. The stories I had heard. Men frozen to death under express-ways, men set on fire by frat boys, men raped to death by cops.

"You got a plan?"

"No plan."

"Well, stick with me, kid," Case said, in fluent fake movie gang-ster. "I got a plan big enough for both of us. Do you smoke?" he asked, flicking out two. I didn't, but I took the cigarette. His fin-gers touched mine. I wanted to say, *It isn't allowed in here,* but Case's smile was a higher law.

"Where's a decent port shop around here? I heard the Bronx ones were all unhygienic as hell."

"Riverdale," I said. "That's the one I go to. Nice office. No one waiting outside to jump you."

"I need to establish a new primary," he said. "We'll go tomor-row." He smiled so I could see it wasn't a command so much as a decision he was making for both of us.

My mother sat on the downtown platform at Burnside, looking across the elevated tracks to a line of windows, trying to see some-thing she wasn't supposed to see. She was so into her voyeurism that she didn't notice me standing right beside her, uncomfortably close even though the platform was bare. She didn't look up until I said *mother* in Spanish, maybe a little too loud.

"Oh my god," she said, fanning herself with a damp *New York Post.* "Here I am getting here late, fifteen minutes, thinking oh my god he's gonna kill me, and come to find out that you're even later than me!"

"Hi," I said, squatting to kiss her forehead.

"Let it never be said that you got that from me. I'm late all the time, but I tried to raise you better."

"How so?"

"You know. To not make all the mistakes I did."

"Yeah, but how so? What did you do, to raise me better?"

"It's stupid hot out," she said. "They got air conditioning in that home?"

"In the office. Where we're not allowed."

We meet up once a month, even though she's not approved for

unsupervised visits. I won't visit her at home because her man is always there, always drunk, always able, in the course of an hour, to remind me how miserable and stupid I am. How horrible my life will become, just as soon as I age out. How my options are the streets or jail or overclocking; what they'll do to me in each of those places. So now we meet up on the subway, and ride to Brooklyn Bridge and then back to Burnside.

Arm flab jiggled as she fanned herself. Mom is happy in her fat. Heroin kept her skinny; crack gave her lots of exercise. For her, obesity is a brightly colored sign that says NOT ADDICTED ANYMORE. Her man keeps her fed; this is what makes someone a Good Man. Brakes screamed as a downtown train pulled into the station.

"Oooh, stop, wait," she said, grabbing at my pant leg with one puffy hand. "Let's catch the next one. I wanna finish my cigarette."

I got on the train. She came, too, finally, hustling, flustered, barely making it.

"What's gotten into you today?" she said, when she wrestled her pocketbook free from the doors. "You upset about something? You're never this," and she snapped her fingers in the air while she looked for the word *assertive*. I had it in my head. I would not give it to her. Finally she just waved her hand and sat down. "Oh, that air conditioning feels good."

"José? How's he?"

"Fine, fine," she said, still fanning from force of habit. Fifty-degree air pumped directly down on us from the ceiling ducts.

"And you?"

"Fine."

"Mom—I wanted to ask you something."

"Anything, my love," she said, fanning faster.

"You said one time that all the bad decisions you made—none of it would have happened if you could just keep yourself from falling in love."

When I'm with my mom my words never come out wrong. I think it's because I kind of hate her.

"I said that?"

"You did."

"Weird."

"What did you mean?"

"Christ, honey, I don't know." The *Post* slowed, stopped, settled into her lap. "It's stupid, but there's nothing I won't do for a man

I love. A woman who's looking for a man to plug a hole she's got inside? She's in trouble."

"Yeah," I said.

Below us, the Bronx scrolled by. Sights I'd been seeing all my life. The same sooty sides of buildings; the same cop cars on every block looking for boys like me. I thought of Case, then, and clean sharp joy pushed out all my fear. My eyes shut, from the pleasure of remembering him, and saw a glorious rush of ported imagery. Movie stills; fashion spreads; unspeakable obscenity. Not blurry this time; requiring no extra effort. I wondered what was different. I knew my mouth was open in an idiot grin, somewhere in a southbound subway car, but I didn't care, and I stood knee-deep in a river of images until the elevated train went underground after 161st Street.

WE ARE THE CLOUD, said the sign on the door, atop a sea of multi-colored dots with stylized wireless signals bouncing between them.

Walking in with Case, I saw that maybe I had oversold the place by saying it was "nice." Nicer than the ones by Lincoln Hospital, maybe, where people come covered in blood and puke, having left against medical advice after spasming out in a public housing stairwell. But still. It wasn't *actually* nice.

Older people nodded off on benches, smelling of shit and hunger. Gross as it was, I liked those offices. All those ports started a pleasant buzzing in my head. Like we added up to something.

"Look at that guy," Case said, sitting down on the bench beside me. He pointed to a man whose head was tilted back, gurgling up a steady stream of phlegm that had soaked his shirt and was dripping onto the floor.

"Overclocked," I said, and stopped. His shoulder felt good against my bicep. "Some people. Sell more than they should. Of their brain."

Sell enough of it, and they'd put you up in one of their Node Care Facilities, grim nursing homes for thirty-something vegetables and doddering senior citizens in their twenties, but once you were in you were never coming out, because people ported that hard could barely walk a block or speak a sentence, let alone obtain and hold meaningful employment.

And if I didn't want to end up on the street, that was my only real option. I'd been to job interviews. Some I walked into on my own; some the system set up for me. Nothing was out there for anyone, let alone a frowning, stammering tower of man who more than one authority figure had referred to as a "fucking imbecile."

"What about him?" Case asked, pointing to another guy whose hands and legs twitched too rhythmically and regularly for it to be a dream.

"Clouddiving," I said.

He laughed. "I thought only retards could do that."

"That's," I said. "Not."

"Okay," he said, when he saw I wouldn't be saying anything else on the subject.

I wanted very badly to cry. *Only retards.* A part of me had thought maybe I could share it with Case, tell him what I could do. But of course I couldn't. I fast-blinked, each brief shutting of my eyes showing a flurry of cloud-snatched photographs.

Ten minutes later I caught him smiling at me, maybe realizing he had said something wrong. I wanted so badly for Case to see inside my head. What I was. How I wasn't an imbecile, or a retard.

Our eyes locked. I leaned forward. Hungry for him to see me, the way no one else ever had. I wanted to tell him what I could do. How I could access data. How sometimes I thought I could maybe *control* data. How I dreamed of using it to burn everything down. But I wasn't strong enough to think those things, let alone say them. Some secrets you can't share, no matter how badly you want to.

I went back alone. Case had somewhere to be. It hurt, realizing he had things in his life I knew nothing about. I climbed the steps and a voice called from the front-porch darkness.

"Awful late," Guerra said. The stubby man who ran the place: most of his body weight was gristle and mustache. He stole our stuff and ate our food and took bribes from dealer residents to get rivals logged out. In the dark I knew he couldn't even see who I was.

"Nine," I said. "It's not. O'clock."

He sucked the last of his Coke through a straw, in the noisiest manner imaginable. "Whatever."

Salvation Army landscapes clotted the walls. Distant mountains and daybreak forests, smelling like cigarette smoke, carpet cleaner, thruway exhaust. There was a sadness to the place I hadn't noticed before, not even when I was hating it. In the living room, a boy knelt before the television. Another slept on the couch. In the poor light, I couldn't tell if one of them was the one who had hurt Case.

There were so many of us in the system. We could add up to an army. Why did we all hate and fear each other so much? Friendships formed from time to time, but they were weird and tinged with what-can-I-get-from-you, liable to shatter at any moment as allegiances shifted or kids got transferred. If all the violence we visited on ourselves could be turned outward, maybe we could—

But only danger was in that direction. I thought of my mom's man, crippled in a prison riot, living fat off the settlement, saying, drunk, once, *Only thing the Man fears more than one of us is a lot of us.*

I went back to my room and got down on the floor, under the window. And shut my eyes. And dove.

Into spreadsheets and songs and grainy CCTV feeds and old films and pages scanned from books that no longer existed anywhere in the world. Whatever the telecom happens to be porting through you at that precise moment.

Only damaged people can dive. Something to do with how the brain processes speech. Every time I did it, I was terrified. Convinced they'd see me, and come for me. But that night I wanted something badly enough to balance out the being afraid.

Eyes shut, I let myself melt into data. Shuffled faster and faster, pulled back far enough to see Manhattan looming huge and epic with mountains of data at Wall Street and Midtown. Saw the Bronx, a flat spread of tiny data heaps here and there. I held my breath, seeing it, feeling certain no one had ever seen it like this before, money and megabytes in massive spiraling loops, unspeakably gorgeous and fragile. I could see how much money would be lost if the flow was broken for even a single second, and I could see where all the fault lines lay. But I wasn't looking for that. I was looking for Case.

And then: Case came knocking. Like I had summoned him up from the datastream. Like what I wanted actually mattered outside of my head.

"Hey there, mister," he said, when I opened my door.

I took a few steps backward.

He shut the door and sat down on my bed. "You've got a Game

Boy, right? I saw the headphones." I didn't respond, and he said, "Damn, dude, I'm not trying to steal your stuff, okay? I have one of my own. Wondered if you wanted to play together." Case flashed his, bright red to my blue one.

"The thing," I said. "I don't have. The cable."

He patted his pants pocket. "That's okay, I do."

We sat on the bed, shoulders touching, backs against the wall, and played *Mega Man 2*. Evil robots came at us by the dozen to die.

I touched the cord with one finger. Such a primitive thing, to need a physical connection. Case smelled like soap, but not the Ivory they give you in the system. Like cream, I thought, but that wasn't right. To really describe it I'd need a whole new world of words no one ever taught me.

"That T-shirt looks good on you," he said. "Makes you look like a gym boy."

"I'm not. It's just . . . what there was. What was there. In the donation bin. Once Guerra picked out all the good stuff. Hard to find clothes that fit when you're six six."

"It does fit, though."

Midway through Skull Man's level, Case said, "You talk funny sometimes. What's up with that?" and I was shocked to see no anger surge through me.

"It's a thing. A speech thing. What you call it when people have trouble talking."

"A speech impediment."

I nodded. "But a weird one. Where the words don't come out right. Or don't come out at all. Or come out as the wrong word. Clouding makes it worse."

"I like it," he said, looking at me now instead of Mega Man. "It's part of what makes you unique."

We played without talking, tinny music echoing in the little room.

"I don't want to go back to my room. I might get jacked in the hallway."

"Yeah," I said.

"Can I stay here? I'll sleep on the floor."

"Yeah."

"You're the best, Sauro." And there were his hands again, rubbing the top of my head. He took off his shirt and began to make a bed on my floor. Fine black hair covers almost all of me, but Case's body was mostly bare. My throat hurt with how bad I wanted to put my hands on him. I got into bed with my boxers on, embarrassed by what was happening down there.

"Sauro," he whispered, suddenly beside me in the bed.
  I grunted; stumbled coming from dreams to reality.
  His body was spooned in front of mine. "Is this okay?"
  "Yes. Yes, it is." I tightened my arms around him. His warmth and smell stiffened me. And then his head had turned, his mouth was moving down my belly, his body pinning me to the bed, which was good, because God had turned off gravity and the slightest breeze would have had me floating right out the window and into space.

"You ever do this before? With a guy?"
  "Not out loud—I mean, not in real life."
  "You've thought about it."
  "Yeah."
  "You've thought about it a lot."
  "Yeah."
  "Why didn't you ever do it?"
  "I don't know."
  "You were afraid of what people might think?"
  "No."
  "Then what *were* you afraid of?"
  Losing control was what I wanted to say, or *giving someone power over me,* or *making a mess.*
  Or: *The boys that make me feel like you make me feel turn me into something stupid, brutish, clumsy, worthless.*
  Or: *I knew a gay kid once, in a group home upstairs from a McDonald's, watched twelve guys hold him down in a locked room until the morning guy came at eight, saw him when they wheeled him toward the ambulance.*
  I shrugged. The motion of my shoulders shook his little body.

I fought sleep as hard and long as I could. I didn't want to not be there. And when I knew I couldn't fight it anymore I let myself sink into data—easy as blinking this time—felt myself ebb out of my cloud port, but instead of following the random data beamed into me by the nearest router, I *reached*—felt my way across the endless black gulf of six inches that separated his cloud port from mine, and found him there, a jagged wobbly galaxy of data, ugly and incongruous, but beautiful, because it was *him,* and because, even if it was only for a moment, he was mine.

Case, I said.

He twitched in his sleep. Said his own name.

I love you, I said.

Asleep, Case said it, too.

Kentucky Fried Chicken. Thursday morning. For the first time, I didn't feel like life was a fight about to break out, or like everyone wanted to mess with me. Everywhere I went, someone wanted to throw me out — but now the only person who even noticed me was a crazy lady rooting through a McDonald's soda cup of change.

Case asked, "Anyone ever tell you you're a sexy beast?" On my baldness his hands no longer seemed so tiny. My big thick skull was an eggshell.

"Also? Dude? You're *huge.*" He nudged my crotch with his knee. "You know that? Like *off the charts.*"

"Yeah?"

I laughed. His glee was contagious and his hands were moving down my arm and we were sitting in public talking about gay sex and he didn't care and neither did I.

"When I first came to the city, I did some porn," Case said. "I got like five hundred dollars for it."

I chewed slow. Stared at the bones and tendons of the drumstick in my hand. Didn't look up. I thought about what I had done, while clouddiving. How I said his name, and he echoed me. I dreamed of taking him up to the roof at night, snapping my fingers and making the whole Bronx go dark except for Case's name, spelled out in blazing tenement window lights. It would be easy. I could do anything. Because: Case.

"Would you be interested in doing something like that?"

"No."

"Not even for like a million dollars?"

"Maybe a million. But probably not."

"You're funny. You know that? How you follow the rules. All they ever do is get you hurt."

"Getting in trouble means something different for you than it does for me."

Here's what I realized: It wasn't hate that made it easy to talk to my mom. It was love. Love let the words out.

"Why?" he asked.

"Because. What you are."

"Because I'm a sexy mother?"

I didn't grin back.

"Because I'm white."

"Yeah."

"Okay," he said. "Right. You see? The rules are not your friend. Racists made the rules. Racists enforce them."

I put the picked-clean drumstick down.

Case said, "Whatever," and the word was hot and long, a question, an accusation. "The world put you where you are, Sauro, but fear keeps you there. You want to never make any decisions. Drift along and hope everything turns out for the best. You know where that'll put you."

The lady with the change cup walked by our table. Snatched a thigh off of Case's plate. "Put that down right this minute, asshole," he said, loud as hell, standing up. For a second the country-bumpkin Case was gone, replaced by someone I'd never seen before. The lady scurried off. Case caught me staring and smiled, *aw-shucks* style.

"Stand up," I said. "Go by the window."

He went. Evening sun turned him into something golden.

Men used to paralyze me. My whole life I'd been seeing confident charismatic guys, and thought I could never get to that place. Never have what they had. Now I saw it wasn't what they *had* that I wanted, it was what they *were*. I felt lust, not inferiority, and the two are way too close. Like hate and love.

"You make me feel like food," he said, and then laid himself facedown on the floor. "Why don't you come over here?" Scissored his legs open. Turned his head and smiled like all the smiles I ever wanted but did not get.

Pushing in, I heard myself make a noise that can only be called a bellow.

"Shh," he said, "everyone will hear us."

My hips took on a life of their own. My hands pushed hard, all up and down his body. Case was tiny underneath me. A twig I could break.

Afterward I heard snoring from down the hall. Someone sobbed. I'd spent so long focused on how full the world was of horrible things. I'd been so conditioned to think that its good things were reserved for someone else that I never saw how many were already within my grasp. In my head, for one thing, where my thoughts were my own and no one could punish me for them, and in the cloud, where I was coming to see that I could do astonishing things. And in bed. And wherever Case was. My eyes filled up and ran over and I pushed my face into the cool nape of his sleeping neck.

My one and only time in court: I am ten. Mom bought drugs at a bodega. It's her tenth or hundredth time passing through those tall tarnished-bronze doors. Her court date came on one of my rare stints out of the system, when she cleaned up her act convincingly enough that they gave me briefly back to her.

The courtroom is too crowded; the guard tells me to wait outside. "But he's my son," my mother says, pointing out smaller children sitting by their parents.

I am very big for ten.

"He's gotta stay out here," the guard says.

I sit on the floor and count green flecks in the floor. Dark-skinned men surround me, angry but resigned, defiant but hopeless. The floor's sparkle mocks us: our poverty, our mortality, the human needs that brought us here.

"Where I'm from," Case said, "you could put a down payment on a house with two thousand dollars."

"Oh."

"You ever dream about escaping New York?"

"Kind of. In my head."

Case laughed. "What about you and me getting out of town? Moving away?"

My head hurt with how badly I wanted that. "You hated that place. You don't want to go back."

"I hated it because I was alone. If we went back together, I would have you."

"Oh."

His fingers drummed up and down my chest. Ran circles around my nipples. "I called that guy I know. The porn producer. Told him about you. He said he'd give us each five hundred, and another two-fifty for me as a finder's fee."

"You called him? About me?"

"This could be it, Sauro. A new start. For both of us."

"I don't know," I said, but I *did* know. I knew I was lost, that I couldn't say no, that his mouth, now circling my belly button, had only to speak and I would act.

"Are you really such a proper little gentleman?" he asked. His hands, cold as winter, hooked behind my knees. "You never got into trouble before?"

My one time in trouble.

I am five. It's three in the morning. I'm riding my tricycle down the block. A policeman stops me. *Where's your mother / She's home / Why aren't you home? / I was hungry and there's no food.* Mom is on a heroin holiday, lying on the couch while she's somewhere else. For a week I've been stealing food from corner stores. So much cigarette smoke fills the cop car that I can't breathe. At the precinct he leaves me there, windows all rolled up. Later he takes me home, talks to my mom, fills out a report, takes her away. Someone else takes me. Everything ends. All of this is punishment for some crime I committed without realizing it. I resolve right then and there to never again steal food, ride tricycles, talk to cops, think bad thoughts, step outside to get something I need.

Friday afternoon we rode the train to Manhattan. Case took us to a big building, no different on the outside from any other one. A directory on the wall listed a couple dozen tenants. *ARABY STUDIOS* was where we were going.

"I have an appointment with Mr. Goellnitz," Case told a woman at a desk upstairs. The place smelled like paint over black mold. We sat in a waiting room like a doctor's, except with different posters on the walls.

In one, a naked boy squatted on some rocks. A beautiful boy. Fine black hair all over his body. Eyes like lighthouses. Something about his chin and cheekbones turned my knees to hot jelly. Stayed with me when I shut my eyes.

"Who's that?" I asked.

"Just some boy," Case said.

"Does he work here?"

"No one *works here*."

"Oh."

Filming was about to start when I figured out why that boy on the rocks bothered me so much. I had thought only Case could get into my head so hard, make me feel so powerless, so willing to do absolutely anything.

A cinderblock room, dressed up like how Hollywood imagines the projects. Low ceilings and Snoop Dogg posters. Overflowing ashtrays. A pit bull dozing in a corner. A scared little white boy sitting on the couch.

"I'm sorry, Rico, you know I am. You gotta give me another chance."

The dark scary drug dealer towers over him. Wearing a wife beater and a bicycle chain around his neck. A hard-on bobs inside his sweatpants. "That's the last time I lose money on you, punk."

The drug dealer grabs him by the neck, rubs his thumb along the boy's lips, pushes his thumb into the warm wet mouth.

"*Do* it," Goellnitz barked.

"I can't," I said.

"Say the fucking line."

Silence.

"Or I'll throw your ass out of here and neither one of you will get a dime."

Case said, "Come on, dude! Just say it."

—and how could I disobey? How could I not do every little thing he asked me to do?

Porn was like cloudporting, like foster care. One more way they used you up.

One more weapon you could use against them.

I shut my eyes and made my face a snarl. Hissed out each word, one at a time, to make sure I'd only have to say it once.

"That's." "Right." "Bitch." I spat on his back, hit him hard in the head. "Tell." "Me." "You." "Like it." Off camera, in the mirror, Case winked.

Where did it come from, the strength to say all that? To say all that, and do all the other things I never knew I could do? Case gave it to me. Case, and the cloud, which I could feel and see now even with my eyes open, even without thinking about it, sweet and clear as the smell of rain.

*

"Damn, dude," Case said, while they switched to the next camera setup. "You're actually kind of a good actor with how you deliver those lines." He was naked; he was fearless. I cowered on the couch, a towel covering as much of me as I could manage. What was it in Case that made him so certain nothing bad would happen to him? At first I chalked it up to white skin, but now I wasn't sure it was so simple. His eyes were on the window. His mind was already elsewhere.

The showers were echoey, like TV high school locker rooms. We stood there, naked, side by side. I slapped Case's ass, and when he didn't respond I did it again, and when he didn't respond I stood behind him and kissed the back of his neck. He didn't say or do a thing. So I left the shower to go get dressed.

"Did I hurt you?" I hollered, when ten minutes had gone by and he was still standing under the water.

"What? No."

"Oh."

He wasn't moving. Wasn't soaping or lathering or rinsing.

"Is everything okay?" Making my voice warm, to hide how cold I suddenly felt.

"Yeah. It was just . . . intense. Sex usually isn't. For me."

His voice was weird and sad and not exactly nice. I sat on a bench and watched him get harder and harder to see as the steam built up.

"Would you mind heading up to the House ahead of me?" he said finally. "I need some time to get my head together. I'll square up things with the director and be there soon."

"Waiting is cool."

"No. It's not. I need some alone time."

"Alone time," I smirked. "You're a—"

"You need to get the hell back, Angel. Okay?"

Hearing the hardness in his voice, I wondered if there was a way to spontaneously stop being alive.

"I got your cash right here," the director said, flapping an envelope at me.

"He'll get it," I said, knowing it was stupid. "My boyfriend."

"You sure?"

I nodded.

"Here's my business card. I hoped you might think about being in something of mine again sometime. Your friend's only got a few more flicks in him. Twinks burn out fast. You, on the other hand —you've got something special. You could have a long career."

"Thanks," I said, nodding, furious, too tall, too retarded, too sensitive, hating myself the whole way down the elevator, and the whole walk to the subway, and the whole ride back to what passed for home.

When the train came above ground after 149th Street, I felt the old shudder as my cloud port clicked back into the municipal grid. Shame and anger made me brave, and I dove. I could see the car as data, saw transmissions to and from a couple dozen cell phones and tablets and biodevices, saw how the train's forward momentum warped the information flowing in and out. Saw ten jagged blobs inside, my fellow cloudbounds. Reached out again, like I had with Case. Felt myself slip through one after another like a thread through ten needles. Tugged that thread the tiniest bit, and watched all ten bow their heads as one.

Friday night I stayed up till three in the morning, waiting for Case to come knocking. I played the Skull Man level on *Mega Man 2* until I could beat it without getting hit by a single enemy. I dove into the cloud, hunted down maps, opened up whole secret worlds. I fell asleep like that, and woke up wet from fevered dreams of Case.

Saturday—still no sign of him.

Sunday morning I called Guerra's cell phone, a strict no-no on the weekends.

"This better be an emergency, Sauro," he said.

"Did you log Case out?"

"Case?"

"The white boy."

"You call me up to bother me with your business deals? No, jackass, I didn't log him out. I haven't seen him. Thanks for reminding me, though. I'll phone him in as missing on Monday morning."

"You—"

But Guerra had gone.

First thing Monday, I rode the subway into Manhattan and walked into that office like I had as much right as anyone else to occupy any square meter of space in this universe. I worried I wouldn't be able to, without Case. I didn't know what this new thing coming awake inside me was, but I knew it made me strong. Enough.

The porn man gave me a hundred dollars, no strings attached. Said to keep him in mind, said he had some scripts that I could "transform from low-budget bullshit into something really special."

He was afraid of me. He was right to be afraid, but not for the reason he thought. I could clouddive and wipe Araby Studios out of existence in the time it took him to blink his eyes. I could see his fear, and I could see how he wanted me anyway for the money he could make off me. There was so much to see, once you're ready to look for it.

Maybe I was right the first time: it *had* been hate that made it easy to talk to my mom. Love can make us become what we need to be, but so can hate. Case was gone, but the words kept coming. Life is nothing but acting.

I could have:

1. Given Guerra the hundred dollars to track Case down. He'd call his contacts down at the department; he'd hand me an address. Guerra would do the same job for fifty bucks, but for a hundred he'd bow and *yessir* like a good little lackey.
2. Smiled my way into every placement house in the city, knocked on every door to every tiny room until I found him.
3. Hung around outside Araby Studios, wait for him to snivel back with his latest big, dumb, dark stud. Wait in the shower until he went to wash his ass out, kick him to the floor, fuck him endlessly and extravagantly. Reach up into him, seize hold of his heart and tear it to shreds with bare bloody befouled hands.

The image of him in the shower brought me to a full and instant erection. I masturbated, hating myself, trying hard to focus on a scenario where I hurt him . . . but even in my own revenge fantasy I wanted to wrap my body around his and keep him safe.

Afterward I amended my revenge scenario list to include:

1. Finding someone else to screw over, some googly-eyed blond boy looking to plug a hole he has inside.

2. Becoming the most famous, richest, biggest gay porn star in history, traveling the world, standing naked on sharp rocks in warm oceans. Becoming what they wanted me to be, just long enough to get a paycheck. Seeing Case in the bargain bin someday; seeing him in the gutter.

3. Burning down every person and institution that profited off the suffering of others.

4. Becoming the kept animal of some rich, powerful queen who will parade me at fancy parties and give me anything I need as long as I do him the favor of regularly fucking him into a state of such quivering sweat-soaked helplessness that childhood trauma and white guilt and global warming all evaporate.

5. Finding someone who I will never, ever, ever screw over.

Really, they were all good plans. None of it was off the table.

Leaving the office building, I ignored all the instincts that screamed *Get on the subway and get the hell out of here before some cop stops you for matching a description!* Standing on a street corner for no reason felt magnificent and forbidden.

I shut my eyes. Reached out into the cloud, felt myself magnified like any other signal by the wireless routers that filled the city. Found the seams of the infrastructure that kept the flow of data in place. The weak spots. The ways to snap or bend or reconstruct that flow. How to erase any and all criminal records; pay the rent for my mom and every other sad sack in the Bronx for all eternity. Divert billions in banker dividends into the debit accounts of cloudporters everywhere.

I pushed, and when nothing happened I pushed harder.

A tiny *pop,* and smoke trickled up from the wireless router atop the nearest lamppost. Nothing more. My whole body dripped with sweat. Some dripped into my eyes. It stung. Ten minutes had passed, and felt like five seconds. My muscles ached like after a hundred pushups. All those things that had seemed so easy—I wasn't strong enough to do them on my own.

Fear keeps you where you are, Case said. Finally I could see that he was right, but I could see something else that he couldn't see. Because he thought small, and because he only thought about himself.

Fear keeps us separate.

I shut my eyes again, and reached. A ritzy part of town; hardly any cloudbounds in the immediate area. The nearest one was in a bar down the block.

"What'll you have," the bartender said when I got there. He didn't ask for ID.

"Boy on the rocks," I said, and then kicked at the stool. "Shit. No. Scotch. Scotch on the rocks."

"Sure," he said.

"And for that guy," I said, pointing down the bar to the passed-out overclocked man I had sensed from outside. "One. Thing. The same."

I took my drink to a booth in the front, where I could see out the window. I took a sip. I reached further, eyes open this time, until I found twenty more cloudporters, some as far as fifty blocks away, and threaded us together.

The slightest additional effort, and I was everywhere. All five boroughs—thousands of cloudporters looped through me. With all of us put together I felt inches away from snapping the city in two. Again I reached out and felt for optimal fracture points. Again I pushed. Gently, this time.

An explosion, faraway but huge. *Con Edison's East Side substation,* I saw, in the six milliseconds before the station's failure overloaded transmission lines and triggered a cascading failure that killed all electricity to the tristate region.

I smiled, in the darkness, over my second sip. Within a week the power would be back on. And I—we—could get to work. Whatever that would be. Stealing money; exterminating our exploiters; leveling the playing field. Finding Case, forging a cyberterrorism manifesto, blaming the blackout on him, sending a pulse of electricity through his body precisely calibrated to paralyze him perfectly.

On my third sip I saw I still wasn't sure I wanted to hurt him. Maybe he'd done me wrong, but so had my mom. So had lots of folks. And I wouldn't be what I was without them.

Scotch tastes like smoke, like old men. I drank slow so I wouldn't get too drunk. I had never walked into a bar before. I always imagined cops coming out of the corners to drag me off to jail. But that wasn't how the world worked. Nothing was stopping me from walking into wherever I wanted to go.

DANIEL H. WILSON

The Blue Afternoon
That Lasted Forever

FROM *Carbide Tipped Pens*

"IT'S LATE AT night, my darling. And the stars are in the sky.
That means it is time for me to give you a kiss. And an Eskimo kiss.
And now I will lay you down and tuck you in, nice and tight, so you
stay warm all night."

This is our mantra. I think of it like the computer code I use
to control deep space simulations in the laboratory. You recite the
incantation and the desired program executes.

I call this one "bedtime."

Marie holds her stuffed rabbit close, in a chokehold. In the dim
light, a garden of blond hair grows over her pillow. She is three
years old and smiling and she smells like baby soap. Her eyes are
already closed.

"I love you, honey," I say.

As a physicist, it bothers me that I find this acute feeling of love
hard to quantify. I am a man who routinely deals in singularities
and asymptotes. It seems like I should have the mathematical vocabulary to express these things.

Reaching for her covers, I try to tuck Marie in. I stop when I feel
her warm hands close on mine. Her brown eyes are black in the
shadows.

"No," she says, "I do it."

I smile until it becomes a wince.

This version of the bedtime routine is buckling around the
edges, disintegrating like a heat shield on reentry. I have grown to

love tucking the covers up to my daughter's chin. Feeling her cool
damp hair and the reassuring lump of her body, safe in her big-girl
bed. Our routine in its current incarnation has lasted one year two
months. Now it must change. Again.

I hate change.

"O.K.," I murmur. "You're a big girl. You can do it."

Clumsily and with both hands, she yanks the covers toward her
face. She looks determined. Proud to take over this task and exert
her independence. Her behavior is consistent with normal child
development according to the books I checked out from the library. Yet I cannot help but notice that this independence is a
harbinger of constant unsettling, saddening change.

My baby is growing up.

In the last year, her body weight has increased 16 percent. Her
average sentence length has increased from seven to ten words.
She has memorized the planets, the primary constellations, and
the colors of the visible spectrum. Red orange yellow green blue
indigo violet. These small achievements indicate that my daughter is advanced for her age, but she isn't out of the record books
or into child genius territory. She's just a pretty smart kid, which
doesn't surprise me. Intelligence is highly heritable.

"I saw a shooting star," she says.

"Really? What's it made of?" I ask.

"Rocks," she says.

"That's right. Make a wish, lucky girl," I reply, walking to the door.

I pause as long as I can. In the semidarkness, a stuffed bear is
looking at me from a shelf. It is a papa teddy bear hugging its baby.
His arms are stitched around the baby's shoulders. He will never
have to let go.

"Sweet dreams," I say.

"Good night, Daddy," she says, and I close the door.

The stars really are in Marie's bedroom.

Two years ago I purchased the most complex and accurate
home planetarium system available. There were no American
models. This one came from a Japanese company and it had to be
shipped here to Austin, Texas, by special order. I also purchased
an international power adapter plug, a Japanese-to-English translation book, and a guide to the major constellations.

I had a plan.

Soon after the planetarium arrived, I installed it in my bedroom.

Translating the Japanese instruction booklet as best I could, I calibrated the dedicated shooting star laser, inserted the disk that held a pattern for the Northern Hemisphere, and updated the current time and season. When I was finished, I went into the living room and tapped my then-wife on the shoulder.

Our anniversary.

My goal was to create a scenario in which we could gaze at the stars together every night before we went to sleep. I am interested in astrophysics. She was interested in romantic gestures. It was my hypothesis that sleeping under the faux stars would satisfy both constraints.

Unfortunately, I failed to recall that I wear glasses and that my then-wife wore contact lenses. For the next week, we spent our evenings blinking up at a fuzzy Gaussian shotgun-spray of the Milky Way on our bedroom ceiling. Then she found the receipt for the purchase and became angry. I was ordered to return the planetarium and told that she would rather have had a new car.

That didn't seem romantic to me, but then again I'm not a domain expert.

My thin translation book did not grant me the verbal fluency necessary to negotiate a return of the product to Japan. In response, my then-wife told me to sell it on the Internet or whatever. I chose to invoke the "whatever" clause. I wrapped the planetarium carefully in its original packaging and put it into the trunk of my car. After that, I stored it in the equipment room of my laboratory at work.

Three months later, my then-wife informed me that she was leaving. She had found a job in Dallas and would try to visit Marie on the weekends, but no promises. I immediately realized that this news would require massive life recalibrations. This was upsetting. I told her as much and my then-wife said that I had the emotional capacity of a robot. I decided that the observation was not a compliment. However, I did not question how my being a robot might affect my ability to parent a one-and-a-half-year-old. Contrary to her accusation, my cheeks were stinging with a sudden cold fear at the thought of losing my daughter. My then-wife must have seen the question in the surface tension of my face, because she answered it anyway.

She said that what I lacked in emotion, I made up for in structure. She said that I was a terrible husband but a good father.

Then-wife kissed Marie on the head and left me standing in the driveway with my daughter in my arms. Marie did not cry when her mother left because she lacked the cognitive capacity to comprehend what had happened. If she had known, I think she would have been upset. Instead, my baby only grinned as her mother drove away. And because Marie was in such good spirits, I slid her into her car seat and drove us both to my laboratory. Against all regulations, I brought her into my workspace. I dug through the equipment stores until I found the forbidden item.

That night I gave my daughter the stars.

The cafeteria where I work plays the news during lunch. The television is muted but I watch it anyway. My plastic fork is halfway to my mouth when I see the eyewitness video accompanying the latest breaking news story. After that, I am not very aware of what is happening except that I am running.

I don't do that very much. Run.

In some professions, you can be called into action in an emergency. A vacationing doctor treats the victim of an accident. An off-duty pilot heads up to the cockpit to land the plane. I am not in one of those professions. I spend my days crafting supercomputer simulations so that we can understand astronomical phenomena that happened billions of years ago. That's why I am running alone. There are perhaps a dozen people in the world who could comprehend the images I have just seen on the television—my colleagues, fellow astrophysicists at research institutions scattered around the globe.

I hope they find their families in time.

The television caption said that an unexplained astronomical event has occurred. I know better than that. I am running hard because of it, my voice making a whimpering sound in the back of my throat. I scramble into my car and grip the hot steering wheel and press the accelerator to the floor. The rest of the city is still behaving normally as I weave through traffic. That won't last for long, but I'm thankful to have these few moments to slip away home.

My daughter will need me.

There is a nanny who watches Marie during the day. The nanny has brown hair and she is five feet four inches tall. She does not have a scientific mind-set but she is an artist in her spare time.

When Marie was ten months old and had memorized all of her body parts (including the phalanges), I became excited about the possibilities. I gave the nanny a sheet of facts that I had compiled about the states of matter for Marie to memorize. I intentionally left off the quark-gluon plasma state and Bose-Einstein condensate and neutron-degenerate matter because I wanted to save the fun stuff for later. After three days I found the sheet of paper in the recycling bin.

I was a little upset.

Perez in the cubicle next to me said that the nanny had done me a favor. He said Marie has plenty of time to learn about those things. She needs to dream and imagine and, I don't know, finger-paint. It is probably sound advice. Then again, Perez's son is five years old, and at the department picnic the boy could not tell me how many miles it is to the troposphere. And he says he wants to be an astronaut. Good luck, kid.

Oh, yes. Running.

My brain required four hundred milliseconds to process the visual information coming from the cafeteria television. Eighty milliseconds for my nervous system to respond to the command to move. It is a two-minute sprint to the parking lot. Then an eight-minute drive to reach home. Whatever happens will occur in the next thirty minutes and so there is no use in warning the others.

Here is what happened.

An hour and thirty-eight minutes ago, the sky blushed red as an anomaly streaked over the Gulf of Mexico. Bystanders described it as a smear of sky and clouds, a kind of glowing reddish blur. NASA reported that it perturbed the orbital paths of all artificial satellites, including the International Space Station. It triggered tsunamis along the equator and dragged a plume of atmosphere a thousand miles into the vacuum of space. The air dispersed in low pressure but trace amounts of water vapor froze into ice droplets. On the southern horizon, I can now see a fading river of diamonds stretching into space. I don't see the moon in the sky but that doesn't mean it isn't there. Necessarily.

All of this happened within the space of thirty seconds.

This is not an unexplained astronomical event. The anomaly had no dust trail, was not radar-detectable, and it caused a tsunami.

Oh, and it turned the sky red.

Light does funny things in extreme gravity situations. When a high-mass object approaches, every photon of light that reaches our eyes must claw its way out of a powerful gravity well. Light travels at a constant speed, so instead of slowing down, the photon sacrifices energy. Its wavelength drops down the visible spectrum: violet indigo blue green yellow orange red.

Redshifting.

I am running because only one thing could redshift our sky that much and leave us alive to wonder why our mobile phones don't work. What passed by has to have been a previously theoretical class of black hole with a relatively small planet-sized mass—compressed into a singularity potentially as small as a pinprick. Some postulate that these entities are starving black holes that have crossed intergalactic space and shrunk over the billions of years with nothing to feed on. Another theory, possibly complementary, is that they are random crumbs tossed away during the violence of the big bang.

Perez in the next cubicle said I should call them "black marbles," which is inaccurate on several fronts. In my papers, I chose instead to call them pinprick-sized black holes. Although Perez and I disagreed on the issue of nomenclature, our research efforts brought consensus on one calculation: that the phenomenon would always travel in clusters.

Where there is one, more will follow.

Tornado sirens begin to wail as I careen through my suburban neighborhood. The woman on the radio just frantically reported that something has happened to Mars. The planet's crust is shattered. Astronomers are describing a large part of the planet's mass as simply missing. What's left behind is a cloud of expanding dirt and rapidly cooling magma, slowly drifting out of orbit and spreading into an elliptical arc.

She doesn't say it out loud, but it's dawning on her: we are next.

People are standing in their yards now, on the sidewalks and grass, eyes aimed upward. The sky is darkening. The wind outside the car window is whispering to itself as it gathers occasionally into a thin, reedy scream. A tidal pull of extreme gravity must be doing odd things to our weather patterns. If I had a pen and paper, I could probably work it out.

I slam on the brakes in my driveway to avoid hitting the nanny. She is standing barefoot, holding a half-empty sippy cup of milk. Chin pointed at the sky. Stepping out of the car, I see my first pinprick-sized black hole. It is a reddish dot about half the intensity of the sun, wrapped in a halo of glowing, superheated air. It isn't visibly moving so I can't estimate its trajectory. On the southern horizon, the crystallized plume of atmosphere caused by the near-miss still dissipates.

It really is beautiful.

"What is it?" asks the nanny.

"Physics," I say, going around the car and opening my trunk. "You should go home immediately."

I pull out a pair of old jumper cables and stride across the driveway. Marie is standing just inside the house, her face a pale flash behind the glass storm door. Inside, I lift my daughter off the ground. She wraps her legs around my hip and now I am running again, toys crunching under my feet, my daughter's long hair tickling my forearm. The nanny has put it into a braid. I never learned how to do that. Depending on the trajectory of the incoming mass, I may not ever have the chance.

"What did you do today?" I ask Marie.

"Played," she says.

Trying not to pant, I crack open a few windows in the house. Air pressure fluctuations are a certainty. I hope that we only have to worry about broken glass. There is no basement to hide in here, just a cookie-cutter house built on a flat slab of concrete. But the sewer main is embedded deep into the foundation. In the worst case, it will be the last thing to go.

I head to the bathroom.

"Wait here for just a second," I say, setting Marie down in the hallway. Stepping into the small bathroom, I wind up and violently kick the wall behind the toilet until the drywall collapses. Dropping to my knees, I claw out chunks of the drywall until I have exposed the main sewer line that runs behind the toilet. It is a solid steel pipe maybe six inches in diameter. With shaking hands, I shove the jumper cable around it. Then I wedge myself between the toilet and the outside wall and I sit down on the cold tile floor, the jumper cables under my armpits anchoring me to the ground. This is the safest place that I can find.

If the black hole falling toward us misses the planet, even by a few thousand miles, we may survive. If it's a direct hit, we'll share the fate of Mars. At the sonic horizon, sound won't be able to escape from it. At the event horizon, neither will light. Before that can happen we will reach a Lagrange point as the anomaly cancels out Earth's gravity. We will fall into the sky and be swallowed by that dark star.

The anomaly was never detected, so it must have come from intergalactic space. The Oort cloud is around a light-year out, mostly made of comets. The Kuiper-Edgeworth belt is on the edge of the solar system. Neither region had enough density to make the black hole visible. I wonder what we were doing when it entered our solar system. Was I teaching Marie the names of dead planets?

"Daddy?" asks Marie.

She is standing in the bathroom doorway, eyes wide. Outside, a car engine revs as someone speeds past our house. A distant, untended door slams idiotically in the breeze. Marie's flowery dress shivers and flutters over her scratched knees in the restless calm.

"Come here, honey," I say in my most reassuring voice. "Come sit on my lap."

Hesitantly, she walks over to me. The half-open window above us is a glowing red rectangle. It whistles quietly as air is pulled through the house. I tie the greasy jumper cable cord in a painfully tight knot around my chest. I can't risk crushing her lungs, so I wrap my arms around Marie. Her arms fall naturally around my neck, hugging tight. Her breath is warm against my neck.

"Hold on to your daddy very tight," I say. "Do you understand?"

"But why?" she asks.

"Because I don't want to lose you, baby," I say, and my sudden swallowed tears are salty in the back of my throat.

Whips are cracking in the distance now. I hear a scream. Screams.

A gust of wind shatters the bathroom window. I cradle Marie closer as the shards of glass are sucked out of the window frame. A last straggler rattles in place like a loose tooth. The whip cracks are emanating from loose objects that have accelerated upward past the speed of sound. The *crack-crack-crack* sound is thousands of sonic booms. They almost drown out the frightened cries of people who are falling into the sky. Millions must be dying this way. Billions.

"What is that?" asks Marie, voice wavering.

"It's nothing, honey. It's all right," I say, holding her to me. Her arms are rubber bands tight around my neck. The roof shingles are rustling gently, leaping into the sky like a flock of pigeons. I can't see them, but it occurs to me that the direction they travel will be along the thing's incoming trajectory. I watch that rattling piece of glass that's been left behind in the window frame, my lips pressed together. It jitters and finally takes flight *straight up.*

A fatal trajectory. A through-and-through.

"What's happening?" Marie asks, through tears.

"It's the stars, honey," I say. "The stars are falling."

It's the most accurate explanation I can offer.

"Why?" she asks.

"Look at Daddy," I say. I feel a sudden lightness, a gentle tug pulling us upward. I lean against the cables to make sure they are still tight. "Please look at your daddy. It will be O.K. Hold on tight."

Nails screech as a part of the roof frame curls away and disappears. Marie is biting her lips to keep her mouth closed and nodding as tears course over her cheeks. I have not consulted the child development books, but I think she is very brave for three years old. Only three trips around the sun and now the sun is going to end. Sol will be teased apart in hundred-thousand-mile licks of flame.

"My darling," I say. "Can you tell me the name of the planet that we live on?"

"Earth."

"And what is the planet with a ring around it?"

"S-Saturn."

"What are the rings made of?"

"Mountains of ice."

Maybe a sense of wonder is also a heritable trait.

"Are the stars—"

Something big crashes outside. The wind is shrieking now in a new way. The upper atmosphere has formed into a vortex of supersonic air molecules.

"Daddy?" screams Marie. Her lips are bright and bitten, tear ducts polishing those familiar brown eyes with saline. A quivering frown is dimpling her chin, and all I can think of is how small she is compared to all this.

"Honey, it's O.K. I've got you. Are the stars very big or very small?"

"Very big," she says, crying outright now. I rock her as we speak, holding her to my chest. The cables are tightening and the sewer main is a hard knuckle against my spine. Marie's static-charged hair is lifting in the fitful wind.

"You're right again. They look small, but they're very big. The stars are so very, very big."

A subsonic groan rumbles through the frame of the house. Through the missing roof I can see that trees and telephone poles and cars are tumbling silently into the red eye overhead. Their sound isn't fast enough to escape. The air in here is chilling as it thins, but I can feel heat radiating down from that hungry orb.

Minutes now. Maybe seconds.

"Daddy?" Marie asks.

Her lips and eyes are tinged blue as her light passes me. I'm trying to smile for her, but my lips have gone spastic. Tears are leaking out of my eyes, crawling over my temples, and dripping up into the sky. The broken walls of the house are dancing. A strange light is flowing in the quiet.

The world is made of change. People arrive and people leave. But my love for her is constant. It is a feeling that cannot be quantified because it is not a number. Love is a pattern in the chaos.

"It is very late, my darling," I say. "And the stars are in the sky."

They are so very big.

"And that means it's time for me to give you a kiss. And an Eskimo kiss."

She leans up for the kiss by habit. Her tiny nose mushing into mine.

"And now . . ."

I can't do this.

"And now I will lay you down . . ."

Swallow your fear. You are a good father. Have courage.

"And tuck you in, nice and tight, so you stay warm all night."

The house has gone away from us and I did not notice. The sun is a sapphire eye on the horizon. It lays gentle blue shadows over a scoured wasteland.

And a red star still falls.

"Goodnight, my darling."

I hold her tight as we rise together into the blackness. The view around us expands impossibly and the world outside speeds up in a trick of relativity. A chaotic mass of dust hurtles past and disappears. In our last moment together, we face a silent black curtain of space studded with infinite unwavering pinpricks of light.

We will always have the stars.

Skullpocket

FROM *Nightmare Carnival*

Jonathan wormcake, the Gentleman Corpse of Hob's Landing, greets me at the door himself. Normally one of his several servants would perform this minor duty, and I can only assume it's my role as a priest in the Church of the Maggot that affords me this special attention. I certainly don't believe it has anything to do with our first encounter, fifty years ago this very day. I'd be surprised if he remembers that at all.

He greets me with a cordial nod of the head and leads me down a long hallway to the vast study, lined with thousands of books and boasting broad windows overlooking the Chesapeake Bay, where the waters are painted gold by an autumn sun. I remember this walk, and this study, with a painful twinge in my heart. I was just a boy when I came here last. Now, like Mr. Wormcake, I am an old man, and facing an end to things.

I'm shocked by how old he looks. I know I shouldn't be; Mr. Wormcake's presence in this mansion by the bay extends back one hundred years, and his history with the town is well documented. But since the death of the Orchid Girl last year, he has withdrawn from public life, and in that time his aspect has changed considerably. Though his bearing remains regal and his grooming is as immaculate as ever, age hangs from him like a too-large coat. The flesh around his head is entirely gone, and his hair—once his proudest feature—is no more. The bare bones of his skull gleam brightly in the late-afternoon sunlight, and the eyes which once transfixed an entire town have fallen to dust, leaving dark sockets. He looks frail, and he looks tired.

To be fair, the fourteen children crowding the room, all between the ages of six and twelve, only underscore this impression.
They've been selected for the honor of attending the opening ceremonies of the Seventieth Annual Skullpocket Fair by the Maggot,
which summoned them here through their dreams. The children
are too young, for the most part, to understand the significance
of the honor, and so they mill about the great study in nervous
anticipation, chattering to each other and touching things they
shouldn't.

Mr. Wormcake's longtime manservant—formally known as
Brain in a Jar 17, of the Frozen Parliament, but who is more af-
fectionately recognized as the kindly "Uncle Digby"—glides into
the room, his body a polished, gold-inlaid box on rolling treads,
topped with a clear dome under which the floating severed head
of an old man is suspended in a bubbling green solution, white
hair drifting like ghostly kelp. He is received with a joyful chorus
of shouts from the children, who immediately crowd around him.
He embraces the closest of them with his metal arms.

"Oh my, look at all these wonderful children," he says. "What
animated little beasts!"

To anyone new to Hob's Landing, Uncle Digby can be unnerv-
ing. His face and eyes are dead, and his head appears to be nothing more than a preserved portion of a cadaver; but the brain inside is both alive and lively, and it speaks through a small voice box
situated beneath the glass dome.

While the children are distracted, Mr. Wormcake removes a
small wooden box from where it sits discreetly on a bookshelf. He
opens it and withdraws the lower, fleshy portion of a human face
—from below the nose to the first curve of the chin, kept moist in
a thin pool of blood. A tongue is suspended from it by a system of
leather twine and gears. Mr. Wormcake affixes the half face to his
skull by means of an elastic band and pushes the tongue into his
mouth. Blood trickles down the jawline of the skull and dapples
the white collar of his starched shirt. The effect is disconcerting,
even to me, who has grown up in Hob's Landing and am accustomed to stranger sights than this.

Jonathan Wormcake has not ventured into public view for
twenty years, since the denuding of his skull, and it occurs to me
that I am the first person not a part of this household to witness
this procedure.

I am here because Mr. Wormcake is dying. We don't know how a ghoul dies. Not even he is sure, as he left the warrens as a boy and was never indoctrinated into the mysteries. The dreams given to us by the Maggot, replete with images of sloughing flesh and great black kites riding silently along the night's air currents, suggest that it's not an ending but a transformation. But we have no experience to measure these dreams against. What waits for him on the far side of this death remains an open question.

He stretches open his mouth and moves his tongue like a man testing the fit of a new article of clothing. Apparently satisfied, he looks at me at last. "It's good of you to come, especially on this night," he says.

"I have to admit I was surprised you chose the opening night of Skullpocket Fair for this. It seems there might have been a more discreet time."

He looks at the children gathered around Uncle Digby, who is guiding them gently toward the great bay window facing east, where the flat waters of the Chesapeake are painted gold by the late-afternoon sun. They are animated by excitement and fear, a tangle of emotions I remember from when I was in their place. "I have no intention of stealing their moment," he says. "This night is about them. Not me."

I'm not convinced this is entirely true. Though the children have been selected to participate in the opening ceremonies of Skullpocket Fair and will be the focus of the opening act, the pomp and circumstance is no more about them than it is about the Maggot, or the role of the church in this town. Really, it's all about Jonathan Wormcake. Never mind the failed mayoral campaign of the midseventies, never mind the fallout from the Sleepover Wars or the damning secrets made public by the infamous betrayal of his best friend, Wenceslas Slipwicket — Wormcake is the true patriarch of Hob's Landing; the Skullpocket Fair is held each year to celebrate that fact, and to fortify it.

That this one marks the one hundredth anniversary of his dramatic arrival in town, and his ritual surrendering of this particular life, makes his false modesty a little hard to take.

"Sit down," he says, and extends a hand toward the most comfortable chair in the room: a high-backed, deeply cushioned piece of furniture of the sort one might expect to find in the drawing room of an English lord. It faces the large windows, through which we are afforded a view of the sun-flecked waters of the Chesapeake Bay. Mr. Wormcake maneuvers another, smaller chair away from the chess table in the corner and closer to me, so we can speak more easily. He eases himself slowly into it and sighs with a weary satisfaction as his body settles, at last, into stillness. If he had eyes, I believe he would close them now.

Meanwhile, Uncle Digby has corralled the children into double rows of folding chairs, also facing the bay windows. He is distributing soda and little containers of popcorn, which do not calm the children but do at least draw their focus.

"Did you speak to any of the children after they received the dream?" Wormcake asks me.

"No. Some of them were brought to the church by their parents, but I didn't speak to any of them personally. We have others who specialize in that kind of thing."

"I understand it can be a traumatic experience for some of them."

"Well, it's an honor to be selected by the Maggot, but it can also be pretty terrifying. The dream is very intense. Some people don't respond well."

"That makes me sad."

I glance over at the kids, seated now, the popcorn spilling from their hands, shoveled into their mouths. They bristle with a wild energy: a crackling, kinetic radiation that could spill into chaos and tears if not expertly handled. Uncle Digby, though, is nothing if not an expert. The kindliest member of the Frozen Parliament, he has long been the spokesman for the family, as well as a confidant to Mr. Wormcake himself. There are many who believe that without his steady influence, the relationship between the Wormcakes and the townspeople of Hob's Landing would have devolved into brutal violence long ago.

"The truth is, I don't want anyone to know why you're here. I don't want my death to be a spectacle. If you came up here any other night, someone would notice, and it wouldn't be hard for them to figure out why. This way, the town's attention is on the fair. And anyway, I like the symmetry of it."

"Forgive me for asking, Mr. Wormcake, but my duty here demands it: are you doing this because of the Orchid Girl's death?"

He casts a dark little glance at me. It's not possible to read emotion in a naked skull, of course, and the prosthetic mouth does not permit him any range of expression; but the force of the look leaves me no doubt of his irritation. "The Orchid Girl was her name for the people in town. Her real name was Gretchen. Call her by that."

"My apologies. But the question remains, I'm afraid. To leave the world purely, you must do it unstained by grief."

"Don't presume to teach me about the faith I introduced to you."

I accept his chastisement quietly.

He is silent for a long moment, and I allow myself to be distracted by the sound of the children gabbling excitedly to each other, and of Uncle Digby relating some well-worn anecdote about the time the Leviathan returned to the bay. Old news to me, but wonderful stuff to the kids. When Mr. Wormcake speaks again, it is to change course.

"You mentioned the dream which summons the children as being intense. This is not your first time to the house, is it?"

"No. I had the dream myself, when I was a kid. I was summoned to Skullpocket Fair. Seventy years ago. The very first one."

"My, my. Now that is something. Interesting that it's you who will perform my death ritual. So that puts you in your eighties? You look young for your age."

I smile at him. "Thanks, but I don't feel young."

"Who does, anymore? I suppose I should say 'welcome back.'"

The room seems host to a dizzying compression of history. There are three fairs represented tonight, at least for me: the Seventieth Annual Skullpocket Fair, which commences this evening; the first, which took place in 1944 — seventy years ago, when I was a boy — and set my life on its course in the church; and the Cold Water Fair of 1914, a hundred years ago, which Uncle Digby would begin describing very shortly. That Mr. Wormcake has chosen this night to die, and that I will be his instrument, seems too poetic to be entirely coincidental.

As if on cue, Uncle Digby's voice rings out, filling the small room. "Children, quiet down now, quiet down. It's time to begin." The kids settle at once, as though some spell has been spoken. They sit meekly in their seats, the gravity of the moment settling over them at last. The nervous energy is pulled in and contained, expressing itself now only in furtive glances and, in the case of one buzz-cut little boy, barely contained tears.

I remember, viscerally and immediately, the giddy terror that filled me when I was that boy, seventy years ago, summoned by a dream of a monster to a monster's house. I'm surprised when I feel the tears in my own eyes. And I'm further surprised by Mr. Wormcake's hand, hard and bony beneath its glove, coming over to squeeze my own.

"I'm glad it's you," he says. "Another instance of symmetry. Balance eases the heart."

I'm gratified, of course.

But as Uncle Digby begins to speak, it's hard to remember anything but the blood.

One hundred years ago, *says Uncle Digby to the children,* three little ghouls came out to play. They were Wormcake, Slipwicket, and Stubblegut: best friends since birth. They were often allowed to play in the cemetery, as long as the sun was down and the gate was closed. There were many more children playing among the gravestones that night, but we're only going to concern ourselves with these three. The others were only regular children, and so they were not important.

Now, there were two things about this night that were already different from other nights they went aboveground to play. Does anybody know what they were?

No? Well, I'll tell you. One was that they were let out a little bit earlier than normal. It was still twilight, and though sometimes ghouls were known to leave the warrens during that time, rarely were children permitted to come up so early. That night, however, the Maggot had sent word that there was to be a meeting in the charnel house—an emergency meeting, to arrange a ritual called an Extinction Rite, which the children did not understand but which seemed to put the adults in a dreadfully dull mood. The children had to be got out of the way. There might have been some discussion about the wisdom of this decision, but ghouls are by nature a calm and reclusive folk, so no one worried that anything untoward would happen.

The other unusual thing about that night, obviously, was the Cold Water Fair.

The Cold Water Fair had been held for years and years, and it was a way for Hob's Landing to celebrate its relationship with the Chesapeake Bay, and to commemorate the time the Leviathan rose to devour the town but was turned away with some clever thinking and some good advice. This was the first time the fair was held on this side of Hob's Landing. In previous years it had been held on the northern side of the town, out of sight of the cemetery. But someone had bought some land and got grumpy about the fair being on it, so now they were holding it right at the bottom of the hill instead.

The ghoul children had never seen anything so wonderful! Imagine living your life in the warrens, underground, where everything was stone and darkness and cold earth. Whenever you came up to play, you could see the stars, you could see the light on the water, and you could even see the lights from town, which looked like flakes of gold. But this! Never anything like this. The fair was like a smear of bright paint: candy-colored pastels in the blue wash of air. A great illuminated wheel turned slowly in the middle of it, holding swinging gondola cars full of people.

"A Ferris wheel!" shouts a buzz-cut boy who had been crying only a few minutes ago. His face is still ruddy, but his eyes shine with something else now: something better.

Yes, you're exactly right. A Ferris wheel! They had never even seen one before. Can you imagine that?

There were gaudy tents arranged all around it, like a little village. It was full of amazing new smells: cotton candy, roasting peanuts, hot cider. The high screams of children blew up to the little ghouls like a wind from a beautiful tomb. They stood transfixed at the fence, those grubby little things, with their hands wrapped around the bars and their faces pressed between.

They wondered briefly if this had anything to do with the Extinction Rite the adults kept talking about.

"Do you think they scream like that all the time?" Slipwicket asked.

Wormcake said, "Of course they do. It's a fair. It's made just for screaming."

In fact, children, he had no idea if this was true. But he liked to pretend he was smarter than everybody else, even way back then.

The children laugh. I glance at Mr. Wormcake, to gauge his reaction to what is probably a scripted joke, but his false mouth, blood pasted to his skull, reveals nothing.

Slipwicket released the longest, saddest sigh you have ever heard. It would have made you cry, it was so forlorn. He said, "Oh, how I would love to go to a place made only for screams." *Uncle Digby is laying it on thick here, his metal hands cupping the glass jar of his head, his voice warbling with barely contained sorrow. The kids eat it up.*

"Well, we can't," said Stubblegut. "We have to stay inside the fence."

Stubblegut was the most boring ghoul you ever saw. You could always depend on him to say something dull and dreadful. He was morose, always complaining, and he never wanted to try anything new. He was certain to grow up to be somebody's father, that most tedious of creatures. Sometimes the others would talk about ditching him as a friend, but they could never bring themselves to do it. They were good boys, and they knew you were supposed to stay loyal to your friends—even the boring ones.

"Come along," Stubblegut said. "Let's play skullpocket."

At this, a transformation overtakes the children, as though a current has been fed into them. They jostle in their seats, and cries of "Skullpocket!" arise from them like pheasants from a bramble. They seem both exalted and terrified. Each is a little volcano, barely contained.

Oh, my! Do you know what skullpocket is, children?

"Yes, yes!"

"I do!"

"Yes!"

Excellent! In case any of you aren't sure, skullpocket is a favorite game of ghouls everywhere. In simple terms, you take a skull and kick it back and forth between your friends until it cracks to pieces. Whoever breaks it is the loser of the game, and has to eat what they find inside its pocket. And what is that, children?

"The brain!"

"Eeeww!"

That's right! It's the brain, which everyone knows is the worst bit. It's full of all the gummy old sorrows and regrets gathered in life, and the older the brain is, the nastier it tastes. While the loser eats, other players will often dance in a circle around him and chant. And what do they chant?

"Empty your pockets! Empty your pockets!" the children shout.

Yes! You must play the game at a run, and respect is given to those who ricochet the skull off a gravestone to their intended target, increasing the risk of breaking it. Of course you don't have to do that—you can play it safe and just bat it along nicely—but nobody likes a coward, do they, children? For a regular game, people use adult skulls which have been interred for less than a year. More adventurous players might use the skull of an infant, which offers a wonderful challenge.

Well, someone was sent to retrieve a skull from the charnel house in the warrens, which was kept up by the corpse gardeners. There was always one to be spared for children who wanted to play.

The game was robust, with the ghouls careening the skull off trees and rocks and headstones; the skull proved hardy and it went on for quite some time.

Our young Mr. Wormcake became bored. He couldn't stop thinking about that fair, and the lights and the smells and—most of all—the screams. The screams filled his ears and distracted him from play. After a time, he left the game and returned to the fence, staring down at the fair. It had gotten darker by that time, so that it stood out in the night like a gorgeous burst of mushrooms.

Slipwicket and Stubblegut joined him.

"What are you doing?" said the latter. "The game isn't over. People will think you're afraid to play."

"I'm not afraid," said Wormcake. And in saying the words, a resolution took shape in his mind. "I'm not afraid of anything. I'm going down there."

His friends were shocked into silence. It was an awed silence, a holy silence, like the kind you find in church. It was the most outrageous thing they had ever heard anyone say.

"That's crazy," Stubblegut said.

"Why?"

"Because it's forbidden. Because the sunlight people live down there."

"So what?"

"They're gross!"

At this, some of the children become upset. Little faces crinkle in outrage.

Now, hold on, hold on. You have to understand how ghouls saw your people at the time. You were very strange to them. Hob's Landing was as exotic to them as a city on the moon would be to you. People went about riding horses, and they walked around in sunlight. On purpose, for Pete's sake! Who ever heard of such a thing?

The children start to giggle at this, won over again.

When they came to the cemetery they acted sad and shameful.

They buried their dead the way a cat buries its own scat. They were soft and doughy, and they ate whatever came to hand, the way rats and cockroaches do.

"We're not cockroaches!" cries one of the children.

Of course not! But the ghouls didn't understand. They were afraid. So they made up wild ideas about you. And it kept their children from wandering, which was important, because they wanted the warrens to stay a secret. Ghouls had been living under the cities of the sunlight people for as long as there have *been* sunlight people, and for the most part they had kept their existence hidden. They were afraid of what would happen if they were discovered. Can you blame them for that?

But young Mr. Wormcake was not to be dissuaded by rumors or legends!

"I'm going down there. I want to see what it's all about."

Back then, the cemetery gate was not burdened with locks or chains; it simply had a latch, oiled and polished, which Wormcake lifted without trouble or fanfare. The gate swung open, and the wide, bright world spread out before them like a feast at the banquet table. He turned to look at his friends. Behind them, the other children had assembled in a small crowd, the game of skullpocket forgotten. The looks on their faces ranged from fear to excitement to open disgust.

"Well?" he said to his friends. "Are you cowards?"

Slipwicket would not be called a coward! He made a grand show of his exit, lifting each foot with great exaggeration over the threshold and stomping it into the earth with a flourish. He completed his transgression with a happy skip and turned to look at Stubblegut, who lingered on the grave side of the fence and gathered his face into a worried knot. He placed his hands over his wide belly and gave it gentle pats, which was his habit when he was nervous.

At that moment of hesitation, when he might have gone back and warned the adults of what was happening, some unseen event in the fair below them caused a fresh bouquet of screams to lift up and settle over the ghouls like blown leaves. Slipwicket's whole body seemed to lean toward it, like he was being pulled by a great magnet. He looked at Stubblegut with such longing in his eyes, such a terrible ache, that his frightened friend's resolve was breached at last, and Stubblegut crossed the threshold himself with a grave and awful reluctance.

He was received with joy.

And before anyone could say jackrabbit, Slipwicket bolted down the hill, a pale little gremlin in the dark green waves of grass. The others followed him in a cool breath of motion, the tall grass like a strange, rippling sea in the moonlight. Of course, they were silent in their elation: the magnitude of their crime was not lost upon them. Wormcake dared not release the cry of elation beating in his lungs.

But, children, they were in high rebellion. They were throwing off the rules of their parents and riding the wave of their own cresting excitement. Even Stubblegut felt it, like a blush of heat over his moss-grown soul.

Naturally, Uncle Digby's story stirs up memories of my own first fair.

The dream of the Maggot came to me in 1944, when I was twelve years old. The tradition of the Cold Water Fair had ended thirty years before, on the bloody night Uncle Digby is speaking of, and Hob's Landing had done without a festival of any sort since. But though we didn't know it yet, this would be the year the Skull-pocket Fair was begun.

I was the sixth kid to receive the dream that year. I had heard of a couple of the others, so I had known, in some disconnected way, that it might happen. I didn't know what it meant, except that parents were terrified of it. They knew it had something to do with the Wormcake clan, and that was enough to make it suspect. Although this was in 1944 and they'd been living in the mansion for thirty years at that point—peacefully for the most part—there were still many in town who considered them to be the very incarnation of evil. Many of our parents were present at the night of the Cold Water Fair, and they were slow to forgive. The fact that the Orchid Girl came into town and patronized the same shops we did, attended the same shows we did, didn't help matters at all, as far as they were concerned.

She's putting on airs, they said. She thinks she's one of us. At least her husband has the decency to keep himself hidden away in that horrible old mansion.

My friends and I were too young to be saddled with all of the old fears and prejudices of our parents, and anyway we thought the Orchid Girl was beautiful. We would watch her from across the street or through a window when she came to town, walking down Poplar Street as proud as you please, unattended by her servants or by any friends at all. She always wore a bright, lovely dress which swirled around her legs, kept her hair pinned just so, and held her head high—almost defiantly, I can say now, looking back. We would try to see the seams on her face, where it would open up, but we never got close enough. We never dared.

We believed that anyone married to the Orchid Girl couldn't be all bad. And anyway, Mr. Wormcake always came to the school plays, brought his own children down to the ice-skating rink in the wintertime, and threw an amazing Halloween party. Admittedly, half the town never went, but most of us kids managed to make it over there.

We all knew about the Church of the Maggot. There were already neighborhoods converting, renouncing their own god for the one that burrowed through flesh. Some people our parents' age, also veterans of that night at the fair, had even become priests. They walked around town in grubby white garb, talking on and on about the flesh as meat, the necessity of cleansing the bone, and other things that sounded strange and a little exciting to us. So when some of the children of Hob's Landing started to dream of the Maggot, the kids worried about it a lot less than the parents or the grandparents did. At first we were even jealous. Christina Laudener, just one year younger than I was, had the first one, and the next night it was little Eddie Brach. They talked about it in school, and word spread. It terrified them, but we wanted it ourselves nonetheless. They were initiates into some new mystery centered around the Wormcakes, and those of us who were left out burned with a terrible envy.

I was probably the worst of them, turning my jealousy into a bullying contempt whenever I saw them at the school, telling them that the ghouls were going to come into their homes while they were sleeping and kidnap them, so they could feed them to their precious Maggot. I made Eddie cry, and I was glad. I hated him for being a part of something I wasn't.

Until a couple of nights later, when I had the dream myself.

I'm told that everyone experiences the dream of the Maggot differently. For me it was a waking dream. I climbed out of bed at some dismal hour of the morning, when both my parents were still asleep, and stumbled my way to the bathroom. I sat on the toilet for a long time, waiting for something to happen, but I couldn't go, despite feeling that I needed to very badly. I remember this being a source of profound distress in the dream, way out of proportion to real life. It terrified me and I felt that it was a sign I was going to die.

I left the toilet and walked down the hallway to my parents' room, to give them the news of my impending demise. In my dream I knew they would only laugh at me, and it made me hate them.

Then I felt a clutching pain in my abdomen. I dropped to my knees and began to vomit maggots. Copious amounts of them. They wouldn't stop coming, just splashed out onto the ground with each painful heave, in wriggling piles, ropy with blood and saliva. It went on and on and on. When I stood up, my body was as wrinkled and crushed as an emptied sack. I fell to the floor and had to crawl back to my room.

The next morning I went down to breakfast as usual, and as my father bustled about the kitchen, looking for his keys and his hat, and my mother leaned against the countertop with a cigarette in her hand, I told them that I had received the dream everyone was talking about.

This stopped them both cold. My mother looked at me and said, "Are you sure? What happened? What does it mean?"

"They're having a fair. I have to go."

Of course this was absurd; there had been nothing about a fair in the dream at all. But the knowledge sat with all the incontrovertibility of a mountain. Such is the way of the Maggot.

"What fair?" Dad said. "There's no fair."

"The Wormcakes," I said. "They're having it at the mansion."

My parents exchanged a look.

"And they invited you in a dream?" he said.

"It wasn't really like an invitation. It's more like the Maggot told me I have to come."

"It's a summons," Mom told him. "That's what Carol was saying. It's like a command."

"Like hell," Dad said. "Who do those freaks think they are?"

"I think I have to go, Dad."

"You don't have to do a goddamned thing they tell you. None of us do."

I started to cry. The thought of disregarding the dream was unthinkable. I felt that clenching in my gut and I feared the maggots were going to start pouring out of my mouth. I thought I could feel them inside me already, chewing away, as though I were already dead. I didn't know how to articulate what I know now: that the Maggot had emptied me out and was offering to fill me again. To ignore it would be to live the rest of my life as a husk.

It was a hard cry, as sudden as a monsoon, my cheeks hot and red, the tears painting my face, my breath coming in a thin hiss. Mom rushed to me and engulfed me in her arms, saying the things moms are supposed to say.

"I have to go," I said. "I have to go, I have to. I have to go."

I watch the children sitting there in profile, their little faces turned to Uncle Digby and his performance like flowers to the sun, and I try to see myself there all those years ago. The sun is setting outside, and in the eastern-facing window darkness is hoarding over the bay. The light in Uncle's glass dome illuminates the green solution from beneath, and his pale dead face is graced with a rosy pink halo of light.

I must have seen the same thing when I sat there with the other kids. But I don't remember it. I only remember the fear. I guess I must have laughed at the jokes, just like the others did.

Skullpocket is, of course, a culling game. It's not about singling out and celebrating a winner. It's about thinning the herd.

Jonathan Wormcake does not appear to be listening to the story anymore. His attention is outside, on the darkening waters. Although her name has not come up yet, the Orchid Girl haunts this story as truly as any ghost. I wonder if it causes him pain. Grieving, to a ghoul, is a sign of weakness. It's a trait to be disdained. The grieving are not fit for the world. I look at the hard, clean curve of his skull and I try to fathom what's inside.

They were clever little ghouls, *Uncle Digby said,* and they kept to the outskirts and the shadows. They didn't want to be discovered. A ghoul child looks a lot like a human child when seen from the corner of the eye. It's true that they're paler, more gaunt, and if you look at one straight on you'll see that their eyes are like little black holes with nothing inside, but you have to pay attention to notice any of that. At the fair, no one was paying attention. There was too much else to see. So Wormcake and his friends were able to slip into the crowd without notice, and there they took in everything they could.

They were amazed by the striped, colorful tents, by the little booths with the competitive games, by the pens with pigs and mules, by the smells of cotton candy, frying oil, animal manure, electricity—everything was new and astonishing. Most of all, though, they marveled at the humans in their excitable state: walking around, running, hugging, laughing, and clasping their hands on each other's shoulders. Some were even crushing their lips together in a grotesque human version of a kiss!

Here the children laugh. They are young enough still that all kissing is grotesque.

There were many little ones, like themselves, and like you. They were swarming like hungry flies, running from tent to tent, waiting in lines, crackling with an energy so intense you could almost see it arcing from their hair.

It was quite unsettling to see humans acting this way. It was like watching someone indulging in madness. They were used to seeing humans in repose, quiet little morsels in their thin wooden boxes. Watching them like this was like watching a little worm before it transforms into a beautiful fly, but worse, because it was so much louder and uglier.

A little girl raises her hand. She seems angry. When Uncle Digby acknowledges her, she says, "I don't think flies are beautiful. I think they're nasty."

"Well, I think you're the one who's nasty," Uncle Digby retorts. "And soon you'll be filling the little tummies of a thousand thousand flies, and they'll use you to lay eggs and make maggots, and shit out the bits of you they don't want. So maybe you should watch your horrid little mouth, child."

The little girl bursts into shocked tears, while the children around her stay silent or laugh unhappily.

Wormcake stirs beside me for the first time since the story began. "Uncle," he says.

"I'm sorry," says Uncle Digby. "Dear child, please forgive me. Tonight is a glorious night. Let's get back to the story, shall we?"

The children are quiet. Uncle Digby forges ahead.

So they made their way among the humans, disturbed by their antics. They knew that it was only a matter of time before the humans all reached their true state, the condition in which they would face the long dark inside the earth; but this brief, erratic explosion of life stirred a fascinated shame in the ghouls.

"It's vile," said Stubblegut. "We shouldn't be seeing this. It's indecent."

"It's the most wonderful thing I've ever seen," said young master Wormcake, and with the courage that had always separated him from the others, he strode out onto the midway, arms a-swing and head struck back like the world's littlest worm lord.

You might be forgiven in thinking that *someone* would notice and cause the humans to flee from them in terror, or cry out in alarm, or gather pitchforks and torches. But human beings are geniuses at self-delusion. Let's be honest, children, you are. You believe that your brief romance with the sun is your one, true life. Our little friend here, for example, becomes upset when contemplating the beauty of the fly. You cherish your comfortable delusions. That evening the humans at the fair just looked at the ghouls as wretched examples of their own kind. Sickly children, afflicted with some mysterious wasting illness that blued their flesh and tightened the skin around their bones. Pathetic creatures, to be mourned and fretted over, even if they also inspired a small thrill of revulsion. So the humans pretended not to see them. They ushered their own children to a safe distance and continued in their revels in a state of constructed ignorance.

Mr. Wormcake leans over to me and whispers in my ear: "Not entirely true. The human adults ignored us, yes. But the human children knew us for what we were. They pointed and quaked. Some burst into tears. It was all such fun."

What was so difficult to tell my parents, all those years ago, was that I *wanted* to go to the fair. The summons was terrifying, yes, but it was also the touch of relevance I'd been wanting so badly. I was just like Christina Laudener now; I was just like weepy Eddie Brach. Two other children had had the dream the same night I did, and by the time a week had finished, there were fourteen of us. The dreams stopped after that, and everyone understood that it was to be us, and only us.

We became a select group, a focus of envy and awe. There were some who felt the resentment I once did, of course, and we were the target of the same bullying I'd doled out myself. But we were a group by this time, and we found comfort and safety in that. We ate lunch together at school, hung out on weekends. The range of ages—six to twelve—was wide enough that normally none of us would give each other the time of day. But the Maggot had changed everything.

The town was abuzz with talk. Of the fourteen summoned children, certainly, but also of the fair itself. Hob's Landing had been without anything like this since the night of Wormcake's arrival, thirty years before. That Wormcake himself should be the one to reintroduce a fair to the town seemed at once sacrilegious and entirely appropriate. Fliers began to appear, affixed to telephone poles, displayed in markets and libraries: The First Annual Skullpocket Fair, to Be Held on the Grounds of Wormcake Mansion, on the Last Weekend of September, 1944. Inaugurated by Select Children of Hob's Landing. Come and Partake in the Joy of Life with the Gentleman Corpse!

People were intrigued. That Mr. Wormcake was himself using the nickname he'd once fiercely objected to—he was not, he often reminded them, a corpse—was a powerful indicator that he meant to extend an olive branch to the people of Hob's Landing. And who were they to object? He and his family clearly weren't going anywhere. Wouldn't it be best, then, to foster a good relationship with the town's most famous citizens?

My parents were distraught. Once they realized I wanted to go, despite my panic of the first night, they forbade me. That didn't worry me a bit, though. I knew the Maggot would provide a way. I was meant to be there, and the Maggot would organize the world in such a way as to make that happen.

And so it did. On the afternoon the first Skullpocket Fair was set to open, I headed for the front door, expecting a confrontation. But my parents were sitting together in the living room, my mother with her hands drawn in and her face downcast, my father looking furious and terrified at once. They watched me go to the door without making any move to interfere. Years later, I was to learn that the night before they had received their own dream from the Maggot. I don't know what that dream contained, but I do know that no parent has ever tried to interfere with the summons.

These days, of course, few would want to.

"Be careful," Mom said, just before I closed the door on them both.

The others and I had agreed to meet in front of the drugstore. Once we'd all assembled, we walked as a group through the center of town, past small gathered clusters of curious neighbors, and up the long road that would take us to the mansion by the bay.

The sun was on its way down.

They rode the Ferris wheel first, *says Uncle Digby*. From that height they looked down at the fair, and at Hob's Landing, and at their own cemetery upon the hill. Away from the town, near the coastline, was an old three-story mansion, long abandoned and believed haunted. Even the adult ghouls avoided the place, during their rare midnight excursions into town. But it was only one part of the tapestry.

The world was a spray of light on a dark earth. It was so much bigger than any of them had thought. As their car reached the height of its revolution and they were bathed in the high cool air of the night, Wormcake was transfixed by the stars above them. They'd never seemed so close before. He sought out the constellations he'd been taught—the Rendering Pot, the Moldy King— and reached his hands over his head, trailing his fingers among them. As the gondola swung down again, it seemed he was dragging flames through the sky.

"Let's never go home again," Wormcake said. If the others heard him, they never said so.

And unknown to them, under the hill of graves, their parents were very busy setting up the Extinction Rite. Were the boys missed? I think they must have been. But no one could do anything about it.

What's next, children? What is it you really came to hear about?

It's as though he's thrown a lit match into a barrel of firecrackers. They all explode at once.

"The freak show!"

"The freak tent!"

"Freak show, freak show!"

Uncle Digby raises his metal arms and a chuckle emits from the voice box beneath the jar. The bubbles churn with a little extra gusto around his floating head, and I think, for a moment, that it really is possible to read joy in that featureless aspect. Whatever tensions might have been festering just a few moments ago, they're all swept aside by the manic excitement generated by the promise of the freaks. This is what they've been waiting to hear.

Yes, well, oh my, what a surprise. I thought you wanted to learn more about ghoul history. Maybe learn the names of all the elders? Or learn how they harvested food from the coffins? It's really a fascinating process, you know.

"Nooooo!"

Well, well, well. The freaks it is, then.

The ghouls stopped outside a tent striped green and white, where an old man hunched beside a wooden clapboard sign. On that sign, in bright red paint, was that huge, glorious word: FREAKS. The old man looked at the boys with yellowing eyes—the first person to look at them directly all night—and said, "Well? Come to see the show, or to join it?"

He tapped the sign with a long finger, drawing their attention back to it. Beneath the word FREAKS was a list of words in smaller size, painted in an elegant hand. Words like *The Most Beautiful Mermaid in the World, The Giant with Two Faces,* and—you guessed it —*The Orchid Girl.*

"Go on in, boys. Just be careful they let you out again."

They joined the line going inside. Curtains partitioned the interior into three rooms, and the crowd was funneled into a line. Lanterns hung from poles, and strings of lights crisscrossed the top of the tent.

The first freak was a man in a cage. He was seven feet tall, dressed in a pair of ratty trousers. He looked sleepy, and not terribly smart. He hadn't shaved in some time, his beard bristling like a thicket down his right cheek and jowl. The beard grew spottily on the left side, mostly because of the second face which grew there: doughy and half formed, like a face had just slid down the side of the head and bunched up on the neck. It had one blinking blue eye, and a nose right next to it, where the other eye should have been. And there was a big, gaping mouth, nestled between the neck and shoulder, with a little tongue that darted out to moisten the chapped lips.

A sign hanging below his cage said, BRUNO: EATER OF CHILDREN.

The ghouls were fascinated by the second face, but the eating children part didn't seem all that remarkable to them. They'd eaten plenty themselves.

Next up was THE WORLD'S MOST BEAUTIFUL MERMAID. This

one was a bit frustrating, because she was in a tank, and she was lying on the bottom of it. The scaly flesh of her tail was pressed up against the glass, so at first they thought they were looking at nothing more than a huge carp. Only after staring a moment did they notice the human torso which grew from it, curled around itself to hide from the gaze of the visitors. It was a woman's back, her spine ridged along her sun-dark skin. Long black hair floated around her head like a cloud of ink from an octopus.

Finally they progressed into the next partition, and they came to THE ORCHID GIRL.

She stood on a platform in the back of the tent, in a huge bell jar. She was just about your age, children. She was wearing a bright blue dress, and she was sitting down with her arms wrapped around her legs, looking out balefully at the crowds of people coming in to see her. She looked quite unhappy. She did not look, at first blush, like a freak; the only thing unusual about her were what appeared to be pale red scars running in long, S-like curves down her face.

Well, here was another disappointing exhibit, the people thought, and they were becoming quite agitated. Someone yelled something at her, and there was talk of demanding their money back.

But everything changed when Wormcake and his friends entered the room. The Orchid Girl sat a bit straighter, as if she had heard or felt something peculiar. She stood on her feet and looked out at the crowd. Almost immediately her gaze fell upon the ghoul children, as though she could sense them through some preternatural ability, and then, children, the most amazing thing happened. The thing that changed the ghouls' lives, her own life, and the lives of everyone in Hob's Landing forever afterward.

Her face opened along the red lines and bloomed in bright, glorious petals of white and purple and green. Her body was only a disguise, you see. She was a gorgeous flower masquerading as a human being.

The people screamed, or dropped to their knees in wonder. Some scattered like roaches in sunlight.

Wormcake and his friends ran, too. They fled through the crowd and back out into the night. They were not afraid; they were caught in the grip of destiny. Wormcake, suddenly, was in love. He fled from the terror and the beauty of it.

*

It was the Orchid Girl who greeted us at the door when we arrived. She looked ethereal. She was in her human guise, and the pale lines dividing her face stood out brightly in the afternoon sun. I was reminded, shamefully, of one of the many criticisms my mother levied against her: "She really should cover that with makeup. She looks like a car accident survivor. It's disgraceful."

To us, though, she looked like a visitation from another, better world.

"Hello, children. Welcome to our house. Thank you for joining us."

That we didn't have a choice—the summons of the Maggot was not to be ignored—didn't enter our minds. We felt anointed by her welcome. We knew we'd been made special, and that everyone in Hob's Landing envied us.

She led us into the drawing room—the one that would host every meeting like this for years to come—where Uncle Digby was waiting to tell us the story. We knew him already through his several diplomatic excursions into town, and were put at ease by his presence. The Orchid Girl joined her husband in two chairs off to the side, and they held hands while they listened.

I sat next to Christina Laudener. We were the oldest. The idea of romantic love was still alien to us, but not so alien that I didn't feel a twinge when I saw Mr. Wormcake and his wife holding hands. I felt as though I were in the grip of some implacable current, and that my life was being moved along a course that would see me elevated far beyond my current circumstance. As though I were the hero of a story, and this was my first chapter. I knew that Christina was a part of it. I glanced at her, tried to fathom whether or not she felt it, too. She caught my look and gave me the biggest smile I'd ever received from a girl, before or since.

I have kept the memory of that smile with me, like a lantern, for the small hours of the night. I call upon it, with shame, even now.

The Maggot disapproves of sentiment.

Do you know what an Extinction Rite is, children? *Uncle Digby asks.*

A few of the children shake their heads. Others are still, either afraid to answer the question or unsure of what their answer ought to be.

On the night of the Cold Water Fair, all those years ago, the ghouls under the hill had reached the end of their age. Ghoul society, unlike yours, recognizes when its pinnacle is behind it. Once this point has been reached, there are two options: assimilate into a larger ghoul city, or die. The ghouls under the hill did not find a larger city to join, and indeed many did not want to anyway. Their little city had endured for hundreds of years, and they were tired. The Maggot had delivered to the elders a dream of death, and so the Extinction Rite was prepared. The Extinction Rite, children, is the suicide of a city.

Like you, I am not a ghoul. I have never seen this rite performed. But also like you, I belong to the church introduced to Hob's Landing by Mr. Wormcake, so I can imagine it. I believe it must be a sight of almost impossible beauty. But I am glad he did not participate that night. Do you know what would have happened here in town if he had?

He looks at the little girl who talked back earlier. What do you think, dear?

She takes a long moment. "I don't know. Nothing?"

Precisely. Nothing would have happened. They would have gone back inside when called, just like old Stubblegut wanted. They would have missed the fair. They would never have met the Orchid Girl, or dear old Bruno, or the lost caravan leader of the mermaid nation. I myself would still be frozen in the attic, with my sixteen compatriots, just another brain in a jar. The Extinction Rite would have scoured away all the ghouls in the hill, and the people of Hob's Landing would have been none the wiser. Their little town would now be just another poverty-ridden fishing village, slowly dissolving into irrelevance.

Instead, what happened was this:

The ghoul children ran out of the tent that night, their little minds atilt with the inexplicable beauties they had just seen. It was as though the world had cracked open like some wonderful geode. They were exhilarated. They stood in the thronged midway, wondering what they ought to do next. Slipwicket and Stubblegut wanted to celebrate; the memory of their unfinished game of skullpocket was cresting in their thoughts, and the urge to recommence the game exerted itself upon them like the pull of gravity. Wormcake thought only of the Orchid Girl, imprisoned like a princess in one of the old tales, separated from him by a thin sheet of glass and by the impossible chasm of an alien culture.

And unbeknownst to them, in the warrens, the Extinction Rite reached its conclusion, and the will of the ghouls was made known to their god.

And so the Maggot spoke. Not just to these children, but to every ghoul in the city under the hill. A pulse of approval, a wordless will to proceed.

The Maggot said, *DO IT.*

What happened then was an accident. The Extinction Rite was not meant to affect the people of Hob's Landing at all. If Wormcake and the others had been at home, where they belonged, the Maggot's imperative would have caused them to destroy themselves. But they were not at home. And so what they heard was permission to indulge the desires of their hearts. And so they did.

Slipwicket fell upon the nearest child and tore the flesh from his skull like the rind from an orange, peeling it to the bone in under a minute. Stubblegut, caught in the spirit of the moment, chose to help him. Bright streamers of blood arced through the air over their heads, splashed onto their faces. They wrestled the greasy skull from the body and Slipwicket gave it a mighty kick, sending it bouncing and rolling in a jolly tumble down the midway.

Wormcake made his way back into the tent, slashing out with his sharp little fingers at the legs of anybody who failed to get out of his way quickly enough, splitting tendons and cracking kneecaps, leaving a bloody tangle of crippled people behind him.

Above them all, the cemetery on the hill split open like a rotten fruit. From the exposed tunnels beneath the upturned clods of earth and tumbling gravestones came the spirits of the extinguished city of the ghouls: a host of buzzing angels, their faceted eyes glinting moonlight, their mandibles a-clatter, pale, iridescent wings filling the sky with the holy drone of the swarm.

People began to scream and run. Oh, what a sound! It was like a symphony. It was just what Wormcake and his friends had been hoping for when they first looked down at the fair and heard the sounds carrying to them on the wind. They felt like grand heroes in a story, with the music swelling to match their achievements.

Slipwicket and Stubblegut batted the skull between them for a few moments, but it proved surprisingly fragile when careening off a fencepost. Of course there was nothing to do but get another. So they did, and, preparing for future disappointments, they quickly decided that they should gather a whole stockpile of them.

Wormcake opened Bruno's cage and smashed the Orchid Girl's glass dome, but he was afraid to smash the mermaid's tank, for fear that she would die. Bruno—who had become great friends with her—lifted her out and hastened her down to the water, where she disappeared with a grateful wave. When he returned to the party, the ghouls were delighted to discover that he was called the Eater of Children for very good reason indeed. The Orchid Girl stood off to the side, the unfurling spirits of the cemetery rising like black smoke behind her, the unfurled petals of her head seeming to catch the moonlight and reflect it back like a strange lantern. Wormcake stood beside her and together they watched as the others capered and sported.

Beautiful carnage. Screams rising in scale before being choked off in the long dark of death, people swarming in panic like flies around a carcass, corpses littering the ground in outlandish positions one never finds in staid old coffins. Watching the people make the transition from antic foolishness to the dignified stillness of death reassured Wormcake of the nobility of their efforts, the rightness of their choices. He recognized the death of his home, but he was a disciple of the Maggot, after all, and he felt no grief for it.

What did the two of them talk about, standing there together, surrounded by death's flowering? Well, young master Wormcake never told me. But I bet I can guess, just a little bit. They were just alike, those two. Different from everyone else around them, unafraid of the world's dangers. They recognized something of themselves in each other, I think. In any case, when they were finished talking, there was no doubt that they would take on whatever came next together.

It was the Orchid Girl who spotted the procession of torches coming from Hob's Landing.

"We should go to the mansion," she said. "They won't follow us there."

What happened next, children, is common knowledge, and not part of tonight's story. The Orchid Girl was right: the people of Hob's Landing were frightened of the mansion and did not follow them there. Wormcake and his friends found a new life inside. They found me, and the rest of the Frozen Parliament, up in the attic; they found the homunculus in the library; and of course, over time, they found all the secrets of the strange old alchemist who used to live there, which included the Orchid Girl's hidden history. Most importantly, though, they made themselves into a family. Eventually they even fashioned a peace with Hob's Landing and were able to build relationships with people in the town.

That was the last night the Cold Water Fair was ever held in Hob's Landing. With fourteen dead children and a family of monsters moved into the old mansion, the citizens of the town had lost their taste for it. For the better part of a generation, there was little celebration at all in the little hamlet. Relations between the Wormcake family and the townsfolk were defined by mutual suspicion, misunderstanding, and fear. Progress was slow.

Thirty years later, relations had repaired enough that Mr. Wormcake founded the Skullpocket Fair. To commemorate the night he first came to Hob's Landing, found the love of his life, and began his long and beneficial relationship with this town, where he would eventually become the honored citizen you all know him as today.

How wonderful, yes, children?

And now, at last, we come to why the Maggot called you all here!

"So many lies."

This is what Mr. Wormcake tells me, after Uncle Digby ushers the children from the drawing room. The sun has set outside, and the purpling sky seems lit from behind.

"You know, he tells the story for children. He leaves out some details. That night in the freak tent, for instance. The people gathered around the mermaid were terrifying. There was a feral rage in that room. I didn't know what it was at the time. I was just a kid. But it was a dark sexual energy. An animal urge. They slapped their palms against her tank. They shouted at her. Said horrible things. She was curled away from them, so they couldn't see her naked, and that made them angry. I was afraid they would try to break the glass to get at her. I think it was only the fear of Bruno the cannibal, in the other room, somehow getting out, too, that stopped them. I don't know.

"And that bit about me recognizing my 'destiny' when I saw the Orchid Girl—Gretchen. Nonsense. What child of that age feels romantic love? I was terrified. We all were. We'd just seen a flower disguised as a girl. What were we supposed to think?"

"I'm curious why you let Uncle Digby call her the Orchid Girl to the kids, when the name obviously annoys you."

"It's simplistic. It's her freak name. But you humans seem so invested in that. She was no more 'the Orchid Girl' than I'm 'the Gentleman Corpse.' I'm not a corpse at all, for god's sake. But when we finally decided to assimilate, we believed that embracing the names would make it easier. And the kids like it, especially. So we use them."

"Is it hard to talk about her?" Probing for signs of blasphemy.

"No," he says, though he looks away as he says it. The profile of his skull is etched with lamplight. He goes on about her, though, and I start to get a sick feeling. "He would have you believe that she was a princess in a castle, waiting to be rescued by me. It's good for mythmaking, but it's not true. She did need rescuing that night, yes, but so did Bruno. So did the mermaid. He doesn't talk about my 'destiny' with them, does he?"

I don't know what to say.

"Nothing but lies. We didn't want to go to the mansion. We wanted to go home. When we saw our home spilling into the sky, transfigured by the Extinction Rite . . . we were terrified."

I shake my head. "You were children. You can't blame yourself for how you felt."

"I was frightened for my parents."

I put a hand up to stop him. "Mr. Wormcake. Please. I can understand that this is a moment of, um . . . strong significance for you. It's not unusual to experience these unclean feelings. But you must not indulge them by giving them voice."

"I wanted my parents back, Priest."

"Mr. Wormcake."

"I mourned them. Right there, out in the open, I fell to my knees and cried."

"Mr. Wormcake, that's enough. You must stop."

He does. He turns away from me and stares through the window. The bay is out there somewhere, covered in the night. The lights in the drawing room obscure the view, and we can see our reflections hovering out there above the waters, like gentlemanly spirits.

"Take me to the chapel," I tell him quietly.

He stares at me for a long moment. Then he climbs to his feet. "All right," he says. "Come with me."

He pushes through a small door behind the chess table and enters a narrow, carpeted hallway. Lamps fixed to the walls offer pale light. There are paintings hung here, too, but the light is dim and we are moving too quickly for me to make out specific details. The faces look desiccated, though. One seems to be a body seated on a divan, completely obscured by cobwebs. Another is a pastoral scene, a barrow mound surrounded by a fence made from the human bone.

At the end of the corridor, another small door opens into a private chapel. I'm immediately struck by the scent of spoiled meat. A bank of candles near the altar provides a shivering light. On the altar itself, a husk of unidentifiable flesh bleeds onto a silver platter. Scores of flies lift and fall, their droning presence crowding the ears. On the wall behind them, stained glass windows flank a much larger window covered in heavy drapes. The stained glass depicts images of fly-winged angels, their faceted ruby eyes bright, their segmented arms spread as though offering benediction, or as though preparing to alight at the butcher's feast.

There is a pillow on the floor in front of the altar, and a pickax leans on the table beside it.

The Maggot summons fourteen children to the Skullpocket Fair every year. One for each child that died that night in the Cold Water Fair, one hundred years ago, when Hob's Landing became a new town, guided by monsters and their strange new god. It's no good to question by what criteria the children are selected, by what sins or what virtues. There is no denying the summons. There is only the lesson of the worm, delivered over and over again: all life is a mass of wriggling grubs, awaiting the transformation to the form in which it will greet the long and quiet dark.

"The church teaches the subjugation of memory," I say. "Grief is a weakness."

"I know," says Mr. Wormcake.

"Your marriage. Your love for your wife and your friends. They're stones in your pockets. They weigh you to the earth."

"I know."

"Empty them," I say.

And so he does. "I miss her," he says. He looks at me with those hollow sockets, speaks to me with that borrowed mouth, and for the first time that night I swear I can see some flicker of emotion, like a candle flame glimpsed at the bottom of the world. "I miss her so much. I'm not supposed to miss her. It's blasphemy. But I can't stop thinking about her. I don't want to hear the lies anymore. I don't want to hear the stories. I want to remember what really happened. We didn't recognize anything about each other at the fair that night. We were little kids and we were scared of what was going to happen to us. We stood on the edge of everything and we were too afraid to move. We didn't say a single word to each other the whole time. We didn't learn how to love each other until much later, after we were trapped in this house. And now she's gone and I don't know where she went and I'm scared all over again. I'm about to change, and I don't know how or into what because I left home when I was little. No one taught me anything. I'm afraid of what's going to happen to me. I miss my wife."

I'm stunned by the magnitude of this confession. I'd been fooled by the glamour of his name and his history; I'd thought he would greet this moment with all the dignity of his station. I stand over him, this diminished patriarch, mewling like some abandoned infant, and I'm overwhelmed by disgust. I don't know where it comes from, and the force of it terrifies me.

"Well, you can't," I say, my anger a chained dog. "You don't get to. You don't get to miss her."

He stares at me. His mouth opens, but I cut him off. I grab the mound of ripe flesh from the altar and thrust it into his face. Cold fluids run between my fingers and down my wrist. Flies go berserk, bouncing off my face, crawling into my nose. "This is the world you made! These are the rules. You don't get to change your mind!"

Fifty years ago, when Uncle Digby finished his story and finally opened the gate at the very first Skullpocket Fair, we all ran out onto the brand-new midway, the lights swirling around us, the smells of sweets and fried foods filling our noses. We were driven by fear and hope. We knew death opened its mouth behind us, and we felt every living second pass through our bodies like tongues of fire, exalting us, carving us down to our very spirits. We heard the second gate swing open and we screamed as the monsters bounded onto the midway in furious pursuit: cannibal children, dogs bred to run on beams of moonlight, corpse flowers with human bodies, loping atrocities of the laboratory. The air stank of fear. Little Eddie Brach was in front of me and without thought I grabbed his shirt collar and yanked him down, leaping over his sprawled form in the very next instant. He bleated in cartoonlike surprise. I felt his blood splash against the back of my shirt in a hot torrent as the monsters took him, and I laughed with joy and relief. I saw Christina leap onto a rising gondola car and I followed. We slammed the door shut and watched the world bleed out beneath us. Our hearts were incandescent, and we clutched each other close. Somewhere below us a thing was chanting, "Empty your pockets, empty your pockets," followed by the hollow *pok!* of skulls being cracked open. We laughed together. I felt the inferno of life. I knew that every promise would be fulfilled.

Six of us survived that night. Of those, four of us—exalted by the experience—took the orders. We lived a life dedicated to the Maggot, living in quiet seclusion, preparing our bodies and our minds for the time of decay. We proselytized, grew our numbers. Every year some of the survivors of the fair would join us in our work. Together, we brought Hob's Landing to the worm.

But standing over this whimpering creature, I find myself thinking only of Christina Laudener, her eyes a pale North Atlantic gray, her blond hair flowing like a stilled wave over her shoulders. We were children. We didn't know anything about love. Or at least I didn't. I didn't understand what it was that had taken root in me until years later, when her life took her to a different place, and I sat in the underground church and contemplated the deliquescence of flesh until the hope for warmth, or for the touch of a kind hand, turned cold inside me.

I never learned what she did with her life. But she never took the orders. She lived that incandescent moment with the rest of us, but she drew an entirely different lesson from it.

"You tell me those were all lies?" I say. "I believed them. I believed everything."

"Gretchen wasn't a lie. Our life here wasn't a lie. It was glorious. It doesn't need to be dressed up with exaggerations."

I think of my own life, long for a human being, spent in cold subterranean chambers. "The Maggot isn't a lie," I say.

"No. He certainly is not."

"I shouldn't have survived. I should have died. I pushed Eddie down. Eddie should have lived." I feel tears try to gather, but they won't fall. I want them to. I think, somehow, I would feel better about things if they did. But I've been a good boy: I've worked too hard at killing my own grief. Now that I finally need it, there just isn't enough anymore. The Maggot has taken too much.

"Maybe so," Wormcake says. "But it doesn't matter anymore."

He gets up, approaches the windows. He pulls a cord behind the curtains and they slide open. A beautiful, kaleidoscopic light fills the room. The Seventieth Annual Skullpocket Fair is laid out on the mansion's grounds beyond the window, carousels spinning, roller coaster ticking up an incline, bumper cars spitting arcs of electricity. The Ferris wheel turns over it all, throwing sparking yellow and green and red light into the sky.

I join him at the window. "I want to go down there," I say, putting my fingers against the glass. "I want another chance."

"It's not for you anymore," Wormcake says. "It's not for me, either. It's for them."

He tugs at the false mouth on his skull, snapping the tethers, and tosses it to the floor. The tongue lolls like some yanked organ, and the flies cover it greedily. Maybe he believes that if he can no longer articulate his grief, he won't feel it anymore.

And maybe he's right.

He removes the fly-spangled meat from my hands and takes a deep bite. He offers it to me: a benediction. I recognize the kindness in it. I accept, and take a bite of my own. This is the world we've made. Tears flood my eyes, and he touches my cheek with his bony hand.

Then he replaces the meat on the altar and resumes his place on his knees beside it. He lays his head by the buzzing meat. I take the pickax and place the hard point of it against the skull, where all the poisons of the world have gathered, have slowed him, have weighed him to the earth. I hold the point there to fix it in my mind, and then I lift the ax over my head.

"Empty your pockets," I say.

Below us, a gate opens, and the children pour out at a dead run. There goes the angry girl. There goes the weepy, buzz-cut kid. Arms and legs pumping, clothes flapping like banners in the wind. They're in the middle of the pack when the monsters are released. They have a chance.

They just barely have a chance.

KELLY LINK

I Can See Right Through You

FROM *McSweeney's Quarterly Concern*

WHEN THE SEX tape happened and things went south with Fawn, the demon lover did what he always did. He went to cry on Meggie's shoulder. Girls like Fawn came and went, but Meggie would always be there. Him and Meggie. It was the talisman you kept in your pocket. The one you couldn't lose.

Two monsters can kiss in a movie. One old friend can go to see another old friend and be sure of his welcome: so here is the demon lover in a rental car. An hour into the drive, he opens the window of the rental car, tosses out his cell phone. There is no one he wants to talk to except for Meggie.

(1991) This is after the movie and after they are together and after they begin to understand the bargain that they have made. They are both, suddenly, very famous.

Film can be put together in any order. Scenes shot in any order of sequence. Take as many takes as you like. Continuity is independent of linear time. Sometimes you aren't even in the scene together. Meggie says her lines to your stand-in. They'll splice you together later on. Shuffle off to Buffalo, gals. Come out tonight.

(This is long before any of that. This was a very long time ago.)

Meggie tells the demon lover a story:

Two girls and, look, they've found a Ouija board. They make a list of questions. One girl is pretty. One girl is not really a part of this story. She's lost her favorite sweater. Her fingertips on the planchette. Two girls, each touching, lightly, the planchette. Is anyone here? Where did I put my blue sweater? Will anyone ever love me? Things like that.

They ask their questions. The planchette drifts. Gives up nonsense. They start the list over again. Is anyone here? Will I be famous? Where is my blue sweater?

The planchette jerks under their fingers.

M-E

Meggie says, "Did you do that?"

The other girl says she didn't. The planchette moves again, a
fidget. A stutter, a nudge, a sequence of swoops and stops.

M-E-G-G-I-E

"It's talking to you," the other girl says.

M-E-G-G-I-E H-E-L-L-O

Meggie says, "Hello?"

The planchette moves again and again. There is something animal about it.

H-E-L-L-O I A-M W-I-T-H Y-O-U I A-M W-I-T-H Y-O-U A-L-W-A-
Y-S

They write it all down.

M-E-G-G-I-E O I W-I-L-L L-O-V-E Y-O-U A-L-W-A-Y-S

"Who is this?" she says. "Who are you? Do I know you?"

I S-E-E Y-O-U I K-N-O-W Y-O-U W-A-I-T A-N-D I W-I-L-L C-O-M-E

A pause. Then:

I W-I-L-L M-E-G-G-I-E O I W-I-L-L B-E W-I-T-H Y-O-U A-L-W-A-Y-S

"Are you doing this?" Meggie says to the other girl. She shakes
her head.

M-E-G-G-I-E W-A-I-T

The other girl says, "Can whoever this is at least tell me where I
left my sweater?"

Meggie says, "Okay, whoever you are. I'll wait, I guess I can wait
for a while. I'm not good at waiting. But I'll wait."

O W-A-I-T A-N-D I W-I-L-L C-O-M-E

They wait. Will there be a knock at the bedroom door? But no
one comes. No one is coming.

I A-M W-I-T-H Y-O-U A-L-W-A-Y-S

No one is here with them. The sweater will never be found. The
other girl grows up, lives a long and happy life. Meggie goes out to
L.A. and meets the demon lover.

W-A-I-T

After that, the only thing the planchette says, over and over, is
Meggie's name. It's all very romantic.

*

(1974) Twenty-two people disappear from a nudist colony in Lake Apopka. People disappear all the time. Let's be honest: the only thing interesting here is that these people were naked. And that no one ever saw them again. Funny, right?

(1990) It's one of the ten most iconic movie kisses of all time. In the top five, surely. You and Meggie, the demon lover and his monster girl; vampires sharing a kiss as the sun comes up. Both of you wearing so much makeup it still astonishes you that anyone would ever recognize you on the street.

It's hard for the demon lover to grow old.

Florida is California on a Troma budget. That's what the demon lover thinks, anyway. Special effects blew the budget on bugs and bad weather.

He parks in a meadowy space, recently mowed, alongside other rental cars, the usual catering and equipment vans. There are two gateposts with a chain between them. No fence. Eternal I endure.

There is an evil smell. Does it belong to the place or to him? The demon lover sniffs under his arm.

It's an end-of-the-world sky, a snakes-and-ladders landscape: low emerald trees pulled lower by vines; chalk and apricot anthills (the demon lover imagines the bones of a nudist under every one); shallow water-filled declivities scummed with algae, lime and gold and black.

The blot of the lake. That's another theory: the lake.

A storm is coming.

He doesn't get out of his car. He rolls the window down and watches the storm come in. Let's look at him looking at it. A pretty thing admiring a pretty thing. Abandoned site of a mass disappearance, muddy violet clouds, silver veils of rain driving down the lake, the tabloid prince of darkness, Meggie's demon lover arriving in all his splendor. The only thing to spoil it is the bugs. And the sex tape.

(2012) You have been famous for more than half of your life. Both of you. You only made the one movie together, but people still stop you on the street to ask about Meggie. Is she happy? Which one? you want to ask them. The one who kissed me in a movie when we were just kids, the one who wasn't real? The one who likes to smoke a bit of weed and text me about her neighbor's pet goat? The Meggie in the tabloids who drinks fucks gets fat pregnant too skinny slaps a maître d' talks to Elvis's ghost ghost of a missing three-year-old boy ghost of JFK? Sometimes they don't ask about Meggie. Instead they ask if you will bite them.

Happiness! Misery! If you were one, bet on it the other was on the way. That was what everyone liked to see. It was what the whole thing was about. The demon lover has a pair of gold cuff links, those faces. Meggie gave them to him. You know the ones I mean.

(2010) Meggie and the demon lover throw a Halloween party for everyone they know. They do this every Halloween. They're famous for it.

"Year after year, the monkey puts on a monkey's face," Meggie says.

She's King Kong. The year before? Half a pantomime horse. He's the demon lover. Who else? Year after year.

Meggie says, "I've decided to give up acting. I'm going to be a poet. Nobody cares when poets get old."

Fawn says, appraisingly, "I hope I look half as good as you when I'm your age." Fawn, twenty-three. A makeup artist. This year she and the demon lover are married. Last year they met on set.

He says, "I'm thinking I could get some work done on my jawline."

You'd think they were mother and daughter. Same Viking profile, same quizzical tilt to the head as they turn to look at him. Both taller than him. Both smarter, too, no doubt about it.

Maybe Meggie wonders sometimes about the women he sleeps with. Marries. Maybe he has a type. But so does she. There's a guy at the Halloween party. A boy, really.

Meggie always has a boy and the demon lover can always pick him out. Easy enough, even if Meggie's sly. She never introduces the lover of the moment, never brings them into conversations or even acknowledges their presence. They hang out on the edge of whatever is happening, and drink or smoke or watch Meggie at the center. Sometimes they drift closer, stand near enough to Meggie that it's plain what's going on. When she leaves, they follow after.

Meggie's type? The funny thing is, Meggie's lovers all look like the demon lover. More like the demon lover, he admits it, than

he does. He and Meggie are both older now, but the world is full
of beautiful black-haired boys and golden girls. Really, that's the
problem.

The role of the demon lover comes with certain obligations. Your
hairline will not recede. Your waistline will not expand. You are
not to be photographed threatening paparazzi, or in sweatpants.
No sex tapes.

Your fans will: Offer their necks at premieres. (Also at restau-
rants and at the bank. More than once when he is standing in
front of a urinal.) Ask if you will bite their wives. Their daughters.
They will cut themselves with a razor in front of you.

The appropriate reaction is—

There is no appropriate reaction.

The demon lover does not always live up to his obligations. There
is a sex tape. There is a girl with a piercing. There is, in the middle of some athletic sex, a comical incident involving his foreskin.
There is blood all over the sheets. There is a lot of blood. There is
a 911 call. There is him, fainting. Falling and hitting his head on a
bedside table. There is Perez Hilton, Gawker, talk radio, YouTube,
Tumblr. There are GIFs.

You will always be most famous for playing the lead in a series of
vampire movies. The character you play is, of course, ageless. But
you get older. The first time you bite a girl's neck, Meggie's neck,
you're a twenty-five-year-old actor playing a vampire who hasn't
gotten a day older in three hundred years. Now you're a forty-
nine-year-old actor playing the same ageless vampire. It's getting
to be a little ridiculous, isn't it? But if the demon lover isn't the
demon lover, then who is he? Who are you? Other projects disap-
point. Your agent says take a comic role. The trouble is you're not
very funny. You're not good at funny.

The other trouble is the sex tape. Sex tapes are inherently
funny. Nudity is, regrettably, funny. Torn foreskins are painfully
funny. You didn't know she was filming it.

Your agent says, That wasn't what I meant.

You could do what Meggie did, all those years ago. Disappear.
Travel the world. Hunt down the meaning of life. Go find Meggie.

When the sex tape happens you say to Fawn, But what does this have to do with Meggie? This has nothing to do with Meggie. It was just some girl.

It's not like there haven't been other girls.

Fawn says, It has everything to do with Meggie.

I can see right through you, Fawn says, less in sorrow than in anger. She probably can.

God grant me Meggie, but not just yet. That's him by way of Saint Augustine by way of Fawn the makeup artist and Bible group junkie. She explains it to the demon lover, explains him to himself. And hasn't it been in the back of your mind all this time? It was Meggie right at the start. Why shouldn't it be Meggie again? And in the meantime, you could get married once in a while and never worry about whether or not it worked out. He and Meggie have managed, all this time, to stay friends. His marriages, his other relationships, perhaps these have only been a series of delaying actions. Small rebellions. And here's the thing about his marriages: he's never managed to stay friends with his ex-wives, his exes. He and Fawn won't be friends.

The demon lover and Meggie have known each other for such a long time. No one knows him like Meggie.

The remains of the nudist colony at Lake Apopka promises reasonable value for ghost hunters. A dozen ruined cabins, some roofless, windows black with mildew; a crumbled stucco hall, Spanish tiles receding; the cracked lip of a slop-filled pool. Between the cabins and the lake, the homely and welcome sight of half a dozen trailers; even better, he spots a craft tent.

Muck farms! Mutant alligators! Disappearing nudists! The demon lover, killing time in the LAX airport, read up on Lake Apopka. The past is a weird place, Florida is a weird place, no news there. A demon lover should fit right in, but the ground sucks and clots at his shoes in a way that suggests he isn't welcome. The rain is directly overhead now, shouting down in spit-warm gouts. He begins to run, stumbling, in the direction of the craft tent.

Meggie's career is on the upswing. Everyone agrees. She has a ghost-hunting show, *Who's There?*

The demon lover calls Meggie after the *Titanic* episode airs, the one where *Who's There?*'s ghost-hunting crew hitches a ride with the International Ice Patrol. There's the yearly ceremony, memorial wreaths. Meggie's crew sets up a Marconi transmitter and receiver just in case a ghost or two has a thing to say.

The demon lover asks her about the dead seagulls. Forget the Marconi nonsense. The seagulls were what made the episode. Hundreds of them, little corpses fixed, as if pinned, to the water.

Meggie says, You think we have the budget for fake seagulls? Please.

Admit that *Who's There?* is entertaining whether or not you believe in ghosts. It's all about the nasty detail, the house that gives you a bad feeling even when you turn on all the lights, the awful thing that happened to someone who wasn't you a very long time ago. The camera work is moody, extraordinary. The team of ghost hunters is personable, funny, reasonably attractive. Meggie sells you on the possibility: Maybe what's going on here is real. Maybe someone is out there. Maybe they have something to say.

The demon lover and Meggie don't talk for months and then suddenly something changes and they talk every day. He likes to wake up in the morning and call her. They talk about scripts, now that Meggie's getting scripts again. He can talk to Meggie about anything. It's been that way all along. They haven't talked since the sex tape. Better to have this conversation in person.

(1991) He and Meggie are lovers. Their movie is big at the box office. Everywhere they go they are famous and they go everywhere. Their faces are everywhere. They are kissing on a thousand screens. They are in a hotel room, kissing. They can't leave their hotel room without someone screaming or fainting or pointing something at them. They are asked the same questions again. Over and over. He begins to do the interviews in character. Anyway, it makes Meggie laugh.

There's a night, on some continent, in some city, some hotel room, some warm night, the demon lover and Meggie leave a window open and two women creep in. They come over the balcony. They just want to tell you that they love you. Both of you. They just want to be near you.

Everyone watches you. Even when they're pretending not to. Even when they aren't watching you, you think they are. And you know what? You're right. Eyes will find you. Becoming famous, this kind of fame: it's luck indistinguishable from catastrophe. You'd be dumb not to recognize it. What you've become.

When people disappear, there's always the chance that you'll see them again. The rain comes down so hard the demon lover can barely see. He thinks he is still moving in the direction of the craft tent and not the lake. There is a noise, he picks it out of the noise of the rain. A howling. And then the rain thins and he can see something, men and women, naked. Running toward him. He slips, catches himself, and the rain comes down hard again, erases everything except the sound of what is chasing him. He collides headlong with a thing: a skin horribly clammy, cold, somehow both stiff and yielding. Bounces off and realizes that this is the tent. Not where you'd choose to make a last stand, but by the time he has fumbled his way inside the flap he has grasped the situation. Not dead nudists, but living people, naked, cursing, laughing, dripping. They carry cameras, mikes, gear for ghost hunting. Videographers, A2s, all the other useful types and the not-so-useful. A crowd of men and women, and here is Meggie. Her hair is glued in strings to her face. Her breasts are wet with rain.

He says her name.

They all look at him.

How is it possible that he is the one who feels naked?

"The fuck is this guy doing here?" says someone with a little white towel positioned over his genitals. Really, it could be even littler.

"Will," Meggie says. So gently he almost starts to cry. Well, it's been a long day.

She takes him to her trailer. He has a shower, borrows her toothbrush. She puts on a robe. Doesn't ask him any questions. Talks to him while he's in the bathroom. He leaves the door open.

It's the third day on location, and the first two have been a mixed bag. They got their establishing shots, went out on the lake and saw an alligator dive down when they got too close. There are baby skunks all over the scrubby, shabby woods, the trails. They come right up to you, up to the camera, and try like hell to spray. But until they hit adolescence, all they can do is quiver their tails and stamp their feet.

Except, she says, and mentions some poor A2. His skunk was an early bloomer.

Meggie interviewed the former proprietor of the nudist colony. He insisted on calling it a naturist community, spent the interview explaining the philosophy behind naturism, didn't want to talk about 1974. A harmless old crank. Whatever happened, he had nothing to do with it. You couldn't lecture people into thin air. Besides, he had an alibi.

What they didn't get on the first day or even on the second day was any kind of worthwhile read on their equipment. They have the two psychics—but one of them had an emergency, went back to deal with a daughter in rehab; they have all kinds of psychometric equipment, but there is absolutely nothing going on, down, or off. Which led to some discussion.

"We decided maybe we were the problem," Meggie says. "Maybe the nudists didn't have anything to say to us while we had our clothes on. So we're shooting in the nude. Everyone nude. Cast, crew, everyone. It's been a really positive experience, Will. It's a good group of people."

"Fun," the demon lover says. Someone has dropped off a pair of pink cargo shorts and a T-shirt, because his clothes are in his suitcase back at the airport in Orlando. It's not exactly that he forgot. More like he couldn't be bothered.

"It's good to see you, Will," Meggie says. "But why are you here, exactly? How did you know we were here?"

He takes the easy question first. "Pike." Pike is Meggie's agent and an old friend of the demon lover. The kind of agent who likes to pull the legs off of small children. The kind of friend who finds life all the sweeter when you're in the middle of screwing up your own. "I made him promise not to tell you I was coming."

He collapses on the floor in front of Meggie's chair. She runs her fingers through his hair. Pets him like you'd pet a dog.

"He told you, though. Didn't he?"

"He did," Meggie said. "He called."

The demon lover says, "Meggie, this isn't about the sex tape."

Meggie says, "I know. Fawn called, too."

He tries not to imagine that phone call. His head is sore. He's dehydrated, probably. That long flight.

"She wanted me to let her know if you showed. Said she was waiting to see before she threw in the towel."

She waits for him to say something. Waits a little bit longer. Strokes his hair the whole time.

"I won't call her," she says. "You ought to go back, Will. She's a good person."

"I don't love her," the demon lover says.

"Well," Meggie says. She takes that hand away.

There's a knock on the door, some girl. "Sun's out again, Meggie." She gives the demon lover a particularly melting smile. Was probably twelve when she first saw him onscreen. Baby ducks, these girls. Imprint on the first vampire they ever see. Then she's down the stairs again, bare bottom bouncing.

Meggie drops the robe, begins to apply sunblock to her arms and face. He notes the ways in which her body has changed. Thinks he might love her all the more for it, and hopes that this is true.

"Let me," he says, and takes the bottle from her. Begins to rub lotion into her back.

She doesn't flinch away. Why would she? They are friends.

She says, "Here's the thing about Florida, Will. You get these storms, practically every day. But then they go away again."

Her hands catch at his, slippery with the lotion. She says, "You must be tired. Take a nap. There's herbal tea in the cupboards, pot and Ambien in the bedroom. We're shooting all afternoon, straight through to evening. And then a barbecue—we're filming that, too. You're welcome to come out. It would be great publicity for us, of course. Our viewers would love it. But you'd have to do it naked like the rest of us. No clothes. No exceptions, Will. Not even for you."

He rubs the rest of the sunblock into her shoulders. Would like nothing more than to rest his head on her shoulder.

"I love you, Meggie," he says. "You know that, right?"

"I know. I love you, too, Will," she says. The way she says it tells him everything.

The demon lover goes to lie down on Meggie's bed, feeling a hundred years old. Dozes. Dreams about a bungalow in Venice Beach and Meggie and a girl. That was a long time ago.

There was a review of a play Meggie was in. Maybe ten years ago? It wasn't a kind review, or even particularly intelligent, and yet the critic said something that still seems right to the demon lover. He said no matter what was happening in the play, Meggie's performance suggested she was waiting for a bus. The demon lover thinks the critic got at something true there. Only, the demon lover has always thought that if Meggie was waiting for a bus, you had to wonder where that bus was going. If she was planning to throw herself under it.

When they first got together, the demon lover was pretty sure he was what Meggie had been waiting for. Maybe she thought so, too. They bought a house, a bungalow in Venice Beach. He wonders who lives there now.

When the demon lover wakes up, he takes off the T-shirt and cargo shorts. Leaves them folded neatly on the bed. He'll have to find somewhere to sleep tonight. And soon. Day is becoming night.

Meat is cooking on a barbecue. The demon lover isn't sure when he last ate. There's bug spray beside the door. Ticklish on his balls. He feels just a little bit ridiculous. Surely this is a terrible idea. The latest in a long series of terrible ideas. Only this time he knows there's a camera.

The moment he steps outside Meggie's trailer, a PA appears as if by magic. It's what they do. Has him sign a pile of releases. Odd to stand here in the nude signing releases, but what the fuck. He thinks, I'll go home tomorrow.

The PA is in her fifties. Unusual. There's probably a story there, but who cares? He doesn't. Of course she's seen the fucking sex tape—it's probably going to be the most popular movie he ever makes—but her expression suggests this is the very first time she's ever seen the demon lover naked, or rather that neither of them is naked at all.

While the demon lover signs—doesn't bother to read anything, what does it matter now, anyway?—the PA talks about someone who hasn't done something. Who isn't where she ought to be. Some other gofer named Juliet. Where is she and what has she gone for? The PA is full of complaints.

The demon lover suggests the gofer may have been carried off by ghosts. The PA gives him an unfriendly look and continues to talk about people the demon lover doesn't know, has no interest in.

"What's spooky about you?" the demon lover asks. Because of course that's the gimmick, producer down to best boy. Every woman and man uncanny.

"I had a near-death experience," the PA says. She wiggles her arm. Shows off a long ropy burn. "Accidentally electrocuted myself. Got the whole tunnel and light thing. And I guess I scored okay with those cards when they auditioned me. The Zener cards?"

"So tell me," the demon lover says. "What's so fucking great about a tunnel and a light? That really the best they can do?"

"Yeah, well," the PA says, a bite in her voice. "People like you probably get the red carpet and the limo."

The demon lover has nothing to say to that.

"You seen anything here?" he tries instead. "Heard anything?"

"Meggie tell you about the skunks?" the PA says. Having snapped, now she will soothe. "Those babies. Tail up, the works, but nothing doing. Which about sums up this place. No ghosts. No read on the equipment. No hanky-panky, fiddle-faddle, or woo woo. Not even a cold spot."

She says doubtfully, "But it'll come together. You at this séance barbecue shindig will help. Naked vampire trumps nudist ghosts any day. Okay on your own? You go on down to the lake, I'll call, let them know you're on your way."

Or he could just head for the car.

"Thanks," the demon lover says.

But before he knows what he wants to do, here's another someone. It's a regular Pilgrim's Progress. One of Fawn's favorite books. This is a kid in his twenties. Good-looking in a familiar way. (Although is it okay to think this about another guy when you're both naked? Not to mention, who looks a lot like you did once upon a time. Why not? We're all naked here.)

"I know you," the kid says.

The demon lover says, "Of course you do. You are?"

"Ray," says the kid. He's *maybe* twenty-five. His look says, *You know who I am.* "Meggie's told me all about you."

As if he doesn't already know, the demon lover says, "So what do you do?"

The kid smiles an unlovely smile. Scratches at his groin luxuriously, maybe not on purpose. "Whatever needs to be done. That's what I do."

So he deals. There's that pot in Meggie's dresser.

Down at the lake people are playing volleyball in a pit with no net. Barbecuing. Someone talks to a camera, gestures at someone else. Someone somewhere smoking a joint. At this distance, not too close, not too near, twilight coming down, the demon lover takes in all of the breasts, asses, comical cocks, knobby knees, everything hidden now made plain. He notes with an experienced eye which breasts are real, which aren't. Only a few of the women sport pubic hair. He's never understood what that's about. Some of the men are bare, too. *O tempora, o mores.*

"You like jokes?" Ray says, stopping to light a cigarette.

The demon lover could leave; he lingers. "Depends on the joke." Really, he doesn't. Especially the kind of jokes the ones who ask if you like jokes tell.

Ray says, "You'll like this one. So there are these four guys. A kleptomaniac, a pyromaniac, um, a zoophile, and a masochist. This cat walks by and the klepto says he'd like to steal it. The pyro says he wants to set it on fire. The zoophile wants to fuck it. So the masochist, he looks at everybody, and he says, 'Meow?'"

It's a moderately funny joke. It might be a come-on.

The demon lover flicks a look from under his lashes. Suppresses the not-quite-queasy feeling he's somehow traveled back in time to flirt with himself. Or the other way round.

He'd like to think he was even prettier than this kid. People used to stop and stare when he walked into a room. That was long before anyone knew who he was. He's always been someone you look at longer than you should. He says, smiling, "I'll bite. Which one are you?"

"Pardon?" Ray says. Blows smoke.

"Which one are you? The klepto, the pyro, the cat-fucker, the masochist?"

"I'm the guy who tells the joke," Ray says. He drops his cigarette, grinds it under a heel black with dirt. Lights another. "Don't know if anyone's told you, but don't drink out of any of the taps. Or go swimming. The water's toxic. Phosphorus, other stuff. They shut down the muck farms, they're building up the marshlands again, but it's still not what I'd call potable. You staying out here or in town?"

The demon lover says, "Don't know if I'm staying at all."

"Well," Ray says, "they've rigged up some of the less wrecked bungalows on a generator. There are camp beds, sleeping bags. Depends on whether you like it rough." That last with, yes, a leer.

The demon lover feels his own lip lifting. They are both wearing masks. They look out of them at each other. This was what you knew when you were an actor. The face, the whole body, the way you moved in it, just a guise. You put it on, you put it off again.

What was underneath belonged to you, just you, as long as you kept it hidden.

He says, "You think you know something about me?"

"I've seen all your movies," Ray says. The mask shifts, becomes the one the demon lover calls "I'm your biggest fan." Oh, he knows what's under that one.

He prepares himself for whatever this strange kid is going to say next and then suddenly Meggie is there. As if things weren't awkward enough without Meggie, naked, suddenly standing there. Everybody naked, nobody happy. It's Scandinavian art porn.

Meggie ignores the kid entirely. Just like always. These guys are interchangeable, really. There's probably some website where she finds them. She may not want him, but she doesn't want anyone else, either.

Meggie says, touching his arm, "You look a lot better."

"I got a few hours," he says.

"I know," she says. "I checked in on you. Wanted to make sure you hadn't run off."

"Nowhere to go," he says.

"Come on," Meggie says. "Let's get you something to eat." Ray doesn't follow; lingers with his cigarette. Probably staring at their yoga-toned, well-enough-preserved celebrity butts.

Here's the problem with this kid, the demon lover thinks. He sat in a theater when he was fifteen and watched me and Meggie done up in vampire makeup pretend-fucking on a New York subway car. The A train. Me biting Meggie's breast, some suburban movie screen, her breast ten times bigger than his head. He probably masturbated a hundred times watching me bite you, Meggie. He watched us kiss. Felt something ache when we did. And that leaves out all the rest of this, whatever it is that you're doing here with him and me. Imagine what this kid must feel now. The demon lover feels it, too. Love, he thinks. Because love isn't just love. It's all the other stuff, too.

He meets Irene, the fat, pretty medium who plays the straight man to Meggie. People named Sidra, Tom, Euan, who seem to be in charge of the weird ghost gear. A videographer, Pilar. He's almost positive he's met her before. Maybe during his AA period? Really, why is that period more of a blur than the years he's spent drunk or high? She's in her thirties, has a sly smile, terrific legs, and a very big camera.

They demonstrate some of the equipment for the demon lover, let him try out something called a Trifield Meter. No ghosts here. Even ghosts have better places to be.

He assumes everyone he meets has seen his sex tape. Almost wishes someone would mention it. No one does.

There's a rank breeze off the lake. Muck and death.

People eat and discuss the missing PA—the gofer—some Juliet person. Meggie says, "She's a nice kid. Makes Whore-igami in her spare time and sells it on eBay."

"She makes what?" the demon lover says.

"Whore-igami. Origami porn tableaux. Custom-order stuff."

"Of course," the demon lover says. "Big money in that."

She may have some kind of habit. Meggie mentions this. She may be in the habit of disappearing now and then.

Or she may be wherever all those nudists went. Imagine the ratings then. He doesn't say this to Meggie.

Meggie says, "I'm happy to see you, Will. Even under the circumstances."

"Are you?" says the demon lover, smiling, because he's always smiling. They're far enough away from the mikes and the cameras that he feels okay about saying this. Pilar, the videographer, is recording Irene, the medium, who is toasting marshmallows. Ray is watching, too. Is always somewhere nearby.

Something bites the demon lover's thigh and he slaps at it.

He could reach out and touch Meggie's face right now. It would be a different story on the camera than the one he and Meggie are telling each other. Or she would turn away and it would all be the same story again. He thinks he should have remembered this, all the ways they didn't work when they were together. Like the joke about the two skunks. When Out is in, In is out. Like the wrong ends of two magnets.

"Of course I'm happy," Meggie says. "And your timing is eerily good, because I have to talk to you about something."

"Shoot," he says.

"It's complicated," she says. "How about later? After we're done here?"

It's almost full dark now. No moon. Someone has built up a very large fire. The blackened bungalows and the roofless hall melt into obscure and tidy shapes. Now you can imagine yourself back when it was all new, a long time ago. Back in the seventies when nobody cared what you did. When love was free. When you could just disappear if you felt like it and that was fine and good, too.

"So where do I stay tonight?" the demon lover says. Again fights the impulse to touch Meggie's face. There's a strand of hair against her lip. Which is he? The pyromaniac or the masochist? In or Out? Well, he's an actor, isn't he? He can be anything she wants him to be.

"I'm sure you'll find somewhere," Meggie says, a glint in her eye. "Or someone. Pilar has told me more than once you're the only man she's ever wanted to fuck."

"If I had a dollar," the demon lover says. He still wants to touch her. Wants her to want him to touch her. He remembers now how this goes.

Meggie says, "If you had a dollar, seventy cents would go to your exes."

Which is gospel truth. He says, "Fawn signed a prenup."

"One of the thousand reasons you should go home and fix things," Meggie says. "She's a good person. There aren't so many of those."

"She's better off without me," the demon lover says, trying it out. He's a little hurt when Meggie doesn't disagree.

Irene the medium comes over with Pilar and the other videographer. The demon lover can tell Irene doesn't like him. Sometimes women don't like him. Rare enough that he always wonders why.

"Shall we get started?" Irene says. "Let's see if any of our friends are up for a quick chat. Then I don't know about you, but I'm going to go put on something a little less comfortable."

Meggie addresses the video camera next. "This will be our final attempt," she says, "our last chance to contact anyone who is still lingering here, who has unfinished business."

"You'd think nudists wouldn't be so shy," Irene says.

Meggie says, "But even if we don't reach anyone, today hasn't been a total loss. All of us have taken a risk. Some of us are sunburned, some of us have bug bites in interesting places, all of us are a little more comfortable in our own skin. We've experienced openness and humanity in a way that these colonists imagined and hoped would lead to a better world. And maybe for them it did. We've had a good day. And even if the particular souls we came here in search of didn't show up, someone else is here."

The A2 nods at Will.

Pilar points the camera at him.

He's been thinking about how to play this. "I'm Will Gald," he says. "You probably recognize me from previous naked film roles such as the guy rolling around on a hotel room floor clutching his genitals and bleeding profusely."

He smiles his most lovely smile. "I just happened to be in the area."

"We persuaded him to stay for a bite," Meggie says.

"They've hidden my clothes," Will says. "Admittedly, I haven't been trying that hard to find them. I mean, what's the worst thing that can happen when you get naked on camera?"

Irene says, "Meggie, one of the things that's been most important about *Who's There?* right from the beginning is that we've all had something happen to us that we can't explain away. We're all believers. I've been meaning to ask, does Will here have a ghost story?"

"I don't—" the demon lover says. Then pauses. Looks at Meggie. "I do," he says. "But surely Meggie's already told it."

"I have," Meggie says. "But I've never heard you tell it."

Oh, there are stories the demon lover could tell.

He says, "I'm here to please."

"Fantastic," Irene says. "As you know, every episode we make time for a ghost story or two. Tonight we even have a campfire." She hesitates. "And of course as our viewers also know, we're still waiting for Juliet Adeyemi to turn up. She left just before lunch to run errands. We're not worried yet, but we'll all be a lot happier when she's with us again."

Meggie says, "Juliet, if you've met a nice boy and gone off to ride the teacups at Disney World, so help me, I'm going to ask for all the details. Now. Shall we, Irene?"

All around them, people have been clearing away plates of half-eaten barbecue, assembling in a half circle around the campfire. Any minute now they'll be singing "Kumbaya." They sit on their little towels. Irene and Meggie take their place in front of the fire. They clasp hands.

The demon lover moves a little farther away, into darkness. He is not interested in séances or ghosts. Here is the line of the shore. Sharp things underfoot. Someone joins him. Ray. Of course.

It is worse, somehow, to be naked in the dark. The world is so big and he is not. Ray is young and he is not. He is pretty sure that the videographer Pilar will sleep with him; Meggie will not.

"I know you," the demon lover says to Ray. "I've met you before. Well, not you, the previous you. Yous. You never last. *We* never last. She moves on. You disappear."

Ray says nothing. Looks out at the lake.

"I *was* you," the demon lover says.

Ray says, "And now? Who are you?"

"You charge by the hour?" the demon lover says. "Why follow me around? I don't seem to have my wallet on me."

"Meggie's busy," Ray says. "And I'm curious about you. What you think you're doing here."

"I came for Meggie," the demon lover says. "We're friends. An old friend can come to see an old friend. Some other time I'll see her again and you won't be around. I'll always be around. But you, you're just some guy who got lucky because you look like me."

Ray says, "I love her."

"Sucks, doesn't it?" the demon lover says. He goes back to the fire and the naked people waiting for other naked people. Thinks about the story he is meant to tell.

The séance has not been a success. Irene the medium keeps saying that she senses something. Someone is trying to say something.

The dead are here, but also not here. They're afraid. That's why they won't come. Something is keeping them away. There is something wrong here.

"Do you feel it?" she says to Meggie, to the others.

Meggie says, "I feel something. Something is here."

The demon lover extends himself outward into the night. Lets himself believe for a moment that life goes on. Is something here? There is a smell, the metallic stink of muck farms. There is an oppressiveness to the air. Is there malice here? An ill wish?

Meggie says, "No one has ever solved the mystery of what happened here. But perhaps whatever happened to them is still present. Irene, could it have some hold on their spirits, whatever is left of them, even in death?"

Irene says, "I don't know. Something is wrong here. Something is here. I don't know."

But *Who's There?* picks up nothing of interest on their equipment, their air ion counter or their barometer, their EMF detector or EVP detector, their wind chimes or thermal imaging scopes. No one is there.

And so at last it's time for ghost stories.

There's one about the men's room at a trendy Santa Monica restaurant. The demon lover has been there. Had the fries with truffle-oil mayonnaise. Never encountered the ghost. He's not somebody who sees ghosts, and he's fine with that. Never really liked truffle-oil mayonnaise, either. The thing in the bungalow with Meggie wasn't a ghost. It was drugs, the pressure they were under, the unbearable scrutiny; a *folie à deux;* the tax on their happiness.

Someone tells the old story about Basil Rathbone and the dinner guest who brings along his dogs. Upon departure, the man and his dogs are killed in a car crash just outside Rathbone's house. Rathbone sees. Is paralyzed with shock and grief. As he stands there, his phone rings—when he picks up, an operator says, "Pardon me, Mr. Rathbone, but there is a woman on the line who says she must speak to you."

The woman, who is a medium, says that she has a message for him. She says she hopes he will understand the meaning.

"Traveling very fast. No time to say goodbye. There are no dogs here."

And now it's the demon lover's turn. He says, "A long time ago when Meggie and I were together, we bought a bungalow in Venice Beach. We weren't there very much. We were everywhere else. On junkets. At festivals. We had no furniture. Just a mattress. No dishes. When we were home we ate out of take-out containers.

"But we were happy." He lets that linger. Meggie watches. Listens. Ray stands beside her. No space between them.

It's not much fun, telling a ghost story while you're naked. Telling the parts of the ghost story that you're supposed to tell. Not telling other parts. While the woman you love stands there with the person you used to be.

"It was a good year. Maybe the best year of my life. Maybe the hardest year, too. We were young and we were stupid and people wanted things from us and we did things we shouldn't have done. Fill in the blanks however you want. We threw parties. We spent money like water. And we loved each other. Right, Meggie?"

Meggie nods.

He says, "But I should get to the ghost. I don't really believe that it was a ghost, but I don't not believe it was a ghost, either. I've never spent much time thinking about it, really. But the more time we spent in that bungalow, the worse things got."

Irene says, "Can you describe it for us? What happened?"

The demon lover says, "It was a feeling that someone was watching us. That they were somewhere very far away, but they were getting closer. That very soon they would be there with us. It was worse at night. We had bad dreams. Some nights we both woke up screaming."

Irene says, "What were the dreams about?"

He says, "Not much. Just that it was finally there in the room with us. Eventually it was always there. Eventually whatever it was was in the bed with us. We'd wake up on opposite sides of the mattress because it was there in between us."

Irene says, "What did you do?"

He says, "When one of us was alone in the bed it wasn't there. It was there when it was the two of us. Then it would be the three of us. So we got a room at the Chateau Marmont. Only it turned out it was there, too. The very first night it was there, too."

Irene says, "Did you try to talk to it?"

He says, "Meggie did. I didn't. Meggie thought it was real. I thought we needed therapy. I thought whatever it was, we were doing it. So we tried therapy. That was a bust. So eventually—" He shrugs.

"Eventually what?" Irene says.

"I moved out," Meggie says.

"She moved out," he says.

The demon lover wonders if Ray knows the other part of the story, if Meggie has told him that. Of course she hasn't. Meggie isn't dumb. It's the two of them and the demon lover thinks, as he's thought many times before, that this is what will always hold them together. Not the experience of filming a movie together, of falling in love at the exact same moment that all those other people fell in love with them, that sympathetic magic made up of story and effort, repetition and editing and craft and other people's desire.

The thing that happened is the thing they can never tell anyone else. It belongs to them. No one else.

"And after that there wasn't any ghost," he concludes. "Meggie took a break from Hollywood, went to India. I went to AA meetings."

It's gotten colder. The fire has gotten lower. You could, perhaps, imagine that there is a supernatural explanation for these things, but that would be wishful thinking. The missing girl, Juliet, has not returned. The ghost-hunting equipment does not record any presence.

Meggie finds the demon lover with Pilar. She says, "Can we talk?"

"What about?" he says.

Pilar says, "I'll go get another beer. Want one, Meggie?"

Meggie shakes her head and Pilar wanders off, her hand brushing against the demon lover's hip as she goes. Flesh against flesh. He turns just a little so he's facing away from the firelight.

"It's about the premiere for next season," Meggie says. "I want to shoot it in Venice Beach, in our old bungalow."

The demon lover feels something rush over him. Pour into his ears, flood down his throat. He can't think of what to say. He has been thinking about Ray while he flirts with Pilar. He's been wondering what would happen if he asked Meggie about Ray. Really, they've never talked about this. This thing that she does.

"I'd like you to be in the episode, too, of course," Meggie says.

He says, "I don't think that's a good idea. I think it's a terrible idea, actually."

"It's something I've always wanted to do," Meggie says. "I think it would be good for both of us."

"Something something closure," he says. "Yeah, yeah. Something something exposure something possible jail term. Are you *insane?*"

"Look," Meggie says. "I've already talked to the woman who lives there now. She's never experienced anything. Will, I need to do this."

"Of course she hasn't experienced anything," the demon lover says. "It wasn't the house that was haunted."

His blood is spiky with adrenaline. He looks around to see if anyone is watching. Of course they are. But everyone is far away enough that the conversation is almost private. He's surprised Meggie didn't spring this on him on camera. Think of the drama. The conflict. The ratings.

"You believe in this stuff," he says finally. Trying to find what will persuade her. "So why won't you leave it alone? You know what happened. We know what happened. You know what the story is. Why the fuck do you need to know more?" He's whispering now.

"Because every time we're together she's here with us," Meggie says. "Didn't you know that? She's here now. Don't you feel her?"

Hair stands up on his legs, his arms, the back of his neck. His mouth is dry, his tongue sticks to the roof of his mouth. "No," he says. "I don't."

Meggie says, "You know I would be careful, Will. I would never do anything to hurt you. And it doesn't work like that, anyway." She leans in close, says very quietly, "It isn't about us. This is for me. I just want to talk to her. I just want her to go away."

(1992) They acquire the trappings of a life, he and Meggie. They buy dishes and midcentury modern furniture and lamps. They acquire friends who are in the business, and throw parties. On occasion things happen at their parties. For example, there is the girl. She arrives with someone. They never find out who. She is about as pretty as you would expect a girl at one of their parties to be, which is to say that she is really very pretty.

After all this time, the demon lover doesn't really remember what she looked like. There were a lot of girls and a lot of parties and that was another country.

She had long black hair. Big eyes.

He and Meggie are both wasted. And the girl is into both of them and eventually it's the three of them, everyone else is gone, there's a party going on somewhere else, they stay, she stays, and everyone else leaves. They drink and there's music and they dance. Then the girl is kissing Meggie and he is kissing the girl and they're in the bedroom. It's a lot of fun. They do pretty much everything you can do with three people in a bed. And at some point the girl is between them and everyone is having a good time, they're having fun, and then the girl says to them, *Bite me.*

Come on, bite me.

He bites her shoulder and she says, *No, really bite me. Bite harder. I want you to really bite me. Bite me, please.* And suddenly he and Meggie are looking at each other and it isn't fun anymore. This isn't what they're into.

He gets off as quickly as he can, because he's almost there anyway. And the girl is still begging, still asking for something they can't give her, because it isn't real and vampires aren't real and it's a distasteful situation and so Meggie asks the girl to leave. She does and they don't talk about it. They just go to sleep. And they wake up just a little bit later because she's snuck back into the house, they find out later that she's broken a window, and she's slashed her wrists. She's holding out her bloody wrists and she's saying, *Please, here's my blood, please drink it. I want you to drink my blood. Please.*

They get her bandaged up. The cuts aren't too deep. Meggie calls her agent, Pike, and Pike arranges for someone to take the girl to a private clinic. He tells them not to worry about any of it. It turns out that the girl is fifteen. Of course she is. Pike calls them again, after this girl gets out of the clinic, when she commits suicide. She has a history of attempts. Try, try, succeed.

The demon lover does not talk to Meggie again, because Pilar, who is naked—they are both naked, everyone is naked, of course —but Pilar is really quite lovely and fun to talk to and the camera work on this show is really quite exquisite and she likes the demon lover a lot. Keeps touching him. She says she has a bottle of Maker's Mark back in one of the cabins and he's already drunker than he's been in a while. Turns out they did meet once, in an AA meeting in Silver Lake.

They have a good time. Really, sex is a lot of fun. The demon lover suspects that there's some obvious psychological diagnosis for why he's having sex with Pilar, some need to reenact recent history and make sure it comes out better this time. The last girl with a camera didn't turn out so well for him. When exactly, he wonders, have things turned out well?

Afterward they lie on their backs on the dirty cement floor. Pilar says, "My girlfriend is never going to believe this."

He wonders if she's going to ask for an autograph.

Pilar's been sharing the cabin with the missing girl, Juliet. There's Whore-igami all over the cabin. Men and women and men and men and women and women in every possible combination, doing things that ought to be erotic. But they aren't; they're menacing instead. Maybe it's the straight lines.

The demon lover and Pilar get dressed in case Juliet shows up.

"Well," Pilar says, from her bunk bed, "goodnight."

He gets Juliet's bunk bed. Lies there in the dark until he's sure Pilar's asleep. He is thinking about Fawn for some reason. He can't stop thinking about her. If he stops thinking about her, he will have to think about the conversation with Meggie. He will have to think about Meggie.

Pilar's iPhone is on the floor beside her bunk bed. He picks it up. No password. He types in Fawn's number. Sends her a text. Hardly knows what he is typing.

I HOPE, he writes.

He writes the most awful things. Doesn't know why he is doing this. Perhaps she will assume that it is a wrong number. He types in details, specific things, so she will know it's not.

Eventually she texts back.

WHO IS THIS? WILL?

The demon lover doesn't respond to that. Just keeps texting FILTHY BITCH YOU CUNT YOU WHORE YOU SLIME etc. etc. etc. Until she stops asking. Surely she knows who he is. She must know who he is.

Here's the thing about acting, about a scene, about a character; about the dialogue you are given, the things your character does. None of it matters. You can take the most awful words, all the words, all the names, the acts he types into the text block. You can say these things, and the way you say them can change the meaning. You can say, "You dirty bitch. You cunt," and say them differently each time; can make it a joke, an endearment, a cry for help, a seduction. You can kill, be a vampire, a soulless thing. The audience will love you no matter what you do. If you want them to love you. Some of them will always love you.

He needs air. He drops the phone on the floor again where Pilar will find it in the morning. Decides to walk down to the lake. He will have to go past Meggie's trailer on the way, only he doesn't. Instead he stands there watching as a shadow slips out of the door of the trailer and down the stairs and away. Going where? Almost not there at all.

Ray?

He could follow. But he doesn't.

He wonders if Meggie is awake. The door to her trailer is off the latch and so the demon lover steps inside.

Makes his way to her bedroom, no lights, she is not awake. He will do no harm. Only wants to see her safe and sleeping. An old friend can go to see an old friend.

Meggie's a shape in the bed and he comes closer so he can see her face. There is someone in the bed with Meggie.

Ray looks at the demon lover and the demon lover looks back at Ray. Ray's right hand rests on Meggie's breast. Ray raises the other hand, beckons the demon lover closer.

*

The next morning is what you would predict. The crew of *Who's There?* packs up to leave; Pilar discovers the text messages on her phone.

Did I do that? the demon lover says. I was drunk. I may have done that. Oh God, oh hell, oh fuck. He plays his part.

This may get messy. Oh, he knows how messy it can get. Pilar can make some real money with those texts. Fawn, if she wants, can use them against him in the divorce.

He doesn't know how he gets in these situations.

Fawn has called Meggie. So there's that, as well. Meggie waits to talk to him until almost everyone else has packed up and gone; it's early afternoon now. Really, he should already have left. He has things he'll need to do. Decisions to make about flights, a new phone. He needs to call his publicist, his agent. Time for them to earn their keep. He likes to keep them busy.

Ray is off somewhere. The demon lover isn't too sorry about this.

It's not a fun conversation. They're up in the parking lot now, and one of the crew, he doesn't recognize her with her clothes on, says to Meggie, "Need a lift?"

"I've got the thing in Tallahassee tomorrow, the morning show," Meggie says. "Got someone picking me up any minute now."

"'Kay," the woman says. "See you in San Jose." She gives the demon lover a dubious look—is Pilar already talking?—and then gets in her car and drives away.

"San Jose?" the demon lover says.

"Yeah," Meggie says. "The Winchester House."

"Huh," the demon lover says. He doesn't really care. He's tired of this whole thing, Meggie, the borrowed T-shirt and cargo shorts, Lake Apopka, no-show ghosts, and bad publicity.

He knows what's coming. Meggie rips into him. He lets her. There's no point trying to talk to women when they get like this. He stands there and takes it all in. When she's finally done, he doesn't bother trying to defend himself. What's the good of saying things? He's so much better at saying things when there's a script to keep him from deep water. There's no script here.

Of course, he and Meggie will patch things up eventually. Old friends forgive old friends. Nothing is unforgivable. He's wondering if this is untrue when a car comes into the meadow.

"Well," Meggie says. "That's my ride."

She waits for him to speak, and when he doesn't, she says, "Goodbye, Will."

"I'll call you," the demon lover says at last. "It'll be okay, Meggie."

"Sure," Meggie says. She's not really making much of an effort. "Call me."

She gets into the back of the car. The demon lover bends over, waves at the window where she is sitting. She's looking straight ahead. The driver's window is down, and okay, here's Ray again. Of course! He looks out of the window at the demon lover. He raises an eyebrow, smiles, waves with that hand again, need a ride?

The demon lover steps away from the car. Feels a sense of overwhelming disgust and dread. A cloud of blackness and horror comes over him, something he hasn't felt in many, many years. He recognizes the feeling at once.

And that's that. The car drives away with Meggie inside it. The demon lover stands in the field for some period of time, he is never sure how long. Long enough that he is sure he will never catch up with the car with Meggie in it. And he doesn't.

There's a storm coming in.

The thing is this: Meggie never turns up for the morning show in Tallahassee. The other girl, Juliet Adeyemi, does reappear, but nobody ever sees Meggie again. She just vanishes. Her body is never found. The demon lover is a prime suspect in her disappearance. Of course he is. But there is no proof. No evidence.

No one is ever charged.

And Ray? When the demon lover explains everything to the police, to the media, on talk shows, he tells the same story over and over again. *I went to see my old friend Meggie. I met her lover, Ray. They left together. He drove the car.* But no one else supports this story. There is not a single person who will admit that Ray exists. There is not a frame of video with Ray in it. Ray was never there at all, no matter how many times the demon lover explains what happened. They say, *What did he look like? Can you describe him?* And the demon lover says, *He looked like me.*

As he is waiting for the third or maybe the fourth time to be questioned by the police, the demon lover thinks about how one day they will make a movie about all of this. About Meggie. But of course he will be too old to play the demon lover.

The Empties

FROM *The New Yorker*

SHE HAD NEVER perfected the trick of moistening the envelope flap with the tip of her tongue so it would stick and lie perfectly flat. In those days, *perfect* meant *as if untouched by hands.* Her flaps were always overwet and lumpy; when she pressed them down, she made them worse. Still, she loved folding the paper twice over, into three equal parts; she loved writing addresses, but especially her name and address in the upper-left corner. *J. Seiden. 29 Portnock Road.* The dignity, the businesslike efficiency of these slim objects, asking nothing, never disclosing more than they needed to. An envelope with only a check inside flapped like a flag, but an envelope containing a two-page letter had a solid integrity on every plane. A writer only in the sense that she loved having written. She slid the envelopes under the metal lid of the mailbox on her parents' porch and stared at them for a few moments. Proof of her existence in the world. Proof the world existed. You could count on it: someone was coming to take them away. Proof you would be sent, proof you would arrive.

She's sitting with Quentin at the Caf Café, set up under an enormous beech tree next to the South Royalton charging tower—a collection of salvaged plastic tables and chairs and a wheelbarrow cut up and welded into a wood-burning stove. The café serves mostly sassafras and stinging-nettle tea, but now and again there are red-market goods, unearthed from a collapsed house or a forgotten box in the pantry: half-rotted Lipton bags or dented cans of Bustelo two years past their expiration date. Dorrie, the owner, is a

strict no-currency Vore, and you have to know her to get in on the
bartering for the really good stuff. But it's worth biking the seven
miles just to bask in the shade of Quentin's unrepentant optimism.
Quentin is a Resurrectionist, a money hoarder. Before that, before
the last supplies ran out, he traded unleaded on the red market.
He's the last one left in South Royalton with a working laptop,
a silver incongruity whenever he takes it from its case and plugs
the white cord into the charging tower's concatenation of rusting
cables. Five minutes of charge keeps the battery alive. People stare
at him until he anxiously gathers the laptop up and slips away. Not
that anyone would steal it. They just don't want to be reminded.
This isn't fucking Starbucks, some crusty Vore always mutters.

She herself takes a bag of nails everywhere she goes, bound up
with fraying rubber bands. Everybody needs nails, and the Rumsons left boxes and boxes of them, sorted by size and type, in the
basement. *Her* basement. Though only in the most accidental
sense: it was Nathan who'd found the house, as a caretaker gig on
Craigslist.

Anyway, Quentin's saying, I was down at the Grange listening
to these guys arguing about the difference between dystopia and
apocalypse. Can you believe that? One of them was saying that we
were living in a dystopian novel, and the other guy, big bearded
dude, from the West Rats Collective, said, No, *dystopia* means an
imaginary place where everything is exactly wrong, and what we're
living in is a postapocalyptic, prelapsarian kind of thing, you know,
a return to nature after the collapse of society as we knew it. Want
some?

He unscrews a Burt's Bees tin and holds it out to her. Pine sap
—milky, resiny, the consistency of caramel. People say it's almost
as good as Nicorette. She shakes her head. He scoops some onto
his thumbnail.

And I must have been three or four shots in—we were drinking
Wayne Peters's sweet-potato vodka—because I said, Look, kiddos,
the truth is *neither,* because we have no idea what might happen,
the infrastructure is still basically in place, especially if people from
certain collectives hadn't stripped out the copper over in White
River—

No copper, no charging tower, she says.

—but my point is really that dystopian and postapocalyptic
narratives are *narratives,* that is, *stories:* things that are inherently

invented or collated ex post facto. Narratives are static. Real life is, is—

Kinetic?

The point is, we need to just let all that shit *go,* because, call it End Times or whatever you want, things are different now. None of the old endings played out, did they? So we have to imagine *new* endings. Hence the possibility for hope.

They must have gone easy on you.

They just started crying. That's the sad thing. Haven't seen so much crying since August of '15. Some people, you get a little liquor in them and it's all about the old times. They want to huddle up and sing Lady Gaga.

The dark is thickening now. Dorrie clanks her step stool from one low-hanging branch to another, lighting the candles inside each red glass globe. Tomas, the glassblower, held out for almost two years, firing the furnace with the last of his stored LPG, then with wood, making thick, indestructible goblets and candle lanterns, heavy and irregular as stones. He'd had exhibits at the Met and the Louvre, had made Christmas ornaments for the White House; now he's buried under a cairn up on Hull Mountain, dead of spring dysentery.

He's right, she's thinking, we have no story for ourselves, we've outlasted the predictions, we're too boring to be apocalyptic. But what would hope mean, after all that's happened? Hope for whom? Quentin's current theory has something to do with Caspar Weinberger, fallout shelters, server farms, and the Strategic Petroleum Reserve. I'm the town crank, he told her once, swigging from a gallon jug of cider on her porch, his face ribboned with tears.

If she didn't want to spare his feelings she would tell him—the way only one liberal-arts college graduate can say to another—that the problem isn't just narrative. It's theory. The era of sensemaking itself has passed. We don't need an analyst, she thinks, or an oracle, God forbid; we need a chronicler, a town recorder, a church Bible full of births and deaths. An inventory with a few highlights, one or two safety tips. A bit of incidental knowledge for whoever comes along next. But who has the hours to sit parked at a desk, smithing words, when there's ten pounds of berries in buckets on the porch, waiting to be picked over and dried on sheets in the sun?

I do.

It's nearly September. Two years ET, they've taken to saying, End Times, as versus BET, Before End Times. Most days the café is empty, Dorrie asleep under a canopy stitched together from banner ads she salvaged from the Catamounts' baseball field: Petco, Ledyard Bank, Murphy's Ace Lumber, National Life. Work now or starve in March. But I, she thinks, I've hit the jackpot, haven't I? Only my one mouth to feed, a roof that doesn't leak, three cords of seasoned wood in the barn, a stone-solid immune system, and hands striated and shiny with scar tissue, hands that can pluck a boiled Mason jar out of a scalding bath. Hands no man would ever love.

The charging towers themselves—top-heavy, buttressed with scrap girders, bits of fencing, broken truck axles—hold ten or twelve solar panels each. The larger ones, like Royalton, have a turbine, too. Whirligigs, Quentin says, works of folk art, the last temples, the only evidence they'll find when we're gone. Built last summer, the second summer, by a group of restless contractors who'd commandeered the Cumberland Farms and its gas tanks. There was a retired engineer from NBC, Davis something, who'd insisted on welding a radio and a TV antenna to each one. She was there the day they flipped the switch. There was only static, snow, the white-noise waterfall of empty air. People wept. Davis left his equipment to rust where it stood and vanished from town. Died later that summer, people said, eating bad freshwater crabs out of the Winooski.

At first there were long lines to charge every conceivable device—battery-powered fans were a big one, of course, PlayStation Portables, dialysis machines (how could anyone survive a year without one?), even vibrators. Twenty minutes a turn, no questions asked. Now the towers sit unused much of the time. Only the diehard and desperate rely on anything electric. There's a nurse from Woodstock who pedals nearly thirty miles with a homemade charger for hearing-aid batteries.

When Dorrie set up the Caf Café, she had a supply of light bulbs and a working refrigerator; a hundred people camped out under the tree every night, holding out for a glass of weak tea with one precious ice cube. There were jugglers, Dobro players, fire eaters, reciters of Shakespeare. Caffeine brought out the best in people. There were plans, speeches, meetings. There was going to be a new society in the ashes of the old. But then August rolled into September: you didn't need a calendar to smell the change in the air. Wood-gathering season. Nothing like the terror of that first night, when the cold lapped under the blankets like a rising sea. People all went back to their holes, Dorrie said to her. Back to their bathtub whiskey and skunk weed. They remember what last winter was like. We'll lose another twenty percent this year, that's my prediction. It's the winnowing.

She thought of the smell a body has after it's lain outside all winter, frozen in a block, even the eyes frozen, the vitreous humor turned to marble, and then the spring thaw hits.

Lucky it's only me, then, she said, and I've been splitting maple all summer.

Oh, honey, Dorrie said. I didn't mean you. God knows I didn't mean you.

Here is a thing that happened today, she wrote at the top of every page of a kelly-green Kate Spade journal, those first few weeks after the blackout. It had been a twenty-first-birthday gift, too pretty to throw away, though she rarely wrote anything by hand, so it had stayed at the bottom of one closet after another for fifteen years. Once her laptop went dead, she unearthed it and afterward kept it under her shirt at all times, in a special sling made of two *Eat More Kale* T-shirts sewn together. *Here is a thing that happened today.* It was the only possible way to begin when the last of the cell towers stopped working. *Spoke to Mom in California yesterday,* she wrote, *should have tried again.* Russell Tyson had his pickup parked on the town green with three generators running in the back, and people were paying twenty dollars for ten minutes of battery life, coaxing their phones back to a single bar, running fingers through their newly matted hair.

A few days later, the gravel around the green was littered with shards of thin, luminous glass: shattered smartphone screens, as disposable now as crack vials had been on North Avenue back in high school.

In those dirty days, she thinks, we were all Resurrectionists — even the most dyed-in-the-wool vegan bicyclists still had Tumblrs to update, still needed ice in their fair-trade coffee on an August afternoon, and a monthly refill of Ritalin in a stapled paper bag from the Rite Aid in Norwich. What was it like to spend every moment a little on edge, thinking that any time now the radio would beep, the air conditioner begin to whir, the lights flood the sullen filthy rooms? What it was like, as a practical matter, was stinky. No one wanting to admit that they needed to go take a bath in the creek. No one wanting to volunteer to build the town latrine. No one who knew *how* to build a latrine. After the third week, people pissed and shat by the side of the road, in the open. It was Elizabethan. And left little white flags of TP everywhere you looked.

That was the worst of it: the weeks of withdrawal when the coffee had run out, then the tea, the cigarettes, the Adderall, the Wellbutrin and Ativan, the Paxil and Zoloft. *Here is a thing that happened today.* She did a tally and counted twenty-three suicides. People disappeared into the woods, carrying knives, plastic bags, rubber bands. Or jumped off the White River Bridge on I-91. It was September, Indian summer, the leaves flaming out, the first nippy nights. The commuters, the office workers, the secretaries and actuaries and lawyers, walked around the town green in a daze, waiting for a sign. The farmers were all hard at work, running out the last diesel in their tractors. Some kids moved into the United Church and hung out a banner: OCCUPY BLACKOUT.

There was a girl, she remembers, who went up on the grassy hillside behind the Montessori school with a basket of scraps and a pair of scissors and began recreating her Pinterest page, squares of bright cloth for each jpeg, strips of blue sheet for the toolbar and browser frame.

One night at the beginning of that first winter—it must have been early in December, Nathan out laying the useless snares he'd built from an illustration in *The Homesteader's Manual*—she panicked when the fire wouldn't start in the kitchen stove and tore out pages in the journal, two or three at a time, as tinder. The living-room shelves sagged with books she could have used for the same purpose—*The Road Less Traveled, Italy on $5 a Day*—but at that moment, she thinks, forgiving herself, no one would have wanted to move a single extra muscle. In the winter, when you're cold, the world extends no more than a foot in any direction. Anyway, she thinks, no one cares about that stuff. The cheap pathos of children losing their toys. Not about the old dead life: only about the life that took its place.

She finds Matilda Barnstone in her rocking chair on the library porch, smoking a pipe, her sawed-off shotgun resting comfortably across the floral sprigs of her lap. The library is the only building left in town with a working lock, chicken wire nailed across the windows. People might share their last finger of motor oil, Matilda says, break a four-inch candle in two, divide a pot of beans to serve eight, but they'll kill you for a book. She sleeps in the basement with a Glock under her pillow. No lending anymore; all books stay on the premises, which means an old schoolhouse groaning on its joists, two floors, people in every nook, sweating, stinking, swatting flies, licking their thumbs as they page through Maeve Binchy and C. P. Snow, Louis L'Amour and George Santayana. Everyone gets patted down before leaving. Matilda blows out a blue cloud of corn-silk smoke and says, Haven't seen you here in an age. Still working through the stash at the Rumsons'?

Never thought I'd get into Trollope. I've read ten so far.

Beats Tom Clancy. We take donations, you know.

Once I get someone to lend me a horse and some saddlebags.

Mmm.

Listen, she says, Matilda, there's a typewriter in the back office, right?

Was last I checked.

Is there paper for it? Ribbons?

Matilda regards her with a faint smile.

I'm working on a town history, she says. August of '15 to the present. A record. There ought to be a record.

An oral history.

Not quite. Just a record. Written by me.

Who's going to read it?

Why, she says, it'll stay here. In the library. For the next generation. For history.

Did I hear right? Did you say "the next generation"? I never took you for a Resurrectionist. Matilda sits up straight in the chair. There is no history, she says. That's over now. No writing, only reading.

But we have a story, too.

We *had* a story. She rocks vigorously. Now we're just poor, she says, outside time. Lumpen proletariat. The subaltern. Outside history. And let's hope history never finds us again. We'll be squashed like bugs on a windshield.

Then a thought seems to strike her.

Stay here for a moment, she says. She shoulders the sawed-off

and disappears inside. Carter, she hears Matilda bellowing, no piss-
ing out the window, please. Use the latrine. Matilda reappears with
a thick padded envelope. Here, she says. Inside there's a stapled
stack of white paper, a manuscript.

Shroud of the Hills
a novel
by
Matilda E. Barnstone
COPYRIGHT 2003

Sent it to some contests, Matilda says. A few agents, one or two
MFA programs. No bites. No notice. Kept getting afraid someone
would steal my ideas. Anyway, you can use it.

Use it how?

Turn it over, dimwit. Use the back. That's three hundred and
thirty-two pages of blank paper.

You don't have another copy?

What would I need it for? Leave it in the library and eventually
some poor unfortunate soul would read the thing. Got pens?

A whole box of ballpoints. Haven't hardly used them since.

Make me look good is all I can say.

At home, later, after she's weeded the tomatoes, harvested the last
of the string beans, hauled a load of wash down to the stream and
spread it out over the long grass, she sits on the porch with a jar of
cold well water and begins:

> Before the last blackout the power had been on and off for weeks. I
> came up to Burlington in 2007 after a bad breakup in Brooklyn. It
> wasn't until Brian Sterling died, in February of the first winter, that we
> knew we were doing it wrong.

All that paper, glorious and terrifying. She riffles the stack through
her fingers. She wonders where her laptop is. Heaped in the back
of a closet somewhere, upstairs, with all the other dead things they
weren't able to cannibalize: the surge protectors and headphones,
Nathan's guitar amp, their digital cameras and printers, iPods,
iPads, the Rumsons' Tivoli stereo receiver and Harman Kardon
speakers. Before End Times, she'd never written anything on paper longer than a single sheet. Even when she kept a journal her
hand cramped up. In college, her writing tutor told her not to

think *essay*, not to think *paragraph*, just think in thought bubbles like comic strips and type them in big letters, hitting *print, print, print* every time, then spread them out across the floor and let the essay appear.

God, she says out loud, not for the first or the thousandth time, the way we built everything on waste.

Now she feels she can't afford a single wasted sheet. It ought to just come to her. Not because she's such a genius. No, because she's the only one, the town scribe, the voice of the people. The living *and* the dead.

For the first few months, before November came and the snow started, you'd still have people rumbling into town in cars, pick-ups, motorcycles—especially motorcycles, because a gallon of gas went so much farther that way. One of the occupiers would climb up and clang the church bell with a hammer, bringing people running from every direction, skidding their bikes, banging strollers along the rutted sidewalks. *Mic check* would come the cry, and then the waves of news in little sentence bundles, tweets amplified in waves through the crowd.

Manhattan is almost empty there are rats running down Broadway

I'm just on my way to look for my kid in Burlington her name's Shelby just started at UVM don't know what it's like up there

Police station torched in Hartford; all the riot gear was stolen

The Chinese are still flying planes into JFK.

Cholera outside Boston, must have been in the water, all southern sub-urbs, hundreds dead in Belmont, Watertown

FEMA set up all these orange tents in Springfield then disappeared

In Albany there's a warehouse full of Wonder bread, ration cards being issued

I've got three bottles of iodine here, one drop for a gallon of water should be enough

Met a guy in Portsmouth who had a basement full of batteries for his radio—said he could get only one station, and it was just the same crazy announcer every day, jabbering about a coup

Look out for a woman with a beetle tattooed on her wrist

I'm a doctor if you have spare antibiotics anything empty your medicine cabinets

It was all so random, you might hear five tendrils of the same rumor in a week, each canceling out the last, and it was almost a relief when the cars and motorcycles stopped coming. People who lived out near the highway still reported seeing vehicles flashing by every now and again, but it was one a day, at most. There was talk of throwing up a checkpoint, a barrier, of collecting tax in some form, but once December started no one had time to think about it. All you heard was the smack of ax on wood. What did people do, she thought, in the places where the old houses had been torn down, where the split-level ranches had baseboard heat and there wasn't a woodstove to be hauled in fifty miles? Thank God for Vermont and its fucking quote rustic unquote charm, Nathan used to say. Every house had a chimney, some two.

Families moved in together that winter; couples learned to grapple in a twin bed or a single sleeping bag. She and Nathan piled up all the comforters in the house, every Boba Fett blanket from the Rumsons' kids' rooms, even the decorative handmade quilts from Mississippi that lined the second-floor hallway; it took her breath away, sliding under twenty pounds of thread and batting, but then she curled up against his shoulder blades, letting him take the weight. She'd never been much for spooning before, but it was a month for counting all your advantages. George Larson converted his barn into a smokehouse and slaughtered every alpaca, llama, and goat on his property, excepting the three best milkers and one buck, walking the piles of smoked meat through town in a wheelbarrow, taking anything he could get as barter: family portraits, Rambo knives, bales of cloth diapers, canned peas, stacks of old *Rolling Stones*.

In the spring there were no reports of cars anywhere.

She wonders what it would be like to see one again. After nearly two years. A car that moved, not a rusting carapace on blocks. Her own car, a '99 Subaru, she'd traded to Dwight Yardley; he made it into a spare chicken coop.

It was one of those tidbits you picked up in middle-school history: the Middle Ages ended when trade began, when roads were built—or rebuilt, the Roman roads—because merchants carried firsthand accounts from town to town, hamlet to castle. BET, she had never made the connection between movement and the news, between cars and information, but how she'd loved the drive to Brattleboro, back when she was temping at Dryvins Parker three days a week, and the richness of the FM signal that boomed through the car: *You're listening to* All Things Considered. *I'm Robert Siegel.*

And I'm Michele Norris. In Syria today, government reprisals claimed new victims, but first we're going to take you to Botswana for a report on new ways to treat waterborne parasites. It was one of the great pleasures of the age, to be safe and warm and dry—showered, deodorized, professionally clothed in espadrilles and a linen jacket, latte steaming up the radio display, taking in the world's troubles three minutes at a time. That was luxury.

Dwight Yardley finds her asleep on the porch the next morning, in the hammock he built for her, the manuscript pages held down by a smooth river stone. Guess that's why they call it a sleeping porch, he says, setting down the milk crate with a solid *clump.* Protein, she thinks, swimming out of her dream. Protein has arrived.

Didn't think you'd be here this early.

It's high summer now. Got to be up with the rooster, then sleep through siesta. World doesn't stop heating up just because we're unplugged. Hotter every year since I can remember.

They've had the same conversation a hundred times. Dwight is not imaginative in his ways. Thank God.

Eggs this week, he says. Netted some crappie and smoked those. Mushrooms. Threw some more jerky in there, too. Know you're sick of it, but still.

Moose are scarce now, is what he's saying. And wickedly labor-intensive. She's never been on one of the group hunts, but Quentin went once, with five other guys. Too big to be hauled away by anything smaller than a pickup, a moose has to be field-butchered, apportioned to the team where it falls. In practice, Quentin says, this means standing around in an inch of blood-soaked snow, like something out of *Fargo,* working frantically to beat nightfall. He sharpened knives all day, that was his task, wiping them against his pants and scrubbing them across the whetstone. For dinner they roasted the heart; it was enough to feed all six of them. Then they hauled the whole bloody mass out, wrapped up and lashed in tarps to the saddles of their horses. It was like Cormac McCarthy, Quentin says, crossed with *The Clan of the Cave Bear.* But you did it, she said, you played your part. Didn't that make you want to cross over and become a Vore, even for a second? And he said, Are you fucking kidding me? I had nightmares for a week. Eating moose still makes me a little queasy. We've advanced since the Pleistocene. That's the *whole point.*

Your appointment's this week, she tells Dwight. Want to come inside?

Can't we do it out here?

In the hammock? Only if you want to repair it.

He grins at her. I was thinking of you leaning over the rail, he says. Got to looking at some of my old magazines.

Oh, Dwight. You know I'm shy.

No one's around to see.

Being so early, it takes him a while to get going, she has some massaging and cooing to do, even puts him in her mouth for a minute, but in the end, with her skirt hiked up over her hips, elbows digging into the flaking paint, he's done before the third grunt. Sorry, he says, pulling up his Carhartts, that's no way for a gentleman to behave.

We can go again if you like, she says, spreading her knees and wiping unashamedly with her bandanna. I didn't even get out the egg timer.

Don't tease. You know I'm good for one a day, if that.

Bet you tell that to all the girls.

She wonders how many there really are. The thing about arrangements is everyone has one, but nobody wants to talk about it. That's what Quentin says. There's no transparency in informal economies.

She remembers what it was like, the transparent world. Walking into a 7-Eleven and looking down the row of coolers, all that glass, all that pure water. Had a vasectomy years back, Dwight said, the first and only time they talked terms, so nothing to worry about on that score. Plus it's only been me and Angela. How was she to know that she wouldn't be puking in a month, heavy with another Yardley in the spring? By demanding his medical records? Asking him to go to Rite Aid and get a pack of Trojans?

We used to say "oppression" only when we talked about the government. Having to survive is also oppression. Necessity is oppression.

Dignity is for people who have options.

We were working so hard to get back to the land; then the land got us back and won't let go.

I would give anything to drink coffee out of a Styrofoam cup. Instant coffee with powdered creamer, the kind they gave out for free at car dealerships and funeral homes. I would give anything to throw something away and never see it again. I think about taking out the trash the way we used to at home, rolling it out to the curb, the trucks passing while we were at school. We are our garbage, Mom always used to say, that was her mantra, and I guess she was right in her way.

In the first couple of weeks there were big piles of trash outside every house. All the stuff you couldn't find another use for and couldn't compost. Yogurt cups, torn trash bags, dirty diapers, hair-spray cans, paper towels. Sometimes you'd see a pile that was as high as your waist. Nathan said it was a purge, a cleanse. But you could just as well say that who we were went out with the empties. We will never get our selves back.

In those days all the terms we had were metaphors. A desktop wasn't a desktop. Mail wasn't mail. Dial didn't mean to use a dial. Ringtones didn't actually ring—

In the winter she dreams of forced-air heating, the *whoosh* of the furnace starting up, the rush through the vents, the toasty smell of radiators, and in the summer she dreams of AC: the blast of frigid air in your face when you turned the key in the car, the cool seeping through a new condo with central air and wall-to-wall ecru carpets, even the oily dampness of an old window unit in an apartment on Second Avenue with sheets over the windows.

And then she thinks, That was the government. That was America. Air conditioning of the mind. We found that out, didn't we? Bob Perl, the Royalton postmaster, hung around the town green in an orange FEMA vest for weeks after the first blackout, showing everyone a thick binder labeled "Disaster Response in Rural Communities." It said that the National Guard would be there within twenty-four hours. There were pictures of tanker trucks, rows of trailers, pallets of MREs.

This isn't science fiction, Quentin says, because if it were we'd have the answers, we'd know what *happened.*

My parents saved everything I ever wrote, all my school projects, my dioramas, my research reports on alligators and elephants. That was what mattered when I was a kid. Good at art. Good at music. Good at lacrosse. Good at Tae Kwon Do. They had a closet to store all my stuff and then it turned into a separate room, the room that was Nana's bedroom before she died. Boxes and boxes, labeled "J. Summer Camp Projects 1995." Of course they kept Peter's things, too. But I was older; they were obsessive about me.

As if they were auditioning me for Jewish sainthood or something.

There was this band that everyone listened to in high school, this creepy metal band, and when I got to Holyoke no one had ever heard of them. It must have been some kind of Westchester cult thing. All their songs were about global warming and the end of the world. This band, they were called Into Another, and their stuff was mystical, insane vegan science fiction. Robot whales and ghost pirates and how we human beings are like the dinosaurs, outdated, redundant: grown too large for our environment—I'm not saying it all made sense, but at least they were ahead of their time. They had this one song that ended, "We are the last of the loved ones."

That's it. We are the last of the loved ones.

Professor Fuller used to say that romantic love was an invention of the Renaissance because it takes so many resources and so much leisure time. Adolescence *itself* was basically invented by the RAND Corporation for marketing purposes in the early fifties.

They could afford to love me because Dad worked in Hartford screwing widows out of their husbands' life insurance. Because Grandpa Stein got the government to declare eminent domain on the Norimco Plant before the EPA designated it a Superfund site. Peter laid it out for me the night he graduated from law school. We're a family of gangsters, he said. I mean, it's great that Mom got Tarrytown to do municipal compost, and it's awesome that you're doing whatever you do up there, but just so you understand: they did a lot of dirty deeds so you could be pretend poor. Isn't that what people call it now? Vermont is like Cuba, a little socialist island saved by huge infusions of cash from abroad.

It hasn't occurred to her to worry about Peter until now. A snapping turtle of a human being, a ridiculer, a fortress builder, with his Land Rover, his fancy skis, his JDate profile, his condo in McLean. She visited him there only once: an empty fridge, an elliptical machine facing a TV the size of a small barn, *Shark Week* playing endlessly on mute. The only certifiable yuppies in Royalton, the summer people, had stayed down in their houses on the far side of McIntosh Pond for months, until someone went down to check on them after the first frost and found them all starving, barricaded in their houses, convinced the townspeople were cannibalizing one another.

No, she decides, he must be dead. Dead for ages. Huddled by the door, still clasping his sand wedge, waiting for the lights to come back on.

Give me a break, she wants to say, rolling out of the hammock on an airless afternoon. The clanging of the church bell rolls across the silent valley in waves: it's something out of *The Sound of Music*, something Bashō would have written a haiku about. There hasn't been a peep from the churchers since last year. She thought they'd left town. Too difficult to heat the place, for starters. But someone is up in that belfry banging away. It could be a fire. That's her best guess. Or a new outbreak.

Not news. She's stopped thinking about news.

There's already a group gathered at the charging station. People tethering horses on the green, toting babies on hips up Division Street. There's a stranger, a new arrival; someone's found him a crate to stand on and rolled him a cone out of poster board. He's freshly bandaged, arm in a sling, his straggling gray hair held back by one of Dorrie's scrunchies.

I was working in corporate headquarters in Norwalk, he's calling out. Chief sustainability officer. Still have my business card here if you want to see it. Case you think I'm some nutcase. My kids were Wilson, Mackenzie, and Dylan. I'm thirty-eight years old. I'm not crazy. Listen to what I have to say, people.

We're listening, someone calls out. Got nowhere else to be.

You've got a good thing going here, he says, looking around at the crowd. I heard as much. I heard there were places up in the mountains where people didn't completely lose their shit. Not to say that we were such a total mess. Norwalk did relatively well, actually, for the first year and a half. It turns out the Salvadorean Mafia is really good at running a city with no centralized authority. They took over the Walmarts and the supermarkets. They enforced things. But supplies finally ran out, down to the last Lunchable, seriously. I was trying to learn to track the deer in our subdivision, but all I had was my grandfather's service revolver. No dice. Our neighbors got one that was roadkill just over the wall on 95. We grilled it on my bench-press rack, tried to get the whole thing evenly well done. Then everybody got sick. Dylan went first. Lauren next. Wilson and Mackenzie—

His face swells up, a rictus of old grief.

I hit the road, he said, no reason to stay. Figured I'd come up here and see if I could find some kind of community. I made it as far as Springfield. Springfield was a mess. Big piles of trash everywhere and roadblocks of old sofas every few blocks. Came across a natural-foods store, still boarded up and mostly intact. I took some

Kashi and soy-nut butter and went back up to the highway. And that's when I saw it. The convoy.

Good one, she thinks, nice timing there. Like a monologue in one of those disaster movies. *And then I saw it.* The audience leans in.

It was this line of Humvees, he says, black Humvees, far as I could see. The bigger boxy ones, troop transports, I guess, and ordinary semis, no markings, no license plates, just white numbers and QR codes on the side. Going north on 91, real slow. So I'm standing there, shading my eyes, getting my bearings, when one of the doors opens and a hand comes out and I hear this voice: Get in.

I mean, this convoy, it's rolling like a slow freight train. I have to run, but I can make it, easily. So there's two guys up on the front seat, the driver and a guy with a big gun between his knees, like something out of a movie, a rocket launcher, and they both have helmets with face shields on. Can't see their faces at all. Where are you going? I ask. No answer. Who are you guys, anyway?

Keep your head down, the driver says. Stay quiet. We're not supposed to pick up civilians.

It's half a day before we make it as far as Northampton. Some of the Humvees and trucks peel off there. Then it's sunset, evening, night, midnight, and we're still chugging along. No headlights. I'm thinking we must have gotten at least as far as Brattleboro.

The guy next to me—rocket-launcher guy? He's asleep. Or seems to be. Head tipped back, long sighing breaths.

We're going as far as Burlington, the driver says all of a sudden. Securing the major population centers first. Whatever that means up here. Then we cover the countryside.

Who are you? I ask him again. The government?

Officially we're Operation Restore Hope.

What the hell does that mean?

It means in about three months you get to eat French fries again, he says. And take a shit in an actual porta-potty. Six months, you'll be back to watching *CSI.* But first we need to reestablish central control. The rule of law. You'd be amazed at some of the crazy catastrophic shit that's been going on out there. We've gotten reports of cannibalism. Pagan rituals. Starvation cults. Hence the heavy machinery. We have to be ready for anything.

If you're the government, what took you so long?

Jesus, he says. Civilians. What took us so long? You should be asking, How'd you get here so soon? Have you noticed how radically things go to shit in this country when you turn off the juice for two hours? You ever notice how no one goes to college for electrical engineering anymore? We've been doing some serious fly-by-night MacGyver magic just to turn the lights back on in the White Zone. That's Pennsylvania Avenue to Capitol Hill.

It's all about priorities, rocket-launcher guy says, out of nowhere. Turns out he's been listening the whole time. Perimeter the strategic areas, he says. I mean, what would you do? Country's friggin' dying, man, you have to triage the motherfucker. Airway, breathing, circulation. Get power to the head. Get somebody looking out from behind those eyeballs. So what if they call it "the Executive Council" now, not "the president"? Now we get the arteries flowing again. Gas. Bleach. Sugar. TV. Little by little, stepping things up. Start from the trunk and worry about the limbs later. And if the limbs die? Well, which would you rather have, no country or a quadriplegic?

They say Vermont's all easygoing, the driver says. But look what they said about Connecticut. In Bridgeport we were fighting house to house. There aren't probably three buildings left standing. I mean, I'm from San Diego. What the hell do I know?

Enough, rocket-launcher guy says. Don't scare him. Look, he says to me, we're letting you out now. Go find some people and spread the word. Remember, it's called Operation Restore Hope. We've got free stickers and water bottles and candy bars, but they're all up in the front of the convoy. Just remember that name. And tell people, whatever they do, don't resist, for fuck's sake. It looks worse than it is.

The driver giggles. Resist, he says, and we'll pulp you like hajjis.

What is this feeling, she's wondering, this creeping numbness, knowing some disaster is happening in some faraway place when you're standing there doing nothing? Not just ordinary fear: fear of winter, fear of sickness, fear of starving. *Dread*. That flushed-my-ring-down-the-drain sensation, like you can't lift your arms. Like Bush in 2000. Wasn't that where it all began, this feeling that there was a master plan, that maybe the crazies were right after all—the assassination freaks, the Chomskyites, the Y2Kers? Remember that song, back in the nineties? she wants to ask someone. In case she imagined it. The one that goes, *We'll make great pets?*

Finally I realized the door was still unlocked, the man's saying, the passenger-side door, and as soon as dawn came up, the first gray in the sky, I opened it and rolled out onto the grass and started running. And here I am.

So what're you telling us? someone calls out.

Hide, he says. Go to ground. Be like the Vietnamese.

This is a bunch of crap, Dorrie says, but she's anxious, chomping a stalk of ryegrass and twisting it around her index finger. It's PSYOPS. Bet you anything there's a war party coming up from White River ready to steal our shit while we go hide in the bushes.

They're standing around the Caf, mostly, some collapsed into chairs. A core of twenty or so. Dwight's there, and Quentin. Matilda sits sunken in a chair, head in hands.

Oh Jesus, Quentin says, stop being such a Vore for a minute and admit you might be wrong. This guy's ID says *Connecticut*. Look, you seriously thought Washington was going to just, like, disappear?

He's trembling, she realizes. Can't keep his knees in place. His downy calves, his clean socks inside ancient, battered Doc Martens. An indefatigable doer of laundry, with a livid scar that runs the length of one forearm, from the first time he tried skimming the bubbling fat, making soap.

There are people who would bear anything, she thinks, to swipe a credit card again, to buy cut flowers, to see the straight furrows in a newly vacuumed carpet. You can't have everyone mourning quietly on a small farm. Someone has to turn a shining face to the Resurrection, to translate loss into profit. That's how we got cotton gins, and B-52s, and Tide.

Look, Matilda says. One thing we know. Someone's coming. We haven't seen the end of this. I'm proposing we arm ourselves and stay together. Who's with me?

Me.

Me.

Me.

Me.

She raises her hand, as if to say not *I agree* but *Present*.

This isn't the way this story ends, she tells herself, pedaling furiously over the last knobby hill before the Rumsons' driveway. We're not like Ewoks, rolling them over with logs, trapezing the soldiers out of their turrets on vines, huddling in tree houses, or like the Cong, trapping them in shit-smeared punji pits, feeding the prisoners to rats. This isn't *Star Wars* and it isn't *The Deer Hunter* and it isn't *Independence Day*. We've got no reason to believe this guy. We've got crops to bring in, tomatoes getting soft on the vine, and we're wasting time acting out *Red Dawn*.

But she'll cycle back with the gun, because she knows she doesn't want to be alone.

Mr. Rumson, who seemed like such a nice man, a mild-mannered professor of something, who evidently didn't believe in sunscreen, the way his nose peeled—she'd met him the one time she picked up the key—he'd left the place well armed, nonetheless. A whole cabinet of guns, unlocked, up in his study, in the attic. She keeps a revolver lying next to her on the bed upstairs and, because Dwight insists, a shotgun in the corner just inside the front door. If a deer comes across the lawn, he says, don't think twice. Aim for the head. And don't worry about the butchering; I'll hear the gun. That's a year's supply of meat for one skinny thing like you.

The gun she wants now is the scary one, with the folding stock and the banana clip. How does she even know those words? It's surprisingly light, when she lifts it out by the strap. The clip slides in and locks just like plugging a battery into a camera. Idiot-proof.

She writes at the table on the porch, the assault rifle laid out just within reach:

> Brian was the first person I'd ever seen die, and it was my fault, or at least I contributed. I mean, I didn't get him sick, but Nathan said not to leave the fire burning so high with the windows closed.
>
> I got better at it after that. For a while we served as the hospital, eleven or twelve patients at a time. There was no reason not to, all these big rooms downstairs and a good supply of wood, two stoves. Maxine was an herbalist and a Reiki healer and a PA, too; she stayed here three months, directing things. That was the best of it.
>
> Then she came down with it and Nathan and I were left handling things on our own. Dwight brought food when he could and took the bodies out, but that was before the last blizzard, the March blizzard.
>
> After Brian I got impatient with them as they died. Knowing that by the time the lips started turning blue there was no stopping it. Hurry up, I used to think, free up the bed. By the time it was Nathan's turn I was just sloppy. Forgetting to bring him water for hours. Things like

that. I was never cut out to be a nurse. There was snow banked halfway up the downstairs windows. Where was I supposed to put the bodies? I laughed at him. I laughed at Nathan when he begged me for things. He was delusional at the end, begging for Klondike bars.

I was never meant to have children I never wanted to.

This isn't our story. There was supposed to be time to tell our story.

I was a decent person. I went to good schools. In my own time I would have been a good person. You can't judge the people on the lifeboats, the crashed soccer players in the stupid Andes.

This is the last time a person will be one person what do I mean I mean a woman living in a house alone Dwight offered to have me stay with them the second winter and I said no I'll cut my own wood no one stays with me this time I'll stock up properly I'm immune now I guess so this is the last time I don't know how to write without drafts I don't know how to write a declarative sentence fuck it I don't know how to declare anything at all

A boil of black smoke rises off the ridge opposite her.

The Macneils. What could they have out there — a forgotten oil drum, a pile of tires? Are they fighting already? Is it the army? The people from White River? A grinding sound, a whining sound. Machinery. Is that what it is? It's been two years; she can't be sure.

And then, trickling through the air, a sick Morse code, a demented tap dancer: gunshots.

This is it, she thinks, not the End Times, the time of the end. What makes her so certain? I have been intimate with death, she thinks, that's how I know. I can smell it, even on myself. She picks up the manuscript: fifteen pages. Scrawl. Notes. Hesitations. Matilda was right, she says to herself. We're not the beginning of anything; we're about to be pulped, right back into the ground. We're about to reenter history.

We were good people. We made it work. We weren't sad. We were proud. We didn't need an ending. We were too grateful. Living was enough.

A flicker of wind, a sudden gust across the yard, takes the pages out of her hand; she doesn't even have to toss them. White flags across the garden; perfect rectangles, perfect things, falling lightly on the gravel, resting in the tall grass. That's done, she says. Picks up the rifle and lays it across her knees.

KELLY SANDOVAL

The One They Took Before

FROM *Shimmer Magazine*

CRAIGSLIST > SEATTLE > ALL SEATTLE > LOST&FOUND
Sat 23 Jul
FOUND: Rift in the Fabric of the Universe — (West Seattle)
Rift opened in my backyard. About six feet tall and one foot wide. Appears to open onto a world of endless twilight and impossible beauty. Makes a ringing noise like a thousand tiny bells. Call (206) 555-9780 to identify.

Kayla reads the listing twice, knowing the eager beating of her heart is ridiculous. One page back, someone claims they found a time machine. Someone else has apparently lost their kidneys.

The Internet isn't real. That's what she likes about it. And if the post is real, the best thing she can do is pretend she never saw it.

After all, she's doing better. She sees a therapist now. She's had a couple of job interviews.

She calls the number.

"Hello?" It's a man's voice. Kayla can't identify his accent.

"Oh. Hi." Her words come out timid and thin, almost a whisper. She stands and starts pacing the length of her apartment, stepping over dirty clothes and cat toys. "I'm calling about your Craigslist ad."

"Oh!" He sounds surprised, but not displeased. "I'm glad to hear from you. So, when did you lose it?"

"Pardon?"

"The rift. When did you lose it?"

Yesterday? A thousand years ago? Time was meaningless there. She's pretty sure it all happened a very long time ago.

"It's complicated," she says.

"Well, can you describe it, then? Tell me what color it is? I just need to be sure it's yours."

It isn't hers. "Have you had a lot of calls?"

"A few crazies," he admits. "Someone claiming to be my evil twin. That sort of thing."

The cats, Ablach and Thomas, twist around her ankles. She leans down to stroke Ablach and presses her face into his fur. He hasn't spoken to her since they got out. Neither of them have. "Have you tried going through it?"

"No. It's not mine." He tries to sound firm, but she knows the longing in his voice. They opened a door for him. It's only a matter of time. "Listen, if this thing isn't yours —"

"Don't go through it," she says. "Even if they ask you to."

She hangs up before he can reply.

The cats watch her, unblinking. Gold eyes and silver. She tries not to imagine their voices.

"What?" she asks them. "I warned him. What else can I do?"

Ablach turns his back on her, tail lashing. Thomas rolls onto his back and lets her stroke his stomach.

"I'm not going back." She repeats the phrase, over and over. Words have power. They taught her that.

After a few hours pass, she tries the number again. No one answers.

The Stranger Lovelab
23 / Man / Cal Anderson
Faerie Queen, saw you in Cal Anderson Park by the tennis courts. You wore a dress of hummingbird feathers and a crown of tiny stars. I asked for a light. I should have asked for more. Coffee?

For two days Kayla avoids the Internet and every local newspaper. If they're hunting again, she doesn't want to know. On the third day, she dares to go out for coffee. A newspaper waits at the only open table, and she flips to the classifieds before she can stop herself.

The ad draws her eye immediately. It's highlighted. She wonders if it was there before she sat down. If it will still be there when she leaves.

Cal Anderson is only a few blocks away. And she's still weak enough to need to know. Kayla leaves her full cup on the table and heads outside, flinching as she enters the sunlight. Long weeks of gray skies and soft rain don't bother her, but these brief days of garish blue leave her longing for twilight.

Shirtless men and girls in bikinis crowd the park, and Kayla tries not to see them. They remind her of someone she was, and she still longs to slip back into that skin. It's best not to think of it. Nostalgia, for either life, is poison.

She keeps her head down, and makes her way to the stand of trees that lines the tennis courts. No hummingbird feathers wait for her there. No tiny stars litter the grass. A group of teens jostle past and one of them reaches up to pluck an apple from the branch above her head. The fruit in his hand is the deep red of exposed muscle. Looking up, she has to tell herself that apples, not hearts, hang heavy on the branches. They are huge and numerous, an out-of-season abundance. Also, it's not an apple tree.

She runs home and sobs quietly until Ablach and Thomas climb into her lap and lick her tears with rough tongues. After that, her sobs aren't quiet at all.

Seattle Times Online
Category: The Blotter
August 1, 2013

King County Sheriff's Office seeks the public's help in locating a Se-attle area woman

Josey Aarons, 24, was last seen on July 30th at the Triple Door on 216 Union Street, where she was performing with her band, The Sudden Sorrows. According to her friends, Aarons was supposed to meet them at an afterparty but never arrived.

Witnesses report Aarons was seen outside the venue with a woman described as having skin the color of a summer moon and eyes as deep as madness. Aarons is 5 feet 9 inches tall, 150 lbs., with short blond hair and brown eyes. She was last seen wearing black jeans and a green trench coat. She was carrying a gray messenger bag.

Anyone with information on the whereabouts of either Ms. Aarons or her companion is asked to call the sheriff's office at 206-555-9252.

Kayla sits, her guitar in her lap, and strokes the smooth wood like it's one of the cats. When she first got back, she took a knife to the strings, sawing through them one by one. It didn't hurt at the time. It hurts now, when she longs for the comfort of melody. But she knows better.

If she plays, they will hear her.

They will take her back.

She is trying so hard. She goes to yoga class. She watches TV.

She rocks in the dark of her apartment, the glow of the computer screen creating a sort of twilight.

Is she loved, this girl that they have taken? Do they kiss her, their lips honey-sweet and dizzying as brandy? Does she realize she is theirs? That they will pet and praise and keep her, drape her in diamonds and bask in her light, but never let her go?

Until they do.

Freedom is its own kind of prison.

In Kayla's apartment, the computer glows, and it is nothing at all like twilight.

She tries to tell herself the girl will be okay. They will keep her for a few eternities, but they will also set her free again. She can rebuild.

Kayla is.

She picks up the phone and dials the number for the sheriff's office. She tells them she knows about Josey.

"Wait a year and a day," she says. "They won't keep her forever."

Except, of course, they will. They kept Kayla even longer than that.

That's two, Kayla thinks. They'll claim one more. They like patterns, cycles, rules.

She tells herself to ignore it. It isn't her problem. She can't save everyone. If she interferes, they'll find her.

She tells herself she doesn't want that. She says it out loud. There's supposed to be power in that.

Seattle Times
August 3, 2013

Explanation sought after fatal hunting trip
The death of James Garcia, a Tacoma area accountant, has left police with more questions than answers. He was hunting in Silwen Falls with his brothers Marcus and Eric Garcia when the fatal accident occurred. While the details are still unclear, the brothers said James Garcia separated from his party early on the morning of August 2 at a blind he was accustomed to using, and where he intended to remain for most of the day.

Sometime around noon, James Garcia left his shelter and removed all his clothing, including his orange safety vest, before approaching the blind his brothers were sharing. In the ensuing confusion, the brothers said they mistook him for, in the words of Marcus Garcia, "a stag of shadow and dream, its antlers cast from sunlight." Eric Garcia admits to taking the fatal shot. Investigations are ongoing, police said.

Kayla remembers the bright cry of horns, horses with hot breath and red eyes, stags with human screams. Her keepers, clad in spider-silk and frost, the mad need in their joy. She tries to think of the dead man. She thinks instead of trays piled high with venison, air spice-laden and thick with laughter. Hunger twists in her stomach and she forgets to be ashamed.

She makes herself a sandwich, ham and cheddar on white bread, but only manages a few bites. Everything tastes like beige.

Thomas jumps into her arms, a furry mass of gold and shadow, and purrs deep and low. The sound usually calms her, reminds her to settle and stay. She should sit down, stroke him, find center.

"I don't need them," she whispers into his fur. She tries turning on the TV, but every show is a meaningless mix of colors and noises.

Ablach paces at the door, his cries high and bright as a hunting horn.

"Don't trust him," she tells herself. "Don't trust any of their gifts."

But he sings her heart, and she sets Thomas aside.

Outside, the stars are hidden behind a thin wash of cloud. Kayla follows Ablach down major roads and through slender alleys lined with overflowing Dumpsters. The route is circuitous and random but she recognizes where he leads her. Cal Anderson Park. She's alone on a tree-lined sidewalk, looking for a shadow in a world of them.

Ablach cries above her. She looks up, finds him watching her from the branches, his eyes like silver coins. She reaches to stroke him and her fingers close around a heavy fruit made russet by the night. It doesn't smell like an apple. It smells of blood and honey, of sex and song.

The juice is silver and she licks it from her fingers when she's done. Ablach lets her carry him home.

*

Seattle Times
August 4, 2013
Obituary

James Carlos Garcia, 43, was lost in a tragic accident on August 2. A man of courage, humor and intelligence, he was an active member of his community and a dedicated husband and father.

He leaves behind three children, Peter Garcia, Mary Winner, and James Garcia Jr. He is also survived by his wife, Alice Garcia.

He loved hunting, Bruce Springsteen's music, and his family.

A celebration of his life will be held on August 10 at 7:30 p.m. at the North Tacoma Community Hall.

The funeral, Facebook tells her, is on the sixth. She sends flowers, the biggest bouquet the florist has. Money isn't an issue; they sent her back decked in gold and strange jewels. She waited weeks for it to fade or turn to leaves but the gold, like the memories, refused to leave her. It means she doesn't have to work, or leave her apartment, or forget.

An obvious trap, and she's been trying to fight it. Of course, she hasn't sent out a job application since she called about the rift. Hasn't answered her phone, or emailed the people she tells herself are her friends.

She doesn't intend to go. The one responsible is sure to be there; they love to watch. Even on the morning of the sixth, as she puts on a dress of black silk and gold lace, she imagines she will stay home. The dress was her favorite, before. Now she can only see it as an echo of something grander. She has worn a cloak of dragonfly skin over a gown woven from the scent of roses. They set her at the feet of the queen, and when she played, they drank the notes from the air.

It will not happen again, Kayla tells herself as she restrings her guitar. And maybe it won't. But she isn't sure anymore.

She lets the cats out before she leaves. Ablach disappears with a confident stride, but Thomas presses himself against her legs, crying to be picked up and trying to follow her into the cab.

"If you would only ask me to stay," she whispers as she sets him back on the pavement, "I might."

But he doesn't ask.

The cab pulls up at the church well after the service is scheduled to begin. She considers going in, makes it all the way to the door before deciding against it. The family already has one voyeur to their pain. She can at least save them a second one.

She waits beside the door and tries to enjoy the feeling of the sun on her skin. She remembers longing for daylight, then screaming for daylight, then forgetting what daylight meant.

It's a difficult thing to learn again.

"They are crying in there." The words settle onto her skin like she's walked into mist, a cat's purr of a sound: low, self-satisfied, demanding. "Painting their faces with ash," it says, "and tearing their clothes with sorrow."

Its skin, Kayla sees, is more the color of an autumn moon than one from the summer, but its eyes are certainly deep as madness, and the iridescent feathers of its hummingbird gown shame her simple dress. She lowers her eyes, curtsies. The gesture is automatic, and she hates herself for it.

"What did he do?" she asks. It's fear, not excitement, that sets her heart racing. She's glad to fear them again.

"Do?" Its purr warms with amusement. "He did nothing. He did not catch me bathing or cross my path to start a riddle game. He sat in his tent and did nothing at all. He bored me."

Yes, that was a sort of crime. What use were humans if they refused to be fun? She stopped being fun, near the end. She sat and rocked and sobbed and would not give them their music.

They sent her home, after that. She thought they freed her. But here she is, standing before one, her guitar at her side.

"You have not played," it says. "We listen, still. And you give us nothing. Are you still broken?"

"Not like I was," she says. And realizes her mistake as it smiles.

"You were her favorite," it says. "Our Lightning Bard."

"You have a new one now," she says. She tries to keep her breathing even, but the scent of it makes her dizzy. "Unless *she's already* broken."

"So unkind. We offer her wonders." It glances up, stares at the sun.

Kayla wants to kiss its neck, drink eternity from its veins. She digs her nails into her palms. "Did you offer her a choice?"

"Of a sort. She followed me."

"She didn't know what she followed you to." But Kayla does.

"Are you jealous?" it asks, voice silken with amusement. "You needn't be. We can still take you."

And yes, she is, isn't she? She wants those first wondering months, before she could see the rot beneath the gilt. She wants the luxury of not yet knowing what it means to love them.

"No." She forces the word out through clenched teeth.

"I have leave to barter," it says. "We have no need for two musicians. And it would be novel to win the same soul twice."

The church door opens and the mourners begin to stream out. Kayla catches sight of a man's face, ugly with pain, and recognizes him as one of the dead man's brothers. It doesn't even glance his way. The man's loss is no more than a daytime rerun of a once amusing show.

"No." She whispers it this time, crossing her arms in a vain attempt at comfort. "It wouldn't last."

"You could be our pretty one again, our summer storm." Its voice is thick and sweet. The world fades and reduces itself, the sun hiding, the mourners hushing their cries.

Kayla's tears are hot on her face and she's afraid to brush them away. She could say yes. She could tell herself she was being generous, playing the sacrifice. "Did you take her just for that? To offer in trade?"

Is it her fault, or does she only want to believe she means that much to them?

"I care little for your questions, Pet. Will you come?"

This is the part where she says yes and it drags her back to that land of endless twilight and impossible beauty. This is the part where she falls.

"No," she says, the third time she's rejected it. She stands straighter, meets its eyes. Her guitar case falls from limp fingers. If it makes a sound as it hits the steps, she doesn't hear it.

"Very well," it says, the purr gone from its voice. "But we will be listening. And you will tire of mortality and dust."

She is already tired of mortality and dust. Tired, too, of being locked into the need of them.

"You can't keep me," she says.

It leans in and kisses the salt from her lips. Its breath smells like storm clouds, all electric promise. "Oh, pretty one. We already have."

The world lurches, empties, and she's alone on the church steps. The mourners are leaving, a long procession of cars already disappearing down the street.

She calls the cab back. Rides home in silence.

A year and a day. An eternity. One doesn't exclude the other.

But they always send back what they take, shattered husks of what they once found beautiful.

Kayla will wait. Apply for jobs. Mark the calendar.

She'll be ready, when the time comes. No one waited for her. No one understood. It can be different, this time. She can help.

And that can be a sort of winning.

T. C. BOYLE

The Relive Box

FROM *The New Yorker*

KATIE WANTED TO relive Katie at nine, before her mother left, and I could appreciate that, but we had only one console at the time, and I really didn't want to go there. It was coming up on the holidays, absolutely grim outside, nine-thirty at night—on a school night—and she had to be up at six to catch the bus in the dark. She'd already missed too much school, staying home on any pretext and reliving all day, while I was at work, so there really were no limits, and who was being a bad father here? A single father unable to discipline his fifteen-year-old daughter, let alone inculcate a work ethic in her?

Me. I was. And I felt bad about it. I wanted to put my foot down and at the same time give her something, make a concession, a peace offering. But even more I wanted the box myself, wanted it so baldly it was showing in my face, I'm sure, and she needed to get ready for school, needed sleep, needed to stop reliving and worry about the now, the now and the future. "Why don't you wait till the weekend?" I said.

She was wearing those tights which all the girls wear like painted-on skin, standing in the doorway to the living room, perching on one foot the way she did when she was doing her dance exercises. Her face belonged to her mother, my ex, Christine, who hadn't been there for her for six years and counting. "I want to relive now," she said, diminishing her voice to a shaky, hesitant plaint that was calculated to make me give in to whatever she wanted, but it wasn't going to work this time, no way. She was going to bed, and I was going back to a rainy February night in 1982, a sold-out show at the Roxy, a band

I loved then, and the girl I was mad crazy for before she broke my heart and Christine came along to break it all over again.

"Why don't you go upstairs and text your friends or something?" I said.

"I don't want to text my friends. I want to be with my mom."

This was a plaint, too, and it cut even deeper. She was deprived, that was the theme here, and my behavior, as any impartial observer could have seen in a heartbeat, verged on child abuse. "I know, honey, I know. But it's not healthy. You're spending too much time there."

"You're just selfish, that's all," she said, and here was the shift to a new tone, a tone of animus and opposition, the subtext being that I never thought of anybody but myself. "You want to, what, relive when you were, like, my age or something? Let me guess: you're going to go back and relive yourself doing homework, right? As an example for your daughter?"

The room was a mess. The next day was the day the maid came, so I was standing amid the debris of the past week, a healthy percentage of it—abandoned sweat socks, energy-drink cans, crumpled foil pouches that had once contained biscotti, popcorn, or Salami Bites—generated by the child standing there before me. "I don't like your sarcasm," I said.

Her face was pinched so that her lips were reduced to the smallest little O-ring of disgust. "What *do* you like?"

"A clean house. A little peace and quiet. Some privacy, for Christ's sake—is that too much to ask?"

"I want to be with Mom."

"Go text your friends."

"I don't have any friends."

"Make some."

And this, thrown over her shoulder, preparatory to the furious pounding retreat up the stairs and the slamming of her bedroom door: "You're a pig!"

And my response, which had been ritualized ever since I'd sprung for the $5,000, second-generation Halcom X1520 Relive Box with the In-Flesh Retinal Projection Stream and altered forever the dynamic between me and my only child: "I know."

Most people, when they got their first Relive Box, went straight for sex, which was only natural. In fact, it was a selling point in the TV ads, which featured shimmering adolescents walking hand in hand along a generic strip of beach or leaning in for a tender kiss over the ball return at the bowling alley. Who wouldn't want to go back there? Who wouldn't want to relive innocence, the nascent stirrings of love and desire, or the first time you removed her clothes and she removed yours? What of girlfriends (or boyfriends, as the case may be), wives, ex-wives, one-night stands, the casual encounter that got you halfway there, then flitted out of reach on the wings of an unfulfilled promise? I was no different. The sex part of it obsessed me through those first couple of months, and if I drifted into work each morning feeling drained (and not just figuratively), at least I knew that it was a problem, that it was adversely affecting my job performance and, if I didn't cut back, threatening my job itself. Still, to relive Christine when we first met, to relive her in bed, in candlelight, clinging fast to me and whispering my name in the throes of her passion, was too great a temptation. Or even just sitting there across from me in the Moroccan restaurant where I took her for our first date, her eyes like portals, as she leaned into the table and drank up every word and witticism that came out of my mouth. Or to go farther back, before my wife entered the picture, to Rennie Porter, the girl I took to the senior prom and spent two delicious hours rubbing up against in the back seat of my father's Buick Regal—every second of which I'd relived six or seven times now. And to Lisa, Lisa Denardo, the girl I met that night at the Roxy, hoping I was going to score.

I started coming in late to work. Giving everybody, even my boss, the zombie stare. I got my first warning. Then my second. And my boss—Kevin Moos, a decent enough guy, five years younger than me, who didn't have an X1520, or not that he was letting on—sat me down in his office and told me, in no uncertain terms, that there wouldn't be a third.

But it was a miserable night, and I was depressed. And bored. So bored you could have drilled holes in the back of my head and taken core samples and I wouldn't have known the difference. I'd already denied my daughter, who was thumping around upstairs with the cumulative weight of ten daughters, and the next day was Friday, TGIF, end of the week, the slimmest of workdays, when just about everybody alive thinks about slipping out early. I figured that even if I did relive for more than the two hours I was going to strictly limit myself to, even if I woke up exhausted, I could always find a way to make it to lunch and just let things coast after that. So I went into the kitchen and fixed myself a gin and tonic, because that was what I'd been drinking that night at the Roxy, and carried it into the room at the end of the hall that had once been a bed-room and was now (Katie's joke, not mine) the reliving room.

The console sat squarely on the low table that was the only piece of furniture in the room, aside from the straight-backed chair I'd set in front of it the day I brought the thing home. It wasn't much bigger than the gaming consoles I'd had to make do with in the old days, a slick black metal cube with a single recessed glass slit running across the face of it from one side to the other. It activated the minute I took my seat. "Hello, Wes," it said, in the voice I'd se-lected, male, with the slightest bump of an accent to make it seem less synthetic. "Welcome back."

I lifted the drink to my lips to steady myself—think of a conduc-tor raising his baton—and cleared my throat. "February 28, 1982," I said. "Nine forty-five p.m. Play."

The box flashed the date and time and then suddenly I was there, the club exploding into life like a comet touching down, light and noise and movement obliterating the now, the house gone, my daughter gone, the world of getting and doing and bosses and work vanished in an instant. I was standing at the bar with my best friend, Zach Ronalds, who turned up his shirt collar and wore his hair in a Joe Strummer pompadour just like me, only his hair was black and mine choirboy blond (I'd dye it within the week), and I was trying to get the bartender's attention so I could order us G&Ts with my fake ID. The band, more New Wave than punk, hadn't started yet, and the only thing to look at onstage was the opening band, whose mem-bers were packing up their equipment while hypervigilant girls in vampire makeup and torn fishnet stockings washed around them in a human tide that ebbed and flowed on the waves of music crashing through the speakers. It was bliss. Bliss because I knew now that this night alone, out of all the long succession of dull, nugatory nights building up to it, would be special, that this was the night I'd meet Lisa and take her home with me. To my parents' house in Pasadena, where I had a room of my own above the detached garage and could come and go as I pleased. My room. The place where I greased up my hair and stared at myself in the mirror and waited for something to happen, something like this, like what was coming in seven and a half real-time minutes.

Zach said what sounded like "Look at that skank," but since he had his face turned away from me and the music was cranked to the sonic level of a rocket launch (give credit to the X1520's parametric speaker/audio-beam technology, which is infinitely more refined than the first generation's), I wasn't quite sure, though I must have heard him that night, my ears younger then, less damaged by scenes like this one, because I took hold of his arm and said, "Who? Her?"

What I said now, though, was "Reset, reverse ten seconds," and everything stalled, vanished, and started up once more, and here I was trying all over again to get the bartender's attention and listening hard when Zach, leaning casually against the bar on two splayed elbows, opened his mouth to speak. "Look at that skank," he said, undeniably, and there it was, coloring everything in the moment, because he was snap-judging Lisa, with her coat-hanger shoulders, Kabuki makeup, and shining black lips, and I said, "Who? Her?," already attracted, because in my eyes she wasn't a skank at all, or if she was, she was a skank from some other realm altogether, and I couldn't from that moment on think of anything but getting her to talk to me.

Now, the frustrating thing about the current relive technology is that you can't be an actor in the scene, only an observer, like Scrooge reliving his boarding-school agonies with the Ghost of Christmas Past at his elbow, so whatever howlers your adolescent self might have uttered are right there, hanging in the air, unedited. You can fast-forward, and I suppose most people do—skip the chatter; get to the sex—but personally, after going straight to the carnal moments the first five or six times I relived a scene, I liked to go back and hear what I'd had to say, what she'd had to say, no matter how banal it might sound now. What I did that night —and I'd already relived this moment twice that week—was catch hold of the bartender and order not two but three G&Ts, though I only had something like $18 in my wallet, set one on the bar for Zach, and cross the floor to where she was standing, just beneath the stage, in what would be the mosh pit half an hour later. She saw me coming, saw the drinks—two drinks—and looked away, covering herself, because she was sure I was toting that extra drink for somebody else, a girlfriend or a best bud, lurking in the drift of shadow that the stage lights drew up out of the murky walls.

I tapped her shoulder. She turned her face to me.

"Pause," I said.

Everything stopped. I was in a 3-D painting now, and so was she, and for the longest time I just kept things there, studying her face. She was eighteen years old, like me, beautiful enough underneath the paint and gel and eyeliner and all the rest to make me feel faint even now, and her eyes weren't wary, weren't *used*, but candid, ready, rich with expectation. I held my drink just under my nose, inhaling the smell of juniper berries to tweak the memory, and said, "Play."

"You look thirsty," I said.

The music boomed. Behind me, at the bar, Zach was giving me a look of disbelief, like *What the* —?, because this was a violation of our club-going protocol. We didn't talk to the girls, and especially not the skanks, because we were there for the *music;* at least that was what we told ourselves. (Second time around I did pause this part, just for the expression on his face—Zach, poor Zach, who never did find himself a girlfriend, as far as I know, and who's probably someplace reliving every club he's ever been in and every date he's ever had, just to feel sorry for himself.)

She leveled her eyes on me, gave it a beat, then took the cold glass from my hand. "How did you guess?" she said.

What followed was the usual exchange of information about bands, books, neighborhood, high school, college, and then I was bragging about the bands I'd seen lately and she was countering with the band members she knew personally—like John Doe and the drummer for the Germs—and letting her eyes reveal just how personal that was, which only managed to inflame me till I wanted nothing more on this earth than to pin her in a corner and kiss the black lipstick right off her. What I said then, unaware that my carefully sculpted pompadour was collapsing across my brow in something very much like a bowl cut (or worse—*anathema*—a Beatles shag), was "You want to dance?"

She gave me a look. Shot her eyes to the stage and back, then around the room. A few people were dancing to the canned music, most of them jerking and gyrating to their own drugged-out beat, and there was no sign—yet—of the band we'd come to hear. "To this?"

"Yeah," I said, and I looked so—what was it?—*needy*, though at the time I must have thought I was chiseled out of a block of pure cool. "Come on," I said, and I reached out a hand to her.

I watched the decision firm up in her eyes, deep in this moment which would give rise to all the rest, to the part I was about to fast-forward to because I had to get up in the morning. For work. And no excuses. But watch, watch what comes next . . .

She took my hand, the soft friction of her touch alive still somewhere in my cell memory, and then she was leading me out onto the dance floor.

She was leading. And I was following.

Will it surprise you to know that I exceeded my self-imposed two-hour limit? That after the sex I fast-forwarded to our first date, which was really just an agreed-upon meeting at Tower Records (March 2, 1982, 4:30 p.m.), and then up to Barney's Beanery for cheeseburgers and beers and shots of peppermint schnapps (!), which she paid for, because her father was a rich executive at Warner Bros.? Or that that made me feel so good I couldn't resist skipping ahead three months, to when she was as integral to my life as the Black Flag T-shirt that never left my back except in the shower? Lisa. Lisa Denardo. With her cat's tongue and her tight, torquing body that was a girl's and a woman's at the same time and her perfect, evenly spaced set of glistening white teeth (perfect, that is, but for the incisor she'd had a dentist in Tijuana remove, in the spirit of punk solidarity). The scene I hit on was early the following summer, summer break of my sophomore year in college, when I gave up on my parents' garage and Lisa and I moved into an off-campus apartment on Vermont and decided to paint the walls, ceiling, and floors the color of midnight in the Carlsbad Caverns. June 6, 1982, 2:44 p.m. The glisten of black paint, a too-bright sun caught in the windows, and Lisa saying, "Think we should paint the glass, too?" I was oblivious of anything but her and me and the way I looked and the way she looked, a streak of paint on her left forearm and another, scimitar-shaped, just over one eyebrow, when suddenly everything went neutral and I was back in the reliving room, staring into the furious face of my daughter.

But let me explain the technology here a moment, for those of you who don't already know. This isn't a computer screen or a TV or a hologram or anything anybody else can see—we're talking retinal projection, two laser beams fixed on two eyeballs. Anybody coming into the room (daughter, wife, boss) will simply see you sitting there silently in a chair with your retinas lit like furnaces. Step in front of the projector—as my daughter had done now—and the image vanishes.

"Stop," I said, and I wasn't talking to her.

But there she was, her hair brushed out for school and her jaw clenched, looking hate at me. "I can't believe you," she said. "Do you have any idea what time it is?"

Bleary, depleted—and guilty, deeply guilty—I just gawked at her, the light she'd flicked on when she came into the room trans-fixing me in the chair. I shook my head.

"It's 6:45 a.m. In the morning. The *morning*, Dad."

I started to say something, but the words were tangled up inside me, because Lisa was saying—had just said—"You're not going to make me stay here and watch the paint dry, are you? Because I'm thinking maybe we could drive out to the beach or something, just to cool down," and I said, or was going to say, "There's, like, maybe half a pint of gas in the car."

"What?" Katie demanded. "Were you with Mom again? Is that it? Like you can be with her and I can't?"

"No," I said, "no, that wasn't it. It wasn't your mom at all . . ."

A tremor ran through her. "Yeah, right. So what was it, then? Some girlfriend, somebody you were gaga over when you were in college? Or high school? Or, what, *junior* high?"

"I must have fallen asleep," I said. "Really. I just zoned out."

She knew I was lying. She'd come looking for me, dutiful child, motherless child, and found me not up and about and bustling around the kitchen, preparing to fuss over her and see her off to school, the way I used to, but pinned here in this chair, like an exhibit in a museum, blind to anything but the past, my past and nobody else's, not hers or her mother's, or the country's or the world's, just mine.

I heard the door slam. Heard the thump of her angry feet in the hallway, the distant muffled crash of the front door, and then the house was quiet. I looked at the slit in the box. "Play," I said.

By the time I got to work I was an hour and a half late, but on this day—miracle of miracles—Kevin was even later, and when he did show up I was ensconced in my cubicle, dutifully rattling keys on my keyboard. He didn't say anything, just brushed by me and buried himself in his office, but I could see that he was wearing the same vacant pre-now look I was, and it didn't take much of an intuitive leap to guess the reason. In fact, since the new model had come on the market, I'd noticed that randy, faraway gaze in the eyes of half a dozen of my fellow employees, including Linda Blanco, the receptionist, who'd stopped buttoning the top three buttons of her blouse and wore shorter and shorter skirts every day. Instead of breathing "Moos and Associates, how may I help you?" into the receiver, now she just said, "Reset."

Was this a recipe for disaster? Was our whole society on the verge of breaking down? Was the NSA going to step in? Were they going to pass laws? Ban the box? I didn't know. I didn't care. I had a daughter to worry about. Thing was, all I could think of was getting home to relive, straight home, and if the image of a carton of milk or a loaf of bread flitted into my head I batted it away. Takeout. We could always get takeout. I was in a crucial phase with Lisa, heading inexorably for the grimmer scenes, the disagreements —petty at first, then monumental, unbridgeable, like the day I got home from my makeup class in calculus and found her sitting at the kitchen table with a stoner whose name I never did catch and didn't want to know, not then or now—and I needed to get through it, not to analyze whether it hurt or not but because it was there and I had to relive it. I couldn't help myself. I just kept picking at it like a scab.

Ultimately, this was all about Christine, of course, about when I began to fail instead of succeed, to lose instead of win. I needed Lisa to remind me of a time before that, to help me trace my missteps and assign blame, because as intoxicating as it was to relive the birds-atwitter moments with Christine, there was always something nagging at me in any given scene, some twitch of her face or a comment she threw out that should have raised flags at the time but never did. All right. Fine. I was going to go there, I was, and relive the minutiae of our relationship, the ecstasy and the agony both, the moments of mindless contentment and the swelling tide of antipathy that drove us apart, but first things first, and as I fought my way home on the freeway that afternoon, all I could think about was Lisa.

In the old days, before we got the box, my daughter and I had a Friday-afternoon ritual whereby I would stop in at the Italian place down the street from the house, have a drink and chat up whoever was there, then call Katie and have her come join me for a father-daughter dinner, so that I could have some face time with her, read into her, and suss out her thoughts and feelings as she grew into a young woman herself, but we didn't do that anymore. There wasn't time. The best I could offer—lately, especially—was takeout or a microwave pizza and a limp salad, choked down in the cold confines of the kitchen, while we separately calculated how long we had to put up with the pretense before slipping off to relive.

There were no lights on in the house as I pulled into the driveway, and that was odd, because Katie should have been home from school by now—and she hadn't texted me or phoned to say she'd be staying late. I climbed out of the car feeling stiff all over—I needed to get more exercise, I knew that, and I resolved to do it, too, as soon as I got my head above water—and as I came up the walk I saw the sad, frosted artificial wreath hanging crookedly there in the center panel of the front door. Katie must have dug it out of the box of ornaments in the garage on her own initiative, to do something by way of Christmas, and that gave me pause, that stopped me right there, the thought of it, of my daughter having to make the effort all by herself. That crushed me. It did. And as I put the key in the lock and pushed the door open I knew things were going to have to change. Dinner. I'd take her out to dinner and forget about Lisa. At least for now.

"Katie?" I called. "You home?"

No response. I shrugged out of my coat and went on into the kitchen, thinking to make myself a drink. There were traces of her there, her backpack flung down on the floor, an open bag of Doritos spilling across the counter, a Diet Sprite, half full, on the breadboard. I called her name again, standing stock-still in the middle of the room and listening for the slightest hint of sound or movement as my voice echoed through the house. I was about to pull out my phone and call her when I thought of the reliving room, and it was a sinking thought, not a selfish one, because if she was in there, reliving—and she was, I knew she was—what did that say about her social life? Didn't teenage girls go out anymore? Didn't they gather in packs at the mall or go to movies or post things on Facebook, or, forgive me, go out on dates? Group dates, even? How else were they going to experience the inchoate beginnings of what the Relive Box people were pushing in the first place?

I shoved into the room, which was dark but for the lights of her eyes, and just stood there watching her for a long moment as I adjusted to the gloom. She sat riveted, her body present but her mind elsewhere, and if I was embarrassed—for her, and for me, too, her father, invading her privacy when she was most vulnerable —the embarrassment gave way to a sorrow so oceanic I thought I would drown in it. I studied her face. Watched her smile and grimace and go cold and smile again. What could she possibly be reliving when she'd lived so little? Family vacations? Christmases past? Her biannual trips to Hong Kong to be with her mother and stepfather? I couldn't fathom it. I didn't like it. It had to stop. I turned on the overhead light and stepped in front of the projector.

She blinked at me and she didn't recognize me, didn't know me at all, because I was in the now and she was in the past. "Katie," I said, "that's enough, now. Come on." I held out my arms to her, even as recognition came back into her eyes and she made a vague gesture of irritation, of pushing away.

"Katie," I said, "let's go out to dinner. Just the two of us. Like we used to."

"I'm not hungry," she said. "And it's not fair. You can use it all you want, like, day and night, but whenever I want it—" And she broke off, tears starting in her eyes.

"Come on," I said. "It'll be fun."

The look she gave me was unsparing. I was trying to deflect it, trying to think of something to say, when she got up out of the chair so suddenly it startled me, and though I tried to take hold of her arm, she was too quick. Before I could react, she was at the door, pausing only to scorch me with another glare. "I don't believe you," she spat, before vanishing down the hall.

I should have followed her, should have tried to make things right—or better, anyway—but I didn't. The box was right there. It had shut down when she leaped up from the chair, and whatever she'd been reliving was buried back inside it, accessible to no one, though you can bet there are hackers out there right now trying to subvert the retinal-recognition feature. For a long moment I stared at the open door, fighting myself, then I went over and softly shut it. I realized I didn't need a drink or dinner, either. I sat down in the chair. "Hello, Wes," the box said. "Welcome back."

We didn't have a Christmas tree that year, and neither of us really cared all that much, I think—if we wanted to look at spangle-draped trees, we could relive holidays past, happier ones, or, in my case, I could go back to my childhood and relive my father's whiskey in a glass and my mother's long-suffering face blossoming over the greedy joy of her golden boy, her only child, tearing open his presents as a weak, bleached-out California sun haunted the windows and the turkey crackled in the oven. Katie went off (reluctantly, I thought) on a skiing vacation to Mammoth with the family of her best friend, Allison, whom she hardly saw anymore, not outside of school, not in the now, and I went back to Lisa, because if I was going to get to Christine in any serious way—beyond the sex, that is, beyond the holiday greetings and picture-postcard moments—Lisa was my bridge.

As soon as I'd dropped Katie at Allison's house and exchanged a few previously scripted salutations with Allison's grinning parents and her grinning twin brothers, I stopped at a convenience store for a case of eight-ounce bottles of spring water and the biggest box of PowerBars I could find and went straight home to the reliving room. The night before, I'd been close to the crucial scene with Lisa, one that was as fixed in my memory as the blowup with Christine a quarter century later, but elusive as to the date and time. I'd been up all night—again—fast-forwarding, reversing, jumping locales and facial expressions, Lisa's first piercing, the evolution of my haircut, but I hadn't been able to pinpoint the exact moment, not yet. I set the water on the floor on my left side, the PowerBars on my right. "May 9, 1983," I said. "Four a.m."

The numbers flashed and then I was in darkness, zero visibility, confused as to where I was until the illuminated dial of a clock radio began to bleed through and I could make out the dim outline of myself lying in bed in the back room of that apartment with the black walls and the black ceiling and the black floor. Lisa was there beside me, an irregular hump in the darkness, snoring with a harsh gag and stutter. She was stoned. And drunk. Half an hour earlier, she'd been in the bathroom, heaving over the toilet, and I realized I'd come too far. "Reset," I said. "Reverse ninety minutes."

Sudden light, blinding after the darkness, and I was alone in the living room of the apartment, studying, or trying to. My hair hung limp, my muscles were barely there, but I was young and reasonably good-looking, even excusing any bias. I saw that my Black Flag T-shirt had faded to gray from too much sun and too many washings, and the book in my lap looked as familiar as something I might have been buried with in a previous life, but then this *was* my previous life.

I watched myself turn a page, crane my neck toward the door, get up to flip over the album that was providing the soundtrack. "Reset," I said. "Fast-forward ten minutes." And here it was, what I'd been searching for: a sudden crash, the front door flinging back, Lisa and the stoner whose name I didn't want to know fumbling their way in, both of them as slow as syrup with the cumulative effect of downers and alcohol, and though the box didn't have an olfactory feature, I swear I could smell the tequila on them. I jumped up out of my chair, spilling the book, and shouted something I couldn't quite make out, so I said, "Reset, reverse five seconds."

"You fucker!" was what I'd shouted, and now I shouted it again, prior to slapping something out of the guy's hand, a beer bottle, and all at once I had him in a hammerlock and Lisa was beating at my back with her bird-claw fists and I was wrestling the guy out the door, cursing over the soundtrack ("Should I Stay or Should I Go"—one of those flatline ironies which almost make you believe everything in this life's been programmed). I saw now that he was bigger than I was, probably stronger, too, but the drugs had taken the volition out of him, and in the next moment he was outside the door and the three bolts were hammered home. By me. Who now turned in a rage to Lisa.

"Stop," I said. "Freeze." Lisa hung there, defiant and guilty at the same time, pretty, breathtakingly pretty, despite the slack mouth and the drugged-out eyes. I should have left it there and gone on to those first cornucopian weeks and months and even years with Christine, but I couldn't help myself. "Play," I said, and Lisa raised a hand to swat at me, but she was too unsteady and knocked the lamp over instead.

"Did you fuck him?" I demanded.

There was a long pause, so long I almost fast-forwarded, and then she said, "Yeah. Yeah, I fucked him. And I'll tell you something"—her words glutinous, the syllables coalescing on her tongue—"you're no punk. And he is. He's the real deal. And you? You're, you're—"

I should have stopped it right there.

"—you're *prissy*."

"Prissy?" I couldn't believe it. Not then and not now.

She made a broad stoned gesture, weaving on her feet. "Anal-retentive. Like, who left the dishes in the sink or who didn't take out the garbage or what about the cockroaches—"

"Stop," I said. "Reset. June 19, 1994, eleven-oh-two p.m."

I was in another bedroom now, one with walls the color of cream, and I was in another bed, this time with Christine, and I'd timed the memory to the very minute, postcoital, in the afterglow, and Christine, with her soft aspirated whisper of a voice, was saying, "I love you, Wes, you know that, don't you?"

"Stop," I said. "Reverse five seconds."

She said it again. And I stopped again. And reversed again. And she said it again. And again.

Time has no meaning when you're reliving. I don't know how long I kept it up, how long I kept surfing through those moments with Christine—not the sexual ones but the loving ones, the companionable ones, the ordinary day-to-day moments when I could see in her eyes that she loved me more than anybody alive and was never going to stop loving me, never. Dinner at the kitchen table, any dinner, any night. Just to be there. My wife. My daughter. The way the light poured liquid gold over the hardwood floors of our starter house, in Canoga Park. Katie's first birthday. Her first word ("Cake!"). The look on Christine's face as she curled up with Katie in bed and read her *Where the Wild Things Are*. Her voice as she hoarsened it for Max: "I'll eat you up!"

Enough analysis, enough hurt. I was no masochist.

At some point I had to get up from that chair in the now and evacuate a living bladder, the house silent, spectral, unreal. I didn't live here. I didn't live in the now with its deadening nine-to-five job I was in danger of losing and the daughter I was failing and a wife who'd left me—and her own daughter—for Winston Chen, a choreographer of martial-arts movies in Hong Kong, who was loving and kind and funny and not the control freak I was. (*Prissy*, anyone? *Anal-retentive*?) The house echoed with my footsteps, a stage set and nothing more. I went to the kitchen and dug the biggest pot I could find out from under the sink, brought it back to the reliving room, and set it on the floor between my legs to save me the trouble of getting up next time around.

Time passed. Relived time and lived time, too. There were two windows in the room, shades drawn so as not to interfere with the business of the moment, and sometimes a faint glow appeared around the margins of them, an effect I noticed when I was searching for a particular scene and couldn't quite pin it down. Sometimes the glow was gone. Sometimes it wasn't. What happened then, and I may have been two days in or three or five, I couldn't really say, was that things began to cloy. I'd relived an exclusive diet of the transcendent, the joyful, the insouciant, the best of Christine, the best of Lisa, and all the key moments of the women who came between and after, and I'd gone back to the Intermediate Algebra test, the very instant, pencil to paper, when I knew I'd scored a perfect 100 percent, and to the time I'd squirted a ball to right field with two outs, two strikes, ninth inning and my Little League team (the Condors, yellow T's, white lettering) down by three, and watched it rise majestically over the glove of the spastic red-haired kid sucking back allergic snot and roll all the way to the wall. Triumph after triumph, goodness abounding—till it stuck in my throat.

"Reset," I said. "January 2, 2009, four-thirty p.m."

I found myself in the kitchen of our second house, this house, the one we'd moved to because it was outside the L.A. city limits and had schools we felt comfortable sending Katie to. That was what mattered: the schools. And if it lengthened our commutes, so be it. This house. The one I was reliving in now. Everything gleamed around me, counters polished, the glass of the cabinets as transparent as air, because details mattered then, everything in its place whether Christine was there or not—especially if she wasn't there, and where was she? Or where had she been? To China. With her boss. On film business. Her bags were just inside the front door, where she'd dropped them forty-five minutes ago, after I'd picked her up at the airport and we'd had our talk in the car, the talk I was going to relive when I got done here, because it was all about pain now, about reality, and this scene was the capper, the coup de grâce. You want wounds? You want to take a razor blade to the meat of your inner thigh just to see if you can still feel? Well, here it was.

Christine entered the scene now, coming down the stairs from Katie's room, her eyes wet, or damp, anyway, and her face composed. I pushed myself up from the table, my beginner's bald spot a glint of exposed flesh under the glare of the overhead light. I spoke first. "You tell her?"

Christine was dressed in her business attire, black stockings, heels, skirt to the knee, tailored jacket. She looked exhausted, and not simply from the fifteen-hour flight but from what she'd had to tell me. And our daughter. (How I'd like to be able to relive *that,* to hear how she'd even broached the subject, let alone how she'd smoke-screened her own selfishness and betrayal with some specious concern for Katie's well-being—Let's not rock the boat and you'll be better off here with your father and your school and your teachers and it's not the end but just the beginning, buck up, you'll see.)

Christine's voice was barely audible. "I don't like this any better than you do."

"Then why do it?"

A long pause. Too long. "Stop," I said.

I couldn't do this. My heart was hammering. My eyes felt as if they were being squeezed in a vise. I could barely swallow. I reached down for a bottle of water and a PowerBar, drank, chewed. She was going to say, "This isn't working," and I was going to say, "*Working?* What the fuck are you talking about? What does work have to do with it? I thought this was about love. I thought it was about commitment." I knew I wasn't going to get violent, though I should have, should have chased her out to the cab that was even then waiting at the curb and slammed my way in and flown all the way to Hong Kong to confront Winston Chen, the martial-arts genius, who could have crippled me with his bare feet.

"Reset," I said. "August 1975, any day, any time."

There was a hum from the box. "Incomplete command. Please select date and time."

I was twelve years old, the summer we went to Vermont, to a lake there, where the mist came up off the water like the fumes of a dream and deer mice lived under the refrigerator, and I didn't have a date or time fixed in my mind—I just needed to get away from Christine, that was all. I picked the first thing that came into my head.

"August nineteenth," I said. "Eleven-thirty a.m. Play."

A blacktop road. Sun like a nuclear blast. A kid, running. I recognized myself—I'd been to this summer before, one I remembered as idyllic, messing around in boats, fishing, swimming, wandering the woods with one of the local kids, Billy Scharf, everything neutral, copacetic. But why was I running? And why did I have that look on my face, a look that fused determination and helplessness both? Up the drive now, up the steps to the house, shouting for my parents: "Mom! Dad!"

I began to have a bad feeling.

I saw my father get up off the wicker sofa on the porch, my vigorous young father, who was dressed in a T-shirt and jeans and didn't have even a trace of gray in his hair, my father, who always made everything right. But not this time. "What's the matter?" he said. "What is it?"

And my mother coming through the screen door to the porch, a towel in one hand and her hair snarled wet from the lake. And me. I was fighting back tears, my legs and arms like sticks, striped polo shirt, faded shorts. "It's," I said, "it's—"

"Stop," I said. "Reset." It was my dog, Queenie, that was what it was, dead on the road that morning, and who'd left the gate ajar so she could get out in the first place? Even though he'd been warned about it a hundred times?

I was in a dark room. There was a pot between my legs, and it was giving off a fierce odor. I needed to go deeper, needed out of this. I spouted random dates, saw myself driving to work, stuck in traffic with ten thousand other fools who could only wish they had a fast-forward app, saw myself in my thirties, post-Lisa, pre-Christine, obsessing over Halo, and I stayed there through all the toppling hours, reliving myself in the game, boxes within boxes, until finally I thought of God, or what passes for God in my life, the mystery beyond words, beyond lasers and silicon chips. I gave a date nine months before I was born, "December 30, 1962, six a.m.," when I was, what—a zygote?—but the box gave me nothing, neither visual nor audio. And that was wrong, deeply wrong. There should have been a heartbeat. My mother's heartbeat, the first thing we hear—or feel, feel before we even have ears.

"Stop," I said. "Reset." A wave of rising exhilaration swept over me even as the words came to my lips, "September 30, 1963, two thirty-five a.m.," and the drumbeat started up, *ba-boom, ba-boom,* but no visual, not yet, the minutes ticking by, *ba-boom, ba-boom,* and then I was there, in the light of this world, and my mother in her stained hospital gown and the man with the monobrow and the flashing glasses, the stranger, the doctor, saying what he was going to say by way of congratulations and relief. A boy. It's a boy.

Then it all went dead, and there was somebody standing in front of me, and I didn't recognize her, not at first, how could I? "Dad," she was saying. "Dad, are you there?"

I blinked. Tried to focus.

"No," I said finally, shaking my head in slow emphasis, the word itself, the denial, heavy as a stone in my mouth. "I'm not here. I'm not. I'm not."

A. MERC RUSTAD

How to Become a Robot in 12 Easy Steps

FROM *Scigentasy*

HOW TO TELL your boyfriend you are in love with a robot:

1. Tell him, "I may possibly be in love with a robot," because absolutes are difficult for biological brains to process. He won't be jealous.
2. Ask him what he thinks of a hypothetical situation in which you found someone who might not be human but is still valuable and right for you. (Your so-called romantic relationship is as fake as you are.)
3. Don't tell him anything. It's not that he'll tell you you're wrong; he's not like his parents, or yours. But there's still a statistical possibility he might not be okay with you being in love with a robot.

On my to-do list today:

- Ask the robot out on a date.
- Pick up salad ingredients for dinner.
- Buy Melinda and Kimberly a wedding gift.

The robot is a J-90 SRM, considered "blocky" and "old-school," probably refurbished from a scrapper, painted bright purple with the coffee-shop logo on the chassis. The robot's square head has an LED screen that greets customers with unfailing politeness and reflects their orders back to them. The bright blue smiley face never changes in the top corner of the screen.

Everyone knows the J-90 SRMs aren't upgradable AI. They have basic customer service programming and equipment maintenance protocols.

Everyone knows robots in the service industry are there as cheap labor investments and to improve customer satisfaction scores, which they never do because customers are never happy.

Everyone knows you can't be in love with a robot.

I drop my plate into the automatic disposal, which thanks me for recycling. No one else waits to deposit trash, so I focus on it as I brace myself to walk back to the counter. The J-90 SRM smiles blankly at the empty front counter, waiting for the next customer.

The lunch rush is over. The air reeks of espresso and burned milk. I don't come here because the food is good or the coffee any better. The neon violet decor is best ignored.

I practiced this in front of a wall sixteen times over the last week. I have my script. It's simple. "Hello, I'm Tesla. What may I call you?"

And the robot will reply:

I will say, "It's nice to meet you."

And the robot will reply:

I will say, "I would like to know if you'd like to go out with me when you're off-duty, at a time of both our convenience. I'd like to get to know you better, if that's acceptable to you."

And the robot will reply:

"Hey, Tesla."

The imagined conversation shuts down. I blink at the trash receptacle and look up.

My boyfriend smiles hello, his hands shoved in his jeans pockets, his shoulders hunched to make himself look smaller. At six foot five and three hundred pounds, it never helps. He's as cuddly and mellow as a black bear in hibernation. Today he's wearing a gray turtleneck and loafers, his windbreaker unzipped.

"Hi, Jonathan."

I can't ask the robot out now.

The empty feeling reappears in my chest, where it always sits when I can't see or hear the robot.

"You still coming to Esteban's party tonight?" Jonathan asks.

"Yeah."

Jonathan smiles again. "I'll pick you up after work, then."

"Sounds good," I say. "We'd better go, or I'll be late."

He works as an accountant. He wanted to study robotic engineering, but his parents would only pay for college if he got a practical degree (his grandfather disapproves of robots). Computers crunch the numbers, and he handles the people.

He always staggers his lunch break so he can walk back with me. It's nice. Jonathan can act as an impenetrable weather shield if it rains and I forget my umbrella.

But Jonathan isn't the robot.

He offers me his arm, like the gentleman he always is, and we leave the coffee shop. The door wishes us a good day.

I don't look back at the robot.

A beginner's guide on how to fake your way through biological social constructs:

1. Pretend you are not a robot. This is hard, and you have been working at it for twenty-three years. You are like Data, except in reverse.
2. (There are missing protocols in your head. You don't know why you were born biologically or why there are pieces missing, and you do not really understand how human interaction functions. Sometimes you can fake it. Sometimes people even believe you when you do. You never believe yourself.)
3. Memorize enough data about social cues and run facial muscle pattern recognition so you know what to say and when to say it.
4. This is not always successful.
5. Example: a woman approximately your biological age approaches you and proceeds to explain in detail how mad she is at her boyfriend. Example: boyfriend is guilty of using her toiletries like toothbrush and comb when he comes over, and leaving towels on the bathroom floor. "Such a slob," she says, gripping her beer like a club. "How do you manage men?" You ask if she has told him to bring his own toothbrush and comb and to hang up the towels. It seems the first logical step: factual communication. "He should figure it out!" she says. You are confused. You say that maybe he is unaware of the protocols she has in place. She gives you a strange look, huffs her breath out, and walks off.
6. Now the woman's friends ignore you, and you notice their stares and awkward pauses when you are within their

proximity. You have no escape because you didn't drive separately.

7. Ask your boyfriend not to take you to any more parties.

Jonathan and I lounge on the plush leather couch in his apartment. He takes up most of it, and I curl against his side. We have a bowl of popcorn, and we're watching reruns of *Star Trek: The Next Generation.*

"I have something to tell you," he says. His shoulders tense.

I keep watching the TV. He knows I pay attention when he tells me things, even if I don't look at him. "Okay."

"I'm . . ." He hesitates. The Borg fire on the *Enterprise* again. "I'm seeing someone else."

"A guy?" I ask, hopeful.

"Yeah. I met him at the gym. His name's Bernardo."

I sigh in relief. Secrets are heavy and hurt when you have to carry them around all your life. (I have to make lists to keep track of mine.) "I'm glad. Are you going to tell anyone?"

He relaxes and squeezes my hand. "Just you right now. But from what he's told me, his family's pretty accepting."

"Lucky," I say.

We scrape extra butter off the bowl with the last kernels of popcorn.

We've been pretend-dating for two years now. We've never slept together. That's okay. I like cuddling with him, and he likes telling me about crazy customers at his firm, and everyone thinks we're a perfectly adorable straight couple on the outside.

The empty spot in my chest grows bigger as I watch Data on-screen. Data has the entire crew of the *Enterprise.* Jonathan has Bernardo now. I don't know if the robot will be interested in me in return. (What if the robot isn't?)

The room shrinks in on me, the umber-painted walls and football memorabilia suffocating. I jerk to my feet.

Jonathan mutes the TV. "Something wrong?"

"I have to go."

"Want me to drive you home?"

"It's four blocks away." But I appreciate his offer, so I add, "But thanks."

I find my coat piled by the door while he takes the popcorn bowl into the kitchen.

Jonathan leans against the wall as I carefully lace each boot to the proper tightness. "If you want to talk, Tesla, I'll listen."

I know that. He came out to me before we started dating. I told him I wasn't interested in socially acceptable relationships either, and he laughed and looked so relieved he almost cried. We made an elaborate plan, a public persona our families wouldn't hate.

I'm not ready to trust him as much as he trusts me.

"Night, Jonathan."

"Goodnight, Tesla."

How to tell your fake boyfriend you would like to become a robot:

1. Tell him, "I would like to be a robot." You can also say, "I am really a robot, not a female-bodied biological machine," because that is closer to the truth.
2. Do not tell him anything. If you do, you will also have to admit that you think about ways to hurt yourself so you have an excuse to replace body parts with machine parts.
3. Besides, insurance is unlikely to cover your transition into a robot.

I have this nightmare more and more often.

I'm surrounded by robots. Some of them look like the J-90 SRM, some are the newer androids, some are computer cores floating in the air. I'm the only human.

I try to speak, but I have no voice. I try to touch them, but I can't lift my hands. I try to follow them as they walk over a hill and through two huge doors, like glowing LED screens, but I can't move.

Soon all the robots are gone, and I'm all alone in the empty landscape.

Eleven reasons you want to become a robot:

1. Robots are logical and know their purpose.
2. Robots have programming they understand.
3. Robots are not held to unattainable standards and then criticized when they fail.
4. Robots are not crippled by emotions they don't know how to process.

5. Robots are not judged based on what sex organs they were born with.
6. Robots have mechanical bodies that are strong and durable. They are not required to have sex.
7. Robots do not feel guilt (about existing, about failing, about being something other than expected).
8. Robots can multitask.
9. Robots do not feel unsafe all the time.
10. Robots are perfect machines that are capable and functional and can be fixed if something breaks.
11. Robots are happy.

It's Saturday, so I head to the Purple Bean early.

The robot isn't there.

I stare at the polished chrome and plastic K-100, which has a molded face that smiles with humanistic features.

"Welcome to the Purple Bean," the new robot says in a chirpy voice that has inflection and none of the mechanical monotone I like about the old robot. "I'm Janey. How can I serve you today?"

"Where's the J-90 SRM?"

Robbie, the barista who works weekends, leans around the espresso machine and sighs. She must have gotten this question a lot. The panic in my chest is winching so tight it might crack my ribs into little pieces. Why did they retire the robot?

"Manager *finally* got the company to upgrade," Robbie says. "Like it?"

"Where's the J-90 SRM?"

"Eh, recycled, I guess." Robbie shrugs. "You want the usual?"

I can't look at the new K-100. It isn't right. It doesn't belong in the robot's place, and neither do I. "I have to go."

"Have a wonderful day," the door says.

How to rescue a robot from being scrapped [skill level: intermediate]:

1. Call your boyfriend, who owns an SUV, and ask him to drive you to the Gates-MacDowell recycle plant.
2. Argue with the technician, who refuses to sell you the decommissioned robot. It's company protocol, he says, and service industry robots are required to have processors and cores wiped before being recycled.

3. Lie and say you only want to purchase the J-90 SRM because you're starting a collection. Under the law, historical preservation collections are exempt from standardized recycling procedures.
4. Do not commit physical violence on the tech when he hesitates. It's rude, and he's only doing his job.
5. Do not admit you asked your boyfriend along because his size is intimidating, and he knows how to look grouchy at eight a.m.
6. The technician will finally agree and give you a claim ticket.
7. Drive around and find the robot in the docking yard.
8. Do not break down when you see how badly the robot has been damaged: the robot's LED screen cracked, the robot's chassis has been crunched inward, the robot's missing arm.
9. Try not to believe it is your fault. (That is illogical, even if you still have biological processing units.)

Two techs wheel the robot out and load it into Jonathan's car. The gut-punched feeling doesn't go away. The robot looks so helpless, shut down and blank in the back seat. I flip open the robot's chassis, but the power core is gone, along with the programming module.

The robot is just a shell of what the robot once was.

I feel like crying. I don't want to. It's uncomfortable and doesn't solve problems.

"What's wrong, Tesla?" Jonathan asks.

I shut the chassis. My hands tremble. "They broke the robot."

"It'll be okay," Jonathan says. As if anything can be okay right now. As if there is nothing wrong with me. "You can fix it."

I squirm back into the passenger seat and grip the dash. He's right. We were friends because we both liked robots and I spent my social studies classes in school researching robotics and programming.

"I've never done anything this complex," I say. I've only dismantled, reverse-engineered, and rebuilt the small household appliances and computers. No one has ever let me build a robot.

"You'll do fine," he says. "And if you need help, I know just the guy to ask."

"Who?"

"Want to meet my boyfriend?"

*

Necessary questions to ask your boyfriend's new boyfriend (a former army engineer of robotics):

1. You've been following the development of cyborg bodies, so you ask him if he agrees with the estimates that replacement of all organic tissue sans brain and spinal cord with inorganic machinery is still ten years out, at best. Some scientists predict longer. Some predict never, but you don't believe them. (He'll answer that the best the field can offer right now are limbs and some artificial organs.)
2. Ask him how to upload human consciousness into a robot body. (He'll tell you there is no feasible way to do this yet, and the technology is still twenty years out.)
3. Do not tell him you cannot wait that long. (You cannot last forever.)
4. Instead, ask him if he can get you parts you need to fix the robot.

Bernardo—six inches shorter and a hundred pounds lighter than Jonathan, tattooed neck to ankles, always smelling of cigarettes— is part robot. He lost his right arm at the shoulder socket in an accident and now wears the cybernetic prosthetic. It has limited sensory perception, but he says it's not as good as his old hand.

I like him. I tell Jonathan this, and my boyfriend beams.

"They really gut these things," Bernardo says when he drops off the power cell.

(I want to ask him how much I owe him. But when he says nothing about repayment, I stay quiet. I can't afford it. Maybe he knows that.)

We put the robot in the spare bedroom in my apartment, which Jonathan wanted to turn into an office, but never organized himself enough to do so. I liked the empty room, but now it's the robot's home. I hid the late payment notices and overdue bills in a drawer before Jonathan saw them.

"Getting a new arm might be tricky, but I have a buddy who works a scrap yard out in Maine," Bernardo says. "Bet she could dig up the right model parts."

"Thank you."

I'm going to reconstruct the old personality and programming pathways. There are subsystems, "nerve clusters," that serve as re-

dundant processing. Personality modules get routed through functionality programs, and vestiges of the robot's personality build up
in subsystems. Newer models are completely wiped, but they usually don't bother with old ones.

Bernardo rubs his shaved head. "You realize this won't be a
quick and easy fix, right? Might take weeks. Hell, it might not even
work."

I trace a finger through the air in front of the robot's dark LED
screen. I have not been able to ask the robot if I have permission
to touch the robot. It bothers me that I have to handle parts and
repairs without the robot's consent. Does that make it wrong? To
fix the robot without knowing if the robot wishes to be fixed?

Will the robot hate me if I succeed?

"I know," I whisper. "But I need to save the robot."

How to tell your pretend-boyfriend and his real boyfriend that
your internal processors are failing:

1. The biological term is *depression,* but you don't have an
   official diagnostic (diagnosis) and it's a hard word to say.
   It feels heavy and stings your mouth. Like when you tried
   to eat a battery when you were small and your parents got
   upset.
2. Instead, you try to hide the feeling. But the dark stain has
   already spilled across your hardwiring and clogged your
   processor. You don't have access to any working help files
   to fix this. Tech support is unavailable for your model. (No
   extended warranty exists.)
3. Pretend the reason you have no energy is because you're sick
   with a generic bug.
4. You have time to sleep. Your job is canceling out many
   of your functions; robots can perform cleaning and
   maintenance in hotels for much better wage investment,
   and since you are not (yet) a robot, you know you will be
   replaced soon.
5. The literal translation of the word depression: you are broken
   and devalued and have no further use.
6. No one refurbishes broken robots.
7. Please self-terminate.

*

I work on the robot during my spare time. I have lots of it now. Working on the robot is the only reason I have to wake up.

I need to repair the robot's destroyed servos and piece together the robot's memory and function programming from what the computer recovered.

There are subroutine lists in my head that are getting bigger and bigger:

- You will not be able to fix the robot.
- You do not have enough money to fix the robot.
- You do not have the skill to fix the robot.
- The robot will hate you.
- You are not a robot.

Bernardo and Jonathan are in the kitchen. They laugh and joke while making stir fry. I'm not hungry.

I haven't been hungry for a few days now.

"You should just buy a new core, Tesla," Bernardo says. "Would save you a lot of headaches."

I don't need a blank, programmable core. What I want is the robot who worked in the Purple Bean. The robot who asked for my order, like the robot did every customer. But the moment I knew I could love this robot was when the robot asked what I would like to be called. "Tesla," I said, and the blue LED smiley face in the upper corner of the robot's screen flickered in a shy smile.

Everyone knows robots are not people.

There's silence in the kitchen. Then Jonathan says, quietly, "Tesla, what's this?"

I assume he's found the eviction notice.

Reasons why you want to self-terminate (a partial list):

1. Your weekly visit to your parents' house in the suburbs brings the inevitable question about when you will marry your boyfriend, settle down (so you can pop out babies), and raise a family.
2. You don't tell them you just lost your job.
3. You make the mistake of mentioning that you're going to your best friend Melinda's wedding next weekend. You're happy for her: she's finally marrying her longtime girlfriend, Kimberly.

4. That sets your dad off on another rant about the evils of gay people and how they all deserve to die.

5. (You've heard this all your life. You thought you escaped it when you were eighteen and moved out. But you never do escape, do you? There is no escape.)

6. You make a second mistake and talk back. You've never done that; it's safer to say nothing. But you're too stressed to play safe, so you tell him he's wrong and that it's hurting you when he says that.

7. That makes him paranoid, and he demands that you tell him you aren't one of those fags, too.

8. You don't tell your parents you're probably asexual and you really want to be a robot because robots are never condemned because of who they love.

9. You stop listening as he gets louder and louder, angrier and angrier, until you're afraid he will reach for the rifle in the gun cabinet.

10. You run from the house and are almost hit by a truck. Horns blare and slushy snow sprays your face as you reach the safety of the opposite sidewalk.

11. You wish you were three seconds slower so the bumper wouldn't have missed you. It was a big truck.

12. You start making another list.

"Why didn't you tell me?" Jonathan asks, more concerned than angry. "I would've helped out."

I shrug.

The subroutine list boots up:

- You are not an adult if you cannot exist independently at all times.
- Therefore, logically, you are a nonoperational drone.
- You will be a burden on everyone.
- You already are.
- Self-terminate.

"I thought I could manage," I say. The robot's LED screen is still cracked and dark. I wonder what the robot dreams about.

Bernardo is quiet in the kitchen, giving us privacy.

Jonathan rubs his eyes. "Okay. Look. You're always welcome to stay with me and Bern. We'll figure it out, Tesla. Don't we always?"

I know how small his apartment is. Bernardo has just moved in with him; there's no space left.

"What about the robot?" I ask.

How to self-destruct: a robot's guide.

1. Water damage. Large bodies of water will short-circuit internal machinery. In biological entities, this is referred to as *drowning*. There are several bridges nearby, and the rivers are deep.
2. Overload. Tapping into a power source far beyond what your circuits can handle, such as an industrial-grade electric fence. There is one at the Gates-MacDowell recycle plant.
3. Complete power drain. Biologically this is known as blood loss. There are plenty of shaving razors in the bathroom.
4. Substantial physical damage. Explosives or crushing via industrial recycling machines will be sufficient. Option: stand in front of a train.
5. Impact from substantial height; a fall. You live in a very high apartment complex.
6. Corrupt your internal systems by ingesting industrial-grade chemicals. Acid is known to damage organic and inorganic tissue alike.
7. Fill in the blank. (Tip: use the Internet.)

Bernardo's family owns a rental garage, and he uses one of the units for rebuilding his custom motorcycle. He says I can store the robot there, until another unit opens up.

Jonathan has moved his Budweiser memorabilia collection into storage so the small room he kept it in is now an unofficial bedroom. He shows it to me and says I can move in anytime I want. He and Bernardo are sharing his bedroom.

I don't know what to do.

I have no operating procedures for accepting help.

I should self-destruct and spare them all. That would be easier, wouldn't it? Better for them?

But the robot isn't finished.

I don't know what to do.

*

How to have awkward conversations about your relationship with your boyfriend and your boyfriend's boyfriend:

1. Agree to move in with them. Temporarily. (You feel like you are intruding. Try not to notice that they both are genuinely happy to have you live with them.)
2. Order pizza and watch the Futurama marathon on TV.
3. Your boyfriend says, "I'm going to come out to my family. I've written an FB update, and I just have to hit Send."
4. Your boyfriend's boyfriend kisses him, and you fist-bump them both in celebration.
5. You tell him you're proud of him. You will be the first to like his status.
6. He posts the message to his wall. You immediately like the update.
7. (You don't know what this means for your facade of boyfriend/girlfriend.)
8. Your boyfriend says, "Tesla, we need to talk. About us. About all three of us." You know what he means. Where do you fit in now?
9. You say, "Okay."
10. "I'm entirely cool with you being part of this relationship, Tesla," your boyfriend's boyfriend says. "Who gives a fuck what other people think? But it's up to you, totally."
11. "What he said," your boyfriend says. "Hell, you can bring the robot in, too. It's not like any of us object to robots as part of the family." He pats his boyfriend's cybernetic arm. "We'll make it work."
12. You don't say, "I can be a robot, and that's okay?" Instead, you tell them you'll think about it.

I write another list.
    I write down all the lists. In order. In detail.
    Then I print them out and give them to Jonathan and Bernardo. The cover page has four letters on it: H-E-L-P.

Reasons why you should avoid self-termination (right now):

1. Jonathan says, "If you ever need to talk, I'll listen."
2. Bernardo says, "It'll get better. I promise it does. I've been

there, where you're at, thinking there's nothing more than the world fucking with you. I was in hell my whole childhood and through high school." He'll show you the scars on his wrists and throat, his tattoos never covering them up. "I know it fucking hurts. But there's people who love you and we're willing to help you survive. You're strong enough to make it."

3. Your best friend Melinda says, "Who else is going to write me snarky texts while I'm at work or go to horror movies with me (you know my wife hates them) or come camping with us every summer like we've done since we were ten?" And she'll hold her hands out and say, "You deserve to be happy. Please don't leave."

4. You will get another job.

5. You will function again, if you give yourself time and let your friends help. And they will. They already do.

6. The robot needs you.

7. Because if you self-terminate, you won't have a chance to become a robot in the future.

"Hey, Tesla," Jonathan says, poking his head around the garage-workshop door. "Bern and I are going over to his parents' for dinner. Want to come?"

"Hey, I'll come for you anytime," Bernardo calls from the parking lot.

Jonathan rolls his eyes, his goofy smile wider than ever.

I shake my head. The robot is almost finished. "You guys have fun. Say hi for me."

"You bet."

The garage is silent. Ready.

I sit by the power grid. I've unplugged all the other devices, powered down the phone and the data hub. I carefully hid Bernardo's bike behind a plastic privacy wall he used to divide the garage so we each have a workspace.

We're alone, the robot and I.

I rig up a secondary external power core and keep the dedicated computer running the diagnostic.

The robot stands motionless, the LED screen blank. It's still cracked, but it will function.

"Can you hear me?" I ask. "Are you there?"

The robot:

I power up the robot and key the download sequence, reinstalling the rescued memory core.

The robot's screen flickers. The blue smiley face appears in the center, split with spiderweb cracks.

"Hello," I say.

"Hello, Tesla," the robot says.

"How do you feel?"

"I am well," the robot says. "I believe you saved my life."

The hole closes in my chest, just a little.

The robot's clean, symmetrical lines and tarnished purple surface glow. The robot is perfect. I stand up.

"How may I thank you for your help, Tesla?"

"Is there a way I can become a robot, too?"

The robot's pixelated face shifts; now the robot's expression frowns. "I do not know, Tesla. I am not programmed with such knowledge. I am sorry."

I think about the speculative technical papers I read, articles Bernardo forwarded to me.

"I have a hypothesis," I tell the robot. "If I could power myself with enough electricity, my electromagnetic thought patterns might be able to travel into a mechanical apparatus such as the computer hub."

(Consciousness uploads aren't feasible yet.)

"I believe such a procedure would be damaging to your current organic shell," the robot says.

Yes, I understand electrocution's effects on biological tissue. I have thought about it before. (Many times. All the time.)

The robot says, "May I suggest that you consider the matter before doing anything regrettable, Tesla?"

And I reply:

The robot says: "I should not like to see you deprogrammed and consigned to the scrapping plant for organic tissue."

And I reply:

The robot says: "I will be sad if you die."

I look up at the frowning blue pixel face. And I think of Jonathan and Bernardo returning and finding my body stiff and blackened, my fingers plugged into the power grid.

The robot extends one blocky hand. "Perhaps I would be allowed to devise a more reliable solution? I would like to understand you better, if that is acceptable." The blue lines curve up into a hopeful smile.

The robot is still here. Jonathan and Bernardo are here. Melinda and Kimberly are here. I'm not a robot (yet), but I'm not alone.

"Is this an acceptable solution, Tesla?" the robot asks.

I take the robot's hand, and the robot's blocky fingers slowly curl around mine. "Yes. I would like that very much." Then I ask the robot, "What would you like me to call you?"

How to become a robot:

1. You don't.
2. Not yet.
3. But you will.

Contributors' Notes

Nathan Ballingrud is the author of *North American Lake Monsters: Stories* and the novella *The Visible Filth*. He lives with his daughter in Asheville, North Carolina.

- The progenitive image of "Skullpocket"—a small group of young ghouls staring longingly through a cemetery gate at a glittering fair—sat in my brain for a couple of years before I finally figured out the story that went along with it. When I did, I was afraid to write it. Until that point I'd been writing what I think of as southern, blue-collar horror stories, and I worried that I wouldn't know how to write something that pulled from such a different aesthetic. Of course, that was precisely the best reason to try. I drew from my deep love of Mike Mignola's comics, Tim Burton's animated gothics, and the universal fear of a wasted life, and threw it all into the pot. Now I feel I'm just getting started. I want to write a book about Hob's Landing, covering the century of the Wormcake family's interactions with the town and how each transformed the other over time. Uncle Digby is already compiling his master's correspondence for me; the work begins soon.

T. C. Boyle is the author of twenty-five books of fiction, including *The Harder They Come* (2015) and the second volume of his collected stories, *T. C. Boyle Stories II* (2013). His stories have appeared in most of the major American magazines, including *The New Yorker, Harper's Magazine, The Atlantic, Esquire, The Paris Review, McSweeney's, Playboy,* and *The Kenyon Review*.

- Though I work in many modes—pride myself on it, in fact—the ones that come most naturally to me are the whimsical, the absurd, and the surreal. I cut my writing chops on Coover, García Márquez, Calvino, Cortázar, Grass, Pynchon, Barthelme, Genet, Beckett, and a host of others who abjured straight-ahead realism and created playful, erudite works that showed me a whole new way of seeing. "The Relive Box" is a recent return to my roots. The story represents my reflections on virtual reality and how absorbing gaming can be (just like entering a story or novel, for that matter, either as author or reader). Of course, as many readers will know, the technology referenced here is very close to being reality, though the downloading of an individual's consciousness hasn't quite been perfected yet. Be pleased to know that I am working out the glitches in my basement lab and that the prototype of the X1520 Relive Box is virtually complete. I expect to begin marketing the first model within a year. So watch out!

Adam-Troy Castro's twenty-six books include the Philip K. Dick Award–winning *Emissaries from the Dead,* first of a trilogy about his profoundly damaged far-future murder investigator, Andrea Cort. His most recent short story collection is *Her Husband's Hands and Other Stories,* published in 2014. This year has seen the penultimate installment of his series of middle-grade novels about a very strange and very courageous young boy who just might save us all, *Gustav Gloom and the Inn of Shadows.* Castro lives in Boynton Beach, Florida, with his wife, Judi, and the usual writerly assortment of cats.

▪ Fiction writing can be a mysterious process in that there are no consistent rules governing which whimsical premise explored as a lark peters out in failure after a thousand not-very-satisfying words and which one develops its own gravity as those words begin to accrue. "The Thing About Shapes to Come" is a manifestation of that phenomenon. When I typed the first sentence about the child born in the shape of a cube, I had absolutely no idea that the story was headed anywhere but escalating absurdity. But the emotions deepened even as the details got sillier, and somehow by midstory I found I was writing a tale of a mother's defiance in the face of all possible barriers to a true relationship with her child. By composition's end, my heart demanded some firm indication that all this devotion was rewarded. None of this was planned before it happened. The story chewed the author like gum. More than one anxious reader, caught up in the strangeness of it all, has fervently begged for some clue to what happens after my protagonist walks through the doorway. I always reply that it was a very private and emotional moment between mother and daughter and that it would be churlish of us to intrude any more than we already have.

Neil Gaiman is the best-selling author of books, graphic novels, and short stories for adults and children. Some of his most notable titles include the novels *American Gods, The Graveyard Book* (the first book ever to win both Newbery and Carnegie medals), and *The Ocean at the End of the Lane* (the U.K.'s National Book Award 2013 Book of the Year). More recently published were his *New York Times* best-selling short story collection, *Trigger Warning,* and the enchantingly reimagined fairy tale *The Sleeper and the Spindle* (with illustrations by Chris Riddell). Born in England, Gaiman now lives in the United States with his wife, the musician and author Amanda Palmer.

▪ I wrote *Neverwhere,* a novel about London Above and London Below, in 1997. About five years later I began to write "How the Marquis Got His Coat Back," but after two pages I put it away and wrote something else instead. It wasn't until the BBC did an adaptation of *Neverwhere* and I spent an afternoon listening to it that I realized how much I missed the characters and the world. *This is great,* I thought. *I wish there was more.* But the only way there would be more was if I wrote it.

So I began this story as a way of finding my way back to London Below. The Marquis de Carabas (I pronounce it *Marquee*) is a rogue and a dealer in favors and obligations. Three quarters of the way through the book he is killed and restored to life. This happens after that. My thanks to Gardner Dozois and George R. R. Martin for offering it a home in their *Rogues* collection, and to the editors of this volume for picking it.

Theodora Goss is the author of the short story collection *In the Forest of Forgetting,* the accordion-style novella *The Thorn and the Blossom,* and the poetry collection *Songs for Ophelia.* With Delia Sherman, she coedited the first *Interfictions* anthology. Her short story "Singing of Mount Abora" won the World Fantasy Award. She lives in Boston and teaches at Boston University as well as in the Stonecoast MFA Program.

▪ "Cimmeria" was inspired by one of my favorite stories, Jorge Luis Borges's "Tlön, Uqbar, Orbis Tertius." I first read it as a college student, around the time I was trying to figure out how to write. I was an immigrant, a Hungarian who had lost her country and language, who had grown up in this strange new society. I took a class on the Latin American magical realists and started reading literature that brought the magical and real together in that way, which made sense to me. My actual lived experience made sense when I read Isabel Allende and Milan Kundera. Toward the end of "Tlön," archaeologists begin finding "hrönir," objects created by expectation, essentially recreating the past. My practical mind, trained as an academic, thought, *They must have journals to write up their findings.* So I came up with a *Journal of Imaginary Archaeology,* and from there it was a logical step to the *Journal of Imaginary Anthropology,* to the creation of entire civilizations. And then I thought about the academics involved: Who would they be, how would they react? Because academics are human, after all: their personal lives intertwine with their research. But the story is also meant to be flipped inside out, because who are these Americans believing that they created the ancient civilization of Cimmeria, which has existed for more than two thousand years? The flip side is a story about hubris and imperialism, about the American and European tendency to believe that Western civilization has somehow created the rest of the world. The story is meant to be both stories at once, its own shadow. And then, right around the time it was published, war broke out in the Crimea.

Alaya Dawn Johnson is the author of six novels for adults and young adults. Her novel *The Summer Prince* was longlisted for the National Book Award for Young People's Literature. Her most recent, *Love Is the Drug*, won the Norton Award. Her short stories have appeared in many magazines and anthologies, including *Asimov's Science Fiction*, *The Magazine of Fantasy & Science Fiction*, *Interzone*, *Subterranean*, *Zombies vs. Unicorns*, and *Welcome to Bordertown*. In addition to the Norton, she has won the Cybils Award and the Nebula Award (for the story included in this anthology) and been nominated for the Indies Choice Award and the Locus Award. She currently lives in Mexico City.

▪ I have a vampire problem. If you asked me five years ago, I would have said I didn't much like vampires. But then I wrote two historical vampire novels. A momentary lapse, I thought. And then came a vampire short story. And another. At this point it occurred to me that I might need some help. I started this particular vampire story four years ago, while attending a conference in Bologna, Italy. I wrote nearly half of the first draft longhand, in my Moleskine, with my Lamy fountain pen (the hipster writing accessories are no surprise to those who know me, but I usually reserve them for note-taking, not drafting). Why northern Italy would inspire a story about a vampire apocalypse in Hawai'i I could not tell you—but there they were. Hungry, insatiable, waiting. At the moment my vampire problem seems to be in remission, but I've learned not to underestimate their temptation, or their bite.

Kelly Link is the author of the collections *Get in Trouble, Stranger Things Happen, Magic for Beginners,* and *Pretty Monsters*. She and Gavin J. Grant have coedited a number of anthologies, including multiple volumes of *The Year's Best Fantasy and Horror* and, for young adults, *Monstrous Affections*. She is the cofounder of Small Beer Press. Her short stories have been published in *The Magazine of Fantasy & Science Fiction, Best American Short Stories,* and *Prize Stories: The O. Henry Awards.* She has received a grant from the National Endowment for the Arts. Link was born in Miami, Florida. She currently lives with her husband and daughter in Northampton, Massachusetts.

▪ Of the various stories that I've managed to write in the last ten years, "I Can See Right Through You" is the one that, when I think about it, I feel a certain sense of satisfaction that stems from the fact that I wrote it at all. I knew how I wanted to start it and I knew how I wanted to end it, and then for over a year I tried to work my way from point A to point B. I wrote so many versions of the first thirteen pages that eventually I began saving them in numbered drafts, just to see if there was something I could figure out from the progression of wrong to different to still-wrong to okay-I-guess to here's-something-salvageable-if-only-I-can-figure-out-how-to-incorporate-it that would make writing other stories easier. The problems, it seemed to me, had to do with speed and motion of the various parts, not to mention the problem of who Meggie and Will ought to be. I had a sense of their relationship, but the characters themselves changed gender, age, sexual orientation, and degree of fame from draft to draft to draft until I had a pair of characters who seemed exactly themselves, as if the true versions had been there all along. I had in mind from the start certain stories—all demon lover stories —by Shirley Jackson, Elizabeth Bowen, and especially Joyce Carol Oates's "Where Are You Going, Where Have You Been?" The other thing I had in mind was something that the writer Holly Black had told me about an interview with either Leo DiCaprio or Kate Winslet and something one of them said about their relationship—first, the intimacy and isolation and strangeness of making a movie like *Titanic* and the kind of closeness that evolves under those circumstances and, afterward, during the promotion of such a monumentally popular movie. Once I got past the first thirteen pages, I still bogged down at certain crucial points in the story. The writers Holly Black, Cassandra Clare, and Sarah Rees Brennan threw me a rope every time.

Carmen Maria Machado is a Nebula-nominated fiction writer, critic, and essayist whose work has appeared or is forthcoming in *The New Yorker, Granta, The Paris Review, AGNI, The Fairy Tale Review, Tin House*'s Open Bar, NPR, *The American Reader,* the *Los Angeles Review of Books,* and elsewhere. Her stories have been reprinted in several anthologies, including *Year's Best Weird Fiction* and *Best Women's Erotica.* She has received the Richard Yates Short Story Prize, a Millay Colony for the Arts residency, the CINTAS Foundation Fellowship in Creative Writing, and the Michener-Copernicus Fellowship. She is a graduate of the Iowa Writers' Workshop and the Clarion Science Fiction & Fantasy Writers' Workshop and lives in Philadelphia with her partner.

▪ A founder of Oulipo, a French literary movement preoccupied with constrained writing, once said, "In the world we live in, we are beholden to all manner of terrible constraints—mental, physical, societal—with death the only way out of the labyrinth. The least we can do is mark off a little section where we get to choose the constraints we are mastered by, where we decide which direction to take." I have always been a fan of formal conceits and constraints, fictional artifacts, and stories that look like other things. There is something deeply satisfying about throwing up obstacles in my own path and having to climb over them; the result is often something unclassifiable, beautiful, or strange.

It wasn't too long after crowdfunding entered the zeitgeist that I became obsessed with the idea of a Kickstarter-shaped story. Here, I decided to use this very modern conceit to illustrate a tragedy about two sisters. There were many decisions to make: Do I put the updates in chronological order or backward, like they appear on the site? Do I try to write a transcription of a video? In what order should I present the comments and messages? Because a Kickstarter page is so visual, I had to try to figure out the most natural and dramatically appropriate order in which to present these sections. But those concerns were a pleasure, a puzzle that I had to sort out for myself. I hope I've done Ursula and Olive justice.

Seanan McGuire is the author of more than a dozen novels and an uncounted number of short stories. (Seriously. She has never counted them.) Her latest work, *A Red-Rose Chain,* was released in September 2015. McGuire won the 2010 John W. Campbell Award for Best New Writer. She lives in a decrepit farmhouse with her two abnormally large blue cats.

▪ I have always worked best from prompts. Say "Write me a story" and I'll stare at you blankly for days. Say "Write me a story about bees" and I'll give you the world. So when an editor friend asked me to write her a story, I requested a prompt, and was given "Women do better on submarines than men do." The story constructed itself from there. I'm constantly doing research into one thing or another, and abyssopelagic marine biology is currently one of my obsessions. Knitting the two together was both natural and surprisingly easy, like making soup using a familiar casserole recipe. Just add water, and everything comes out fine at the end.

Sam J. Miller is a writer and a community organizer. His fiction has appeared in *Lightspeed, Asimov's Science Fiction, The Minnesota Review, Arts & Letters,* and *Strange Horizons,* among many others. He is a nominee for the Nebula Award, a winner of the Shirley Jackson Award, and a graduate of the Clarion Writers' Workshop. He lives in New York City and at www.samjmiller.com.

▪ "We Are the Cloud" is science fiction, but it's also not. Sauro's world is *our* world, plus some futuristic technology to further oppress the poor. The story extrapolates from the interconnected systems of exploitation I was seeing up close through my work as a community organizer with homeless people. The moms I met in shelters had lost kids to the foster care system; the folks I met at soup kitchens had aged out of foster care . . . so had the boys I saw hanging out in Morningside Park, who got arrested and fed into the prison system by cops looking to fill their quotas, and who also starred in the super-low-budget gay porno flicks some guys I worked with would share. So this is our world, where the systems that are supposed to help people end up hurting them, not for lack of resources (NYC really does spend four times as much to keep someone in a shelter as it would cost to provide someone housing) but because these systems are in place to disempower and divide certain communities. A world where, as in ours, big businesses make a ton of money profiting off the bad decisions that people in a tough spot are forced to make to survive. And in a world like that (in a world like ours) none of us come out clean. We're all culpable. One person's comfort is another person's nightmare. I love my smartphone, but workers in the factories that make them are committing suicide because of how bad conditions are. With that said, of course, people have an astonishing capacity for resistance, and I like to think of "We Are the Cloud" as a supervillain origin story: Sauro's exploitation by the status quo gives him the power to destroy it.

Susan Palwick is an associate professor of English at the University of Nevada, Reno, where she teaches creative writing and literature. Her most recent novel, *Mending the Moon,* was published in 2013 and followed three previous novels: *Shelter* (2007), *The Necessary Beggar* (2005), and *Flying in Place* (1992). Her story collection, *The Face of Mice,* appeared in 2007. Recent short fiction has appeared in *The Magazine of Fantasy & Science Fiction,* in *Asimov's Science Fiction,* and on the Clarkesworld and Tor.com websites. Palwick's fiction has been honored with a Crawford Award from the International Association for the Fantastic in the Arts, an Alex Award from the American Library Association, and a Silver Pen Award from the Nevada Writers Hall of Fame. She has also been a finalist for the World Fantasy Award and the Mythopoeic Award.

  ▪ The son of a family friend is in prison, under very different circumstances from Graham's. "Windows" is drawn partly from my friend's stories of long, expensive—and sometimes futile—trips to visit him. But Vangie is a fictional character, not this friend. I'm fascinated by narratives about people who are marginalized or forgotten. A more conventional science fiction story would focus on Zel's experience, on what's happening in the generation ship. My own impulse is always to look for the untold story, to think about the people left behind. Vangie navigates her life within tolerances arguably as narrow as those faced by either of her children. This is a story about different kinds of confinement and survival, and about what it sometimes takes for us to acknowledge common humanity.

Cat Rambo lives and writes in the Pacific Northwest. Her short stories have appeared in such places as *Asimov's Science Fiction Magazine, Tor.com,* and *Clarkesworld Magazine.* She has produced four story collections and a novel, *Beasts of Tabat,* whose sequel, *Hearts of Tabat,* will appear in late 2015. She has been nominated for Endeavour, Nebula, and World Fantasy Awards and is the former editor of *Fantasy Magazine.* She is the current president of the Science Fiction and Fantasy Writers of America. Find links to her online work as well as information about her online classes at www.kitty wumpus.net.

▪ I actually have a tortoiseshell cat named Taco, and the story grew out of learning that you can't clone one and expect the same fur pattern because of the way X-linked inactivation works. At the same time, I'd been thinking about clones and personality for a while, and that led me to mulling over why you'd want to clone someone, and if the results would be what you expect. When the title, "Tortoiseshell Cats Are Not Refundable," came to me, the story clicked into place.

Jess Row is the author of the novel *Your Face in Mine* and the story collections *The Train to Lo Wu* and *Nobody Ever Gets Lost*. His fiction has appeared in *The New Yorker*, *Granta*, *Tin House*, *The Atlantic*, and many other venues, as well as three times in *The Best American Short Stories*, and he has received a Whiting Award, a PEN/O. Henry Award, and two Pushcart Prizes. He's at work on a new novel and story collection as well as a collection of essays on race and American fiction, *White Flights*. He teaches at the College of New Jersey and the City University of Hong Kong.

▪ It's weirdly fitting, to me, that "The Empties" has found its way to a collection of science fiction and fantasy writing. I'm not an active reader, let alone writer, of science fiction or fantasy as genres—if I had to say what kind of writer I am, I would steal an old line from Trollope and say I'm much more interested in "the way we live now," in lived human experience, in all its complexity, in the present. But in our present present, the world as it is in 2015, the line between actual technology and science fiction, between satire and sincerity, between what we expect of "the real" and what appears to be only fantasy, is obviously blurry. We have American politicians today who treat Margaret Atwood's *The Handmaid's Tale* like a governance handbook—politicians who, needless to say, view science itself as fiction. In my own work, it's not so much that I found science fiction; I feel more like it found me.

In "The Empties" I was trying to create a gentle satire of what life might be like among people who are experiencing an actual apocalyptic event through the filter of all the other apocalypses they've ever imagined—in movies, in books, on TV. (Which is, of course, what would happen to us if the lights went off.) I kept trying to keep it lighthearted and metafictional, and yet the story kept pulling me toward the intimate details of one woman's lived experience. And that was before Cressida Leyshon, who edited the story for *The New Yorker*, started asking pointed questions that forced me to create a plausible Vermont-invasion scenario. In the end it seemed many people found the story quite disturbing and also wanted to know if there would be a sequel—a question I've never fielded before. The answer is no. I'm really quite comfortable not knowing how it ends.

Karen Russell is the author of the story collections *St. Lucy's Home for Girls Raised by Wolves* and *Vampires in the Lemon Grove,* the novella *Sleep Donation,* and the novel *Swamplandia!,* which was named one of the five best fiction books of 2011 by the *New York Times Book Review* and a finalist for the Pulitzer Prize. She is a graduate of the Columbia MFA program (SOA '06), a 2011 Guggenheim Fellow, and a 2013 MacArthur Fellow.

▪ I love stories of metamorphoses. One of my favorite Ovid stories was Daphne's flight from Apollo—she escapes him by becoming a laurel tree. The Greek Witness Protection Program. When I was a young reader, this exit strategy struck me as alternately miraculous and horrifying: to become a tree, to forfeit your life as a woman. I don't remember exactly what sent me back to Ovid, but I reread Daphne's story and I started to imagine a reverse Leap—what would a tree do if it were changed into a human?

And then I visited Joshua Tree National Park and saw my first Joshua tree, a Dr. Seussical species that looks like God's first draft of a tree, or maybe Satan's melting telephone poles. I grew up in Florida, and the desert was an alien landscape to me—sublime in the old sense of the word. And the Joshua trees are nothing like the eastern deciduous trees, with their even arpeggios of branches. They seem to be bristling with strange life, as if they are only holding those poses, seconds from uprooting themselves and strolling through the desert. I thought that Florida had prepared me for dinosaur foliage, but the Joshua seems to be an emissary from another planet entirely. And a good candidate for a hitchhiking spirit that jumps into a human woman.

Darwin has written about the coevolution of the Joshua tree and the yucca moth, its exclusive pollinator—it's one of the most extraordinary partnerships in nature. One species cannot survive without the other. That fed into this story, too—two strangers evolve into a couple, and that interdependency both sustains them and makes them doubly vulnerable.

A. Merc Rustad is a queer nonbinary writer and filmmaker who lives in Minnesota. Favorite things include robots, dinosaurs, monsters, and tea. Rustad's stories have appeared in *Fireside Fiction, Escape Pod, Inscription Magazine, Scigentasy, Ideomancer, Daily Science Fiction,* and *Vitality Magazine.* When not buried in the college homework mines or working, Merc likes to play video games, read comics, and wear awesome hats. You can find Merc on Twitter @Merc_Rustad or at the website http://amercrustad.com.

▪ This is one of the most personal stories I've ever written. It took years before I could understand, growing up, why I felt different and why it was (and is) so hard to interact in a world when your programming doesn't match what everyone tells you you should be.

It started as two different projects, actually. I'd written all the lists in one document, thinking it was going to be a collection of to-do slips assembled into a loose narrative. But then I had this other story chewing its way out (this was the first-person sections) and I was like, *Well, they're both good but I don't know how to make them work individually.* Which was when I realized they were all one story. When I stitched the two bits together, it was this epiphany moment: this is the story I have needed to tell for years and didn't know how, until I saved a new Word document with the title "How to Become a Robot in 12 Easy Steps."

I owe a huge debt of thanks to my friend Ada Hoffmann, who helped me refine the ending and clarify what I needed this story to do. And also much gratitude to Sara and Mary at *Scigentasy* for giving it its first home! I've been so humbled and delighted that this story has resonated with readers. I write because I want to connect to other people and robots, and when a story makes that connection, it is the best feeling in the world.

Sofia Samatar is the author of *A Stranger in Olondria* (2013), winner of the Crawford Award, the British Fantasy Award, and the World Fantasy Award for Best Novel. She teaches literature and writing at California State University Channel Islands.

▪ "How to Get Back to the Forest" was inspired by three pieces of writing: "Everyday Barf" by Eileen Myles, "Barf Manifesto" by Dodie Bellamy, and "Apoplexia, Toxic Shock, and Toilet Bowl: Some Notes on Why I Write" by Kate Zambreno. They're all about narrative and bodily excesses and ecstasy and control. They're also about, as Zambreno puts it, the revolt and the revolting, about women in a state of sickness and defiance. In "How to Get Back to the Forest" I wanted to explore that connection. I was also interested in the fact that nausea is catching, and the idea of rebellion as a kind of sympathetic reaction. Of course it's no accident that my rebels are a bunch of girls whose bodies are controlled and who get up to a secret vomit-fest in the bathroom. Feminist writing has always been concerned with the body and its potential, the body as a site of resistance, and how that affects writing.

In the library of the University of Wisconsin-Madison, as a graduate student, I came across a book called *A Picnic Party in Wildest Africa* by C.W.L. Bulpett, published in 1907. It's an account of a hunting trip, full of admiration for the animals and loathing for the people of East Africa. I found it almost mesmerizingly vile. The hunter in "Ogres of East Africa" is loosely based on Bulpett. I think of the story as a kind of speculative excavation of history, and also as a space for language play, for the sheer joy of imagining what escapes bullets and indexes, what goes on in the margins, in the deep forest. The ogres, of course, are real.

Kelly Sandoval's fiction has appeared in *Asimov's Science Fiction, Esopus, Shimmer, Grimdark, Flash Fiction Online,* and *Daily Science Fiction.* In 2013 she attended Clarion West with some of the best writers she's ever had the pleasure of reading. By day she works as a procedure writer at a bank, where she's developed strong feelings about the use of the word *verbiage.* She's currently writing an urban fantasy novel about the fall of Faerie and a steampunk game about the adventures of Bernadette Charity Darlington. You can find her online at kellysandovalfiction.com.

• When I first moved to Seattle, I noticed everything. The woman with piercings all down her spine, the nude cyclists, the homeless teens camping by the overpass. There was so much beauty and so much pain everywhere I looked. But that was five years ago. Eventually, I stopped looking. When there's always something to see, you get overloaded. You stop noticing anything. I think that's tragic.

I wrote "The One They Took Before" to remind myself to look. To show that sometimes magic is right there, leaking in at the edges. We just need to see it. There's magic in winter roses. In the guy on the bus with the punk outfit and the pink umbrella. In the people who remember to be kind.

Of course, magic has its costs. So does noticing. Once you see, you start to feel responsible. Beauty and pain can both get under your skin.

Jo Walton has published twelve science fiction and fantasy novels, three poetry collections, and a book of essays about rereading. She won the John W. Campbell Award for Best New Writer in 2002, the World Fantasy Award for her novel *Tooth and Claw* in 2004, and the Hugo and Nebula Awards for her novel *Among Others* in 2012. Her most recent books are fantasies set in Plato's Republic, *The Just City* and *The Philosopher Kings.* She comes from Wales but lives in Montreal, where the food and books are more varied.

• I very rarely have short-story-length ideas. I had been interested in the idea of a Soviet sleeper who gets left behind by the unexpected collapse of the USSR since reading a bunch of Cold War thrillers at the time when the Cold War was ending. I came across the commonplace assertion that all biographers fall in love with their subjects. When disputing this and pointing out exceptions, I suddenly thought of a future where biographies routinely featured an artificial intelligence that replicated the subject but was programmed by the biographer. This came together in my mind with the idea of a left-behind Soviet sleeper who is, like King Arthur, sleeping until his country needs him. The details of the future world were manufactured out of wondering what kind of country would lead anyone to need that particular sleeper woken.

Daniel H. Wilson is a Cherokee citizen and the best-selling author of nine books, including *Robopocalypse, Amped, A Boy and His Bot,* and *Robogenesis.*

He coedited the science fiction anthologies *Robot Uprisings* and *Press Start to Play*. His playable short story, *Mayday! Deep Space,* is available in the App Store. He publishes a monthly comic, *Earth 2: Society,* and his graphic novel, *Quarantine Zone,* is forthcoming. *Robopocalypse* was purchased by DreamWorks and is currently being adapted for film by Steven Spielberg. Wilson earned a PhD in robotics from Carnegie Mellon University. He lives in Portland, Oregon.

▪ I made a terrible mistake. In "The Blue Afternoon That Lasted Forever," I included the exact bedtime routine, word for word, that I used for my daughter when she was three years old. She is nearly five at this moment, and so, of course, that particular bedtime routine has disintegrated. The rituals that we have with our children are so special and so personal —yet they are rendered ephemeral by a child's constant growth and development. Letting go hurts a little. Sometimes it hurts a lot. The instinct to memorialize those special patterns is strong. We want to hold on forever. At the event horizon of a black hole, this becomes a physical possibility. Drawing on conversations with my brilliant friend-since-childhood-and-now-physicist, Dr. Mark Baumann, I was able to thread these two elements together as hard science fiction. In my mind, the black hole represents the terrible actuality of holding on forever. It violently demonstrates what we all know to be true in our hearts: we must always be letting go. Life itself is a long, slow letting go. Sad and beautiful. So why the terrible mistake? Quite simply, this story triggers a nostalgia in me so deep that I cannot read it out loud without leaking from the eyes in a deeply embarrassing manner. That's life for you.

Other Notable Science Fiction and Fantasy Stories of 2014

Selected by John Joseph Adams

ALEXANDER, WILLIAM
The War Between the Water and the Road. *Unstuck 3*
ANDERS, CHARLIE JANE
The Day It All Ended. *Hieroglyph,* ed. Ed Finn and Kathryn Cramer (William Morrow)
Palm Strike's Last Case. *The Magazine of Fantasy & Science Fiction,* July-August
ARNASON, ELEANOR
The Scrivener. *Subterranean,* Winter

BACIGALUPI, PAOLO
Moriabe's Children. *Monstrous Affections,* ed. Kelly Link and Gavin J. Grant (Candlewick Press)
Shooting the Apocalypse. *The End Is Nigh,* ed. John Joseph Adams and Hugh Howey (Broad Reach)
BLACK, HOLLY
Ten Rules for Being an Intergalactic Smuggler (The Successful Kind). *Monstrous Affections,* ed. Kelly Link and Gavin J. Grant (Candlewick Press)

BROADDUS, MAURICE
The Iron Hut. *Sword & Mythos,* ed. Silvia Moreno-Garcia (Innsmouth Free Press)
BROCKMEIER, KEVIN
The Invention of Separate People. *Unstuck 3*
BUCKRAM, OLIVER
The Black Waters of Lethe. *Beneath Ceaseless Skies,* June

CORREIA, LARRY
The Great Sea Beast. *Kaiju Rising,* ed. Tim Marquitz (Ragnarok)

DELANCEY, CRAIG
Racing the Tide. *Analog,* December
DUE, TANANARIVE
Herd Immunity. *The End Is Now,* ed. John Joseph Adams and Hugh Howey (Broad Reach)

EL-MOHTAR, AMAL
The Lonely Sea in the Sky. *Lightspeed,* June (special issue: Women Destroy Science Fiction!)
ERDRICH, LOUISE
Domain. *Granta,* October

EVENSON, BRIAN
The Blood Drip. *Granta,* October

FINLAY, C. C.
The Man Who Hanged Three
Times. *The Magazine of Fantasy
& Science Fiction,* January-
February
FRIED, SETH
Hello Again. *Tin House,* Spring

GILBOW, S. L.
Mr. Hill's Death. *The Dark,* May
GRIFFITH, NICOLA
Cold Wind. *Tor.com,* April

HANKS, TOM
Alan Bean Plus Four. *The New
Yorker,* October 27
HEADLEY, MARIA DAHVANA
The Tallest Doll in New York City.
Tor.com, February
Who Is Your Executioner?
Nightmare, November
HOWARD, KAT
The Saint of the Sidewalks.
Clarkesworld, August

IRVINE, ALEX
For All of Us Down Here. *The
Magazine of Fantasy & Science
Fiction,* January-February

JEMISIN, N. K.
Stone Hunger. *Clarkesworld,* July
JONES, KIMA
Nine. *Long Hidden,* ed. Rose Fox
and Daniel Jose Older (Crossed
Genres)
JONES, RACHAEL K.
Makeisha in Time. *Crossed Genres,*
August

KELLY, JAMES PATRICK
Someday. *Asimov's Science Fiction,*
April-May

KENDALL, MIKKI
If God Is Watching. *Revelator,* April
KENYON, SHERRILYN, AND
KEVIN J. ANDERSON
Trip Trap. *Dark Duets,* ed.
Christopher Golden (Harper
Voyager)
KIERNAN, CAITLÍN R.
Bus Fare. *Subterranean,* Spring

LAVALLE, VICTOR
Lone Women. *Long Hidden,* ed.
Rose Fox and Daniel Jose Older
(Crossed Genres)
LEE, YOON HA
The Contemporary Foxwife.
Clarkesworld, July
LE GUIN, URSULA K.
The Daughter of Odren. ebook
(HMH Books for Young Readers)
LIBLING, MICHAEL
Draft 31. *The Magazine of Fantasy
& Science Fiction,* April-May
LIPPMAN, LAURA
Ice. *Games Creatures Play,* ed.
Charlaine Harris and Toni Kelner
(Ace)
LIU, KEN
The Long Haul: From the
ANNALS OF TRANSPORTATION,
The Pacific Monthly, May 2009.
Clarkesworld, November

MACLEOD, CATHERINE
Sideshow. *Nightmare,* October
(special issue: Women Destroy
Horror!)
MARCUS, DANIEL
Albion upon the Rock. *The
Magazine of Fantasy & Science
Fiction,* March-April
MCINTOSH, WILL
Dancing with Death in the Land
of Nod. *The End Is Nigh,* ed. John
Joseph Adams and Hugh Howey
(Broad Reach)

MOHANRAJ, MARY ANNE
Communion. *Clarkesworld,* June

MORAINE, SUNNY
Singing with All My Skin and
Bone. *Nightmare,* September

NELSON, SHALE
Pay Phobetor. *Lightspeed,*
December

PERALTA, SAMUEL
Hereafter. *Synchronic,* ed. David
Gatewood (David Gatewood)

PRATT, TIM
Ghostreaper, or, Life After
Revenge. *Nightmare,* January

REED, ROBERT
Blood Wedding. *Asimov's Science
Fiction,* July

SCHROEDER, KARL
Kheldyu. *Reach for Infinity,* ed.
Jonathan Strahan (Solaris)

SIGLER, SCOTT
Complex God. *Robot Uprisings,* ed.
Daniel H. Wilson and John Joseph
Adams (Vintage)

STALKER, GABRIELLA
In the Image of Man. *Lightspeed,*
June (special issue: Women
Destroy Science Fiction!)

STEWART, ANDY
The New Cambrian. *The Magazine
of Fantasy & Science Fiction,*
January-February

SWIRSKY, RACHEL
Tender. *Upgraded,* ed. Neil Clarke
(Wyrm)

TOLBERT, JEREMIAH
In the Dying Light We Saw a
Shape. *Lightspeed,* January

VAN EEKHOUT, GREG
The Authenticator. *Flytrap,* March

VAN LENTE, FRED
Neversleeps. *Dead Man's Hand,* ed.
John Joseph Adams (Titan)

VOGEL, NIKKI
The Past, of Course. *One Throne,*
Winter

WASSERMAN, ROBIN
Dear John. *The End Is Now,* ed.
John Joseph Adams and Hugh
Howey (Broad Reach)

WATTS, PETER
Collateral. *Upgraded,* ed. Neil
Clarke (Wyrm)

WILLIS, CONNIE
Now Showing. *Rogues,* ed. George
R. R. Martin and Gardner Dozois
(Bantam)

YANT, CHRISTIE
This Is as I Wish to Be Restored.
Analog, January-February

YAP, ISABEL
Have You Heard the One About
Anamaria Marquez? *Nightmare,*
March

THE BEST AMERICAN SERIES®

FIRST, BEST, AND BEST-SELLING

The Best American series is the premier annual showcase for the country's finest short fiction and nonfiction. Each volume's series editor selects notable works from hundreds of periodicals. A special guest editor, a leading writer in the field, then chooses the best twenty or so pieces to publish. This unique system has made the Best American series the most respected—and most popular—of its kind.

Look for these best-selling titles in the Best American series:

The Best American Comics

The Best American Essays

The Best American Infographics

The Best American Mystery Stories

The Best American Nonrequired Reading

The Best American Science and Nature Writing

The Best American Science Fiction and Fantasy

The Best American Short Stories

The Best American Sports Writing

The Best American Travel Writing

Available in print and e-book wherever books are sold.
Visit our website: *www.hmhco.com/popular-reading/general-interest-books/
by-category/best-american*